MOUNTAIN LAUREL

Jude Deveraux

G.K.HALL & CO.
Boston, Massachusetts
1991

British Commonwealth rights courtesy of
Random Century Group.

Published in Large Print by arrangement with
Pocket Books, a division of Simon
and Schuster, Inc.

G.K. Hall Large Print Book Series.

Set in 16 pt. Plantin.

Library of Congress Cataloging-in-Publication Data

Deveraux, Jude.
    Mountain laurel / Jude Deveraux.
        p.   cm.—(G.K. Hall large print book series)
    ISBN 0-8161-5124-5 (lg. print)
    1. Large type books.   I. Title.
[PS3554.E9273M6   1991]
813'.54—dc20   91-11204

Acknowledgments

First and foremost I would like to thank Antonia Lavanne, who so very kindly allowed me to spend the afternoon in her studio and listen to her give singing lessons. It was a wonderful experience.

I would like to thank the students and teachers and Mannes College of Music, where I spent an evening listening to such wonders as a live performance of the quartet from *Cinderella*.

I would like to apologize to my readers and to Bizet for lying about the date of *Carmen* and having my heroine sing the opera a few years before it was written.

I would also like to thank the late Thomas Armor for his name. I made you a hero, Tom.

And, as always, I'd like to thank Linda Marrow for listening . . . and listening and listening and listening and . . .

ROCKY MOUNTAINS

Summer 1859

CHAPTER 1

Colonel Harrison read the letter a second time, then leaned back in his chair and smiled. The answer to a prayer, he thought. That was the only way to describe the letter: the answer to a prayer.

Just to make sure it did indeed say what he thought it did, he looked at the letter again. General Yovington had issued orders from Washington, D.C., that Lieutenant L. K. Surrey was to leave the post of Company J, Second Dragoons, for a special assignment. But since Lieutenant Surrey had died just last week, Colonel Harrison would have to choose someone to take the assignment in his place.

Colonel Harrison's smile grew broader. He was choosing Captain C. H. Montgomery to take Lieutenant Surrey's place. The lieutenant, now replaced by Captain Montgomery, was "requested" to escort a foreign opera singer into the gold fields of the Colorado Territory. He was to remain with her and her small band of musicians and servants as long as the lady needed him. He was to protect her from any dangers she would possibly encounter on her journey and to do what he could to make her travels more comfortable.

Colonel Harrison put the letter down, handling

it as though it were a precious relic, and smiled so broadly his face nearly cracked. Lady's maid, he thought. The high and mighty Captain Montgomery was being ordered to be nothing more than a lady's maid. But, more important, Captain Montgomery was being ordered away from Fort Breck.

Colonel Harrison took a few deep, cleansing breaths and thought about having his own fort to command, and about not having to deal with the perfection, the cool knowledge of Captain Montgomery. No longer would the men look to their captain for confirmation of every order, for permission to do what their colonel asked of them.

Colonel Harrison thought back to when he first came to Fort Breck a year ago. His predecessor, Colonel Collins, had been a drunken, lazy old fool. Collins's only concern had been surviving until he could retire, get out of Indian country and go back to Virginia, where people lived in a civilized manner. He was content to turn over all responsibility to his second-in-command, Captain Montgomery. And why not? Montgomery's record had to be seen to be believed. He'd been in the army since he was eighteen, and in the ensuing eight years he'd worked himself up through the ranks. He'd started as a private, and, after extraordinary heroism on the field of battle, he'd been made an officer. He'd gone from second lieutenant to captain in a mere three years, and at the rate he was going he'd outrank Colonel Harrison in another few years.

Not that the man didn't deserve everything he'd ever earned in the army. No, as far as Colonel Harrison could tell, Captain Montgomery was perfect. He was cool under fire, never losing his head. He was generous, fair, and understanding with the enlisted men, and as a result they pretty much thought he ran the fort. The officers went to him with their problems; the officers' ladies fawned over him and asked his advice about social events. Captain Montgomery didn't drink, didn't patronize the whores outside the fort; he'd never lost his temper as far as anyone knew, and he could do *anything*. He could ride like a demon and, while at a full gallop, shoot the eye out of a turkey from a hundred yards away. He knew Indian sign language and a smattering of several Indian languages. Hell, even the Indians liked him, said he was a man they could respect and trust. No doubt Captain Montgomery would die before he broke his word.

Everyone in the world seemed to like, honor, respect, even revere Captain Montgomery. Everyone, that is, except Colonel Harrison. Colonel Harrison loathed the man. Not just disliked him, not just hated him, but *loathed* him. Everything the captain could do that the colonel couldn't made the colonel despise him more. The enlisted men saw within a week after the colonel's arrival that Harrison didn't know anything about the West, and the truth was, this was the first time in his life the colonel had been west of the Mississippi. Captain Montgomery hadn't volunteered

5

to help the colonel learn the ropes; no, he was much too polite for that, but, in the end the colonel had had to ask him some questions. The captain had always known the answer, always known the best way to settle any dispute.

It was after Colonel Harrison had been at Fort Breck for five months that he began to hate the man who had all the answers. Of course, having a sixteen-year-old daughter who practically swooned at the sight of the man, didn't help matters.

Colonel Harrison's resentment had come to a head one hot morning the previous summer when, in a vile mood, the colonel had ordered a man who had done no more than oversleep reveille to be punished with twenty lashes. He was sick unto death of the drunkenness of his men and meant to make an example of the private. He ignored the looks of hatred from the other men, but his stomach began to hurt. He wasn't a bad man; he just wanted to enforce discipline at his post.

When Captain Montgomery stepped forward to protest the punishment, Colonel Harrison saw red. He informed the captain that *he* was in charge of the fort and unless the captain meant to take the man's punishment, he was to stay out of this. It wasn't until Montgomery began removing his jacket that the colonel realized what he meant to do.

It was the worst morning of the colonel's life, and he dearly wished he could go back to bed and start the day over. Captain Montgomery—the

6

fearless, perfect Captain Montgomery—took all twenty of the man's lashes. For a while the colonel thought he was going to have a mutiny on his hands when all the enlisted men refused to wield the whip. In the end a second lieutenant applied the whip to Montgomery's broad back, and when he was finished he threw the whip into the dirt and turned on the colonel, his eyes blazing with hatred. "Anything else . . . *sir?*" he'd asked, sneering the last word.

For two weeks hardly anyone on the post spoke to the colonel—including his own wife and daughter. As for the captain, he was back on duty the next morning without so much as a grimace of pain for a back that must have been killing him. That he wouldn't even commit himself to the infirmary for a few days was the last straw. From that day on, Colonel Harrison didn't even bother trying to conceal his loathing for the captain. Of course the captain never once betrayed what he felt for the colonel; no, perfect human beings like Montgomery don't give away what they feel. He just continued to be the perfect officer: a friend to the men, a charming escort to the ladies. A man trusted by all. A man who, as far as Colonel Harrison could tell, had no feelings. A man who never woke up on the wrong side of the bed. A man who never tripped on his horse's stirrup or missed whatever he was aiming to shoot. A man who would probably smile in the face of death.

But now, Colonel Harrison thought, now he was going to get rid of this perfect man. Now General

7

Yovington had requested an escort for some opera singer through gold country, and he was going to send the illustrious Captain Montgomery. "I hope she's fat," the colonel said aloud. "I hope she's *real* fat."

"Sir?" his corporal asked from his desk on the other side of the room.

"Nothing," the colonel barked. "Send Captain Montgomery to me, then leave us." The colonel ignored the look the corporal gave him.

Promptly, as always, Captain Montgomery appeared and the colonel tried to keep from frowning. There wasn't a speck of dust on the captain's dark blue uniform, which he suspected had been privately tailored to fit the captain's six-foot-three-inch frame.

"You wanted to see me, sir?" Captain Montgomery asked, standing at attention.

Colonel Harrison wondered if the man *could* slump. "I have orders for you from General Yovington. Ever hear of him?"

"Yes, sir."

What had the colonel expected, that Montgomery *didn't* know the answer to something? He rose from behind his desk, put his hands behind his back, and began to walk about the room. He must try to keep the joy from his voice. "As you know, General Yovington is a very important man and he has reasons for what he does. He does not allow people like you and me to know those reasons, but then, you and I are mere soldiers and ours is to obey, not to question the reason behind an order." He looked at the captain. There was no impatience on his face, no annoyance, just that calm look he always wore. Perhaps the colonel could break that perfect calm. He'd give a month's pay to be able to do that.

The colonel went to the desk and picked up the letter. "I received this by special courier this morning. It seems to be of utmost importance. The general, for whatever reasons, seems to have formed an, ah . . . attachment to an opera singer and now that . . . lady wants to sing for the gold miners. He wants her to have an army escort."

The colonel looked hard at Captain Montgomery, his eyes wide, for he didn't want to miss the man's reaction. "The general requested Lieutenant Surrey, but as you well know, the poor unfortunate man won't be able to make it, therefore I've thought long and hard about a suitable replacement, and I have chosen you, Captain."

Colonel Harrison almost did a little jump of joy when Montgomery blinked twice and then tightened his lips. "You're to keep her out of trouble, see that the Indians don't bother her, keep the miners from making advances toward her, see that she's comfortable. I guess that means see that's she's fed and that her bath water's hot and—"

"I respectfully decline the assignment, sir," Captain Montgomery said, his back straight, his eyes straight ahead, which was some inches over the colonel's graying head.

Colonel Harrison's heart swelled. "This is not a request, it's an order. You are not being asked, you are being told. It is not an invitation you can refuse."

To the colonel's astonishment, Montgomery dropped his rigid posture and, without being given permission, he sat down in a chair, then withdrew a thin cigar from inside his jacket. "An opera singer? What the hell do I know about an opera singer?"

The colonel knew he should reprimand the captain for sitting without permission, but if he'd learned nothing else in the last year, he'd at least learned that the western army was not like in the East, where discipline was understood. Besides, he was enjoying the perfect captain's consternation too much.

"Oh, come now, Captain, you can figure it out. Who better than you? Why, in all my twenty years of service I've never seen a man with a better record. Commissioned on the field of battle, an indispensable right-hand man to any officer. You've fought Indians and whites. You've rounded up outlaws and renegades. You're a man's man and yet you can advise the ladies on how to set a table, and according to what I hear from the ladies, you dance divinely." He smiled when Captain Montgomery gave him a malevolent look. He hadn't broken that façade even on the day he'd taken the twenty lashes for the private.

"What's Yovington to her?"

"*General* Yovington didn't make me his confidant. He merely sent his orders. You're to leave in the morning. As far as I can tell, the woman has already reached the mountains on her own. You'll recognize her by . . ." He picked up the letter, trying hard to conceal his smile. "She's traveling in a modified Concord wagon. It's red and it has, ah . . . let's see, the name LaReina painted on the side. LaReina is the woman's name. I hear she's very good. At singing, I mean. I don't know what else she's good at besides singing. The general didn't tell me that."

"She's traveling in a stagecoach?"

"A red one." Colonel Harrison permitted himself a small smile. "Oh, come now, Captain, surely this isn't a *bad* assignment. Think how this will look on your record. Think where this could lead. If you perform this duty well, you could start escorting generals' daughters. I'm sure my own daughter would give you a recommendation."

Abruptly, Captain Montgomery stood. "With all due respect, sir, I cannot do this. There is too much unrest now and I am needed elsewhere. There are white settlers to protect, and what with this slavery controversy and the possibility of war, I do not believe I can desert my post to—"

Colonel Harrison lost his sense of humor. "Captain, this is *not* a request. This is an order. Whether you like it or not, you are on an assignment of indefinite length. You are to stay with this woman as long as she wants, go wherever she wants, do whatever needs to be done, even if it is no more than pull her coach out of the mud. If you don't do this, I will slap you in jail, court-martial you, find you guilty, and have you shot.

11

And if I have to, I'll pull the trigger myself. Is that understood? Do I make myself clear?"

"Very clear, sir," Captain Montgomery answered tightly.

"All right, then, go and pack. You're to leave at dawn tomorrow." The colonel watched as the captain seemed to be trying to say something. "What is it?" he snapped.

"Toby," was all the captain could get out through a jaw tight with anger.

So, the captain *did* have a temper, the colonel thought, and he was tempted to antagonize him further by insisting that the orders had not included the garrulous, scrawny little private who was never more than a few feet from the captain's side. But the colonel remembered too well the anger of the enlisted men the day the captain had taken an enlisted man's lashes. "Take him," the colonel said. "He'll be of no use here."

The captain nodded his thanks but didn't speak them as he turned on his heel and left the colonel's office.

After the captain was gone, the colonel sank onto his hard chair and let out a sigh of relief, but at the same time he was a little nervous. Could he control this unruly fort, where most of the "soldiers" were farmers who'd signed up merely to fill their bellies? Half of them were drunk most of the time, and desertion was rampant. For the last year his record had been excellent, but he knew that was due a great deal to Captain Montgomery. Could he rule the fort on his own?

12

"Damn him!" he said, and slammed a desk drawer shut in anger. Of course he could command his own fort!

'Ring Montgomery stared at the woman through the spyglass for a long moment, then angrily slammed it closed.

"That her?" Toby asked from behind him. "You sure she's the one?" He was a foot shorter than 'Ring, wiry, and had skin the color of walnut juice.

"How many other women would be fool enough to travel alone to a town of forty thousand men?"

Toby took the spyglass and looked through it. They were standing on a hill looking down into a pretty valley where a bright new red stagecoach sat, glittering in the setting sun, a tent not far away. In front of the coach was a woman sitting at a table, slowly eating her dinner while a thin, blonde woman served her.

Toby lowered the glass. "What d'you think she's eatin'? It looks like somethin' green on her plate. Do you think it's peas? Maybe string beans. Or is it just green meat like the army has?"

"I couldn't care less what she's eating. Damn Harrison! Damn him to hell and back! Incompetent bastard! Just because he can't run a fort the size of Breck, he sends me off to do his dirty work."

Toby yawned. He'd heard this a thousand times. He'd been with 'Ring since 'Ring was a boy, and he might seem stoic to others but Toby

13

knew the truth. "You oughta be thankin' the man. He got us out of that godforsaken fort and put us out here where the gold's ours to be had."

"We have an assignment, and I mean to fulfill it."

"*You* is right. I ain't part of the army."

'Ring started to remind Toby of the uniform he wore, but he knew it was a waste of breath. Toby had joined the army because 'Ring had and for no other reason. The purpose of the army, the work that needed to be done, meant nothing to Toby.

But it meant everything to 'Ring. He'd joined the army before his first beard had fully grown, and he'd always tried to do his best, to always be fair, to see what needed to be done and do it. He'd been quite successful and quite happy until last year, when Colonel Harrison had become his commanding officer. Harrison was an incompetent fool, a man who'd never seen any action, a desk officer who had been sent west and had no idea what to do. He'd dumped his anger at his own incompetency on his captain's shoulders, making 'Ring take the blame for what the colonel couldn't do.

"She's eatin' somethin' else too," Toby said, looking through the spyglass. "You think it's lettuce? Maybe carrots. You think it's somethin' besides hardtack?"

"What the hell do I care what she's eating?" He walked away from the ridge. "We have to make a plan. First of all, she's either a good woman or a bad one. If she's good, she has no business being out here alone, and if she's bad, she doesn't need an escort. Either way, she has no need for me."

"What's that say on her door?"

'Ring paused in pacing and grimaced. "La-Reina, the Singing Duchess." He looked back down at the red coach. "Toby, we have to *do* something about this. We cannot allow this young woman to go into the gold-mining area. I'm sure she knows nothing about what she's getting into. If she knew the many dangers she faced, I'm sure she would return to her point of origin."

"Her point of—?" Toby said.

"Origin. Where she came from."

"You know, I was just wonderin' how she got this far by herself. You think she drove that coach herself?"

"Heavens, no! A Concord isn't easy to drive."

"Then where are her drivers?"

"I don't know," 'Ring said, waving his hand in dismissal. "Perhaps they've deserted her to work in the gold fields. Perhaps the woman will be grateful if I explain to her the hazards involved in a journey such as she's planning."

"Humph!" Toby snorted. "I ain't never yet seen or heard tell of a woman that was grateful for anything."

'Ring took the spyglass from Toby and looked through it again. "Look at her, sitting there calmly eating, and unless I miss my guess, that is very fine china she's eating from. She doesn't look like a woman who is used to the hardship of a gold camp."

15

"She looks pretty fine to me. Big top on her. I like the top half to be big. And the bottom half, too, if the truth be told. I can't see her face from here."

"She's an opera singer!" 'Ring snapped. "She's not a dancehall girl."

"I see. Dance-hall girls sleep with miners and opera singers sleep with generals."

'Ring glared at him and Toby glared back until 'Ring walked away. "All right, here's the plan: We show her a little of what the West is really like, what she can expect in the camps."

"You ain't plannin' to use her for target practice, are you?"

"Of course not. I'll just, maybe, well, scare her a little bit. Put some sense into her."

"Great," Toby said with a sigh. "Then we can go back to Fort Breck and Colonel Harrison. That man's gonna be as glad to see you as he would be to see a pack of Apaches. He don't like you none at all."

"The feeling is mutual. Yes, we'll return to Fort Breck, but I'll put in for a transfer."

"Good. In four, five years we should be able to get out of the place. By then you ain't gonna have no skin left on your back from tryin' to play the hero and impress the men."

"It was something that had to be done, and I did it," 'Ring said as though from rote, for he'd said this a thousand times to Toby.

"Like you gotta go scare this lady now, is that

16

it? How come you don't just go tell her you don't wanta ride around the gold fields with her?"

"It must be the woman's decision to return to civilization. Otherwise, I am not free from my duties and obligations to her."

"So maybe you're plannin' to scare her for yourself and not to save any of her skin."

"You have a very pessimistic outlook on life. It would be the best thing for both of us if she were to turn back. Now, are you coming with me or not?"

"I wouldn't miss this for the world. Maybe she'll offer us somethin' to eat, but I sure hope she don't sing. I sure do hate opery."

'Ring straightened his uniform, adjusted the heavy, long saber at his side. "Let's get this over with. I have many things to do back at the fort."

"Like keepin' ol' man Harrison from killin' you?"

'Ring didn't answer as he mounted his horse.

CHAPTER 2

Maddie pulled the photograph of her little sister from the trunk and looked at it. She was so absorbed, she didn't hear Edith enter the tent.

"You ain't gonna start cryin', are you?" Edith said as she spread a blanket over the hard cot that was Maddie's bed.

"Of course not!" Maddie snapped. "Have you cooked anything yet? I'm starved."

17

Edith pushed a strand of dishwater-blonde hair out of her eyes. Neither it nor her dress was too clean. "You thinkin' of changin' your mind?"

"No, I'm not. I've never considered doing anything but what I have to. If I have to sing for a bunch of dirty, thieving, illiterate miners in order to save my sister, I'll do it." Maddie looked at this woman, who was part maid, part companion, part pain-in-the-neck to her. "*You* aren't getting cold feet, are you?"

"Ain't me who's got a sister they're gonna kill and, besides, I wouldn't care if they did hold my sister. I'm plannin' to get me a rich gold miner and make him marry me and set me up for life."

Maddie looked at the photograph once more, then put it away. "I just want to get this done as quickly as possible and get my sister back. Six camps. That's all I have to do, and then she'll be returned to me."

"Yeah, well, you hope. I don't know why you trust them so much."

"General Yovington promised he'd help me, and he's the one I trust. When this is all over, he's going to help me prosecute her kidnappers."

"You have a lot more faith in men than I do," Edith said, jerking the bed covers. "You ready to—" She stopped as she saw a large, dark form at the tent flap. "He's here again."

Maddie looked up, then slipped out of the tent. She returned in minutes. "There may be some trouble," she said to Edith. "Be very cautious tonight."

An hour later, just as Maddie was finishing her dinner, she looked up to see two soldiers approaching. Or, she thought, perhaps a soldier and a half, as one man was splendidly dressed in a perfectly cut, perfect-fitting uniform, sitting on top of a horse that must have bloodlines back to Adam's horse. The other man, half the size of the first one, looked as though he'd made his shirt out of a bunch of dirty rags. There were large patch pockets sewn all over the front of the shirt, and each pocket seemed to be bulging.

"Hello," she said, smiling. "You are just in time to join me for a cup of tea and perhaps a piece of apple pie."

The larger man, who Maddie could now see was a very handsome man, with dark hair curling from under the broad brim of his hat, dark, frowning eyes, heavy dark brows, and a thick dark mustache, just scowled at her.

"Real tea?" the smaller man asked, his brown skin crinkling as he spoke. One of his incisors was missing. "Real apples? Real pie?"

"Why, yes, of course. Please share it with me." He was off his horse in a second, before Maddie could pour the tea. When he took the cup, his hand trembled a bit in anticipation. She poured another cup and held it out. "Captain," she said to the younger man, noting his rank by the double silver bars on his shoulders.

He ignored the tea and rode his horse very close to the table. Glaring down from atop the enormous horse, he seemed to be twelve feet tall, she

19

thought, and felt a cramp in her neck as she looked up at him.

"You're LaReina?"

He had a nice voice but not a nice tone to it. "Yes." She smiled as graciously as possible, trying to ignore the cramp in her neck. "LaReina is my stage name. My name is actually—"

She didn't get to finish, as the man's horse did a sidestep and she had to keep the dishes from tipping over.

"Quiet, Satan," the man said, and brought the big horse under control.

To her right the small man choked on his tea.

"Are you all right?"

"Fine," the little man said, grinning. "Satan, is it?" He was laughing.

Maddie cut him a generous wedge of pie, put it on a plate, and handed it to him. "Would you care to sit down?"

"No, thank you, ma'am. I'm gonna watch this show from over here."

Maddie watched him walk away, then looked back up at the man on the horse. The animal was so near that its switching tail was about to knock the dishes off the table. "How can I help you, Captain?" She moved a teacup out of the tail's way.

He reached inside his short blue jacket and withdrew a folded piece of paper and handed it to her. "I have orders from General Yovington to escort you about the gold camps."

Maddie smiled as she opened the paper. How

thoughtful of the general to provide even more protection for her. "You've been promoted," she said, looking at the name on the paper. "Congratulations, Captain Surrey."

"Lieutenant Surrey died last week and I have been ordered to fulfill his duties. General Yovington is unaware of Lieutenant Surrey's death and has not yet been informed of my taking Surrey's place here."

For a moment Maddie was speechless. She was sure the general had chosen a man who would know why she was in the gold fields. She was sure the general would have given private orders to the man, but now what was she to do? How in the world was she to do what she had to do if she had a couple of soldiers snooping about her? Somehow, she *had* to get rid of this man.

"How kind of you," she said, folding the letter. "How very kind of General Yovington, but I don't need an escort."

"Nor does the army need to spare officers to accompany a traveling singer," the man said, looking down at her.

Maddie blinked at him. Surely, he hadn't meant that as rudely as it sounded. "Please, Captain, won't you join me for a cup of tea? It's growing cold. And, besides, your horse is destroying my coach." She nodded to where the animal was beginning to chomp on the red-painted wood of the wagon.

The man, using his knees, backed the horse up, then a few feet away he dismounted, leaving the

21

reins dangling. Well trained, Maddie thought, and watched the man come toward her. He seemed almost as tall off the horse as on and she had to strain to look up at him. "Please do sit down, Captain."

He did not sit but kicked a stool from under the table and put his foot on it, then, leaning on his knee, he took a long, thin cigar from the inside of his jacket and lit it.

Maddie looked at him, and she was not amused by his presumption and insolence.

"I think, ma'am, that you have no idea what lies ahead of you."

"Gold miners? Mountains?"

"Hardship!" he said, looking down at her.

"Yes, I'm sure it will be difficult, but—"

"But nothing. You are . . ." He looked down at the table with its porcelain dishes. "You obviously know nothing of hardship. What could you know after having lived the cosseted life of an opera singer?"

He didn't know her, of course, or he would have been aware of the way her green eyes turned greener. "May I take it that you are a connoisseur of opera, Captain? You've spent a great deal of time near opera stages? Do you sing? Tenor perhaps?"

"What I do or do not know about opera makes no difference. The army has ordered me to escort you, and it is my belief that if you knew anything of the dangers that lie ahead, you would give up this foolhardy scheme of wanting to enter the mine fields." He stepped off the stool and turned his back to her. "Now, I'm sure," he said in a fatherly tone, "that your purposes are of the highest order: You want to bring a little culture to the miners." He looked back at her and almost smiled. "I commend you for your noble attitude, but these are not the type of men who will appreciate good music."

"Oh?" she said softly. "And what kind of music would they like?"

"Crass, vulgar tunes," he said quickly. "But that's neither here nor there. The point is that the gold fields are no place for a lady."

At that Maddie felt as well as saw him look her up and down—and there was nothing flattering about his look. It was as though he'd said, If you *are* a lady. "Bad places, are they?" Her voice was very soft yet carried. Years of training had given her absolute control over her voice.

"Worse than you can imagine. There are things that go on there that— Well, I don't want to burden you with the horrors. There is no law except a vigilance committee. Hangings are rampant, and hanging is the cleanest way a man can die. Thieves." He put his hands on the table and leaned forward. "There are men there who take advantage of women."

"Oh, my. My goodness," she said, blinking up at him, her eyes wide. "And you think I shouldn't go into the camps?"

"Definitely not." He leaned away from the table

and again nearly smiled. "I was hoping you'd see reason."

"Oh, yes, I can see reason when it is there to see. Tell me, Captain, ah . . ."

"Montgomery."

"Yes, Captain Montgomery, if you are released from your duty of escorting me, what do you plan to do?"

He frowned a bit, obviously not liking any questions from her about himself. "I will return to Fort Breck and to my duties there."

"Important duties?"

"Of course!" he snapped. "All duties a soldier performs are important."

"Includin' cleanin' the latrine," the little man said as he walked toward the table, his empty plate held out. "It's all day long of important cuttin' firewood and haulin' water and buildin' more army buildin's and—"

"Toby!" Captain Montgomery snapped.

Toby quit talking as Maddie gave him another slice of pie.

"I apologize for my private," Captain Montgomery said. "Sometimes he doesn't quite grasp the true purpose of the army."

"And you do?" Maddie asked sweetly. She cut him a slice of pie, put it on a fragile plate, and handed it to him with a heavy silver fork.

"Yes, ma'am, I do. The army is here to protect this country. We protect the white settlers from Indians, and—"

"And the Indians from the white settlers?"

24

Toby gave a snort of laughter, but Captain Montgomery gave him a look to silence him, then the captain noticed his plate and the half-eaten pie in horror, as though he'd just sold out to the enemy. He put the plate down and straightened. "The point is, ma'am, you cannot go into the gold fields."

"I see. I take it that if I don't go, then you are free of your orders to accompany, a . . . what did you call me? A traveling singer, is that right?"

"Whether I am free or not means nothing. The point is that you are not safe in the gold fields. Even I might not be able to protect you."

"Even you, Captain?"

He stopped speaking and looked at her. This was not going as he'd hoped. "Miss LaReina, you may find this an occasion for jesting, but I assure you it isn't. You are an unprotected woman here alone, and you have no idea what lies ahead of you." He lifted one eyebrow. "Perhaps I am wrong in assuming your desire is to sing. Perhaps you are hoping to partake of the gold rush. Perhaps you are planning to win some unsuspecting miner's hard-won gold from him by using—"

"That's it," Maddie said, standing, her hands on the table and leaning toward him. "You are right in the first part, Captain: You are wrong in assuming. You know *nothing* about me, absolutely nothing, but I'm going to tell you something about me: I am going into the gold fields and neither you nor your entire army is going to stop me."

He lifted an eyebrow at that and, as quick as a

snake, he put his hand on Maddie's arm. He meant to do whatever must be done to get the woman to listen to reason.

Out of the twilight stepped two men, one a short, stocky man who had a face that looked as if he'd spent years slamming it against brick walls. The other man was the largest, blackest man 'Ring had ever seen. 'Ring wasn't used to seeing men taller than he was, but this man topped him by inches.

"Would you release me?" Maddie said softly. "Neither Frank nor Sam like for any harm to come to me."

Reluctantly, 'Ring let go of her arm and stepped back.

Maddie walked around the table, and as she did so, the two men closed in beside her. The shorter man wasn't much taller than she was, but even through his clothes one could see that he was all muscle, a couple of hundred pounds of it. As for the other man, not any human on earth—at least one who had any sense anyway—would have wanted to tangle with him.

"Captain," Maddie said slowly, giving him a little smile, "you were so busy telling me what you assumed I didn't know that you didn't bother asking me what precautions I had taken. Allow me to introduce my protectors." She turned to the shorter man. "This is Frank. As you can see, Frank has been in a few pugilistic contests. He can shoot anything that moves. Besides that, he can play the piano and the flute."

26

She turned to the tall black man. "This is Sam. I guess I don't have to tell you what Sam can do. He once won a wrestle with a bull. See the scar around his neck? Someone tried to hang him once, but the rope broke. No one's tried again."

She looked at Captain Montgomery, saw his dark eyes glittering. "Behind you is Edith. Edith has a special affection for knives." Maddie smiled. "And she isn't bad with a fluting iron either."

She smiled even more broadly. It was a lovely feeling having beaten this pompous, know-it-all man. From the look of him she had an idea he wasn't used to being bested at anything. "Now, you have my permission to return to your army fort and tell them I don't need anyone to escort me. You can tell them that you've seen that I am in trustworthy hands. To save your conscience I will write a letter to General Yovington about Lieutenant Surrey's untimely death and explain that while I appreciate his kind offer of an escort, I am not in need of one at this time."

She tried to stop herself but she couldn't help gloating. "I especially don't need someone as obviously clumsy as you. Frank knew two days ago that you were searching for us. Your inquiries weren't exactly subtle, and all the time you were on the hill watching us, Sam was watching you. And when you were riding into camp . . . Heavens, Captain, the chorus of *La Traviata* makes less noise than you did. For the life of me I cannot understand why the army would choose a man like you to protect anyone."

She knew she should stop, but she didn't seem able to. The way the dreadful man had called her a traveling singer was enough to make her pull out all the stops. "It seems that if the army was concerned for my safety from Indians, the least they could do is send me a man who could move about the world with a little more subtlety and a lot less noise. Tell me, Captain, have you ever been in the West before? Ever seen an Indian? Can you tell a Ute from a Crow from a Cheyenne? Or is trying to intimidate women what you do best? Is it, perhaps, the *only* thing you can do?"

She gave him a sweet smile. Throughout her speech he'd just stood there, his handsome face a stone mask, his body rigid. She wouldn't have known he was alive except for eyes that blazed with black fire.

"You may return to your army now, Captain," she said. "I'm done with you."

'Ring looked from one man to the other, then at Maddie and gave a little pull to the brim of his hat. "Good evening, ma'am," he said, then turned, walked around Edith, and went to his horse. A step behind him was Toby, who looked with some awe at Sam, then he winked at Maddie before he mounted his army-issue horse.

They weren't completely out of earshot before Maddie started laughing. Frank chuckled too, and even Sam smiled, but Edith didn't.

"He ain't gonna like what you said to him," Edith snapped.

"I didn't like what he said to me!"

"Yeah, well, a woman was born to take whatever a man gives her, but a man ain't used to it."

"Then I shall start a new trend of women not taking what a man offers," she snapped, then calmed. "Oh well, it doesn't matter, we've seen the last of him." Sam made a movement, nodding his head toward the hill where the two men had sat, and watched them through a spyglass. "Yes," Maddie said. "I think an extra watch tonight might be appropriate."

She turned away as Frank lit the lamps. She thought she might go to bed so that she could get an early start in the morning. She smiled again. So much for the army, she thought.

"Scare her, huh?" Toby was saying as they sat around the campfire eating army hardtack. "That lady don't seem like she's scared of nothin'!" He chuckled in admiration. "I didn't see either one of them men, didn't even know they was there until they stepped out. Where do you think they was? That big one, I could believe he was in hell and just come up through the earth, but the other one—"

"Could you keep your mouth shut for a few minutes?" 'Ring snapped.

Toby didn't have the least intention of being quiet. "She sure is a looker, ain't she? You think a woman pretty as she is can sing?"

'Ring tossed out the dregs of his coffee. "No. If she's a singer, I'm a liar."

"And you ain't that, are you, boy?" Toby's eyes

29

were dancing. "You just told her the truth, that she didn't know nothin' about nothin'. 'Course you never asked her if she had a couple of plug-uglies to take care of her, you just told her. She sure didn't like that, did she? Said you made more noise than . . . what was that?"

"An opera," 'Ring said loudly. "She mentioned the name of an opera. Don't you have something else to do, old man, besides flap your jaws?"

"Oooeee, I hope you don't scare me as bad as you scared that little lady. Where you goin'?"

'Ring mounted his horse. "Don't expect me back before morning."

Toby frowned. "I hope you ain't plannin' nothin' stupid. That big one looks like he could break you in half."

"That's more difficult than it seems." 'Ring reined his horse away into the trees. When he was some distance away from Toby and away from the singer's coach, he dismounted, removed his saddle bags, and pulled out everything. In the very bottom was a roll of leather and inside of the roll was a round tin box. He hadn't looked at these objects for a couple of months, but he knew he needed them now.

As he began to undress, his mind went back to the evening. It wasn't the humiliation that bothered him, or even that he was humiliated by a woman, no, a man could stand words, but what bothered him was that she was getting in the way of an order. The army had given him an order, and no matter how much he didn't want to carry

30

out the order, he meant to do it no matter what was said to the contrary.

So, she thought she was safe in this country, did she? She thought she was safe because she had two men watching over her. It was true 'Ring hadn't been aware of the men skulking in the shadows of the coach—he accepted the blame for that—but when he had seen them, he hadn't been intimidated. The short one, Frank, had a cloudy left eye. If he wasn't blind on that side, he was close to it. With the black man, for all that his skin was tight and he appeared to be ageless, 'Ring detected a slight stiffness in his movements, and when he stood, he favored his right knee. It was his guess that the man was older than he looked and his right leg gave him a great deal of pain. As for the woman and her knives, he dismissed her. There was lust and longing in her eyes and he suspected he had merely to smile at her and she'd drop her knives.

As for the singer, this LaReina, she was the most difficult to read. He thought he'd known her when he first saw her. She seemed soft and wide-eyed. She seemed as though she was listening to every word he said. She appeared to be a lady, what with her manners of offering Toby tea from her fine dishes. None of the officers' wives would have offered a private, especially one who looked like Toby, so much as a smile. Yet this opera singer had.

As 'Ring removed the last of his clothing, he knew that the woman did need an escort. Perhaps

31

General Yovington had realized that and that's why he'd asked for an army man. The choice of Lieutenant Surrey was an odd one, though. 'Ring remembered him as a quiet man who kept to himself. There wasn't much else to remember about him except that once he'd been accused of cheating. The general must have had good reasons for his choice.

Whoever he'd chosen to escort her, the general had certainly been perceptive enough to realize that she did indeed need someone with her. Perhaps the general could tell that she was a woman who was as soft as talcum powder but believed herself to be tough and invincible. She seemed to think she'd have no trouble in the gold country in spite of the fact that she was the prettiest thing he'd seen in years.

When he was nude, he fastened the breech cloth about his hips, stepped into tall, soft moccasins, tied a knife about his waist, then opened the can of vermilion.

Her prettiness was a problem. Maybe he could keep the miners away from her, but how was he going to keep her away from the miners? Perhaps the general meant the woman's escort to keep her pure and chaste, to see that she didn't have trysts with other men.

As he dipped his fingers in the powdered vermilion, he shrugged. He was a soldier. He had no reason to question what was behind his orders. He just meant to obey them.

Maddie was deeply asleep, dreaming that she was singing at La Scala with Adelina Patti. The audience booed and hissed at Patti, then began chanting, "LaReina, LaReina."

She was smiling in her sleep when the bright light of a match being struck then a lamp being lit woke her. She blinked a few times, not wanting to open her eyes. "Edith, put out that light," she murmured, and started to turn over. Something was holding her hand above her head. Sleepily, she pulled on it, then awakened a bit to pull harder. Her hand wouldn't move. Suddenly, in a panic, she started to sit up, but it seemed that both her hands and both her feet were tied to the cot. She opened her mouth to scream.

"Go ahead and scream. I can assure you that no one will come to your rescue."

She closed her mouth and turned to see Captain Montgomery sitting on the floor in the middle of the tent, calmly smoking a thin cigar. But it was such a different Captain Montgomery that at first she almost didn't recognize him. He wore only a leather loincloth, leaving his long, strong-looking legs bare, as well as a good portion of his muscular buttocks. His chest was bare except for a great deal of hair and three marks of vermilion at one shoulder. He also had stripes of the brilliant red-orange powder across one cheek.

Perhaps she should have been afraid of him, but she'd never been less afraid of anyone in her life. She knew exactly what he was doing: She'd hurt his pride and now he was getting her back—just like any little boy would do.

"How kind of you to drop in on me like this, Captain, and what an interesting play-outfit. But you'd better release me before Sam finds out. He doesn't have the sense of humor that I do."

He took a long draw on his cigar. "I took care of both men and your maid before I came in here."

She pulled against the ropes holding her. "If you've hurt any of my people, I'll see you're hung."

"Hanged."

"What?"

"The word is *hanged*, not hung. Hung is when God gives a man a special gift. Hanged is when men put a rope around somebody's neck."

"A special gift? I have no idea what you're talking about."

"Oh? I would have thought you knew a great deal, what with the general and all."

It was at that moment that Maddie understood what he was saying. His playing dress-up and tying her to a bed to prove a point didn't make her angry, but his insinuation that there was something between her and the general did. "How dare you!" she gasped. "I'll report you to your commanding officer for this. I'll see that you're hung—hanged—damn you, drawn and quartered, if you don't release me this minute."

"Careful. You're making enough noise that the chorus of . . . what was that? La something, wasn't it?"

34

"*La Traviata*, you boorish, backwoods, over-grown army mule! Release me!"

He slowly stood up and stretched. "If I'd been an Indian, I could have had your scalp by now, or a white man could have had anything he wanted."

"Is that supposed to frighten me? Why in the world would an Indian want to risk starting a war just for my scalp?"

He sat down on the edge of the cot and looked at her. "Haven't you heard how the Indians rav-age white women, how they lust for their beauty?"

"Does all your reading matter consist of dime novels?"

He looked away and took a deep draw on the cigar. "You seem to know some about Indians. How does a duchess from Lanconia, isn't it, know about Indians?"

Maddie started to tell him the truth but decided she'd be damned if she would. She wasn't going to give this man the time of day if she could get out of it. "How very perceptive of you, Captain," she said, practically purring at him. "The truth is that an old mountain man—you know, the men who used to trap the furs in the West—came to Lanconia and lived with us. As a child he used to dandle me on his knee and tell me lots of won-derful stories—*true* stories."

"So now you've come west to see the land he told you about."

"Oh, yes. And to sing too. I'm rather good at singing."

35

He moved away from the cot, and while his back was turned Maddie struggled with the ropes, but the knots were intricate and well tied.

Abruptly, he glanced back at her, but she was quicker, and when he looked she was lying there peacefully, smiling at him.

"I've told you I don't think you should go into the camps. They're a rough lot and I'm afraid for your safety."

Afraid you'll have to follow me around, she thought, but she continued smiling. "I'll be safe and you can return to your army. I promise I will write General Yovington the nicest letter possible. He's a sweet man."

"I would imagine you'd know."

She clamped her teeth together. "I assure you, sir, that the general's interest in me is purely artistic."

"Artistic?"

Yes, you half-naked dodo bird, she thought. Artistic. But she smiled at him. "My singing. The man likes to hear me sing. If you would be so kind as to remove these ropes, I would sing for you."

He gave her a patronizing little smile that made anger run through her like oil on a hot skillet: she was almost sizzling.

"Opera?" he asked. "No thanks."

She gave a sigh of exasperation. "All right, Captain, let's get down to it and stop this charade. You've bested my men, my maid, and me. You win. Now, what do you want?"

"The army has ordered me to accompany you, and that's what I plan to do. That is, if you don't have sense enough to listen to reason."

"Reason being my doing whatever it is you want me to do, is that right? No, sorry. I didn't mean to say that." She took a breath. "Captain, you may be one of the few people left on earth who doesn't like to hear a singer of my caliber, but I can assure you that millions of people around the world are not so—" She meant to say pigheaded, stubborn, or stupid, but thought better of it. "Not so unaware. *They* would like to hear me sing."

"Good idea. I'm all for music, but—"

"How generous of you."

He ignored her remark. "But I think you should go back to the States, wait a few years until this land is more settled, and then return to sing."

She took another breath to calm herself, and when she spoke, she spoke as though to a not very bright child. "Captain Montgomery, perhaps you've heard this before, but a singer's voice is not a permanent thing. It is an unfortunate fact of life, but I will not always be able to sing. As it is now, I'm twenty-five and not even at my peak, but I need to sing while I can, and I want to sing for these poor, lonely men. No, more than that, I am *going* to sing in the gold camps."

He looked down at her. "You're stubborn, aren't you?"

"Me? *I* am stubborn? You have been told in every way possible that you are not wanted, not needed, yet here you are playing Indian in the middle of the night and tying up some poor, defenseless female."

He almost smiled at her, but he did sit on the cot and lean over her to untie her hands. His skin was warm and tan, and she thought he must run around in just a breech cloth a great deal to be tanned all over as he was.

When her hands were untied she sat up and rubbed her wrists and watched while he untied her ankles. The moment she was free, she pushed at him and sprang off the cot. He caught her around the waist before she reached the tent flap and dropped her onto the cot, then towered over her, glowering.

"You have any whiskey?" he asked after a long moment of glowering. "I think I need some."

"Serving firewater to Indians is illegal."

"Don't push me anymore. I've had all I'm going to take from you."

"In the little trunk is a bottle."

He went to the trunk, turning his back on her, but when she so much as moved her foot, he looked back at her, but she just smiled.

He took a glass from the trunk also and poured himself a healthy shot, downed it, and poured another. "The way I see it is that there are two choices: You either don't go on your singing tour or you go with me as your escort."

"That's like giving me a choice of different ways to die."

He raised one eyebrow at her. "I can assure that my company isn't generally considered to be bad."

"Please spare me the listing of your romantic conquests. I am not interested."

The whiskey seemed to be having an effect on him, as he could feel himself relaxing. "What *are* you interested in, ma'am?"

"Singing, singing, and singing. And my family also. That's about it."

He was beginning to feel so relaxed that he thought he'd better sit down, so he sat on the floor, leaning against the trunk. "Your family. Little dukes and duchesses. Do they sing too?"

"Not much, but they're great with buffalo guns."

"Ah, yes, hunting." His eyes were feeling heavy. "If you must go and sing, I'll go with you and protect you."

"But, Captain Montgomery, what you don't seem to understand is that I don't *want* you with me. I never asked for the army's help; I never wanted it. And I especially didn't want someone like you. Under no circumstances do I want you with me."

"Orders," he murmured. "Orders."

"*Your* orders, not mine."

He rubbed his hand across his eyes, then looked at the bottle of whiskey. "What's in this?"

"Opium," she said brightly. "It was Edith's idea. She used to give a free drink to any of her, ah . . . customers if she took a dislike to them. When they woke up, she used to tell them they had been magnificent lovers. Not one man ever doubted her."

He could barely keep sleep from overtaking him. "You drugged me?"

"You're the one who asked for the whiskey. I was the one who reaped the benefits." She got off the cot and went to him, patted him on the head. "Don't worry, Captain, you'll wake up in a few hours, none the worse for wear. And when you do, would you please go find someone else to annoy? I have plans for my life, and they don't include a pompous, overbearing, know-it-all army captain who calls me a traveling singer."

She took a step toward the tent flap, and he made a motion as though he meant to go after her, but he was too sleep-weakened. "Good night, Captain," she said sweetly. "Sweet dreams." She left the tent.

CHAPTER 3

Maddie glanced up at the sun through the trees to confirm her direction, then leaned forward to pat her horse's neck. It hadn't been easy getting away from Frank and Sam, but she'd done it. Whatever made men assume she was helpless? Why did men like Frank and Sam take it for granted that she didn't know up from down? Frank had grown up in New York City and Sam had spent his life in the South—until they'd hung—hanged, she corrected herself—him, then he'd gone north and that's where Maddie had first been introduced to him.

She removed the cap from her canteen and took a drink. It didn't seem to matter that neither man had ever crossed the Mississippi, each still believed he knew more about tracking and trailing in these parts than a female who'd spent most of her life west of the river.

Just as that captain did, she thought. Whereas neither Frank nor Sam made her angry, *he* did.

For a moment, anger made her tighten her jaw, but then she smiled. She'd won in the end, though. After he'd fallen asleep from the opium, she'd gone to where he'd tied both Frank and Sam, and after some work released them.

"Sailors' knots," Frank had muttered, and then said a few things about no man being able to sneak up on him.

Maddie hadn't answered him. When she'd hired the two men she'd known she should have hired men who knew more about Indian country, at least men who knew a badger from a beaver, a Ute from a Crow, but there hadn't been time, so she'd taken the men General Yovington had sent her. Frank's face and Sam's size were enough to frighten most people. Sam, as usual, hadn't said anything when Maddie had released him. Sam acted as though words were precious jewels and he'd become a pauper if he gave any away.

She found Edith under the coach, bound and gagged—and enraged. It seemed that Captain Montgomery had slipped into bed with her before tying her to the wagon wheel. "I thought he wanted *me*," she spat out. "All he wanted was to tie me up. Even then I thought he'd planned somethin' interesting, but he just left me. Left me there! Untouched!"

Maddie just worked at the knots in the thin ropes and didn't ask any questions about "something interesting."

They broke camp immediately. Sam carried the slumbering captain outside the tent and dumped him at the edge of a steep hillside, then, with his foot, gave him a little push so he went rolling down the hill.

Maddie hoped the captain didn't freeze in the cool mountain air, but she thought a man such as Captain Montgomery, with as much audacity as he harbored, would have enough to keep him warm until morning.

They had struck out for the gold fields, traveling slowly on the rutted trail that passed for a road until the sun came up, then Sam had whipped the horses forward, and they'd put many miles between themselves and the determined Captain Montgomery.

Now it was three days later and they hadn't seen him in all that time. Perhaps he had frozen to death. Or, more likely, he'd gone back to his army post and complained about an opera singer who wouldn't listen to "reason." Whatever had happened, she was very glad to get rid of him.

She hung the canteen over her saddle horn and once again removed the map from inside her tight wool jacket and looked at it. She knew it by heart now, but she still wanted to make sure she was in the right place at the right time.

When she took the letter out she also pulled out a lock of Laurel's hair. It had come with the first letter, and there had been a note saying one of Laurel's fingers would be included with the next letter if Maddie missed today's meeting.

With trembling hands she folded the map and put it and the lock of hair back into her pocket and kicked her horse forward up the steep, rocky slope.

They had Laurel, she thought. These anonymous, faceless men, or women for that matter, had taken an innocent twelve-year-old child from her home in Philadelphia and used her to force Maddie to do what they wanted.

Six months ago Maddie had made her American debut. She'd already conquered Europe, having sung throughout the continent for nine years, always to great acclaim, but she'd longed to return to America. Her manager, John Fairlie, had booked her in Boston and New York, and for three glorious months she'd sung to Americans, who'd been enthusiastic and generous in their praise of her.

But then three months ago her aunt, who had a small house in Philadelphia, had sent a message saying that Maddie must come to Philadelphia as soon as possible.

Here's where Maddie's memory troubled her. Why hadn't she gone immediately? Why hadn't she walked out the door and boarded the first train to Philadelphia? Instead, she'd waited three days, until after she'd sung three more roles before she went to see her aunt. After all, the woman was old and a bit daffy and maybe even a little senile, so she could wait.

By the time Maddie got to Philadelphia it was too late to change anything. Laurel, Maddie's little sister, had been sent east to live with her father's brother's widow and to go to school. Maddie had known her sister was but a few hundred miles away but, what with her performances and the demands of singing, she'd had no time to make the journey to Philadelphia—hadn't *made* the time, she corrected herself.

So for several months Maddie had been within a few hundred miles of her little sister and hadn't been to see her.

Now, urging her horse forward, she remembered her sister as a chubby, awkward child following her around, sitting under the piano while Maddie sang. Their father used to say that he didn't know if Laurel would ever be a singer herself, but he was sure she'd be an opera lover.

In the nine years Maddie had been singing in Europe, she'd written letters and exchanged photographs with her faraway family and she'd received adoring letters from Laurel as she grew up. Laurel couldn't sing as her sister Maddie could, or draw as her sister Gemma could, but she could adore her talented older sisters. She could keep scrapbooks about them and worship them from afar.

Maddie knew she'd taken her little sister's adoration for granted, and over the years she'd sent her copies of programs signed by a king or the czar or a little gold fan or even a pearl necklace, yet she hadn't taken the time to visit her when she was so near.

By the time Maddie got to Philadelphia, her aunt was in bed, prostrate with anxiety and nerves. It had been nearly a week since a man had come to her house and told her he was holding Laurel captive and that he wanted to talk to Maddie.

"Your father will never forgive me," her aunt kept saying. "Oh, Maddie, I did my best. Laurel is such a sweet child. She was never noisy or messy like other children and she loved her new school. Why, oh, why did this happen to her?"

Maddie gave her aunt a healthy dose of laudanum and went downstairs to wait. It was a long, nerve-racking day before anyone contacted her, and then a man came to see her. He kept his hat on and stood in the shadows, but she memorized every feature of his face.

He told her that she would get Laurel back if she would go to the new gold fields on the Colorado River and sing in six cities. At each of these places someone would contact her and give her a map, and she was to go to the place on the map and a man would give her a letter. She was to take the letter back to her camp, keep it, and deliver it to the next point.

"What's in the letters?" Maddie had asked without thinking.

45

"None of your business," he'd snapped. "Don't ask no questions and your sister will be returned to you alive."

He'd warned her more about not bringing any outsiders into this, and to keep her mouth shut. He said that if she obeyed all orders, she'd get to see her sister at the third town and keep her when she reached the sixth camp.

Maddie didn't think any more about her planned singing tour of the eastern United States. She instructed her manager to cancel all performances. John was furious. He said she was abandoning America to Adelina Patti, that Patti would become the darling of America, and if Maddie canceled her performances, Americans would despise her.

She knew that what John said was true, but she also knew that she had no choice. She didn't want to go west and sing for a bunch of gold miners who thought opera was "when the fat lady sang." She had enough problems in her life without trying to sing for ruffians who didn't want to hear her.

In the end John had done what she wanted and canceled her performances, but he'd also quit her service and sailed back to his native England. They'd been together since she was seventeen years old; he'd practically made her what she was, yet she'd lost him because of these men and their letters.

She was in a frenzy of packing and planning the trip west when General Yovington came to her.

Since her arrival in America he'd been her staunch-est fan, visiting her after every performance, tak-ing her to supper, even giving her gifts now and then, a ruby here, an emerald there. She knew he'd love to make her his mistress, but she knew how to flatter men into believing she'd love to be theirs alone but she just couldn't.

The man who came to her house that day, how-ever, was different from the fawning, loving man who'd kissed her hand over dinner. He practically pushed into her house and told her he knew about Laurel.

To her shame, Maddie burst into tears. The general had held her for a while, then firmly set her to one side. He told her a lot that she didn't understand. It was all about American politics, something that didn't interest Maddie much. It had to do with slavery and whether this new ter-ritory where gold had recently been discovered would join the union as for or against slavery.

"What does this have to do with Laurel?" she'd asked, blowing her nose. "Or to do with me?"

"They need a courier, someone no one will sus-pect. Someone like a singer, who can travel about freely and arouse no suspicions."

"*Who* needs a courier?"

"I don't know. I don't know whether you're being asked to carry messages that are for or against slavery."

"I don't care about slavery. I've never owned anyone in my life, nor do I plan to. I just want my little sister back. Maybe my father—"

"No!" the general half shouted, then calmed. "These men are fanatics. They'll kill your sister if you bring someone else in. You'd better do exactly what they say." He took her hand in his. "But I'm going to help you."

Three days later she found herself following the thousands of other people going west, either as settlers or seeking their fortune in the gold fields. Except that she was riding in her own stagecoach, painted bright red, and she had in her employ three of the oddest people she'd ever met. There was Frank, who looked out of his battered face with angry eyes, and Sam, who rarely spoke so you never knew what he was thinking, and Edith, who called herself Edith Honey and constantly regaled Maddie with stories about her life as a prostitute.

Both the coach and the people had been chosen for her by the general. Maddie had wanted a smaller wagon, but the general had pointed out the ruggedness of the Concord and he'd also pointed out the usefulness of the three people he'd hired, telling her in detail each person's violent talents. At the time she'd been so eager to get started on her journey that she couldn't have cared less who went with her.

So now she was in this wild country traveling up the side of a mountain, when just a few months before she'd been wearing satin and sleeping on a feather bed. During the day she had been surrounded by people who spoke of her trills and her cadenzas, and now she was sleeping in a tent on a hard cot, surrounded by people like Edith, who spoke of men tying her up. And men like Captain Montgomery, who crept into her tent at night and told her what she was going to do and how she was going to do it.

Thank heavens she'd been able to get rid of him! She could rather easily outwit Frank and Sam and Edith. After all, they felt like it was her business if she wanted to ride off into the woods alone and risk getting herself killed, but Maddie sensed that Captain Montgomery wouldn't have let her do anything without his permission. She didn't think he'd have taken calmly the announcement that she was riding off into the woods alone and she'd see him when she returned.

What if he did travel with her? What if he prevented her from meeting the man with the letters? What if he demanded to know what she was doing and why? Because Edith had been hired by General Yovington, Maddie had told her about the contents of the letters, but Edith had merely yawned. She cared even less about politics than Maddie did. But, of course, Edith usually couldn't think past what was being served for dinner.

But Maddie sensed that Captain Montgomery was different. If he were to travel with her, he'd no doubt stick his nose into every aspect of her life. And if he found out about the letters, she had no doubt *he* would have an opinion of the slavery question and he wouldn't like her to interfere with people choosing of their own free will. He'd probably do what he could to prevent her from "helping" the territory decide whether it was for or against slavery.

And it was imperative that he didn't interfere, for if he did, Laurel would be killed. A sweet, innocent child of twelve years would die because some overzealous captain had done what he thought was "right."

She kicked her horse forward, urging it up the steep hill. She was to meet the man in four hours.

"What d'you see?" Toby asked, lounging back on the grass, half asleep in the midday sun.

'Ring lowered the spyglass and looked off through the trees to where the woman was forcing her horse to climb a steep hill. With Toby close beside him, 'Ring had been following the woman for three days now. He'd kept his distance, never letting her know he was near. So far, she'd done nothing unusual. She'd traveled inside her coach all day, the men setting up her tent at night. She'd done nothing even very interesting, but he'd watched her so intently that it had been a day before he'd seen the other people who were following her.

At the beginning of the second day he'd seen the two men. They were heavy-footed men, not used to the mountainous terrain, and they made no attempt at concealment. For a few hours he watched them watching her, looking like vultures waiting for someone to die. As he was watching them, he saw a movement in the distance, many yards behind and above the men and, extending his glass to its full length, he saw a shape he could barely distinguish as being a man. And if he wasn't mistaken, he was an Indian. Alone. There seemed to be no one with him. Was the Indian watching the woman or the two men who were watching the woman?

It was during the third night that he saw the new campfire. The two men watching LaReina always built a fire, the Indian never did, and 'Ring had so concentrated on them that he had almost missed the fourth man on the ridge behind him. Far away, high on the same ridge as 'Ring, was a small fire and somehow 'Ring knew this man was also interested in the woman.

Now 'Ring put down his glass. "The woman has more people following her than the Pied Piper."

Toby scratched his arm. "You think they want to hear her sing?"

'Ring snorted. "Not likely. Something is going on or else the woman wouldn't have worked so hard to get rid of me."

Toby looked up at the trees overhead and grinned. It had been a sore, bruised, cold, angry man who'd returned to camp three nights before, and no amount of questions would make 'Ring tell him what had happened. Since then 'Ring and Toby had followed the woman, and had watched her and the countryside around her, but always from a distance.

Now they were resting, or at least Toby was,

51

as 'Ring, on his belly in the grass, watched the woman from across a deep ravine.

"How could they let her go off into the woods alone?" 'Ring muttered. "I thought those thugs of hers were supposed to protect her." He rolled to his back. "An old man and another one blind in one eye."

"Not to mention that little blonde," Toby said. "Pretty little thing she is. Not as pretty as the lady, but—"

'Ring, looking again through the glass, stiffened. "Those two men are making their move." He lifted the glass to look at a spot higher on the ridge facing him. "And so is the Indian." In one movement he came to his feet. "I'm going after her."

"And how are you gonna get across that canyon?" Toby asked. "Jump? Fly?"

"I'm going to the top and across the ridge."

Toby looked up. Sheer rock wall was above them. "Nobody can climb that," he said, but 'Ring was already pulling off his boots and putting on his moccasins. He removed the confining army jacket, his saber, and his revolver, until he wore nothing but trousers, shirt, and belt. He fastened his canteen to the back of his belt. "You can't go without a gun," Toby protested. "You don't know nothin' about them people."

'Ring didn't answer, but he slipped a knife inside his boot, then stood up and looked down at Toby, his weathered old face wrinkled into a grimace of worry. "I'll be all right," 'Ring said.

52

"Don't be such an old woman. It's something I have to do. I don't know why those fools allowed her to go off on her own, but they did and now those men who were following her are closing in. I have to—"

"Like you *had* to carry me out that time?" Toby snapped.

'Ring grinned. "Just like that. Now, sit down and stop your worrying. I'll get the woman and take her back to the coach and give those . . . guards of hers a piece of my mind. I'll meet you at the coach later today, and from now on we'll travel with her." He rolled his shirt-sleeves to above his forearms. "I'm beginning to see why General Yovington wanted someone with her. She needs protection." He stopped. "And I mean to find out what she's up to, what she's so eager to conceal." He turned away toward the rocks, then turned back, and for a second clasped Toby's shoulder. No one would have guessed that the old man who seemed so quarrelsome was often like a second mother to 'Ring. "Go on or I'll put you up for a promotion and when we get back to the post you'll have a whole troop of men under your care."

"Hell," Toby snorted. "I'll desert. You go on. I got more to do than concern myself with your attempts to get yourself killed."

Maddie stopped moving and listened. She could hear the man she was to meet thrashing through the underbrush. Slowly, as silently as creaking

53

leather would permit, she dismounted and began to lead her horse up the hillside. As the noise grew louder, her heart began to pound. In spite of her anger and outrage at the kidnapping scheme of which this man was a part, she must not offend him. She must be as gracious and polite as possible. She must—

She took in her breath sharply as Captain Montgomery dropped from a tree, no more than a foot in front of her. She put her hand to her heart. "You frightened me!" she complained, then recovered herself. "What in the world are *you* doing here?" Her mind was beginning to race. She *had* to get rid of him.

"I could ask you the same thing," he said. "You told me you had people to protect you, yet here you are alone."

"I want to be alone." She took a deep breath and tried to think. "Captain Montgomery, you must go away. I have something I must do and I must do it alone. It has to do with, ah . . . being a female." Perhaps he'd be put off by the mystery of that statement.

He leaned against a tree and folded his arms across his chest. "Now, what could that possibly be?" He looked her up and down. "Couldn't be childbirth. I don't imagine your monthlies necessitate your leaving camp, nor—"

"You are a despicable man, and I won't listen to any more of your vulgarities. I've told you before that I don't need or want your protection." Holding her horse's reins, she started out around

54

him, but he blocked her path, and when she went another way, he blocked that too. "All right, what do you want?"

"Information. Who're the men you're meeting?"

She couldn't tell him the truth and jeopardize Laurel. Think, Maddie, think, she told herself. "One of them is my lover," she said at last, and hoped she looked sincere.

"So why didn't he visit you at your camp?"

She turned away from him while she thought. "Because . . . because . . ." She looked back at him. "Because he's an outlaw. Oh, Captain, I know he's done wrong. I mean, he's not a murderer, but he has robbed a few banks so he can't show himself and I do want to see him." She took a step closer to him. Usually, men who'd heard her sing didn't need any more from her in the way of flirtation, but this was one of those stupid men who had preconceived ideas about opera. She smiled up at him. He was a soldier, a man who'd been living at a fort with lots of other men, so she probably wouldn't have to do much to flatter him.

"Surely, Captain, even you must understand about love. I love the man even if he has done some things wrong." She stepped even closer. His arms were down at his sides, his shirt half unbuttoned, and there was a tear just at the top of his ribs on his left side. She ran her fingertip across the skin showing through the tear. "You wouldn't begrudge me a few minutes alone with the man I love, would you?"

He didn't answer, so she looked up at him. He was looking down at her with such a patronizing, knowing smirk that she stepped away.

"Tell me, do you lie out of habit or just to get your own way? And do most people believe your lies?"

She glared at him. "Why, you sleep-insider, what do you know about truth and lies? What do you know about survival?" Before she thought about what she was doing, she ran at him, her head down, and rammed him in the stomach, and when he gave a quiet whoosh of air, she kicked his shin hard with her stiff-soled boots, then bit him on the chest.

He grabbed her around the waist, and they went tumbling to the ground as he put his hand below her chin to keep her from biting him again. When he had her pinned, her small body under his large one, he looked at her. "What the hell's wrong with you? What are you up to? What are you doing in these mountains?"

"Don't hurt my throat," she whispered. "Anything but that."

He saw that there were tears forming in her eyes and he released his hold on her chin, but he still lay on top of her, not allowing her to get away from him. He watched as she turned her face away, not wanting him to see her tears, and that seemed unusual to him. Most women liked for men to see them cry, he thought.

"Tell me what's going on," he said softly, his face close to hers.

"I can barely breathe with your weight on me, much less talk and, besides, you are bleeding on me."

He glanced down at his arm, saw the blood running and dripping onto her expensive riding habit. "Sorry. About the blood, I mean. It wasn't easy getting to you. I had to come up that rock face over there."

Maddie twisted to look at it, saw the sheerness of it. She looked back at him. "Not possible. Even my father couldn't climb that."

He gave her an odd look. "I could and did climb it."

As he looked down at her, his body on top of hers, his face close to hers, she saw his eyes darken and she began to twist to get away from him.

"You won't succeed in getting away, and I don't mind telling you that I find the sensation of your struggles not unpleasant. You might as well tell me the truth."

She opened her mouth to speak, then cocked her head and listened. "He's here," she whispered. "He's waiting for me."

"He has been for some while. Makes more noise than *La* . . ."

She looked at him and her eyes were pleading. "Please release me. Please, I beg you. I beg you with all my heart and soul. Please release me and let me go to him."

"Maybe this man *is* your lover. Maybe you're sneaking away so General Yovington won't hear of this."

"Are all your brains in your trousers?" she hissed. "Isn't there more in life to you than this?" She gestured, meaning his body on hers.

He looked surprised. "Many things mean more to me than . . . this."

"He's leaving. Oh, my God, he's leaving." At that Maddie became a frenzy of activity as she struggled to get away from him.

He watched her for a moment, easily holding her but fascinated by the fact that she would fight him so hard. Whatever she wanted, she wanted it very, very much.

"Anything," she choked out through a mixture of tears and rage and desperation. "I will give you *anything* if you'll let me go to him alone. Money. Jewels. I'll . . . I'll . . ." She looked into his eyes. "I'll go to bed with you if you let me have thirty minutes alone with him."

At that, he rolled off her and sat up. "Go," he said softly. "I will give you thirty minutes, then I come after you. Understand?"

Quick tears came to her eyes. "Thank you," she murmured, and started running up the steep hill, tripping over branches, a scrub oak scraping her face, falling against a rock and bruising her hands, but never even pausing in her scramble up the hill.

He watched her until she was out of sight, then leaned back against a tree and listened. He could hear when she found the man, and for some reason he gave a small smile. Somehow, it was gratifying to know she had received what she so much wanted.

And what was it she wanted, he wondered. What was she after? All in all, just what in the world was going on around this woman? The longer he knew her, the more she seemed to resemble the eye of a cyclone, with people and events moving around her. He wondered if she knew about the other men following her, about the Indian, and the man even farther away than the Indian.

He listened and could hear the raised voice of the man. 'Ring was on his feet instantly. Whoever the man was, relative, friend, or enemy, he wasn't going to be allowed to harm her. 'Ring hadn't taken ten steps when an arrow came sailing into the tree in front of him. Instantly, he dropped to his belly and reached for his revolver, but it wasn't there.

He looked around him but could see no one, hear nothing. The arrow was a warning, he knew that, for if it'd been meant to, that arrow would have hit him. But a warning of what? To stay away from the woman? If so, why hadn't the Indian shot when 'Ring had been wrestling with her? Was the arrow a warning to leave the singer alone with this man?

Slowly, cautiously, while searching the trees for any sign of the Indian, he stood and put his hand on the arrow, then pulled it from the tree. Crow, he thought. Odd, for the Crow weren't a violent people. In fact, frequently the Crow welcomed the whites, 'Ring knew, because the whites brought wonderful goods that the Crow could steal—and they were thieves of the first caliber. 'Ring had heard that they could take a man's horse and leave him sitting in the saddle.

He looked at the arrow, at the little steel tip. Indians today liked firearms, but often used a bow and arrow when they wanted to be quiet. This Indian didn't seem to mind that 'Ring knew he was there, but either he didn't want the woman to know—or she knew already. And the Indian didn't seem to want 'Ring to interfere with whatever she was doing.

He lifted the arrow in a silent salute to the Indian then slipped it into one of his tall moccasins as he heard the woman who called herself LaReina come down the hill. His blood was dried on her habit, her hands and neck were scratched, and he imagined she had a few other bruises on her as well.

She was silent as she went to her horse and he didn't speak either. He'd already heard and seen enough to know that there was no use asking her what she was doing and why. But he meant to find out. No matter what he had to do or say, he meant to find out all the answers to his questions.

CHAPTER 4

Hours later Maddie was alone in her tent and at last she could allow herself to give in to her fear.

The man she'd had to meet was dreadful. He had mean, hard eyes and, worse, he was stupid. She knew there would never be any reasoning with him about Laurel or anything else. He'd given her the letter, but he'd also demanded she give him the little pearl and diamond brooch she wore. It wasn't worth much, not in money, but it had been a gift from her mother and it had belonged to her grandmother as well. Forgetting herself, she'd protested when he'd demanded the pin and she'd seen him grow angry. He'd yelled at her and she was ashamed to remember that she had been afraid. She was afraid for Laurel, yes, but she was afraid for herself too.

She put her face in her hands. All her life she seemed to have been given whatever she wanted. She had her talent, the adoration of thousands of people, and she had her family, who had always supported her in whatever she wanted to do.

Now, rather abruptly, her luck seemed to have run out and she was so utterly, totally alone.

She glanced up when she heard someone enter the tent, and to her consternation she saw Captain Montgomery. They'd had to ride down the mountain together, on the same horse, but she'd refused to speak to him, and for once he hadn't asked his hundreds of questions.

"What do you think you're doing?" she demanded. "This happens to be *my* tent, my private place, such as it is. If I want you in here, I'll invite you, and furthermore—"

"We have a bargain, remember?"

She frowned at him. "I have no idea what you're—" She broke off because she did remember what she'd said. "You couldn't possibly mean . . ."

"You said you'd go to bed with me if I'd let you have thirty minutes alone with the man. I did, and I'm here to collect."

"I didn't mean . . ." she whispered.

"Didn't mean what you said? Do you lie about everything? Is there even an ounce of truth in you?"

"I am not a liar. I never lie. I never have the need to lie," she said, her back straight, but her hands were trembling.

"Good, then." He smiled at her in a way she found particularly insidious. "Let's get to it."

Laurel, Maddie thought. I'll do this for Laurel. Besides, maybe it would be better this way. Perhaps if he were her lover, she could more easily persuade him the next time she had to meet a man to exchange letters.

She tried not to think as she put her hands to the buttons at the front of her habit. She looked up at him. He'd put his foot on the trunk at the side of the tent, leaned his arms on his knee, and was watching her. "Sh-shouldn't we turn down the lamp?"

"No," he said slowly. "I want to see what I'm getting."

Her face turned red and she had to look down to keep him from seeing the hatred in her eyes. She thought she might possibly kill him after this

62

night. She would like to see him lying dead and bleeding.

She finished unbuttoning her jacket and was about to slip it off her shoulders when he put his hands on hers and stopped. When she looked up at him, all her hatred, all her rage, was blazing in her eyes.

"I'm glad those eyes of yours aren't daggers," he said, amusement in his voice.

She jerked out of his grasp. "Let's get this over with, shall we? I'm to pay you for *allowing* me" —she spat the word out—"to use my own God-given freedom. What does it matter what I think or feel? You're the stronger one, Captain Montgomery. You're the one with the strength to take what you want." She jerked the jacket off her shoulders, and when it caught in her hair, she pulled harder.

"Stop it," he said, and pulled her into his arms, trapping her hands between them. "Quiet," he soothed, and began to stroke her back. "It's over now, no one's going to hurt you."

"You!" she gasped, her nose smashed against his chest, but she didn't struggle against him; she was fighting too hard to keep her tears in check to do anything else. *"You're* going to hurt me." She was swallowing hard and fast to keep the tears at bay.

"No, I'm not, and I never meant to. I just wanted to know something and I found that out."

She pushed away from him so she could see his

face. He seemed to be amused about something. "What have you found out?" she asked softly.

"How much you wanted whatever you were doing today. You must have wanted to do whatever it was with all your soul if you were willing to go to bed with someone you dislike as much as you dislike me in order to get it. And . . ."

He smiled at her so that she could see his bottom lip disappearing under his heavy mustache.

"And what, Captain?"

"And I found out about General Yovington." He gave her a knowing look. "Undressing for a man is not something you've done very often."

"Oh?" She barely whispered the word.

"In fact"—he smiled broader—"in fact, I'll even go so far as to guess that you've *never* done this before." He gave a little chuckle. "I also found out what you think of me." He lost his smile. "I can assure you, ma'am, that I am not the sort of man to force a woman to trade sexual favors for . . . for whatever happens. I am a man of reason, and you may discuss anything with me without resorting to unseemliness."

He was silent for a moment, standing there, looking at her as though he expected her to thank him for his noble act.

"Man of reason?" she whispered. "You, Captain Montgomery, are the most unreasonable man I have ever come across. I have met mules who are more reasonable than you. At least with mules one can hit them over the head with a board to

64

get their attention. I doubt very much if any such solution is possible with you."

"Now, just a minute—"

"No! You wait just a minute." She might not be able to outwrestle him, but the volume of her voice was a match for anyone's. "Since I met you, you have done nothing but insult me."

"I would never insult a lady."

"You called me a traveling singer. You told me I *must* do what you want. Can't you understand that you have no rights over me?"

"My orders—"

"Damn your orders to hell! *You* are in the army, I am not. I have done everything in my power to explain to you that I don't want you or need you, yet here you are and this . . ." She pulled her jacket closed. "This! You humiliate me, ridicule me so that I am reduced to playing the harlot for you, and—" Her head shot up. "And for your information, I have undressed for many men, hundreds of men. Frenchmen, Italian men, Russian men. And not one of them ever called me a traveling singer!"

"I never meant—"

"Of course you didn't!" she snapped. "You were just doing your duty, weren't you? Imposing your will on someone else, weren't you?"

Quite suddenly, her strength seemed to leave her. She felt dizzy, her knees weak. It was all too much for her. Since the day she'd walked into her aunt's house and heard about Laurel, she hadn't had a moment's rest. Since then her life, a life of music and good food and laughter, had disappeared. In its place was fear and hard beds and dirt and strangers. Her manager was gone; his comfort and humor were somewhere in England now. All the people who knew her, who knew her music and loved it, were on the other side of the world.

She put her hand to her forehead and started to sink, but he caught her before she hit the floor, lifted her into his arms, and carried her to the cot. He went to the bucket of water—no pretty porcelain dishes anymore—dipped in a cloth, wrung it out, then sat on the cot and put it to her forehead.

"Don't touch me," she whispered.

"Shhh. There's nothing wrong with you that some rest and food wouldn't cure."

"Rest and food," she murmured. All the food in the world wouldn't make Laurel safe.

"Now, Miss LaReina, no, be quiet and rest. I have something to say to you and I mean to say it. First of all, it's true the army has ordered me to escort you, and I have always meant to fulfill those orders. Lie still." He said it as though it were an order but his voice was quiet and didn't anger her as it usually did. She closed her eyes and he adjusted the cloth on her head, then lightly touched the hair at her temples.

"At first I just wanted to get you to leave, to go back east where you belong."

She wanted to say that she had no choice but

to remain in the gold fields, but she didn't. Better to let him know as little as possible.

He touched her other temple, then, very gently, he put both hands on her head and his thumbs began to make little circular motions on her temples. She could feel herself relaxing all the way to her toes. "Where did you learn to do that?" she whispered.

"One of my sisters has headaches. I learned to soothe them away."

She could feel tension slipping from her shoulders and her back. "How many sisters?"

"Two."

She smiled. "I have two sisters as well. Gemma is a year older and Laurel is . . ." She took a breath. "Laurel is just twelve."

"That's a coincidence." His big hands were massaging the back of her head. "My little sister is just fourteen."

"The family pet?"

"More than you can know. With seven older brothers, it's a wonder she isn't a monster."

"But she isn't?"

"Not in my eyes," he said softly.

"Neither is Laurel. She smiles all the time. She used to follow me around when she was a baby and she loved to hear me sing."

"She's in Lanconia now?"

For a moment, Maddie couldn't remember who or what Lanconia was, then she opened her eyes. "Yes, she's at home in the palace now," she said flatly, and the moment was broken.

"Thank you for the . . . the cloth, Captain Montgomery, but now, if you don't mind, could you please send Edith to me?"

"Of course," he answered, then looked at her for a moment. "What happened to the brooch you were wearing?"

She put her hand to her throat. "I—I lost it when I was hurrying up the mountain."

"And didn't stop to search for it? It looked old."

She looked away from him. "It was my grandmother's," she said softly, then turned on him. "Would you please leave me? Get out of my tent and go away? Would you just go back to your army post and leave me alone?"

He didn't seem in the least bothered by her outburst. "I'll see you in the morning, ma'am," he said pleasantly, and left the tent.

Two hours later he was bedded down near Toby on a rise not far from the coach. When he'd left the tent he saw the others standing outside and unabashedly listening to what had been going on inside. 'Ring hardly noticed them as he chose a place to camp, a place near enough that he could hear if there was any danger. Toby had snared a rabbit and he put it to roast over the small fire that 'Ring built, and then he insisted on looking at the cut on 'Ring's arm, so 'Ring took his shirt off and Toby rather roughly doctored the four or five cuts on 'Ring's upper body.

"She's somethin', ain't she?" Toby said.

"If you like liars." 'Ring sipped the hideous concoction Toby called coffee and stared into the fire. "As far as I can tell, she hasn't told me the truth once."

"Sometimes people have reasons for lyin'."

"Hmph!" 'Ring snorted.

"We can't all be as pure as you," Toby said, pouring whiskey on a cut. "If you think she's so all-fired bad, why don't you just leave her here and go back to the fort?"

"She's not bad," 'Ring snapped, then looked away at Toby's grin. "I have no idea what she is. Hell, getting any information out of her is like . . . like . . ."

"Fightin' Blackfeet?"

"Almost as bad." He stood up and stretched. "I'm going to get some sleep. With this woman I need all the strength I can get." He put his shirt back on, then sat on his blanket spread on the ground to remove his tall moccasins. "Toby?"

"Yeah."

"You ever hear the term *sleep-insider?*"

"Can't say as I have. Where'd you hear it?"

"From our little—" He paused and smiled. "Traveling singer." When he'd called her that he certainly hadn't meant to offend her. Not that he hadn't meant to be offensive that day, he had, but he'd also meant to scare her. So far he'd tried tying her up, dressing like a savage, jumping down from a tree in front of her, wrestling her to the ground, and even demanding that she go to bed with him. He'd made her angry, he'd annoyed her, but he hadn't come close to frightening her. Yet today, when she'd come down from that mountain, she'd

69

been very frightened. And later when he'd walked into her tent she'd been fighting tears.

He smiled as he remembered the two of them in the tent. He'd certainly succeeded in stopping her tears. She'd gone from tear-filled eyes to eyes filled with hatred. When she looked at him like that he was glad she didn't have a weapon in her hand. If she had a weapon, could she use it? She could certainly ride a horse. She could ride down the side of a mountain, across streams, under tree branches. She hadn't learned to ride like that in a park on a ducal estate. She—

"What's that?" Toby asked, interrupting 'Ring's thoughts.

'Ring looked absently at the arrow he'd taken from his moccasin. "An arrow. Crow, don't you think?"

"How would I know? One Injun's like all the others. Where'd you get it?"

'Ring held it out and looked at it. "It was sent to me, I think, perhaps, as a warning."

"Warnin' you about what?"

"I don't know exactly." He thought over the time he and the woman were rolling about on the ground. The Indian hadn't seemed to mind that. "I think perhaps he's her guardian."

"How can a duchess from . . ."

"Lanconia."

"Yeah, right. How can a foreign lady have an Indian guardian?"

'Ring laughed and lay down on the blanket. "That's the *least* of my questions about that little

70

lady. Tomorrow I'm going to start finding out some answers. Good night," he said, and closed his eyes.

Maddie sat on the hard horsehide seat inside the coach and glared out the window. She utterly refused to look at the man sitting across from her. This morning Captain Montgomery had told her he was going to ride in the coach with her. Not asked. Told. He said he'd like a break from horseback, but she knew he planned to try to get information out of her.

This morning, after she'd awakened from a restless night, her first thought had been that last night, when she'd been so tired and he'd used his hands to relax her, she'd almost told him something about Laurel.

What if she'd let something slip? She could just hear him saying "My orders, ma'am, are to take into custody any man, woman, child, or animal that is trying to interfere in the freedom of this country." She imagined pleading with him for her sister's life and hearing him say that duty and orders mean more than one insignificant little girl's life.

"I beg your pardon," she said as she became aware that Captain Montgomery was speaking.

"I asked if LaReina was all there is to your name."

"Yes," she said, looking into his eyes. She'd tried once to tell him that LaReina was a stage name and he wouldn't listen then so she wasn't going to make a second effort.

"That's odd, then, that Miss Honey calls you Maddie and your trunks all have the initials MW on them."

"If you must know, LaReina is my middle name. It's Madelyn LaReina . . ." She was trying to think of an appropriate Lanconian surname but couldn't.

"No last name, as in all royalty, or, should I say, aristocracy?" he asked. "Is your family from royal dukes or just aristocratic dukes? Or do they distinguish them in Lanconia?"

She had no idea what he was talking about. Ask me the difference between a trill and a cadenza, she thought. Or the range of a mezzo compared to a soprano. Ask me the words, in Italian, French, German, or Spanish to most operas, but don't ask me anything outside the world of music. "They don't distinguish," she said, giving him what she hoped was a confident smile. "A duke is a duke is a duke."

"That makes sense, but then, I guess the king is a relative of yours."

"Third cousin," she said without blinking an eye. It was amazing that lying seemed to get easier with practice. Maybe it was like scales.

"On your mother's side or your father's?"

She opened her mouth to say *mother's,* but he spoke before she could answer.

He stretched his long legs out when the coach gave a violent lurch. "That was a foolish question.

It would have to be on your father's side for the title to pass down." His eyes sparkled. "This father of yours who can't climb very well. Unless Lanconia has a matriarchal link or your mother has one of those rare titles that a woman can inherit, in which case your father probably couldn't take her title." He paused at another lurch. "But then, if *you* have inherited the title, then presumably your parents are dead and there *is* a matriarchal link."

"Look," Maddie said, "there's an elk. Perhaps tomorrow, after my performance tonight, I can go see some of the countryside. It's so different here from my home."

"Which is it?"

"Which is what?" she asked, knowing exactly what he was asking.

"Is your title a matriarchal link?"

She gritted her teeth. If the man was nothing else, he was persistent. "Please, this is America. While I'm here I want to be as American as I can be. Being a duchess is so . . . so . . . ."

"Fraught with duties?"

"Yes. Exactly. It was such a boring life in the palace. All I ever cared about was singing. I spent all my days with Madame Branchini. I cared for nothing but my lessons." At last there was a bit of truth. She straightened her bonnet. Maybe if she told him a story he'd shut up. "Once, outside Paris, after I'd sung *I Puritani* three nights in a row, a Russian prince invited me to a dinner party at his house. There were about half a dozen women there that night, all great ladies: English, French, an Italian lady, and a beautiful, sad-looking Russian princess. The first course was a lovely, thick creamy soup with a bit of sherry in it and, as we reached the bottom of our bowls, each lady found a pearl in the bottom of the bowl. Quite a lovely pearl, rather large."

He looked at her thoughtfully for a while. "After a childhood in a palace and dinners with pearls in the soup, you came to America. America must be a great letdown for you."

"It's not so bad. I mean, America and Americans have a lot to say for themselves."

"You are very kind to say that, but a lady like you . . . you should have champagne and roses and gentlemen giving you diamonds."

"No, really," she said, leaning forward. "I'd just as soon not. I mean, I've had that all my life. Even as a child I had to wear a little crown when I went out among my people." It's a wonder God doesn't strike me dead, she thought.

He smiled at her. "And what were your sisters' titles?"

She knew this was a trap. As little as she knew, she knew there was only one duchess to a family. "I find I have a terrible headache, Captain."

"Shall I massage your head for you?"

"I'd as soon play with a rattlesnake," she answered, leaning her head back and closing her eyes, not even opening them at his chuckle. She wasn't sure what game they'd just played, but she somehow felt as though she'd lost.

It was noon when they reached Denver City, along with a few hundred other people. It was a "town" consisting of a couple of hundred log shacks, some tents, and a few thousand men who were all bent on making their fortunes.

As soon as their coach stopped, men ran to greet them with the news: There was no gold whatsoever; there were nuggets as big as hen's eggs in the streams. There were men begging for grubstake money, others who were just curious. There was a camp of Utes not far on the outskirts of town and they came to see the red coach and the woman wearing the bright blue dress.

Maddie was unruffled by the noise and confusion and the questions about her name and the legend "Singing Duchess" painted on the side of the coach. She smiled at all of them graciously, then instructed Frank and Sam to erect her tent, then to start passing out handbills announcing tonight's performance. When the tent was up, she went inside to change into a dark wool skirt that was only ankle-length and a plain white cotton blouse. Captain Montgomery was waiting for her outside the tent.

"Good day, Captain," she said, and started past him, but he blocked her way. She sighed. "All right, what is it you want?"

"Where are you planning to go?"

"Not that it's any of your business, but I plan to eat luncheon and then take a walk around town."

"With whom as your guard?"

"I plan to go all by myself, just as I've been walking all alone since I was about a year old."

"You can't go out among these ruffians alone."

She pressed her lips together, tried to walk past him, and when he got in her way, she elbowed him in the ribs. He gave a grunt and she walked past him. Edith had the table set. All along the way from St. Louis to Denver City they'd stopped at farmers' houses and purchased fresh produce, and they'd brought smoked, preserved meat. Now she ate ham and green beans.

"If you must stand over me and glower, Captain, at least have the courtesy to sit down. Have something to eat."

He sat down on the stool, but he shook his head when Edith offered to fill a plate. "I mean no offense, ma'am, but I wouldn't touch food or drink you'd been near."

For the first time Maddie gave him a genuine smile. "At last, some wisdom from the perfect Captain Montgomery. Too bad you're so timid. The ham is excellent."

From out of nowhere Toby came and stood by the table. Maddie nodded to Edith and she heaped a plate full for him.

"I hope you like it, Private."

"I do. I surely do," Toby said, his mouth full as he took a seat on the ground near them. "And it's Toby, just Toby. I ain't a private, not a real private anyway. I don't have nothin' to do with the army if I can help it. The army's what the boy here does, though why he'd want to leave Warbrooke—"

"Toby!" 'Ring snapped. "Forgive him, ma'am, he sometimes talks too much."

"Oh?" She smiled at Toby. "And where is War-brooke?"

"In Maine. The boy here left—"

"Toby!"

Toby put down his fork. "Hell, might as well stop tryin'. I don't know what's got stuck in his craw." He stood up, took his plate, and went out of sight behind the tent.

"What *is* in your craw, Captain?"

"Just trying to keep you alive, that's all."

"Alive? Who would possibly want to harm me?"

Abruptly, he took her hand, holding it even when she tried to pull away, and turned it palm-up. There was a deep scratch across her palm and a bruise on her wrist.

She snatched her hand away, then stood. "Now, Captain, if you'll excuse me, I'm going to take a walk around town."

"Not alone, you're not."

She closed her eyes for a moment and prayed for strength. Her first thought was to try reasoning with him. Appearances to the contrary, no one was trying to harm her. But she couldn't reassure him of that fact without telling him more than she meant to. As she started walking, she thought she'd try to ignore him, but it wasn't easy to ignore a man six feet three inches tall and weighing, she'd guess, somewhere over two hundred pounds. And, too, he glowered.

Since it was quite unusual in Denver City to see a woman who wasn't for sale, she caused quite a bit of commotion as she walked down the wide, dirty paths that served as streets. She stopped at tents with crude tables set up outside them, the tables covered with goods from the East. Often, people in the East sold everything they owned to outfit themselves with wagons and basic necessities for the journey to the gold fields, and when they arrived they sold it all for a few pans and shovels and maybe for a bit of land near a stream.

Maddie looked at lanterns, then picked up a very pretty lace collar. As she did so, three dirty miners stopped, their hats crushed to their chests, and stared at her. She turned and smiled at them. "Good morning."

They nodded back to her.

"Have you found any gold yet?"

One of the men reached into his pocket, but as he withdrew his hand, Captain Montgomery was there, a big hand clamped down on the smaller man's wrist.

Maddie was embarrassed as well as outraged. She grabbed the captain's wrist. "My apologies, gentlemen," she said, and turned away.

"He could have had a gun in his pocket," 'Ring said from behind her. "I was just protecting—"

"Protecting me from what? A few lonely miners?" She turned and faced him. "Captain Montgomery, go away! Leave me alone!"

"I am going to protect you no matter what I have to do. No matter how unpleasant this is for both of us."

That did it, she thought as she turned away. Now he was insinuating that it was a burden to have to spend time with her. She marched ahead of him, her fists clenched at her sides. All along the road were curious men stopping to look at this tall, elegant-looking woman being followed by an even taller man. The men began to nudge each other since they could tell that the woman was very angry.

Now I'm an object of ridicule, Maddie thought, and wondered how in the world her life had come to this.

It was at that thought that she decided to stop this charade. She turned to him and gave him her sweetest smile. "Captain Montgomery, I'm hungry."

"But you just ate."

What happened to men who were eager to do the bidding of a woman? "Yes, I did, but I'm hungry again. Couldn't we find someplace to eat?"

He looked over her head. To tell the truth, he was very hungry. He had been living on dried beef and hardtack while everyone else ate fresh meat and, even better, fresh vegetables. But after the opium in the whiskey, he wasn't going to trust eating at her table. "There's a wagon over there, and I think they're selling food."

Within minutes she had both his hands loaded down with plates of food and a loaf of fresh bread

79

to take back to Edith. She smiled up at him. "Could you please hold this for me while I make a trip to the . . . you know?"

He looked at the food, steam rising from it. Beef. Potatoes. Corn bread. Peas. He hardly heard what she was saying, but nodded and went to sit on a bench at the side of the wagon. He was so hungry that he'd finished his plate of food and was halfway through hers before he realized she hadn't returned.

"Damn her," he muttered. "Damn *me*," he amended, and set off to find her. There was no way to track her in a town, but she was distinctive enough to cause people to notice her wherever she went, so he asked questions. There didn't seem to be a man in town who hadn't seen her, but their directions were all contradictory.

It was nearly an hour before he found her, standing in a group of Ute women and laughing. He had only a moment to wonder how they were communicating before he bore down on her.

The squaws saw him first and warned Maddie. She started to run straight into the camp, with 'Ring behind her, yelling at her to stop. The Indian women, always ready for a laugh, did everything they could to block 'Ring's progress, until he had to pick one of the women up and set her aside.

Maddie ran through the village as fast as she could, dodging children and dogs, once bumping into a brave and apologizing profusely, but not slowing down her run. When she reached the end of the camp, she doubled back and ran toward town.

As soon as she reached the edge of town she slowed to catch her breath and smiled. She'd out-witted him as well as outrun him.

A few seconds later she felt a hand on her shoulder, and when she looked up and saw him with something akin to triumph in his eyes, she gave him an I'll-show-you look, then screamed. "Help me! Help me! Please don't hit me again!"

Eight men leaped on 'Ring at once, and she went scurrying away. Twenty minutes later he was close on her heels again. Looking over her shoulder, she saw that his usually perfectly combed hair was mussed, there was a red place on his cheek and dust all over his clothes. She grinned and kept running.

She wasn't sure when she began to enjoy the game, but enjoy it she did. She hid in an empty barrel and nearly giggled aloud when he stood not a foot from her and looked around. She ran into a group of men who were rolling dice on the ground, grabbed the hat off one of the men, and crouched down into the group. The men swarmed closer to help hide her. In fact, one of the men crouched much, much too close and she gave a squeal of protest when, she wasn't positive, but she thought he pinched her thigh. She jumped, then saw Captain Montgomery turn and see her, so she started running again.

She ran into one of the many saloon tents, paused at the high, rough bar, her head on her hand, and whispered, "Whiskey." She downed the shot in one swallow, held out the glass for another shot, then saw Captain Montgomery in the doorway. "He's payin'," she said, and ran toward the back. The bartender and a couple of men held the captain while he dug money out to pay for her whiskey.

Outside, she quickly asked two men to give her a boost to the top of one of the few buildings in Denver City that had a roof. The men did so gladly, but with a great deal of fumbling hands all over her body.

She stood on top of the building and watched Captain Montgomery looking for her. She had to put her hand over her mouth to keep from laughing out loud. She took a deep breath, put her arms out and her head back. It was the first time she'd enjoyed herself in months. How precious freedom is, she thought.

When she opened her eyes, Captain Montgomery was standing below and watching her.

"Oops," she said, laughing, and ran to the far side of the building and started scrambling down a stack of barrels and old wagon wheels. Just as she reached the ground, Captain Montgomery was there. She started to run but he caught her skirt and pulled her to him.

She fought him. Oh, heavens, she fought him, but he kept her hands away from his face, and at last he grabbed her around the waist and slung her over his hip.

"You bite one part of me and you won't be able to sit down for a week. You understand me?"

She felt rather like a sack of feed as she was slung across his arm, but she could tell he was very angry, and angry men sometimes did unpredictable things. So, instead of fighting him, she went limp so that he had her full weight tucked under his one arm. But it didn't seem to make any difference to him as he stomped away from the town and into the woods with her.

At last, when they were some distance from the noisy town, he dumped her onto a soft, grassy bank.

"Captain Montgomery, I—"

"Don't you say a word, not a *word!* I have been ordered to protect you and I damned well plan to do it. You may think your little escapade was clever, but you have no idea what's going on. These are people you know nothing about. They—"

"You're the one who knows nothing," she said calmly, and lay back against the grass. The exercise in the clear, thin mountain air had made her feel wonderful. It was the first time since she'd heard Laurel was taken that she hadn't felt as tense as a violin bow. "Oh, Captain, don't you have any sense of humor? Any at all?" she said languidly. It was the first time in a long while that she'd noticed wildflowers and trees and blue sky high above her head.

He didn't say anything for a while, and she didn't look at him, but then he lay down on the grass about a foot away from her. "I have a rather well developed sense of humor, actually. But in the last year I seemed to have lost it."

"Oh?" she said in an encouraging way, but he said nothing. She took a breath of the clear air. "I can't imagine a man who names his horse Satan having a sense of humor. As far as I can tell, you are all business and no play. Your idea of dealing with women is to frighten them, to intimidate them. I'm sure some women like that, but you couldn't have had much success."

"You know nothing about me," 'Ring said with some anger. "Nothing whatever."

"Then I guess we're even, for you know nothing about me."

He turned on his elbow to look at her, but she kept looking skyward. "Now, there you're wrong. The truth is, Miss LaReina, I know a great deal about you."

She gave a derisive little chuckle. "Nothing. Absolutely nothing."

He rolled to his back. "Shall we make a wager?"

"More of your go-to-bed-with-me deals?" There was some bitterness in her voice.

"No," he said softly. "We'll wager for something more important." He didn't acknowledge the glare she sent his way. "For twenty-four hours you won't run away. For twenty-four hours I can sleep knowing you won't do anything foolish."

"And you get to define foolish?"

"Yes."

"What do I get?"

"For twenty-four hours I'll stay away from you."

She smiled up at the trees. "All this is to see whether you know anything about me or not, is it?" She didn't think she was wagering much. First of all, she was supposed to meet someone about the letters that night right here in Denver City and she had no doubt she could do that under his nose. And second, from her observation, he was a man who couldn't see beyond the end of his own nose. He seemed to think women were frail creatures, and she knew he had preconceived ideas about opera singers. "All right, it's a deal. What do you know about me?"

"First of all, if you're a duchess, I'm Queen Victoria. You know almost nothing about aristocratic lineages, and you know nothing about Lanconia. And the brooch you, ah . . . lost, the one that belonged to your grandmother, very pretty little thing but neither the diamonds nor the pearls were quite the quality of a duchess. What you *do* know about is this country. You climb these hills like you were born and raised here. You can ride a horse better than most men, and you down a shot of rotgut whiskey as though you've done it many times before. How am I doing so far?"

"I haven't fallen asleep yet."

"Also you are at ease around Indians. Unusual in a European lady, don't you think? You don't know Sam or Frank very well and you don't like Edith much. It makes me wonder if you were the one who chose them. Am I right?"

85

"Perhaps."

"Let's see, what else? My guess is that you're a virgin, or very near to being one."

"I don't like this, Captain." She started to rise, but he wouldn't allow it.

"I certainly don't mean to offend you. I'm sure that a woman as pretty as you has had more than a few offers, but I don't think men interest you much."

"Men who are forced on me certainly hold no interest for me. I think I need to go back to camp now."

He caught her arm. "There's more, and if I must remind you, you were the one who said I know nothing about you. Now, where was I? Oh, yes, someone is blackmailing you. I haven't figured out why yet, but I feel sure it isn't some former lover. No, it's something more serious—much, much more serious. You don't frighten easily yet you're deathly afraid of whatever is going on in your life now."

Maddie didn't say anything; she couldn't.

Very softly, very gently, he took her hand in his. "I am an honorable man . . . Maddie," he whispered, using the name he'd heard Edith call her. "If you would confide in me, I will do all in my power to help you, but you have to trust me."

It took every bit of Maddie's willpower not to tell him about Laurel. She wanted to tell someone who might understand. Someone who might react differently from Edith who had merely shrugged her shoulders. And she wanted advice too. What would she do if she got to the third camp and they didn't let her see Laurel? What if—

To keep herself from giving in to temptation, she jumped up, standing over him. "Oh, very good, Captain Montgomery, very, very good. If you ever leave the army, perhaps you can go on the stage." She straightened her shoulders and looked down her nose at him. "But you forgot the most important thing about me: my voice. Until you have heard me sing, you know nothing about me. All else is superficial."

He smiled up at her. "Do you really think that bunch of drunken, greedy men are going to appreciate opera?"

"One doesn't have to appreciate opera, or even music, for that matter, to love the sound of my voice."

He laughed at that, genuinely laughed, a deep, sweet sound. "Vain, aren't you?"

Her face was serious. "Absolutely not. I haven't a vain bone in my body. My voice is a gift from God. Were I to say that it is less than it is would be a slight to God."

"That's one way of looking at it."

She sat down beside him. "No," she said earnestly. "I'm speaking the truth. Where else does talent come from but God? I have been singing since I was three. I was on the stage at sixteen. Every day I thank God for blessing me with the voice He gave me and I try to honor Him by taking care of it."

He knew she deeply, sincerely believed what

she was saying and, with the way she spoke, it made sense. "And you think these miners are going to love your songs? Love your *La . . .*"

"*Traviata.*"

"Ah, yes, the fallen woman."

She gave him a look of speculation. "You speak Italian?"

"A little. You think these miners will love your songs?"

"Not the songs. My *voice*. There is a great deal of difference."

"All right," he said, smiling, "then show me. Sing a song for me."

At that she stood and smiled down at him. "I apologize, Captain Montgomery, for doubting you. You *do* have a sense of humor. An incredible, outrageous sense of humor."

"Oh, I see, you need, what? An orchestra? Opera singers can't sing *a cappella?*"

"I could sing underwater if need be, but I sing only when I want to. Were I to sing here for you, just you, it would be a gift of great value. You have done nothing to earn such a gift."

"The miners who fork over ten dollars tonight have earned this . . . gift?"

"Tonight I will not sing for one man alone but for many. There is a great, great deal of difference."

"Oh, I see," he said in a patronizing way, then pulled his big gold watch out of his jacket pocket. "Gift or not, it's time for you to get back to camp now to get ready to sing tonight."

"How do you think I functioned for twenty-five years without you to tell me what to do and when to do it?"

"I really don't know. It bewilders me." As he stood, he grimaced with pain.

"Getting old, Captain?"

"I think perhaps climbing rock walls to protect you from unknown men, being bitten, kicked, and elbowed, not to mention fighting off eight men this morning, are beginning to take their toll."

"You could always go back to your fort and rest."

"Harrison would love me to come back with my tail between my legs," 'Ring muttered.

"And who is Harrison?"

"I'll answer your questions as soon as you answer mine."

"Then hell shall freeze over," she said sweetly as she started to walk back to camp.

"Whatever, but don't forget that I won our wager. For twenty-four hours you don't run away."

"You did *not* win the wager, Captain. I explained that to you. If you had said, 'You are a singer,' then you would have won, for singing is all to me."

"I *did* say you were a singer."

She turned and glared at him. "You did not so much as mention my singing."

His eyes sparkled. "I said you were a singer." His voice lowered. "Who travels."

Her mouth tightened in anger, then she had to

hide a smile. "Ha!" She turned on her heel and walked away. "You will see," she said over her shoulder. "Tonight you will learn who and what I am."

He stood, watching her walk away. She was damned interesting is what she was, he thought. And pretty, and smart—and in trouble. And she didn't need more trouble than what she already had. He liked the way she told him she was great, no, that she had a magnificent voice. Sometimes he got so tired of women who constantly asked him if he liked their dress or hair. Maybe Toby was right. He'd said all the Montgomery boys had it too easy when it came to women. They had looks and money, and women didn't usually ask for more. Toby'd said it wasn't fair, for he, Toby, had never had either, so, to win women, he'd had to be nice to them, to court them.

'Ring watched Maddie walk ahead of him. His good looks hadn't seemed to make an impression on her, and he doubted if she'd care one way or the other if he told her of his family's money. After all, how could money impress someone who'd spent her childhood wearing a little crown and traveling amid her people? He laughed out loud, then regained control when a couple of people stared at him. She was a liar, true, but she was an interesting one and a creative one. Maybe she needed less protection than he'd originally thought, but he was going to stick around her, if for no other reason than to see what happened next. Chasing her around a dirty gold mining town sure beat the army life that, as Toby frequently pointed out, for the most part, could bore a dead man.

He smiled and watched the sway of her skirt across ample hips.

CHAPTER 5

"All right," 'Ring said to Toby. "You understand everything I told you? Remember everything?"

They were in a tent set up at the back of the large log shell that would someday be a hotel but for tonight was a stage for Maddie's singing.

"I can't very well forget," Toby said in disgust. "You've told me twenty times in the last ten minutes. We're to keep the audience quiet and if anybody acts like he don't like her singin', we're to break his head."

"More or less," 'Ring said, looking at his watch again.

"What's eatin' you anyway? I ain't never seen you so nervous. You act like you're about to have a baby."

"Not quite but close. She thinks these drunks will like her singing."

"I thought she was smarter'n that."

'Ring sighed. "You should hear her. She thinks her voice is a gift from God. Maybe it is, but it's a gift to men in cutaways, to men who drink champagne. To men who live on Taos Lightning, I think they're going to want to see her legs."

"That ain't a bad idea."

'Ring shot him a look of disgust.

"We can't all be as high-minded as you. I heard about you two in town today. I ain't never heard of you chasin' a woman in public or private. Did you really carry her off into the trees?"

'Ring didn't answer but just looked at his watch again.

"You two get up to somethin' in the woods?"

"Yes," 'Ring snapped. "We *talked*. Ever try doing that with a woman?"

"Why would I want to? Bein' in the army gives me the chance to hear more talkin' than I ever wanted to hear. You even kiss her?"

"Toby, shut up."

Toby grinned.

Maddie looked at her music one more time. She was to sing a few familiar arias, songs with catchy tunes, a couple of songs that showed off her voice to its best advantage, and then "America the Beautiful" to close the program.

Frank had come up with a piano, dented and scarred from its trip across the plains, but he'd worked on tuning it and had it working well enough. Frank was fairly talented and she thought he might once have been a musician, but he must have left the possibility of a musical career behind when he'd entered the ring. She had never asked him about his life. A face like his tended to put one off exchanging confidences.

She looked up as Captain Montgomery, Toby

behind him, entered the little makeshift dressing room outside the back door of the half-finished building.

"They're serving drinks," the captain said glumly. "And gambling. They're not used to civilized entertainment. Toby and I will do our best to keep them under control, but I can't guarantee anything."

"*I* will control them, Captain. My voice and I will control the men."

He gave her a look that said she wasn't too bright, then smiled and winked at her. "Sure. Of course. God'll probably send a bolt of lightning down to strike them dead if they don't behave."

"Out," she said softly. "Out!"

He gave a mocking little bow and left the tent, but Toby hesitated. "He sure do make a body mad, don't he, ma'am?"

"More than I can say. Tell me, has anyone ever told him he was wrong?"

"A few, but in the end he was always right."

"No wonder his family sent him away to the army."

Toby chuckled. "Ma'am, his whole family's just like him."

"That I don't believe. The earth couldn't hold them."

"Yes, ma'am." Toby grinned. "Good luck tonight."

"Thank you."

As she stepped onto the stage, built just that afternoon to Sam's specifications, Maddie did feel a little nervous, and she knew it was thanks to Captain Montgomery. Now he stood at the back of the big room, behind what looked to be about three hundred men, with his pistol on his hip, sword by his side and a knife or two showing. He looked ready to fight a ship full of pirates. Toby stood on the other side of the room picking his teeth with a knife big enough to cut through buffalo bones.

Heaven help me, she thought, I'm singing in a prison, but in this case the prisoners are happy and the guards are lunatics.

She started the program with the beautiful *"Ah, fors' è lui"* from *La Traviata,* but she hadn't sung more than the first few lines before trouble broke out in the back. And it was all Captain Montgomery's fault. Some poor, tired miner had tipped his chair back too far, the chair had crashed to the floor, and the captain had pounced on the man, pistol drawn.

"Fight!" someone yelled, and after that all was chaos as the brawl began. Fists were flying; chairs were sailing through the air.

What does one do with unruly boys? Maddie wondered. One calls them down, that's what.

She took a breath, a deep, deep breath, filling her body with oxygen in the way she'd been trained, and then she hit a note, a high, clear note, a very loud note.

She immediately had the attention of the men nearest her as they paused, fists aimed at each

94

other's faces, and looked at her, eyes wide, blinking.

Maddie held the note and more men began to look at her. The men in front began to slowly clap their hands in rhythm, marking the beats with their claps. The men in the middle of the room added their feet to the rhythmic beat. The men in the back were the last to realize what was going on and to stop trying to kill men who an hour earlier had been their friends.

"By damn!" Toby said, watching her as she held that one single note, and held it.

'Ring let go of the hair of the man he was pummeling and looked at her. She had everyone's attention now.

Maddie continued holding the note. And holding it. And holding it. Tears ran down her face. Her lungs emptied of oxygen, but still she held it. She drew air from every part of her body, from her legs, her arms, her fingertips, her toes, even from the ends of her hair. She depleted everything she had while the men kept up their rhythmic clapping. One, two, three, four. She held it. Her backbone was touching her navel. Her corset was loose, but still she held that note.

At long, long last she spread her arms wide and balled her hands into fists. Her body hurt; every muscle ached, but she didn't let go of that note.

She put her head back and then, quickly, abruptly, she brought her fists together, bent her elbows, brought her fists to her forehead and *down!*

She stopped and for a moment she thought she might collapse, but she gasped for air like a person drowning—and the crowd went wild. They cheered and fired pistols, rifles, and shotguns into the air. They grabbed one another's arms and danced around. They might be uneducated and their morals might leave something to be desired, but they certainly recognized when something miraculous had just happened.

When Maddie recovered herself, she looked over the heads of the jubilant miners to where Captain Montgomery stood at the back. His eyes were as wide with wonder as the men's. She gave him the smuggest smile she could manage and pointed skyward. He smiled back, then put one hand in front of him, one in back, and bowed deeply. When he straightened, she gave him a condescending nod that any queen would have been proud of.

After that, those lonely, tired, half-drunken men belonged to Maddie. She sang and they listened. It often annoyed her that the American people had such odd ideas about opera. They seemed to think opera was for kings, for people with great education, but the truth was, opera had started out being very common: common stories for common people.

She told the miners of poor Elvira not being able to have the man she loved, then sang *"Tui la voce sua soave,"* where the young woman goes mad. At the end there were some tears wiped away.

She sang *"Una voce poco fa"* after telling them that Rosina was vowing to marry the man she loved no matter what. They thought that was more sensible than going mad.

After six arias the men were making requests for repeats. She hadn't sung for such a genuinely appreciative audience since she'd left her parents' home.

"Go mad again," they called.

"No, marry the country man," someone else yelled.

She sang for almost four hours before Captain Montgomery walked onto the little stage and told the men the show was over. He was booed and hissed and at first Maddie started to tell him that she would decide when she'd stop singing, but then common sense won over pride and, gratefully, she took the arm he offered as he led her through the door and out to the tent that served as a dressing room.

The applause behind them was thunderous—helped by the explosion of many firearms. The audience no longer consisted of a mere three hundred men, but, while Maddie had sung, hundreds more had quietly, respectfully, tiptoed into the building, and when no more people could be held inside, they climbed the walls and sat on them. They opened the doors and stood, sat, lay, outside to hear her sing.

"I have to do an encore," Maddie said, but Captain Montgomery held her fast.

"No, you don't. You're tired. It must be enormous work to sing like that."

She looked up at him, saw his eyes were wide with wonder and appreciation. "Thank you," she said, and leaned a bit against him. Her former manager had never cared whether she was tired or sick; he felt that the singing was Maddie's concern and not his. He never quarreled with her if she said she was too ill to perform—which she rarely was. His interest was booking her and in how much money she made from the box office.

Now it was rather nice to have someone realize that she was tired. She smiled at him. "Yes, I am rather tired. Perhaps, Captain, you'd like to join me in a glass of port. I always carry the finest Portuguese port with me, and I always have some after singing. It soothes my throat."

All around them were hundreds of shooting men, but they might as well have been alone. The moonlight glistened off the rose pink of her silk dress, and her bare shoulders were white and round and smooth. "I would like that," he said softly.

He held back the tent flap for her, and Maddie started inside, but then she saw that hideous man inside, the man who knew where Laurel was. His gun was pointed straight at Maddie, and she realized that if she didn't get rid of 'Ring, they'd probably both get shot. She turned around and jerked the flap out of Captain Montgomery's hand.

"Tell me, Captain, are you trying to seduce

98

me?'' she snapped at him. "Is that why you wanted me off the stage?''

"Why, no, I—''

"No? Isn't that what all men want? Isn't that why you carried me through town today? Isn't all your concern for me so you can have what you want from me? I've dealt with men like you all over the world.'' With each word she saw his back stiffen until he was standing at a soldier's attention. She didn't like herself much for what she was saying because, if she were honest, she had to admit that so far all he'd really done was try to protect her. But she *had* to get rid of him. The man inside could shoot one or both of them and no one would notice, what with all the noise surrounding them.

"Is that it, Captain? Do you think that a traveling singer like me is a woman of easy virtue?'' Since just a few hours earlier he'd said he believed her to be a virgin, she knew the statement made no sense. "Is the hope of gain what is keeping you from returning to the army?''

He looked down at her, his face cold and hard. "I apologize for having given you such an impression of my character. I will wait for you to . . . to have your port, then I will escort you to your camp.'' He touched the brim of his hat, then turned on his heel and walked smartly away.

Maddie refused to think about what she'd said. She had done what she had to. The man was waiting for her inside, slipping his pistol into his belt.

"Quick thinker, ain't you?''

"When necessary." She went to the little trunk Sam had moved for her and from under the lining she took the letter. He pulled another one from inside his shirt. The letter was folded to make an envelope, and there was nothing written on it, but it was sweaty and crumpled from being next to the man's skin. She had to resist holding it by one corner and at arm's length.

He smirked at her as though he could read her thoughts, then pulled another paper from inside his shirt and handed it to her.

She took it to the lantern light which she left turned low so the shadows inside the tent couldn't be seen clearly from the outside. What she saw was a map. Tomorrow she was to sing in a place on Tarryall Creek, and two days later she was to sing in an isolated little town called Pitcherville. At Pitcherville she was to use the map and go fifty miles up into the Rockies, where she was to deliver the next letter.

"And Laurel will be there?" she asked the man. "I was told I'd see her after the third camp."

"If you can find the place."

"I can find it all right."

"Alone? You show up with your fancy captain and the three of you are dead."

"You couldn't kill a child."

The man chuckled. "After what she's been through, she might rather be dead."

At that Maddie lunged at the man, but he caught her in his arms and held her easily. "How about a kiss?"

It was sometime later that Maddie emerged from the tent and Captain Montgomery was waiting to escort her back to her camp. They walked silently.

It was 'Ring who at last spoke. "You don't seem to have enjoyed your port much. You keep wiping your mouth."

"What I do or do not do is none of your concern!"

At her own tent she ordered Edith to put kettles of water on the fire to heat. "I'm going to take a bath."

"A whole one?" Edith asked.

"Yes. As hot as I can stand. As thorough as I can stand." She went inside the tent.

"What's eatin' her?" Toby asked. "I'd a thought she'd been real happy tonight."

"She was," 'Ring said stiffly. "She was until she thought I had dishonorable intentions toward her."

"She don't know you very well, does she?" Toby said, meaning his words as an insult, but 'Ring didn't take them as such.

"No, she doesn't. One minute she was offering me port and the next minute she looked inside her tent and acted like I was a satyr about to attack her. The woman makes no sense. She—" He stopped. "Toby, I've been a fool," he said, then turned and took off running.

Four men were taking down the tent they'd set up for Maddie to use, but he examined the ground by lantern light. The ground was too trampled to tell anything from the tracks, but he picked up the butt of a cigar. "Does this belong to one of you?" he asked the men moving the tent.

"Naw, you can have it."

"No, I mean, did one of *you* smoke it?"

One man punched another with a knowing look. "That pretty little singer leadin' you a chase? Her other fella already left."

"You saw someone leave the tent?"

"I didn't see nothin'," the man said. "You see anything, Joe?"

'Ring knew the men weren't going to volunteer any information. They'd fallen in love with Maddie and they meant to protect her. He grabbed a man by the collar. "You want to keep that face of yours? Then tell me what you saw. I think he's trying to kill her."

Four pistols were placed near 'Ring's head and the triggers cocked. The man jerked out of 'Ring's grasp. "Why didn't you say so? I just saw him slippin' out. Couldn't say if I'd ever seen him before."

'Ring frowned at the men still holding guns on him. They didn't seem dangerous unless one of them tripped on a rock. "Short? Tall?"

"Medium. About medium, I'd guess."

"Light? Dark?"

"About medium."

"Hell!" 'Ring said, and clasped the cigar butt in his hand. He walked away from the men, cursing himself. What was wrong with him? He knew she was a liar, yet this time he'd believed her. If he weren't already so bruised, he'd have smacked himself because he'd believed her. She'd hurt his damned pride. All she had to do was give him a few insults and he'd gone off like a hurt little boy.

What—who—had been waiting inside that tent for her? Had the man been holding a gun? She could have seen that when he opened the flap. Had she possibly saved his neck by making him angry? 'Ring realized that had she allowed him to walk inside that tent, unprepared for an ambush, he might not be alive now.

Fool, he thought. I'm a damned fool for not having seen through her.

He stopped walking, for he remembered the way she'd kept scrubbing at her lips, the way she'd demanded a bath when she'd returned. What was she being blackmailed about? What could someone hold over her that was causing her to do what she was doing?

He slowed his steps as he neared the camp. As bodyguards, Sam and Frank seemed to be nearly worthless. And, unfortunately, he hadn't been much better. He had been so blinded by the sound of her voice that he'd completely forgotten about any possible blackmail plot, had lost all sense of danger.

As he saw the camp before him, his first impulse was to charge into her tent and demand that she tell him what was going on. And what was he going to use to force her to tell him? Physical violence? If at times he was less than brilliant, she didn't seem to be. From the first she'd never believed he'd harm her. She'd never been afraid of him in the least. And she was right, for he would never in his life hurt a woman.

So, how was he going to make her trust him enough to tell him? As soon as he thought it, he knew that the key word was *trust*. She had to trust him.

He saw Edith coming out of the tent. "She finish her bath?"

"Yeah, and my back is finished from carryin' the buckets."

'Ring fished a gold piece out of his pocket and gave it to her. "You give her anything she wants."

"I'll give you anything *you* want," Edith purred.

'Ring ignored her and strode into the tent.

"Captain Montgomery!" Maddie snapped. "How dare you—"

"I came for the port you offered me. That is, if you and the man who was in here earlier haven't drunk it all."

"I'd *never* serve him port." She clapped her hand over her mouth.

"Oh? What do you serve him, then?"

Maddie looked away. "I have no idea what you mean. Now, Captain, I'm tired and I'd like to go to bed."

He flicked open the little stool and sat on it. "Go ahead, but I'm going to have some port." He smiled at her. "Wouldn't you like to have something to drink? It might calm you down."

"I'm perfectly calm. I'm always like this after a performance."

"Is that so? Sure it wasn't the man's kisses that did this?"

Maddie looked away from him and began to tremble at the memory of that odious man touching her. Never in her life had she had to put up with anyone touching her if she didn't want to be touched. Since she was a child she'd known she was different, special even, and she'd treated herself with respect. When she was twenty, there had been a quick tumble on a couch with a French count, but she'd found the encounter so unpleasant she'd never repeated the experience. Men had been content to hear her sing; she'd not had to give more.

But tonight . . . oh, God, tonight he'd touched her. He might have done more except for Edith bursting into the tent.

Now, as a strong arm went around her shoulders, she panicked and began to fight.

"Shhh, it's just me," 'Ring said. "You're safe now. You have the greatest voice in the world, a God-given voice, and I've never had so much pleasure as I had hearing you tonight. What was that song you sang about the lady going mad?"

"Tui la voce sua soave," she said against his chest.

"It was the most beautiful. . . ?" he said, purposely mistranslating.

"No. 'It was here in sweetest accents.'"

"Ah, yes. That was my favorite."

She smiled up at him. "Favorite so far. You haven't heard much."

"Oh, but I have. I've heard Adelina Patti sing."

"What!" She pushed away from him. "Patti? That scarecrow? Her F sharps are a disaster. She shouldn't be allowed out of the chorus."

"She sounded good to me."

"But then, what do you know? You are but a poor Colonial soldier while I am—"

"A duchess from Lanconia?" He looked at her with one eyebrow raised.

Quite suddenly she realized what he was doing. She had been trembling when he'd entered and near to tears, but now she was better—a lot better. "How about a glass of port, Captain?"

He knew she understood, and it made him feel good. "I'd rather have a song. A song just for me."

"Ha!" she said, but she was smiling. "You must slay dragons for that reward. Tonight all you deserve is a glass of port. But it is the finest port in the world." It pleased her that he'd gone from ridiculing her singing to wanting her to sing for him.

"Then I'll have to take what I can get, but I mean to earn that song."

She poured the rich liquid into two crystal glasses that she kept in a box specially made to hold and protect them.

"To truth," he said, raising his glass.

Maddie drank the toast, but she fully expected to be struck dead on the spot. She gave him a weak smile over the top of the glass and vowed to not give him another piece of information.

The next day they traveled and Maddie was once again stuck inside the rocking coach with Edith, who slept and snored. Captain Montgomery had asked to be allowed to ride inside with her, but she'd refused. She would very much have liked his company, someone to talk with, but he'd gotten too much information out of her.

At midmorning Frank stopped the coach and the captain came to the window. "I'm afraid I have a favor to ask of you. Toby isn't feeling well, so could he ride inside the coach?"

"Of course. He can sit by Edith."

"That's the whole idea," 'Ring said softly.

"I beg your pardon."

He motioned for her to lean toward him. "I think they're in love," he whispered in her ear.

"Oh?" She straightened and looked from Edith to Toby, who looked perfectly fit.

'Ring motioned her down again. "They want to be alone."

She still wasn't understanding.

"You can ride with me."

"I see. If this is an attempt to get me alone with you, you can forget—"

"You can ride my horse."

She didn't question how he'd known she could ride his stallion, or that she was greedy to do so, but she wasn't going to turn down the offer. She flung open the coach door so quickly she caught Toby on the shoulder.

"I'm sorry, I—"

'Ring practically lifted Toby and thrust him into the coach, then slammed the door behind him. "Edith can take care of him." He moved his arm in a sweeping gesture toward that gorgeous horse of his.

She smiled up at the animal. "Here, Satan," she called, but the horse didn't move. "Satan?"

'Ring took off his hat and scratched his head. "Try, ah . . . Buttercup."

She looked at him. "Buttercup?"

"It wasn't my idea. My little sister named him. He eats anything. My brothers wanted to name him Sawdust, but I thought Buttercup was the lesser of the two evils."

"No Satan?"

He looked down at his hat. "I would have been laughed out of my family. You ready to ride him?"

"Come, Buttercup," she called, and the horse trotted straight to her, went past her outstretched hand, and started munching on the coach's red paint.

She laughed, took the reins, and mounted.

"He's not used to anybody but me, so your lighter weight may disturb him," 'Ring said as he shortened the stirrups for her.

She patted the horse's neck. "I'll manage. My father taught me to ride. We'll get along fine, won't we, you big, beautiful male?"

Frank looked at 'Ring and 'Ring shook his head. Women and horses.

Maddie handled Buttercup easily. It was wonderful to once again be on the back of such a spirited animal, and she went up the steep hill ahead of the coach so that 'Ring, on Toby's horse, had trouble keeping up with her. She would have loved to try him out on a flat stretch of ground, but in the Rockies, flat land was not to be had.

When 'Ring pulled up beside her, she was grinning broadly.

"It must be wonderful to be back in the country where you grew up," he said casually.

"Oh, it is. It's heavenly. The air is so clear and cool and—" She realized he'd trapped her again. She looked at him, and he was smiling smugly. She looked away. "Captain," she said slowly, "what is your name? I mean besides 'boy' as Toby calls you?"

"Or 'devil incarnate' as *you* call me?"

She kept her face turned away from him.

"It's 'Ring."

She turned and gave him an odd look. " 'Ring? I see. And all these brothers and sisters you have, what are their names? Necklace? Bracelet? Anklet, perhaps?"

He chuckled. "No, actually it's Christopher Hring Montgomery. My middle name is spelled with an H on the front of it, but the H isn't pronounced. My mother always spelled my name with an apostrophe on the front of it. I guess it kept people from calling me Huh-ring."

She was silent for a while, enjoying the air and the wonderful horse beneath her. "Where did you get such a name?"

"My father has a big old family Bible full of names for our family."

"Such as?"

"Jarl and Raine and Jocelyn."

"Jocelyn's pretty."

"Not when it's given to a boy, as it is in our family."

"Perhaps you'd have to give the boy another name, such as . . . well, I don't know. Lyn, maybe."

"Lyn! He'd have to defend himself with a gun from the time he was six."

"Lyn isn't any worse than 'Ring. Why didn't they call you Chris?"

"Christopher is my father's name. I would have been 'Young Chris' or, in our family, 'Young Kit.' All in all, 'Ring is all right, just so it's not Huhring."

He smiled at her. "And where did you get the name Maddie?"

"From the queen, of course. She names all the little duchesses."

"I guess she named your little sister Laurel after some Lanconian plant. I'll bet—"

He stopped because all humor left her face. He searched his mind for what he'd said wrong. "Laurel," he said softly, and saw her wince. "Look! Was that a mountain bluebird?" He watched her turn away, and when she looked back she had herself under control again. Laurel, he thought. Perhaps all this had to do with her little sister Laurel.

He didn't try to provoke her again but let her enjoy the day as he vowed to keep an even closer watch on her than he had.

CHAPTER 6

Maddie's second performance needed no showy display to make the miners listen to her, for word of her first performance had spread across the mountain and men had traveled from camps all over to hear her.

She told Captain Montgomery that she would sing outside. He'd protested, but relented when he saw how determined she was. The men built her a stage of sorts, large enough for her and for Frank behind her, this time playing a flute. Captain Montgomery stood at one end and Toby at the other.

While she was singing she glanced once at Captain Montgomery. He was leaning against a tree, his eyes closed in pleasure. Whatever else she had to say about him, he was coming to genuinely like her music. By the end of the performance she found herself singing for him, watching out of the corner of her eye as, when she played with notes, holding them, trilling them up and down, he'd smile ever so sweetly.

When, after four hours, he led her from the

stage, he wrapped her arm tightly in his, his fingers closing over hers. "You were right," he said. "You cannot say enough about your voice."

She thought perhaps it was the most sincere compliment she'd ever received. The compliment was so sincere and the moonlight was so lovely that she didn't invite him into her tent for a glass of port, and once she was alone inside the tent she got out her photograph of Laurel and looked at it for a long while. Whatever she must do she must trust no one, at least not anyone who might possibly interfere. She imagined Captain Montgomery charging up the mountainside, sword drawn, and challenging that dreadful man with the letters. And in payment they might harm Laurel.

By the time she went to bed she remembered only Laurel.

There were no opening or closing hours for the saloons in the Pikes Peak gold fields. Since getting drunk was as much of an occupation as looking for gold, the drink flowed as freely as the mountain streams.

Inside one of the many tents there were two empty whiskey bottles on the table that would have been full of splinters except for the layer of gray grease coating it, and the four men were rapidly emptying the third bottle.

"Ain't never heard nothin' like her," one man said.

"An angel can't sing no better."

"Member how Sully said she'd not be any good?"

"I would have liked the boys to hear her."

"We could ask her to sing up at Bug Creek."

"Takes a day to get there and there's only fifty men. Wouldn't even pay her way. She ain't gonna do that."

They called for bottle number four and drank half of it. "I think she ought to sing for us. Sully'd like to hear her, even if he thinks he don't want to, and he can't leave the fields, what with claim jumpers all around."

They silently finished the bottle, and when they called for bottle number five their courage was at its highest. "I think she *ought* to sing for us."

"Yeah," the three others said. "Yeah."

'Ring heard the men near Maddie's tent and woke instantly. He couldn't tell, but he thought there were two of them. Silently, he rolled out of his blankets, his pistol in his hand, and made for the trees. He was barely on his feet before he saw the shadow of a man near a tree.

'Ring stuck his pistol in the man's ribs, and when the man turned, he grinned in the moonlight, and his breath was enough to knock a person down. "Evenin'," the man said.

It was the last thing 'Ring heard before a pistol butt came crashing down on his head and he crumpled to the ground.

He woke to a pair of large hands shaking him vigorously. Groggily, he opened his eyes, but it was so dark he could hardly see the black face in front of him. Besides that, his head hurt abominably. It took a moment for his memory to come back, and then he tried to leap up but instead found himself staggering. He clutched at the big shoulder of the man. "Sam," he whispered.

"She's gone," Sam said in a surprisingly soft voice for a man so large.

"Gone?" 'Ring couldn't quite comprehend what was happening since his head was splitting in half. He blinked a few times to clear his vision, then looked again at Sam. "Gone? Maddie is gone? Where? Who's she meeting this time?"

"She was taken. Four men."

'Ring stood still for a moment, trying to take this in. "Who?"

"Don't know."

"Well, where the hell were you?" 'Ring shouted, then grabbed his head in both hands. When his brain stopped moving about in his skull, he realized it didn't matter who or why, it just mattered where.

He went down the little rise to her tent. Edith was inside going through Maddie's clothes. "Tell me all you know," he said to her, the light hurting his eyes, but he squinted through it at her.

"There were four of them. They came into the tent and took her. I think they were drunk."

His head hurt so much that he was having trouble thinking. "Where were you? And Frank? And you?" he said to Sam.

Edith answered. "I was sleeping outside and

114

didn't do nothin' or say nothin'. I'd like to live awhile longer." She glared at him, daring him to say anything. "Frank ain't here, I don't know where he is, and I think they hit Sam."

'Ring turned to see the man, and because of his darker skin the blood running down his neck hadn't been immediately visible. 'Ring knew Sam's head must be hurting as much as his own did, but Sam gave no indication of it. 'Ring's opinion of the man rose a bit. He looked at Edith, barely able to keep the sneer from his voice. "Which way did they head?"

"Through the town."

"West," he murmured, then turned and left the tent. He woke Toby when he was saddling Buttercup and quickly, tersely, answered Toby's questions.

"You ain't goin' by yourself, are you?" Toby asked.

He knew he had to. Toby wasn't especially good on a horse and, besides, he was getting old, and on top of that 'Ring didn't want to put him at risk. He trusted no one else. "I want you to stay here and find out what you can about what's going on. Where was Frank and—?"

"Gamblin'. The man's a heavy gambler."

'Ring turned to Toby. "And the cowardly Miss Honey?"

"Takes in customers after ever'body's asleep."

It was amazing that a person could know someone as long as he'd known Toby and still find out new things. He'd had no idea Toby could be so observant. "And Sam?"

"He's real hard to figure."

'Ring mounted his horse. "Find out what they know. Find out whose side they're on and—" He paused. "Find out who hired them." He reined his horse away. "I'll see you when I have her."

He rode through the camp, concentrating hard to ignore the pain in his head and the anger in his soul. He blamed himself for her having been taken, for not looking more and seeing more.

There was no way to track her in the dark through a camp of several hundred men who did anything but keep regular hours. All 'Ring could do was ask. After an hour he found a couple of men who said yes, they'd seen four men riding west and the opera singer had been sitting in front of one of the men.

"How did she look? Hurt?"

"Pretty," one man said. "I told her her singin' was real good, and she nodded toward me. Didn't smile though."

"You have any idea where they were taking her?"

"I didn't ask, but there's only five or so camps up that road. 'Course I ain't been up there for a couple of weeks now, so there might be more 'n that now."

'Ring thanked the men and started up the steep, rutted trail. On each side of the road the trees had little bark left on them because the miners had used block and tackles to get their wagons up and down the road.

The sun came up and still he rode, his eyes searching the ground for any clues to the direction she took. Perhaps she knew something about tracking, at least enough to leave something behind so someone could follow her. The sun was high in the sky, and he saw nothing that gave him a hint as to where she'd been taken. At about eleven he came to a fork in the trail and he halted his horse, removed his canteen, and drank.

He had a fifty-fifty chance of taking the right way. With resignation he started down the right-hand trail. He'd gone no more than fifty feet when, from overhead, came an arrow, which stuck into a tree ahead and to his left. For a moment 'Ring stood still. It was a Crow arrow, exactly like the one shot near him before.

Slowly, he rode forward and took the arrow out of the tree. Was it another warning? As he looked at the tip, he suddenly knew: the arrow was meant as a barrier. He was going the wrong way. So the Crow must know where she'd been taken. He knew but he wasn't going after her. Why?

'Ring looked up in the mountains, but saw no one. Because she's not in danger, he thought. She might have been taken, but she wasn't in danger.

'Ring turned his horse around, then started down the other trail. He felt sure of himself now. Ten miles down the road he came to another branch and this time, when he took the right branch, there was no arrow. He kept going until, at sundown, he reached a little camp of no more than fifty men living in shacks and tents and under overhanging rocks.

Maddie wasn't difficult to find. She was sitting on a stump surrounded by very sad-looking men.

"Just one song?"

"Please, ma'am?"

"We'll pay you."

"We'll sign a claim over to you."

"Please."

'Ring almost smiled at the scene. She sat there in a dusty dress, her hair hanging down her back, looking as regal as a princess. "Might as well give up, boys," 'Ring said from behind the men. "She's the most stubborn female on earth. Can't make her do anything she doesn't want to do." He smiled across the men at her, and she gave a little smile back. It was a smile that said I knew you'd come, but what took you so long?

He made his way through the men, stepping over a few sprawled on the ground, and when he reached her he held out his hand. She took it and stood, then followed him through the men. They groaned and made a few muffled pleas for her to sing for them, but no one made any vigorous actions.

Slowly, 'Ring led her to his horse, lifted her onto it, then mounted behind her. Slowly, his hand near his pistol, he rode out of the camp, but not one of the sad-faced men followed them.

"You can relax now," she said. "They won't follow us."

"Bastards!" he said under his breath. "As soon as we're farther down the road, I'm going back and—"

She put her hand on his on the reins. "No, please. They meant no harm."

"Harm! My head feels as though a wagon ran over it, Sam's head was bleeding, and you say they meant no harm."

"They were drunk, but it's not something that hasn't happened to me before."

"I see, you're a regular kidnap victim. Is that what that man the night before last wanted? To hear you sing?"

She wasn't going to answer that. "*These* men," she said pointedly, "wanted to hear me sing, and for a singer of my quality, abduction is not so unusual. In Russia, after I sang for the czar, the students unhitched the horses from my carriage and pulled it to a dreary little boardinghouse. They could not afford even the cheapest tickets, but they very much wanted to hear me."

"And did you sing for them?"

"No. I wanted to because I was very flattered by their attentions, but I was afraid that if it were told that, like a bird in a cage, I would sing in captivity, then someone might permanently put me in a cage."

After a moment he spoke to her gruffly. "Here, lean back."

She hesitated, but she was so tired that she couldn't help leaning back against him. Her head fit exactly under his chin.

119

"Who was with you during all these years of travel?" His voice was still full of anger.

"John. John Fairlie, my manager, was with me."

She could feel the front of him against her back, feel the anger that still raged in him.

"Where's all the money you've earned? For that matter, who takes care of the money you've earned in the gold camps?"

"I don't know," she said sleepily. "John took care of money. Frank does now or maybe Sam does. I don't think Edith does."

"How much do you know about the three of them?"

"Could you *please* stop asking me questions?"

He didn't answer her, and his silence gave her peace to close her eyes and relax against him.

She was asleep in his arms within minutes, but she jolted awake when he stopped. "What's wrong?"

"Nothing, but Butter's tired, you're exhausted, and I wouldn't mind some sleep too."

She was more tired than she wanted to admit, and when he put up his arms for her she slid into them. He stood close to her for a moment and removed a leaf from her hair. "You are a damned infuriating woman. You know that?"

She was too tired to argue. "I knew you'd find me. You are the most persistent man I have ever encountered."

"I guess you're used to men losing sleep to find

you. I guess your manager came after you when the Russian students took you?"

"No, he didn't. He had a nice dinner and went to bed. John always thought I was able to take care of myself. Which I am. They would have returned me before long."

"Maybe," he snapped. "But who knows what could have happened?"

She felt herself swaying toward him. Maybe it was the moonlight. "I am not your responsibility."

"Yes you are. I have orders from the army." Supporting her, he put his arm around her shoulders and led her to a little clearing. When he told her to sit down and be quiet, she didn't bother to protest, but leaned against a tree, hugged her arms about her, and closed her eyes.

She wasn't about to tell him so, but the miners' abduction of her had frightened her. It was some time after they'd burst into her tent before she realized that they'd only wanted her to sing. Had she known they were merely drunks looking for someone to entertain them, she might have protested, but she had been afraid they were from Laurel's captors.

When she'd realized they'd merely wanted her to sing, she'd been furious and had then just sat and waited, waited for Captain Montgomery to find her.

She sat up with a start when he touched her shoulder and handed her a cup of coffee.

"I didn't bring much to eat. I left in a bit of a hurry."

She watched him as he tended to the fire and his horse, then spread blankets on the ground for a bed. He gave her a couple of the horrible dried army crackers called hardtack to eat, and when she'd finished, he took her by the hand and led her to the blankets.

"Where will you sleep?"

"Don't worry about me. I'm not the one who gets into trouble every five minutes."

"I wasn't in trouble. I was perfectly safe. I—"

"But none of us knew that, did we? Sam had blood running down his neck, and you ought to feel the size of the lump on my head. My head still hurts so bad I can hardly see straight, while you just say that you weren't in danger. You—"

"Let me see," she said, interrupting him. Anything to make him shut up. She sat down on the blanket and motioned for him to bend to her. She put her hands in his thick, dark hair and immediately felt an awful lump and she also felt somewhat guilty. She hadn't meant for anyone to get hurt because of her.

On impulse, she leaned forward and kissed the lump. "There, does that make it feel better?"

"Not much," he said, and when she looked at him he was still frowning.

"Really, Captain, don't you have any sense of humor at all? I apologize for causing you so much trouble, but, may I remind you that I never have yet asked for your help or your interference. I've never wanted, or felt I needed, an army escort. You are free to return to your post at any time you want."

He turned toward the fire, sitting not a foot from the blankets. "And who would protect you?" he asked softly.

"Sam and—"

"Ha! You're better at protecting yourself than they are."

"Was that a compliment? If it was, I want to mark it down in my diary."

"I've complimented you. I told you I like your singing."

She frowned into the fire. "True, you like my singing but you've said nothing but dreadful things about me as a person. You call me a liar and—"

"As far as I can tell, most of what you say to me is lies."

"Don't you understand that there are sometimes reasons why a person *must* lie? Or has your life always been so easy that you've never found a lie necessary? Are you perfect, Captain Montgomery, utterly perfect?"

He was quiet so long that she turned to look at him, and by his face she knew she'd hit some chord in him.

"No, I'm not perfect," he said. "I have fears just like everyone else."

"Such as?" she whispered. At the moment they didn't seem like an army officer and his captive, but just two people, alone, sitting by a campfire, surrounded by darkness. "What do you fear?"

He opened his mouth to speak but closed it again. "When you're ready to tell me your secrets, I'll tell you mine. Until then, let's keep this on a different plane. Now, Miss Whatever-your-true-name-is, get between those blankets and sleep."

He stood and walked away into the darkness, allowing her some privacy as she made herself ready to sleep. When the miners had burst into her tent she'd asked to please be allowed time to change out of her nightgown. She'd dressed as hurriedly as possible, not bothering with her corset, but without it she couldn't fasten her skirt and was glad for the concealing tail of the jacket she'd slipped over her blouse.

It was cold in the mountains at night so she snuggled under the top blanket fully clothed, put her head on Captain Montgomery's saddlebag, and went to sleep. As a child, she'd slept this way often, with a campfire crackling and stars overhead.

During the night she was awakened by a voice and, startled, she sat up abruptly.

Captain Montgomery came to her and pushed her back down on the blanket.

"I was dreaming," she murmured. "I was with my father."

"He's not here now, so go back to sleep."

He started to move away, but Maddie caught his hand. "Worth," she whispered.

"Worth what?"

"My last name is Worth. Madelyn Worth."

"Ah, yes, the M. W. on the trunks."

She yawned and turned on her side away from him. "Thank you, Captain, for coming to my rescue even if I didn't need you."

"I just hope I don't have to do it again."

"Me too," she murmured, and went to sleep.

'Ring went back to his place against the tree. He was cold and since he'd given her the last of his hardtack he was hungry, so what sleeping he did was very light. For the most part he spent the night watching her and trying to put together all the pieces.

His head and back still ached in the morning and his mood felt worse. "Get up," he snapped. "This isn't the Paris opera house, where you can sleep late."

She stretched and yawned. "You certainly got up on the wrong side of the bed."

"I wasn't in any bed to get out of."

He didn't know it, of course, but Maddie had spent a great deal of her life around men and knew when one was in a sulk. "What's the matter, Captain? Angry because a woman won't do what you want?"

He lifted one eyebrow as he looked over the coffeepot at her.

"I guess you haven't had much trouble with women, have you? I'm sure that your fabulous good looks have enabled you to get what you want from women."

He perked up at "fabulous good looks."

"I can just hear all your young ladies." She cast her eyes skyward and put on a simpering look. "Oh, 'Ring," she said in a honeyed voice while batting her lashes. "You dance so beautifully and it's so good to have such a *strong* man to lean on. Do you like my dress?" She glanced back at him and continued. "Oh, Captain, I find it's awfully hot in here. Couldn't we walk outside? Just the two of us? Alone? In the moonlight?"

She looked back at him and grinned. "Your life story?"

He had to bite his lips to keep from laughing because what she'd said was so close to reality. At the fort Toby had had to warn 'Ring whenever the colonel's daughter, or even his wife, was approaching, or else 'Ring would have spent half of his time carrying things or giving his opinion on ribbon colors, or just commenting on the heat or cold or dust or state of the world in general.

"Not even close," he said, handing her a cup of coffee.

"Now who's lying? You'll never make a good liar. Your cheeks are almost pink under your manly tan." She laughed when the pink deepened.

He quit scowling and smiled at her. "Actually, my problem with women has been the opposite, which is why my father hired Toby. Are you ready to go? We need to leave soon if we're—"

"I thought Toby was in the army with you."

"He is. He joined because I did." He looked at her in reproach. "He told you that, remember? I'm glad I'm a better detective than you are. You'd

126

better fasten your skirt, or have you put on weight?"

"I haven't put on weight. I left my corset—" She broke off, annoyed that he'd made her mention her undergarment. "Tell me about Toby."

"Here, can you clean a coffeepot or can you only sing?"

"I can do a great deal that you don't know about. What about breakfast?"

"It'll have to wait. You ate all the hardtack and we don't have time to go hunting."

"I could snare a rabbit, or shoot one, for that matter."

He looked directly at her. "Oh? And where did you learn to do that?"

"My father," she said as she took the coffeepot to the stream and scoured it with sand. When she returned, the fire was out and his bedding rerolled and put on the back of his horse. Maddie rubbed Buttercup's soft nose. "Why did your father hire Toby?" She didn't want to ask him, but her curiosity was eating at her. From the moment she'd seen him she'd felt as though she knew all there was to know about him. It had been her unfortunate experience that big, good-looking men were very much alike. They had never had much denied them in their lives and always expected more to be given to them. But Captain Montgomery had surprised her from the first. Come to think of it, where had he learned to wear a breech cloth and sneak about so quietly?

He helped her onto his horse, then mounted behind her. "Why do you think a father would hire a man like Toby for his son?"

She smiled. "Easy. To keep you out of trouble. For all his complaining, Toby takes care of you like a mother. He worries about you. No doubt he's had to pull you out of scrapes with daughters whose fathers were after you with shotguns. Did you join the army to perhaps escape marriage to some poor innocent girl?"

She twisted to look at his face, sure she was right, but he was smiling.

"I have no idea what has given you such a low opinion of me. Have I ever said or done anything to you that could be considered unseemly?"

"Other than threatening me with having to go to bed with you to make you give me freedom that is mine by right?"

"Yes, other than that." His eyes sparkled.

"No, but then, you don't like me much."

"I don't think *like* has much to do with ah . . . what we're talking about, does it? I may not like you, but you're not exactly painful to look at."

"Thank you," she said softly. "I think." What an odd conversation to have, especially when she was riding so close to him and they were so alone in the mountains. "Why was Toby hired?"

"To get me into trouble."

She turned and looked at him.

"My father worried that I thought of duty before anything else in life." 'Ring grimaced. "My father was also concerned that I lacked a sense of

128

humor, so when I was sixteen he hired Toby to introduce me to, ah . . . life."

"Life?"

"Girls."

"You didn't—don't—like girls?"

"I thought you wanted to know about Toby."

She was a little confused as to what she did want to know about. "Did he? Did he introduce you to girls?"

"More or less."

She had to try to figure out what that meant. "I've never heard of a father hiring someone to show his son about . . . life."

"He was worried that I spent too much time involved in our family business, that's all. So he chose the man who knew more about living than anyone else he'd ever met."

"Toby?"

"Toby."

She was quiet a moment. "So, I suppose he probably succeeded. I don't guess with your face and—" She refused to give him the satisfaction of saying physique. "I would imagine you were an apt pupil."

"I did what was required of me."

What in the world did he mean by that, Maddie wondered.

"But I joined the army at eighteen, and here I am."

"No doubt leaving a wake of bereaved females behind you," she said, laughing.

"No," he answered.

"But surely—"

"Enough about me. Let's talk about you."

But she didn't want to talk about herself. "Captain, I don't understand any of this."

"Nor do I understand much about you."

For the most part he'd been polite to her over the few days she'd known him. Save for the few moments when she'd thought he meant to force her to lie with him, she'd felt in no danger, but now it seemed rather odd that he'd never so much as kissed her hand. And that now with her sitting so close to him, his hand had never strayed. "Your father had to hire someone to introduce you to women because by inclination you are not interested in them?"

"My father didn't *have* to hire Toby."

"All right, then. He *chose* to hire Toby. That's not the point. The point is whether you're interested in women or not."

"Whose point?"

"*My* point!" she snapped at him. "Are you or are you not?"

"Not what?"

"Interested in women, you idiot."

"Interested in women as opposed to what?"

She started to speak, then stopped. "You're not going to answer me, are you?"

"Who was the man in your tent after your first performance? Who hired Sam and Frank and the delightful Miss Honey?"

"Is she the type of woman you like?"

"Do all the men you like smoke cigars and hide

130

in tents? What makes you so violently opposed to having an army escort? Why do you pretend to be a duchess? What happened to your brooch? Where does your family live? Who—"

"All right!" She laughed. "You win. How about if I teach you a little about singing?"

"I would like you to sing for me," he said softly.

"No, not sing for you. Teach you. Now, listen." She sang a single note. "That's B flat." She sang another note. "C. This is F sharp."

"The one Patti can't sing?"

"What an annoyingly good memory you have. Now, listen while I put them together. See if you can hear the difference."

"C, F sharp, B flat," he said.

"Very, very good. I'll add more notes." She sang more notes for him, put them together, and each time he could tell her what she'd sung. "Perfect pitch," she said. "You can identify the notes perfectly. You have perfect pitch. Did you know this?"

"Never gave it a thought. No one in my family knows anything about music."

"Sing me a song," Maddie demanded.

"You've slain no dragons for me."

"I highly doubt that your untrained singing is worth even the smallest dragon. Sing, or I'll ask more about Toby."

He sang "Row, Row, Row Your Boat," and she waited until the end before speaking. "Amazing, Captain. Really amazing."

"Not bad, huh?"

"It is amazing that someone could have as pleasant a speaking voice as you, an ear so refined as to be able to hear slight sound variations in notes, and yet . . ."

"And yet what?"

"Be such a bad singer."

"Watch out," he said, and pushed her nearly off the horse, but caught her before she fell. She threw her arms around him to keep from falling, then looked up at him, laughing. He, too, was laughing, and quite suddenly she wanted him to kiss her. Maybe it was all their talk of girls and his "doing what was required."

She moved her face closer to his and she saw him move toward her. She closed her eyes—but the kiss never came. When she opened her eyes he was looking down at her with an expression she didn't understand. Embarrassed, she removed her arms from around his neck, straightened, and turned around.

"How long before we get to camp?"

"I figure you know as well as I do."

She did. She could think of nothing else to say to him. Their good mood was broken and she had no idea why, but she didn't ponder the question. She snuggled back against him and enjoyed the ride down the mountain.

CHAPTER 7

At the camp the others were waiting for them, only Toby showing concern at their absence. Maddie allowed Sam to help her off Captain Montgomery's horse, and the captain rode away to the place where he stayed, on the ridge overlooking the camp.

She went inside the tent and Edith followed her.

"He came while you were gone."

"Who did?"

"You have such a good time with your captain that you forgot about your little sister?"

Maddie was immediately alert. "But why? I wasn't supposed to see him until after tomorrow's performance. And not even that night. He gave me a map."

"Yeah, he said all that. He just wanted to make sure you'd be there. And he said for you to wear somethin' pretty. Somethin' that sparkled. I think maybe he's gettin' worried about your captain friend."

Maddie sat down on the cot. "What did he say about Captain Montgomery?"

"Said it'd take a buffalo gun to kill a so-and-so as big as he is."

Maddie put her face in her hands. "What am I going to do? Tomorrow I'm supposed to go into the mountains to meet him. I'm to see Laurel. I cannot, under any circumstances, annoy the man.

133

Annoy him!" she said bitterly. "He's already said that Laurel has . . . has been . . . I can't think about it. I have to do what he says."

"Then maybe you'd better not go up that mountain with your army friend taggin' along behind you. And the little one is askin' questions too."

"Little one?"

"Toby. He's sniffin' around Frank and Sam as well as me, wantin' to know all about you."

Maddie stood up and walked to the side of the tent. What was she going to do? What could she do? I *have* to get rid of Captain Montgomery, she thought. I can't tell him what's going on for fear he might interfere. And tomorrow he'll be even more alert than usual after the fiasco of the last few days. As for that, no one had seen the drunken miners take her, yet somehow, he'd found her. If he could find her once, he could find her again, but this time it wouldn't be men merely wanting to hear her sing. This time it would be the men holding Laurel.

"What are you gonna do?" Edith asked.

"I don't know. Somehow, I have to make him stay behind when I leave day after tomorrow."

"I've got some more opium."

"He won't take any food or drink from me."

"Club him over the head?"

"I don't want to hurt him." She remembered how he'd given her his blankets and sat up cold all night. He really was only trying to protect her.

"How about women? I could get a couple more girls together and we could—"

"No!"

Edith looked at her awhile. "Too bad you can't spend the night in bed with him yourself."

"I have more important things to think about than seducing a man. Although . . ." She thought it wouldn't hurt if he trusted her more. "You say that Toby is asking questions? Perhaps I can ask Toby a few in return. Go now and set the table for luncheon. I can think better with a full stomach."

Edith had purchased some chickens, scalded them, plucked them, and fried them in hot grease. Maddie invited Toby to join her for luncheon, and she would allow him to sit nowhere else but at the table with her.

"You've known the captain for a long time, haven't you, Toby? Please have some more chicken."

"Ten years now. Don't mind if I do."

She smiled at him as graciously as she knew how. "Tell me about him."

Toby didn't even glance her way. He was used to women asking him about 'Ring. If he were a man who ran to fat, he would have been a keg on legs long ago from all the women feeding him to get to 'Ring. For the first few years Toby had felt trapped because on the one hand he knew he should keep his mouth shut about 'Ring, but at the same time he didn't want to cut off his food supply. "Ain't much to tell. He ain't so different from most men."

"Most fathers don't hire someone to show their sons the seamier side of life."

Toby was startled. "He tell you about that?"

"Yes, he did. Please, have some more butter on your roll. I was wondering why he doesn't . . . I guess I mean, why he doesn't pay attention to women."

"Beats me," Toby said.

"Perhaps a lost love somewhere in his past. Someone he loved but couldn't have."

"Oh, you mean like them songs you sing. Naw, nothin' like that. He just don't pay attention to girls. Why, I've seen them do some of the all-fired orneriest things you can imagine to get him to take an interest in 'em, but he just don't."

"Here, have another tomato. Perhaps his lack of interest in women is a family trait."

"No, ma'am. In fact, that's one of the things that worried his father. All six of his younger brothers is *real* interested in girls. Even the little ones. 'Course it could have somethin' to do with the fact that the boy is the ugly one in the family."

She paused with her fork on its way to her mouth. "Captain Montgomery, this man here with us is the ugly one?"

"Yes, ma'am, he is. And his little brothers never let him forget it. They say they own dogs better-lookin' than their oldest brother."

At that moment Maddie realized that in spite of the sincere look on Toby's face, surely he was teasing her. She smiled at him indulgently. "If he

136

isn't interested in women, what *is* he interested in?"

"Duty. Honor. That kind of thing." Toby said the words as though they were dreadful qualities. He looked at her over a mouthful of skillet bread. "You interested in him?"

"Of course not. I was just wondering how trustworthy he is."

Toby set the bread down and, when he looked at her, his old eyes were intense. "He's trustworthy. You can trust him with your life. If he says he's gonna protect you, he means it. He'll give up his own life 'fore he'd let anything happen to you."

She frowned. "I don't imagine he'd ever involve himself in anything illegal." Such as trying to influence a territory about becoming slave or free, she thought.

"Hell no! Oh, sorry, ma'am. He'd agree to be tortured 'fore he'd do anything bad." Toby grimaced. "I tell you, the boy can wear a man down. He don't lie, he don't cheat, he don't do nothin' that ain't upholdin' to the laws of man and God."

Maddie gave him a weak smile. It was just as she'd thought. If Captain Montgomery found out about the letters, would he turn her over to the army for discipline? Haul her back to the capital and have her tried for treason? Would he say that the good of the country was more important than the good of one child?

"You're sure thinkin' hard on somethin', ain't you, ma'am?"

137

"I guess I am."

"He's a good boy," Toby said. "You can trust him with your life."

But can I trust him with my secrets, she wondered. "What is he doing now?"

"Watchin'."

"Watching what?"

"Watchin' out for you. There's men followin' you, and he sets up on a hill and watches 'em, what he can see of 'em anyway. Two of 'em keep pretty well hidden, but the other two are bumblefoots."

She stopped eating. "You mean he just sits up there and watches? Watches everything I do?"

Toby gave her a little half smile. "He's tryin' to find out what you're hidin'. You oughta just tell him so he can get some sleep. I can't even get him to eat anything 'cept hardtack, and thank the Lord we're runnin' out of that."

Just tell him, Maddie thought. She would if it all weren't so very serious. "Edith, put the rest of this chicken and some tomatoes in a bag."

"You gonna go see him?"

I'm going to give him something else to think about besides the men who are following me, she thought. "Yes. Perhaps he'd like a little company."

"He'd rather read than visit with a female," Toby said, and could hardly keep the laughter inside. He'd said that a hundred times to a hundred females and every one of them had considered it a personal challenge. He was glad to see

138

this opera singer was no different from other women.

"Oh? Perhaps I can persuade him otherwise." She took the bag of chicken and tomatoes from Edith and went up the hill.

"Captain?" she asked. He was sitting on the ground, leaning against a tree, looking for all the world as though he were asleep, but she knew he wasn't. His breathing was too even, too deep. She settled on the ground near him. "You can stop pretending now. You're too good a mess captain to let someone walk up on you."

Slowly, he opened his eyes but he didn't smile at her. "What are you doing up here?"

"I brought you some fried chicken."

"I've eaten, thank you."

"Toby told me what you eat. Have I done something to offend you?"

"You mean besides lying and getting kidnapped?"

"And telling you you can't sing? I know your sense of humor is, as far as I can tell, nonexistent, but surely I didn't hurt your feelings."

"No, you didn't hurt my feelings. Now, will you please return to your own tent?"

"And leave you up here alone to spy on me?" Before he realized what she was doing, she reached behind him and grabbed the spyglass. He made a lunge for it, but she put it behind her back. He leaned back against the tree.

"This is old," she said, looking at the beautiful, worn brass case. "Isn't it the kind sailors use?"

"Perhaps."

She pulled the glass out to its full length. "Ah, yes, now I remember. You tied up Frank and Sam with sailor's knots. It is my guess, Captain, that you've had something to do with the sea in your life. Am I right?"

He snatched the glass from her hands without answering.

"What in the world has made you so grumpy?"

"I have things to do and I'd rather you went back to your own camp."

She opened the bag Edith had given her and withdrew a somewhat scrawny chicken breast. "I brought you something good to eat."

"Oh? Is it poisoned? I'm not eating any food you give me."

"You drank the port I gave you."

"You poured us both glasses from the same bottle and you drank first."

"All right," she said with resignation, stripped a piece of meat from the chicken, and ate half of it. She held out the other half to him.

"Thank you, but I've eaten."

"It's awfully good," she said, holding the chicken in front of his face. "The very best I've ever eaten. Mmmmm."

He gave a bit of a smile and snapped at the chicken, but she jerked it away from him, laughing.

He lunged at her, then caught her around the

waist, pushed her to the ground, and caught the chicken and her fingers in his mouth.

At first she was laughing, but then, abruptly, she became aware of his body on hers and her fingers inside the warmth of his mouth. She stopped laughing and looked at him. She did not take her fingers from inside his mouth.

" 'Ring," she whispered.

For a moment she thought he was feeling the same as she was, but the moment passed and he caught her wrist and pulled her hand from his mouth. "Chicken, yes, but human fingers, no."

It seemed that he'd refused her at every opportunity she had given him. It was difficult not to throw the entire bag of chicken at him and go back to her own tent. Instead, she reminded herself that she had to be nice to him for Laurel's sake. If she was to meet one of the kidnappers after her performance the following day, she had to have Captain Montgomery's trust.

She forced herself to smile at him. "If you are through trying to smash me with your oversized body, I'd like to get up."

"Sure," he said cheerfully, rolling away from her. "I guess the chicken is safe, but I want you to take a bite of each piece before I do."

"Really, Captain, you'd think I was a master poisoner."

"A Lucrezia Borgia?"

"Who's that?"

He looked at her over a chunk of chicken. "How many languages do you speak?"

141

"Including the American ones?" She was pleased to see his eyes widen at that.

"Including the language that uses such terms as *sleep-insider* and *mess captain*. What is a mess captain, by the way?"

He was really, truly, the most observant man she'd ever encountered. She doubted if her pulse rate was unknown to him. "Mess captain is a trapping term and means the leader, or an experienced trapper. I told you I've had some contact with mountain men."

"Ah, yes, in Lanconia. Have you ever even been to Lanconia?"

"How is your chicken? Would you like a tomato?"

He accepted the tomato and took a bite of it. "It seems odd to me that you know so much about music and languages yet know next to nothing about history. And as far as I can tell, you know as little about arithmetic as anyone on earth."

"I came all the way up this hill to bring you food, and here you sit, insulting me. I don't know why I bother being friendly to you."

"I don't either. I'm sure you had a reason for coming up here, but it wasn't merely to bring me chicken. What was waiting for you in the tent when we returned?"

She looked away, unable to meet his eyes.

"Someday, Miss Worth, I hope that you will realize that you can trust me."

"My father told me that people have to earn trust."

142

"And we know that whatever Daddy says is the law."

"Just what is that supposed to mean?"

"You've mentioned your father before . . . repeatedly." He filled his mouth with chicken. "Do you know that when you speak of your father you sound as though you're speaking of God? I imagine your father is a good mess captain."

"My father is the best! The absolute best there is. He is honest and kind and good and . . ." She hated the way he was smirking at her. "And *he* has a sense of humor."

"Anybody who has been through what I have in the last few days and is still sane has to have a sense of humor."

"All of it brought on by yourself." In spite of her good intentions, she could feel herself getting angry. "Why don't you go back where you came from and leave me alone?"

"And leave you to all the men who are watching you?"

"The only person watching me who bothers me is you." She stood up and started to go back down the hill, but he caught her skirt.

"What's the matter, don't you have a sense of humor? What's making you so grumpy?"

She looked down at him, not knowing whether he was serious or laughing at her.

"Come on, you don't want to leave, and you know it. You know what I think, Miss Worth?"

"No, and I don't care to know."

"I think that for years now you've been treated

as a legend rather than as a person. I don't think you've allowed anyone close enough to you to question your story of being a duchess from Lanconia. All you've had to do was sing, and with that voice of yours, all sense leaves a person and he can't use what brains he was given."

"Is that so?" she said, trying to sound haughty but not quite accomplishing her goal.

"You've spoken about that manager of yours, but as far as I can tell, all he cared about was the money you brought in. Tell me, how long has it been since you saw anyone in your family?"

To Maddie's disbelief, she felt tears forming in her eyes. "Let me go," she said softly, tugging on her skirt. "I don't have to listen to this."

"No, you don't," he said quietly, and there was a hint of apology in his voice. "I didn't mean—"

He broke off, for they both heard the sound in the bushes at the same time. It was in the opposite direction from where her camp was. Whoever had made the noise had to have come down the mountain.

Maddie didn't think she'd ever seen anyone move so fast. One second Captain Montgomery was on the ground and the next he was on top of her, pulling her down with him, his arms wrapped around her back and one leg wrapped about her legs, the other leg guiding them as they rolled down the hill, away from the camp, away from the sound in the bushes.

They rolled for some distance, Maddie's body rarely touching the ground as his big body enveloped and protected her. He stopped fifty feet down the hill, hiding them in the scrub oaks. She started to speak, but he put his hand at the back of her head and buried her face in his neck. He was protecting her completely, so that should any danger—a shot, an arrow—come, he would receive it and not her.

The thrashing in the bushes became louder, and she recognized it at the same time that he did.

"Elk," she whispered against his neck, and he nodded.

Still on top of her, still covering her, he turned his head, allowing her to do so also, and they saw not an elk, but a mule deer standing on the hill, where they had just been. The deer stood still and watched them for a moment, not knowing what they were, then, as 'Ring lifted his arm, the deer hurried off into the woods with its springy gait.

"Are you all right?" he asked, rising on one elbow to look at her.

"Perfectly." She started to move out from under him but stopped when she felt something sharp pricking her. "I seem to have a thorn in my shoulder."

He moved off her, sat up, and turned her over. He pulled two cactus thorns from her shoulder. "There. Any more?"

She sat up and moved her shoulders. "No, I think that's all of them." She looked back up the steep hill they had just rolled down and saw it was covered with flat-leaved cacti, and she was glad for the protection of her skirt and petticoats, her corset and corset cover. She looked back at him. "I've never seen anyone react so quickly. Thank you."

"Nothing a good mess captain wouldn't do— or your father."

She started to tell him what she thought of his little jest, but instead she smiled. "Do I really talk of my father in worshipful tones?"

He smiled and nodded at her. "You ready to go back to your tent now?"

She said, "Yes," and looked down at her skirt to brush it off. There were cactus thorns sticking out of it everywhere. She looked back up the hill at the path they'd made as they'd rolled and looked at the many cacti they'd rolled over, then looked back up at him.

"Turn around," she said.

"I think you'd better get back. You've had a hard two days and tomorrow you have a performance and—"

"Turn around, I said."

"Miss Honey will be looking for you."

"Edith couldn't care less if I started rolling down a hill and kept going." She was still smarting from his comment about her lack of education. "If you don't understand English, how about Italian? *Distògliere il viso.* French? *Traiter avec dédain.* Or maybe Spanish is something you understand. *Dejar libre.*" She was very pleased to see his puzzled look. That should teach him to denigrate her education.

"Which do you want me to do? Turn around,

turn aside, turn a cold shoulder, or turn something free."

He had translated all three languages perfectly. "You are a truly infuriating man." She grabbed his arm and pulled on him. He was much too big for her to move if he hadn't helped her, but she did get to see the back of him. He was covered with cactus thorns, some of them hidden by his cotton army blouse, but all of them embedded in his skin. There were more thorns protruding from his trousers, but the sturdy army wool had kept most of them from going through to his skin.

"You've mentioned that before, about my being infuriating. I'm afraid that your languages don't impress me. It might impress me if you had any idea what has happened to all the money you've earned over the years."

She used her fingertips to pull out a thorn. "Are you after my money?"

"I can't tell that you have any. If you have as little concern for what you've made in the past as you do for what you've earned on this trip, then I doubt very much that you do have any. Besides, it's a tradition in my family that we take care of money. My father made me invest twenty percent of all my pocket money from the time I was three years old."

She pulled out three more thorns, but then his shirt got in her way and hid more thorns than it exposed. She pushed him at the waist. "Up the hill and take that shirt off. Money has never been a concern of mine. I want to sing. Singing is what

147

matters, not money. The sound of the music and the appreciation of the audience is what matters in life."

He climbed the hill, her behind him. "You say that you'll not always have your voice. What will you live on when you can no longer sing?"

"I don't know. It's not something that has ever interested me much. Perhaps I'll marry some fat, rich old man and let him support me." They were at the top of the hill now, and he paused, turning to face her.

"What about children?"

"Take that shirt off, give me that tooth-picker of yours, and lay down on the ground. I want to get those thorns out."

He began unbuttoning his shirt. "You never thought about children?"

In spite of the fact that he was acting as though the thorns weren't bothering him, she knew they must be very painful. She walked behind him and helped peel the shirt off, moving the thorns as little as possible. "Is this a marriage proposal, Captain? If it is, I'm not interested. To sing I have to travel around the world a great deal. I don't have the time or inclination to tie myself to a man. Nor do I want—" She broke off at the sight of his broad, muscular back, for it was covered with thin white scars.

"Stretch out there on the grass," she said softly, and when he'd done so, she ran her fingertip over one of the scars. "How did this happen?"

"I ran into something."

"The wrong end of a whip? I didn't think they whipped officers. And, besides, I can't imagine you doing anything that could possibly get you into trouble. I'd think the army would give men like you medals—not whippings."

"I haven't always been an officer," he said as he watched her go to his saddle gear and remove his big skinning knife. "You planning to do some skinning?"

She laughed at the nervousness in his voice, then cut a piece of greasy canvas from the bag containing the chicken and wrapped it around her thumb. "Be still," she said, pushing at his shoulder as she knelt by him. "I've removed a few of these before, and I know what I'm doing." She used the back of the knife blade against her padded thumb to pull the first of the many, many thorns from his back.

When she'd cleared enough of his back that she could put her palm on it, she touched the scars. "For all your flippancy, I know how much pain a whipping like this must have caused you. I know something of pain."

He could hear the tears in her voice. "Don't tell me you feel sorry for yourself? What do you know of pain or even hardship? An opera singer's life isn't full of what I'd call agony. What do you usually do? Sing all day? Or do you spend most of the time at your dressmaker's?"

"You know nothing about being a singer of my caliber. If you'll behave yourself, I'll tell you how I came to be a singer. I guess I was about seven years old. My father was helping some settlers. They were coming west to open a trading post and—"

"In Lanconia?"

"All I have to do to cause you great discomfort is wiggle one of these thorns. Now, be still and listen. There was a woman who was ill with this group of settlers, and her husband had been killed on the journey. She—"

"Indians?"

"No, actually, he'd been killed by a rattlesnake, if I remember correctly, but I'm not sure because, as I said, I was quite young. The other people with her were very annoyed at having a lone female with them, and a sick one at that, and, from what my father said, they let her know she was a burden to them. My father had no sympathy for them, as he thought all settlers were a nuisance and a plague on the earth. He—"

"But then, your father was a settler too, wasn't he?"

"Are you going to listen or talk?"

"I can hardly wait to hear more about your illustrious father."

"You *should* be honored. Now, where was I?"

"With your father, a settler, being annoyed with more settlers coming in."

"Oh, sorry," she said, tweaking one of the thorns very slightly, "did I hurt you? I'll try to be more careful, but if you don't stop interrupting me, I may not remember to be gentle. Now, let's see, I was talking about Mrs. Benson. My father thought my mother might like to have some company, so he brought the woman home, planning to take her back east in the spring. She ended up staying with us for four years, then she fell in love with some passing easterner and married him, but by then I had Madame Branchini."

"And she taught you opera?"

"I'm getting ahead of myself. Mrs. Benson had taught piano and singing in the East and my mother thought it would be nice if she tried to do something with me, because I was awfully jealous of my older sister, Gemma. You see, my mother is an artist and my sister had inherited every bit of my mother's talent. Even at five years old Gemma could paint and draw rather well, while I could draw not at all. I was jealous that my mother spent so much time with Gemma."

"So, your mother turned you over to the music teacher and immediately you started singing arias."

"No, I sang funny little popular songs and things my father's friends taught me and—"

"Songs about hailing the queen, that sort of thing? Are your father's friends also dukes?"

She ignored him. "No one thought much about my singing for years, then, one day, Mrs. Benson was looking through a trunk my father had found. It had been thrown from a settler's wagon—the idiots take everything they own with them and then at the first rough place they have to start lightening their wagons."

'Ring had seen some of the "rough" places.

151

Ravines a hundred and fifty feet deep. "What was in the trunk?"

"Sheet music. My father hauled it home because he thought maybe Mrs. Benson and I could use it." Maddie pulled another thorn from his back and smiled. "In the bottom was a piece of music such as I'd never seen before. It was '*Air des bijoux*,' you know, from *Faust*."

"Jewel Song," he said softly, translating.

"Yes, exactly."

"I don't know the song, but maybe you could sing it for me and I'd recognize the tune."

"You should have so much luck. Anyway, Mrs. Benson helped me with the words, and since my father's birthday was approaching, I thought I'd learn the song and sing it for him."

"And so you did."

"No, not quite that easily. Mrs. Benson is an American."

"A curse on a person if I ever heard it."

"You don't understand. Americans have a horror of opera. They think opera is for rich people, for snobs. If an American says he has even *seen* an opera, he will probably be ridiculed. When I asked Mrs. Benson about the piece of music in the trunk, she dismissed it, said it was opera and it wasn't for a little girl like me. I guess I was about ten then."

"And that was like waving a red flag in front of you, wasn't it? Nobody anywhere can tell you not to do anything, can they?"

"Would you like me to send Edith up here to

do this? I'm sure she would love to get you with your clothes off."

He didn't say anything, but he turned his head and gave her an odd look that she didn't understand, and she continued.

"I did feel rather challenged by her warning, and I was quite curious, so I took the music to Thomas." Before he could ask, she told him who Thomas was. "There were several men who lived with us, friends of my father's. Thomas is one of them, and he could play a little and sing a little. Not as well as my father, of course, but—"

"Of course not as well as Daddy," 'Ring said under his breath.

"Thomas could play and sing a little," she repeated pointedly, "so I went to him with the music. By then I could read music rather well and I've always had perfect pitch."

"The best people do."

She smiled. "Thomas and I together pieced the song out and I rehearsed it. At my father's birthday, after everyone had eaten and my father had been given gifts from everyone else, Thomas played his flute and I sang the song."

"And you became an opera singer after that."

She gave an unladylike snort. "Not quite 'just like that.' After I finished my song, no one spoke, they just sat there and stared at me. I knew that I didn't know how to pronounce the Italian words properly, but I didn't think my singing was too bad, so I was hurt when they said not a word."

She paused a moment, remembering that most

eventful day in her life. "After what seemed like forever, my mother turned to my father and said, 'Jeffrey, in the morning you are to leave here, go east, and find my daughter a teacher—a singing teacher. A real teacher. The best teacher that money can buy. My daughter is going to be an opera singer.' After she said that, the dam broke. Everybody started whooping and my father put me on his shoulders and—"

"His incredibly broad shoulders?"

"As a matter of fact, yes. It was the most wonderful night of my life."

"Oh? None of your hundreds of men since then have equaled the experience?"

"Not even close."

"And I guess your father got your teacher. I can't imagine he ever failed at anything. Madame what-was-her-name?"

"He was gone for months, and when he returned, he had this thin, sour-looking woman with him. I disliked her immediately, and I almost hated her when my mother welcomed her and the little woman ignored my mother. Madame Branchini said, 'Let me hear this child and see if she is worth all I have gone through.' Behind her, I could see my father grimacing and I knew she must have been a trial to him on the trip."

"But she heard you sing and she agreed to stay with you forever and teach you everything you know."

"Not exactly. In fact, you couldn't be further from the truth. She had me play the piano—by

154

then my father had brought me one from the East—and—"

"Did he haul it in on his back?"

"And so I played the piano for her and sang a bit." She stopped and shook her head. "I was a vain little thing. I had been adored by my family and told that I was the best singer in the world. I believe I thought that Madame Branchini was honored to get to hear me sing."

"I'm glad you're so different now. None of this telling people that they'd be privileged to hear a singer of 'your caliber.'"

"I have earned it now. Back then I was a child who was vain without any reason for her vanity. Now I but speak the truth. You have heard me sing. Have I ever lied or even exaggerated about my voice?"

"No," he said honestly. "That is the *one* thing you haven't lied about."

"But that day I was lying to myself. Looking back, I must have been dreadful, really dreadful. The raw talent was there, of course."

"Of course."

"But that day I did not get praise as I did from my family. I finished singing my little song and looked up at Madame Branchini with expectation. I expected praise, even hugs. If the truth were told, I expected her to fall to her knees in gratitude at being privileged to hear me sing. Instead, she did not say a word. She turned on her heel and left the room. Of course, my parents and the rest of my family were standing just outside the door. I think they, too, were expecting her to praise their precious daughter. I think that in order to get Madame there, my father had praised my talent rather lavishly."

"He would."

"Yes, he would. But Madame Branchini did not praise me. Instead, she told my family that I was lazy and spoiled and that I was much too vain to do anything with. She told my father he had to take her back to New York immediately, that he had wasted his time and hers on this worthless child."

'Ring turned his head to look at her.

"Yes, difficult to believe, isn't it? But she knew what she was doing. Everyone started talking at once, with my father telling her she had to at least stay the winter and the others telling her that she had a tin ear. I stood in the doorway and listened, and it was all quite gratifying to my young heart. How dare the old crow say that I had no talent? Why, I was going to be the greatest singer in all the world. I imagined her coming backstage after a performance and begging my forgiveness for ever doubting me."

Maddie pulled out another thorn and chuckled. "Thank heaven that even at that tender age I had some sense. It quite suddenly occurred to me to wonder *how* I was going to become an opera singer. Was Mrs. Benson going to teach me? Was I going to learn on my own? Was I going to wait until I was an adult and go east and then start training? What was I going to do in the meantime?

In the few years that Mrs. Benson had been with me, I had realized that the thing I liked best in the world was singing. I sang all the time, wherever I was, whatever I was doing."

Maddie took a breath. "I made the most important decision of my life at that moment. I suddenly realized that Madame Branchini was right and I *was* lazy. I went to her and asked her to please teach me. She refused. I went on my knees to her and *begged* her to teach me."

She paused and stared for a moment, unseeing. "My family hated my begging. They all hated Madame. My father tried to pull me off the floor, but after her continued refusal to give me what I wanted, I was trying to kiss her feet."

'Ring looked back at her. He couldn't imagine her groveling.

She smiled at him. "I would have done anything to be able to sing, and this woman was the key to what I wanted."

"She relented," he said softly.

"Oh, yes, she did, but only after I'd promised to be her slave. My family didn't like it, but I think I had an idea of what was necessary. She stayed with us for seven years, and she taught me what I know. It was difficult."

"Just singing all day?"

"What do you know? You probably spent your childhood outside in the sunshine. I did not. Rain or shine, good weather or bad, I was inside with Madame, practicing. The same note over and over. The same syllable. The Italian lessons, the

157

French lessons. Outside, I could hear other people laughing and having a good time, but I was always inside, practicing."

"You must have had some time off."

"Very little. I faltered in my resolve once and only once. I fell madly in love with a young man my father had hired to help with the work. I wanted to be near him almost as much as I wanted to sing."

"And what did your little Madame say to that?"

"She said that I could be a singer or I could subject myself to a man's tyranny for life. It was my choice."

"Spoken like a true spinster."

Maddie made a face at him. "Why do men always think that the worst state in life for a woman is to live without a man? Yes, she was a spinster. And because she was, she'd been free to come to me in the middle of—" She hesitated. "In the middle of nowhere."

"So I assume that you chose your singing over the cowboy?"

"Obviously. I saw him years later and wondered what I had ever seen in him."

"But you made up for lost time with your many hundreds of lovers."

"My what? Oh, yes, all the men. It's true that men do love women with talent."

"Not to mention women with figures like yours."

She laughed. "I believe that has been an, ah . . . added attraction. Opera singers do tend to be a bit plump, so I've always been careful not to follow that particular fashion. I had no idea *you* had noticed, though."

"The last time I checked, I was alive and I was a male. You know, one of those creatures out to make a woman's life miserable by not allowing her to remain a spinster."

When she laughed the second time, he turned to look at her. "No sense of humor, huh?"

"None. I'm sure you were serious. Now that I've told you a story, you tell me one."

"Such as?"

"Why you're doing this. Why you're taking care of me."

"I was ordered to, remember? Your beloved General Yovington ordered me here, and I'm doing my job."

"No, General Yovington ordered Lieutenant—"

"Surrey."

"Yes, Lieutenant Surrey to escort me. You, Captain Montgomery, are an error. Why did your commanding officer choose you?"

"Now, *there's* a man with a sense of humor. I think he thought it would be a great joke to send me out to baby-sit an opera singer."

"How many of these thorns are sticking in you from the waist down?"

"Not enough to make me strip off in front of a lady."

"How ridiculous. Especially after the way you sneaked into my tent wearing practically nothing the night you were trying to scare me."

"Little did I know that an attack of Blackfeet couldn't frighten you."

"There you're wrong. Bug's Boys scare me to death. Take off those trousers and let me see. I promise not to be shocked at the sight of your bare backside."

He stood up and grinned down at her. "I hate to disappoint you, but I have on underwear. And it's a good thing, too, since otherwise I might have frozen to death in the last few days while chasing you around these mountains." He unbuttoned the fly of his trousers and, after removing his boots, dropped them and stepped out of them. He wore long, red summer underwear under his trousers, and when he turned his back to her, there were several long thorns sticking out of his legs.

On her knees, she began pulling the thorns from his legs. He stood quietly and she became aware of her hands on his body. He'd said that she'd never allowed people close to her. Always, there had been the knowledge that if she'd allowed herself to love anything but her singing, she would have to give up too much. Over the ten years that she'd been singing professionally, she'd seen so many good singers give up a career to marry a man and have babies. Maddie had never wanted to have to make such a choice, so, by necessity, she'd kept to herself. And John Fairlie had helped a great deal by keeping her so busy with lessons and rehearsals and performances that she'd had little time for a social life. What little social life she did have had been booked by John. He had always arranged for her to socialize with rich, influential people who could further her career.

But now, in these mountains where she'd grown up, in this wild and beautiful country, the drawing rooms of the East and Europe seemed far away. She'd bragged to Captain Montgomery that she'd had hundreds of affairs, yet the truth was that she'd had none. Her fingers tightened on the muscle of his leg.

"There," she said at last, and then, to make sure that he had no more thorns in him, she ran her hands up and down his legs. She had never touched a man like this before and, if the truth were known, she'd never had an urge to, at least not since she was sixteen years old and had fallen for the cowboy. At that time Madame Branchini had made it so clear to her that it was either singing or men, Maddie had made her choice and had never once regretted it.

Now, as she touched him, it was as though she were in a trance and couldn't stop herself. He stood perfectly still as she ran her hands over him, down the back of his heavy, muscular legs, down his calves, then to his heels. She wished he weren't wearing the underwear so she could feel his skin. Vividly, the memory of the night he'd appeared in her tent wearing only the loincloth came to her. She hadn't paid much attention to him that night, but now she remembered the color of his skin.

Still silent, she stood, letting her hand trail up his body, over his buttocks to his naked waist. With both hands she touched the smooth, warm skin of his back, traced the faint white scars, the red places the thorns had made.

It was as though she'd never seen a man's body before, although she'd grown up around men who in the summer rarely wore much besides a breech cloth. But at that time music had meant more to her than any well-put-together male.

Her hands went to his shoulders, to the round strength of them. She moved to the right and ran her hands down his arm to his hand, then back up again. She didn't look at his face; for all she cared, he could have been a warm, living statue. When she reached his shoulder again, she moved her hands over his chest. He was hard and muscular, a body used to exercise, to a life spent outdoors. Her fingers entwined in the hair on his chest, then moved down to the hard flatness of his stomach.

When her hands lingered at his waist, he caught her wrists. "No," he whispered, and she looked into his eyes.

His eyes broke her trance, and she pulled away from him, terribly embarrassed. She turned away. "I . . . I was looking for more thorns."

"There are no more thorns," he said quietly.

"I . . . I have to go now," she said, and ran down the hill as fast as she could. She couldn't bear to look at him again.

CHAPTER 8

When Maddie awoke the next morning, she knew that something was wrong. At first she wasn't sure what it was, but then she vividly remembered her embarrassment over Captain Montgomery.

Edith brought her washing water. "You two were sure up there a long time last evenin'. And you sure came down that hill in one big hurry. He try somethin' you didn't like?"

Maddie recalled all too well that nothing had come from Captain Montgomery in the way of an improper advance, but she'd certainly made a fool of herself. She could still hear him saying "No" to her when her hands had strayed too far.

She turned to Edith. "Absolutely nothing happened. Captain Montgomery was a perfect gentleman at all times."

"So *that's* what you're so mad about."

"I am not angry in the least," she snapped. "Don't you have a breakfast to cook?"

"You want me to feed him?"

"If you're referring to Captain Montgomery, you'll have to ask him if he wants to eat with us. Whether he eats or not is none of my business."

Edith left the tent, chuckling.

As Maddie washed herself and dressed in her sturdy traveling clothes, she told herself that she wasn't angry, that Edith was a stupid woman with no morals and even less sense. But the more she thought, the more the muscles in her body began to tense up. How dare he treat her like some woman of the evening? All she was doing was removing thorns from him, yet he'd thought she was trying to make advances toward him. Of all the presumptions of any man, this was the worst. She wasn't interested in him. If she was going to be interested in a man, it would be in a man who was . . . was more romantic. A man who gave her a compliment now and then—at least a compliment better than "You're not painful to look at."

By the time she was dressed and left the tent, she was no longer embarrassed, but good old-fashioned angry at Captain Montgomery for taking advantage of her and misunderstanding her intentions. Outside, Edith had fried eggs and ham, and had thrown slices of stale bread in the grease and fried them too. Frank, Sam, Toby, and Captain Montgomery were all sitting on the ground and eating heartily.

The first one to meet her eyes was Captain Montgomery. To Maddie's mind he gave her a look of smug knowing. So, she thought, he thinks I'm one of his women, does he? He thinks that I'm one of those weak-headed, simpering females who follows handsome men around and begs them for attention.

She put her nose in the air and looked away from him, but she smiled at the other three men. "Good morning," she said cheerfully. "I hope everyone slept well. I know I did. Not a care in the world."

She sat down at the table and looked at the plate of greasy food Edith had put in front of her and lost her appetite completely. She pushed the food around for a while, then looked at Frank. "Did you look at that music I gave you?"

"Yeah," he said without much interest.

"Did you like it?"

"It's all right."

She looked back at her food. So much for conversation with Frank. She turned to Sam. "How are the horses faring on the trip?"

All Sam did was nod at her, so she looked right past Captain Montgomery as though he weren't even there and smiled at Toby. "How's your breakfast?"

"Beats army food."

She took a small bite of egg. "Toby, tell me something about yourself."

"Ain't much to tell. I got born and I ain't died yet. Ain't been much in between."

With great concentration she avoided Captain Montgomery's eyes on her and looked back at her plate. She was *not* going to try to make conversation with him. From now on she was going to let him know that she had no interest in him whatsoever. None. Not any.

After breakfast, as Edith was clearing up the dishes, packing Maddie's china in its special case, and the men were taking down the tent, Edith said, "I thought you were gonna be real nice to him so that he'd let you go the next time you have to meet that man about your little sister."

"I do not have to ask anyone's permission to go wherever I want to go. Neither Captain Montgomery nor the entire army has any right to tell me what I can and cannot do."

"But he thinks he has the right. It's been my experience that men take what they want and do what they want. If a woman stands in their way, they consider that about as much hindrance as a mosquito flyin' around 'em."

"Captain Montgomery isn't like that. He's an educated man. He's a sensible man. I shall explain to him that I have to go somewhere and I need to go alone."

Edith's reply was a great howl of laughter as she turned away.

"If he won't listen to reason, then there's always more opium," she said under her breath.

As the crow flies, it wasn't more than fifteen miles to the next town where Maddie was to sing, but it was difficult going. Riding inside the coach was dreadful, as she was flung from one side to the other, her head hitting the frame, her back bouncing on the hard, horsehide seats, her knees banging into the side panels. Once Captain Montgomery asked her if she'd like to ride his horse with him, but she'd haughtily refused. Edith had spent an hour in the coach and decided that walking was the easier way to travel, so she'd left Maddie alone. Maddie wouldn't walk because she was sure that Captain Montgomery would ride beside

166

her and laugh at her, and she was mortified at the thought that he might remark on her behavior of the day before. She repeatedly practiced what she was going to say to him when he did mention the event. Every phrase she rehearsed was guaranteed to give him the setting down that he so richly deserved. Several times she wished she'd left the thorns in him. But twice she remembered the feel of his legs under her hands.

Not long after noon they had to stop the coach to ford a branch of the Colorado River. Frank came to tell her that she'd better get out in case there was some trouble and the coach turned over. With Frank's help, she gracefully stepped down from the high step and climbed the rutted trail that served as a road.

At the top of the ridge she turned and looked back to watch the men trying to get the coach across the rocks and through the water. When the coach got stuck in the rocks, she watched as Captain Montgomery dismounted, took off his shirt, tossed it inside the coach, and went to help Sam turn the big wheel.

"He's one mighty fine-lookin' male, ain't he?" Edith said from behind her.

Maddie stared at the man's broad, tan back.

"Fair makes a body's teeth hurt, don't he?"

"Can't you find something else to do?" Maddie snapped, making Edith glare at her and walk away.

Maddie thought she should use the time out of the coach to get some exercise, but she stood right where she was and watched Captain Montgomery's every movement. She watched the play of muscles under his skin as he strained against the wheel, saw his leg muscles bulge as he pushed. Once, he paused and looked directly at her, as though he knew she was watching him. She looked away quickly, but not before he'd seen her.

When the coach was across the water, Captain Montgomery turned and motioned for her to come down the hill. She looked the other way, as though she hadn't seen him, and started walking off into the woods.

Within minutes he was beside her, on his horse, his shirt still off. "I've come to give you a ride across the river."

She had been so absorbed in watching him that she hadn't thought about how she was going to get across the water. "No, thank you. I'll walk."

"You can't walk across that river. It's too deep and too slippery, as well as being too cold."

"The cold doesn't seem to bother you," she said, giving him a sideways glance.

He followed along beside her. "What is wrong with you this morning? Yesterday you couldn't stay away from me and today you won't get near me."

She turned and gave him a look of such anger that Buttercup took a sidestep away from her.

He tried to make a joke of it. "You're scaring my horse." When she didn't react, he sighed. "Whatever I've done this time, Maddie, I apologize for it. I never meant—"

"I prefer Miss Worth. I have never given you permission to call me Maddie."

"Oh, hell," he muttered, then leaned over and grabbed her just under the arms and lifted her off the ground. "Everyone's waiting for you."

"Put me down! You're hurting me. I'll walk back to the coach."

"You cannot walk across that river, and there isn't time for you to try it so that you can prove to me that you can do it. Besides that, I don't trust you not to go wandering off into the woods. Either I carry you like this across the river in front of the others or you ride with me."

"Captain Montgomery, I don't like you at all. Not one little bit," she said as she allowed him to help her onto his horse in front of him. She could feel his warm, bare skin through her cotton blouse.

"That's odd," he said into her ear. "Yesterday I got the impression that you liked me a lot. A whole lot."

Maddie's entire body turned red in embarrassment, and she did her best to sit up straight so that she didn't touch him, but that was impossible to do on the ride across the river. She could swear that he led his horse into every hole so that she was thrown back against him.

Once, when Buttercup's front hoof slipped, 'Ring's arm tightened around her rib cage. "I don't care how mad you are at me," he snapped. "Lean back against me and don't risk falling."

She had sense enough to obey him. She leaned

169

back and found that she fit against him as though her body had been made for his.

On the other side of the river, as she dismounted, she didn't look at him. "Thank you," she murmured, and went quickly to the coach. His shirt was on the seat, and she sat as far away from it as possible.

The coach had just started rolling when the door was thrown open and Captain Montgomery entered.

"This coach is the heaviest thing I've ever tried to push. What's in those trunks of yours? Lead?"

"I don't want any company," she said, and looked out the window.

"Well, I do. Both Frank and Sam leave something to be desired as conversationalists, and Toby mostly complains, and that maid of yours is . . ."

She looked at him and wished she hadn't, because he still wore no shirt. "What's wrong with Edith?"

"She keeps offering herself to me, that's all. Said that for me it would be free."

She turned angry eyes to him. "And we know you're much too good to take her up on the offer, don't we?"

He rubbed his arms against the cold, then looked for his shirt, which he was sitting on. He withdrew it and began to put it on. "I don't know how I've come to be classified as a prude but, for the record, I'm not."

She didn't look at him, but she snorted.

"Should I throw myself on a woman to prove that I'm not?"

"I don't know what gives you the idea that I care what you do. Except that I wish you'd ride somewhere else. I didn't invite you into this coach with me, nor did I invite you on this trip. I really wish you'd go away."

He didn't say anything for a while. In fact, he was so silent that Maddie turned to look at him. He was watching her intently. "Do I have dirt on my face, Captain?"

"No," he said slowly. "Not dirt." He didn't say a word more, but opened the door, grabbed the outside overhead rail, and pulled himself out of the coach, going up to ride on the top with Sam and Frank.

Maddie lectured herself for the next hour for being such a fool. She was making an ass of herself and everyone was taking note of it. She vowed that she'd keep her feelings to herself from then on. Captain Montgomery meant absolutely nothing to her. She wasn't interested in him in any way, shape, or form, and the sooner he understood that, the better. From now on she was going to be polite to him and nothing else. He was no different, of no more interest to her than Frank was.

"You can't go out there," 'Ring said softly. "I mean it, you can't go out there. Those men are drunk. They've taken days to get drunk and they're getting mean."

They were in her tent that they'd set up outside the only building in the little town of Pitcherville. When they'd arrived in the dirty little camp a few hours before, every man and all the women who serviced them had come out to meet the singing duchess. Word of LaReina's impending visit had reached them the previous day, and everyone had taken time off from the monotony of trying to find gold to get drunk in anticipation of hearing the opera singer. Six men had even made the trek back to Denver City to get the piano for her. They'd hauled it up the steep mountain trail, dropping it three times, and now Frank was trying to put it back together.

"Of course I can sing for them," Maddie said, turning away from him, trying to sound confident. But she could hear the shouts and the occasional gunfire from the men.

He caught her arm and turned her to face him. "What's wrong with you? What's made you so angry at me?"

"I have no idea what you're talking about. I am the same as I've always been to you. Nothing's changed."

"Yes, it has. For a while there I thought maybe we could be friends. I know I certainly enjoyed our conversations."

"Conversations? Is that what you call them? Where you tell me what I can and cannot do? Where you ask me questions about every aspect of my life?"

He took a step back from her. "I beg your

172

pardon. I guess I was under the wrong impression." He took a breath. "But forget our differences. Those men out there are getting mean and I'm afraid for you."

"Why? Afraid that if your charge gets knocked over the head with a whiskey bottle, it will go on your record and tarnish your perfect image?"

He looked at her for a long while. "If you were injured, I wouldn't like it at all."

Again she looked away from him. "You can't stop me. I'm going out there."

He grabbed her by the shoulders and turned her to face him. "Maddie, don't do this just to prove to me that you can do whatever you want to. Use your common sense. I can't control a crowd that size and that mean. And this time you won't be able to make them hear one single note."

She knew that he was telling her the truth, and if it were up to her alone, she'd leave right then, in the dark, and head back to Denver City, but her orders were to sing in six camps and in six camps she was going to sing. "I have to," she whispered.

He held her at arm's length for a few moments, looking into her eyes. "I sure wish you'd tell me what is going on that makes you have to go on this trip in the first place. Both our lives would be a lot easier if you'd trust me."

If I trust you, she thought, maybe it would make our lives easier but it just might end the life of one little girl. "I have no idea what you're talking about." She moved out of his grasp. "I am going to bring a little culture to these poor men and—" She had to stop as a series of gunshots rang out.

"I'll do the best I can," he said at last, then left the tent.

Maddie stood still for a moment and looked after him. She wasn't the fool she portrayed herself to be. It was one thing to impress men with her voice who were lonely and mostly sober, but she'd seen too many drunks not to know that many men who otherwise were respectfully nice often became violent when they drank.

About a dozen shots rang out, making her jump, and when her heart stilled, she thought back over the years to other performances. She remembered all the roses thrown at her feet in Florence. In Venice she'd gone riding in a gondola with a tenor—what was his name? It was amazing how forgettable the names of other performers were— and they'd sung duets. All the other gondolas had stopped, and the people of Venice had opened the windows of their houses to listen. When she and the tenor had finished singing, the bravos had echoed through the canal. Now she was going to have to persuade a crowd of drunken, dirty miners to like her.

"You look like you're about to cry," Edith said, coming into the tent.

"Of course not." Maddie smacked herself in the face with a powder puff.

"If I had to face them men singin' the songs

you do and lookin' the way you do, I'd be scared too."

"What does that mean? 'Looking the way I do.'"

"This is one of Harry's towns. She's this big redhead. Well, not really red, but close enough, and she heard you was comin' and she don't like it. She considers these men hers and she don't wanta share 'em."

"I can assure you—and her—that I do not want any of these men. I merely want to, shall we say, borrow them for a while."

"Whatever, she don't like it none. She's talked against you so much, sayin' that you're a snob and a lady and that you'll look down your nose at 'em that the men are preparin' to hate you. She's also told 'em that you're an iceberg and that opera is for men with ice water in their veins."

"That's ridiculous. All the opera stories are full of passion and love."

"But they're in foreign languages and nobody can understand 'em, can they? And the way you stand there singin' 'em . . ." Edith straightened her spine, put her hands in a prayerful attitude, a proud, haughty look on her face, and pursed her mouth. "You don't look like you're singin' a song about love when you're up there." Edith's eyes turned sly. "I don't think that Captain Montgomery thinks about you and love in the same breath either."

That did it. Maddie threw down the powder

175

puff. "Edith, I want to borrow that red and black corset of yours, that really gaudy one."

"What?"

"You heard me. Go and get it now. This minute."

"It ain't gonna fit over that chest of yours."

"Good. I shall have to allow a great deal of it to hang out."

Edith's eyes widened. "Yes, ma'am," she said, and scurried out of the tent. Maddie began to change out of her lovely, simple silk dress.

Forty-five minutes later, Captain Montgomery came to the tent so that he could lead her onto the stage that Sam had put together. He'd planned to try one more time to persuade her not to sing, but he took one look at her set jaw and didn't say a word. He walked in front of Maddie, and she wondered how he could move with the weight of all the weapons he was wearing. A serious-looking Toby followed her.

Maddie did her best to hide her nervousness, both about the coming crowd and about what she planned to do. She wasn't sure that she had the nerve.

She walked onto the stage, and the noise of the men quieted to a dull roar. They weren't going to welcome her; they were going to make her prove herself.

She could see by their eyes that they thought she was just what this woman called Harry said she was. But perhaps her voice could change their minds.

She took the stance that Madame Branchini had taught her, the stance that the rest of the world expected from an opera singer, and began to sing a beautiful aria from *Don Giovanni*.

She hadn't sung five minutes before they started booing. A couple of shots were fired and some of the men started muttering in loud tones.

She glanced at Captain Montgomery, saw that his eyes were scanning the crowd, one hand on his pistol, the other on his sword, ready to draw them if need be.

Maddie stopped singing. She turned and went to Frank. "Do you have the music from that new opera?"

"*Carmen?*"

She nodded. "Give me some of the overture and then play the '*Habanera.*' Play it three times. Play it as though your life depended on it."

He looked out over the crowd with an uneasy eye. "In this place it might."

She tried to get the attention of the men to tell them the story of Carmen and about the song she was going to sing, but no one listened to her. She looked at Captain Montgomery and saw the worry on his face.

I shall show them, she thought. I shall *be* Carmen, the lusty girl who works in a cigarette factory.

Frank started playing some of the overture, and Maddie began to unbutton her blouse. What her singing couldn't do her skin did. She had the attention of the first row now. And when she unpinned her hair, letting it flow down her back, she gained the attention of the next five rows.

Carmen was a mezzo soprano's role and Maddie's voice didn't have quite the necessary darkness, but she had the emotion. The first words to the *"Habanera"* were "Love is a rebellious bird that nobody can tame, and it's all in vain to call it if it chooses to refuse."

As she sang the words about love being a Gypsy child, she acted them out. She swished her skirt so that her ankles in their black silk stockings were exposed. When she got to where she sang *"L'amour"* several times, she drew it out as seductively as she knew how.

She'd never done anything like this in her life, but as she started to sing the song for the second time, Maddie began to regret that she had never before acted like this. She could feel the captain's eyes on her. Yesterday she'd been forward with him and he'd told her no, but the wide eyes of the men in the audience told her that none of them would tell her no.

She left the stage and went down among the men. Her blouse was open to her waist now and, as Edith had predicted, a great deal of her was coming up over the top of the bright, gaudy red satin corset. She leaned over men and sang, speaking of love, "You think you can hold it, it escapes you," and as she did so she slid away from the men's clutching hands.

By the third rendition of the *"Habanera,"* she was practically slithering around the room, from table to table. She was the promiscuous, luscious Carmen and she could entice any man in the world—but they couldn't have her.

When she finished the song for the third time, Maddie looked at Frank. He was trying to keep the surprise off his face, but he wasn't succeeding. Captain Montgomery was scowling at her. She smiled at him and then slid into the next song from *Carmen,* the song where she tells Don José that her heart belongs to no one.

She suspected that most of the men could not understand the French words, but she knew that Captain Montgomery did. She sang the song with real feeling, giving it all she had when she said that she'd take her lover with her to keep her from being bored. Then when she remembers that she's between lovers, Maddie put her back to a post in the building and rubbed up against it, moving down, her knees bent but slightly wide as she asked who wanted to love her. Who wanted her heart?

The miners might not have understood the words, but at her actions and her tone about five of them made a lunge for her. She slipped away from their grasp and sang that she was going to Lillas Pastia's tavern to drink manzanilla.

It was at the end of the chorus that Maddie got what must have been the surprise of her life, for out of the crowd came a scruffy-looking older man, who marched to her and told her, in French, in a quite pleasant tenor, to keep quiet, not to speak.

Maddie recovered from her shock and sang to him that she could sing all she wanted, that she was thinking of a certain army officer who she could possibly love. Her eyes slid to Captain Montgomery, who was watching her with the intensity of a hawk watching its prey.

The gray-haired man sang, "Carmen!"

Maddie sang to him that she was a Gypsy in love with a man other than him and she could make do with that man, hinting that she didn't need an officer like Don José.

The man, singing Don José's part, asked her if she could love him, and Maddie said yes.

The miners were grinning and punching one another as they watched ol' Sleb sing to this beautiful woman. They watched as Maddie, as Carmen, teased him, her face and body showing that she may or may not love him, as the mood took her. Poor Sleb looked like all the men there felt: that he would sell his soul to the devil if he could have her and that he might end his life if he could not.

Sleb sang his agony while Maddie sang the role of the woman in command, her voice so powerful that every note could be heard above all the movement and noise of the many men around her.

They cheered when Sleb pretended to be untying Maddie's hands from the rope that bound them, and then they watched as she sang again that she was going to the tavern to drink and dance, while poor Sleb looked at her with lust and longing.

They cheered more when the two voices blended in a short duet.

At the last chorus, Maddie made her way back to the stage. Her blouse was open all the way down to her waist now and hanging out of her skirt. She flipped her skirt and sang one last time about going to the tavern and ended with a magnificent tra-la-la-la-la.

When the miners' cheers shook the foundations of the building, it was a gratifying sound. She looked at Captain Montgomery and was pleased to see that he was frowning at her. She bowed to the audience and held out her hand to the man who had so unexpectedly sung the part of Don José.

But the men weren't going to allow her to have an ordinary ending. In one frightening motion they surged toward the stage. Maddie saw 'Ring make a leap for her, but he was lost to her sight as the men grabbed her and put her on their shoulders. She yelled, "'Ring!" a couple of times, but no one could hear her over the noise and confusion.

CHAPTER 9

As Maddie was carried along on the men's shoulders, she held on for dear life. She could .smell the stench of whiskey and unwashed bodies rising from them. This wasn't the same as having Russian students pull her carriage, for these men were so drunk that by sheer accident, they could drop her and trample her. They were so drunk that if they did drop her, it would probably be an hour before they realized it. Also, she was worried that some of the men would think that she had meant her performance and believe that she was Carmen.

It was with great relief that she saw Captain Montgomery making his way through the crowd to her. He was at least a head taller than the other men, and he was a man with a mission, so he was perhaps using more force than was necessary. As she buried her fingers in the hair of one of the men holding her and tried her best to keep her seat, she realized she wouldn't have minded if Captain Montgomery had made his way toward her by using a cannon.

When he got near her, she could see that he was very angry, but when he put his arms up for her, she didn't hesitate. She let go of the hair of the man holding her and fell into Captain Montgomery's arms. She hid her face against the wool of his jacket and snuggled against him as tightly as possible. She could hear the sound of his heart over the angry shouts of the miners, but she heard some other shouts and knew without looking that Toby and Frank and Sam were there also.

Captain Montgomery carried her back to her tent, which Sam had moved into the trees during her performance, away from the camps of the miners.

He dropped her without much gentleness on the cot, then turned his back on her and poured some whiskey. "Here," he said, holding the glass out to her.

He can't be too angry if he's offering me food, she thought. She took a sip, then he jerked the glass from her hand and drank the whiskey himself.

"You don't deserve any and I don't trust any whiskey that you keep," he said, scowling down at her. "That was some exhibition you put on in there. Did your Madame Branchini teach you that?"

"It was done purely on my own instincts." She smiled at him. "Did you like it?"

"I'm glad the men couldn't understand the words of the songs. Gypsy love, indeed." He turned away to refill his glass.

She leaned back on the cot on her elbows. Her blouse was still open, Edith's corset showing, and she just happened to notice that with her arms back as they were, her breasts plumped up rather nicely. "I've never done anything like that before. I think I did rather well, don't you?"

He turned back and some whiskey splashed out of his glass when he looked at her.

She smiled as innocently as she knew how.

"If you keep playing with fire, you're going to get burned."

"Oh? And who is going to add fuel to my fire?"

"Not me, if that's what you're hinting at."

That cooled her off. She sat up. "I should have known I wouldn't get a compliment out of you."

"Is that what you want? Your singing was magnificent. I have never heard anything like it in my life. Every note was like a precious jewel being given to the earth."

She blinked a few times, hearing the sincerity in his voice. "But what about my acting?"

"Acting?" He snorted. "You weren't acting. You *were* Carmen." He gave her a look up and down. "But you can stop now."

She snatched her blouse together and got off the cot. "Thank you so much for rescuing me from the miners, Captain, but I'd like to get ready for bed now, so perhaps you should leave."

"I'm not going anywhere tonight. I'm not letting you out of my sight."

"You can't spend the night with me."

"No, not spend the night with you, at least not the way it sounds. I am going to try to keep those men who you did your best to entice from coming in here to get you. Sam and Frank and Toby are going to sleep just outside."

This made Maddie feel rather like an extraordinarily desirable woman.

"You can stop looking so pleased with yourself. I hope no one gets hurt."

"I do too, and I'm sure they won't with you looking out for me." She smiled at him. "They did like me, didn't they?" She began to hum the *"Habanera"* and, with her skirt held out, she moved about the tent as though she were dancing.

He watched her, frowning. "Is that who you want to like you, men like them?"

"You don't understand."

"Explain it to me."

She took his empty glass from his hand, refilled it, and then drank from it. "People have such odd ideas about opera singers. They think we're not quite human, as though we are creatures closer to divinity than to flesh and blood. They think just as you did, that we were born singing and that it has all been easy for us. They don't see that we are human and that we want the same things that all women want."

He caught her wrist, pulling her close to him. "And what do you want, Maddie? To be a saloon singer who swells out of the top of a too-small corset?"

"No, I want what I have, but tonight it was . . . I don't know, it was nice to be liked for my womanly characteristics and not just for my voice."

"But your voice—"

She pulled away from him. "I *know* that my voice is magnificent. I wanted to know that the men like my . . . I wanted to know that they liked me as a woman also. And they did."

"How could you possibly doubt that?" he asked softly.

She turned and looked at him, and for a moment she was again Carmen, the lusty cigarette girl who knew that she had power over men. She wanted him to take her in his arms, to kiss her, possibly to make love to her.

"Save your seductions for your miners," he said, and turned away.

Maddie felt as though she'd been kicked in the stomach, and it took a moment to recover her breath. She walked to the cot. "I don't want you here tonight, Captain. If you feel that I'm not safe, then send Toby or Frank or Sam to stay with me."

"After the display you made tonight, I wouldn't trust my own father alone in here with you. My own grandfather."

"But I'm perfectly safe with you, aren't I, Captain?" To her horror, she could feel tears beginning to form in her eyes. Tonight, as she had been singing about the army officer that Carmen had loved, she knew she had been singing to this army officer who was beginning to fill her thoughts.

"I would protect you with my life, but you have to trust me."

"I trust you with *my* life, but—" She broke off, the emotion of the night too much for her. "Leave me for a while, please."

He walked behind her, then turned her and pulled her into his arms. She struggled against him. He wouldn't touch her when she wanted him to, but the minute she couldn't bear the sight of him, he held her close. "I hate you."

"No, you don't." He stroked her hair. "You have no idea how you feel about me."

"But I guess you do know?" she asked angrily.

"I think I know better than you do."

She pushed away from him. "You say that I'm vain, but it's your vanity that knows no bounds. I imagine you think I care about you. Well, I don't. I care nothing at all about you."

"You sure looked like you cared nothing about me when I plowed my way through those men to get to you tonight. I never saw such joy on a person's face as when I held up my arms for you and you fell into them with absolute and total trust."

"I would have gone to any man I knew. The men who were carrying me didn't have me balanced properly."

"Oh? From the moment the men picked you up, Sam was not a foot from you, and since he's somewhat taller than I am, why didn't you see him and go to him?"

"I saw him," she lied. "I just didn't choose to go to him, that's all."

The way he grinned made her turn away.

"I wonder if we could stop arguing just long enough for you to patch me up? I'm bleeding."

She whirled on him, immediately putting her hands on his waist and turning him about. "Where?" There was a large bloody patch on his back and at the top of it his shirt was cut. "Oh, 'Ring, you fool. This looks serious. Why didn't you say anything? Did someone use a knife on you?" She glanced up at him and saw the way he was smiling. "Not that I care in the least. I don't. I would help anyone in my employ, even men I don't like. Oh, do stop smirking and take that shirt off. I have bandages in the trunk."

"You will do anything to get me undressed, won't you?"

"Truthfully, I like the look of you better than what comes out of your mouth."

She saw him wince when he moved his arms out of his shirt. "Sit," she ordered, and he did.

She'd bandaged men before and knew something about wounds. The cut wasn't deep, and she didn't have to sew it, but it looked grimy. "What did you do, roll in a pigsty after you were cut?"

"More or less. Somebody hit me in the knees and I went down, then about thirty or forty others decided to walk across me."

"I saw you go down, but there was nothing I could do."

"And I heard you call out to me. I'm sorry I couldn't get to you," he said softly.

She looked back at him, but his eyes were on the part of her anatomy that was bulging over the top of her corset. *Now* he looks at me, she thought angrily, and poured whiskey onto the cut.

He sat up straight, drawing in his breath. "A little gentler, if you don't mind."

"I'm being as gentle as you deserve."

"Then I deserve the best. If it weren't for me, you'd probably be in some miner's tent right now, at the mercy of half a dozen men."

She stepped away from him. "At least they'd

know that I was a woman. At least *they* wouldn't look at me on the sly."

He put his hand up to the side of her face, burying his hand in her hair, his thumb at the corner of her mouth. "Don't you understand anything? Anything at all? You're the most desirable woman I've ever met in my life. Between your body and that voice of yours, I— Never mind what I feel, but I don't want you if you want just any man. I want you only when you want me. Me, 'Ring, not Captain Montgomery, not a man you don't trust, not a man you consider an enemy. You're much too important for anything less than that."

There was too much of him unclothed, too much of her uncovered, and they were too close together. She backed away from him. "You want information from me."

"I want a lot more than that from you."

"To sing for you?" she whispered.

He sighed and turned away. "Do you think this cut needs sewing?"

"No." She was confused by his words, didn't at all understand what he was saying. In fact, the more she was around him, the less she understood about him. She didn't want to talk anymore about whatever it was that they were talking about.

"Who was the man who sang with me?" she said as she began bandaging the cut on his back, winding clean strips of linen around his shoulder, under his arm, and across his back. She tried to ignore the way her nearly bare breasts rubbed

189

against his bare back and chest as she reached around him.

"I didn't have much time, and, if the truth be known, I could hardly take my eyes off the spectacle you were making of yourself, but, from what I gather, he is the town drunk of a town of drunks. Comes from a place called Desperate."

"Not a bad voice. I can't imagine where he got the music to *Carmen*. I wouldn't have thought it had come west yet. There, that should hold you."

He caught her hand. "Thank you." He looked at her hand, then turned it over and kissed the palm, holding it for a moment against his lips. She put her hand on his thick, dark hair. When he looked up at her, she felt a little weak-kneed. "You were great tonight. I imagine you changed a few minds about opera."

Now she was far enough away from her performance to remember it with embarrassment— including her performance in the tent with him. "I'm afraid I went a little too far in the other direction. I'm afraid they're going to have a new opinion of opera that is as bad as their old one."

"They are certainly going to think of opera *singers* in a new way." He looked pointedly at her bosom which was about three inches from his face.

Maddie nearly jumped away from him and pulled her dress together. "I don't know what came over me."

"Carmen did," he said, then stretched, his hands touching the canvas of the tent. "But I'm glad you're back. Carmen's not the kind of woman

I'd choose. Tell me, what happens to her in the opera?"

"Don José kills her."

"That would have been my guess. You ready to go to bed? You may be willing to stay up all night, but I need my sleep."

She was staring at him. What did he mean by, "the kind of woman I'd choose"?

"You plan to wear that to bed?"

That shook her out of her trance. "You expect me to undress in front of you?"

"From what you were wearing tonight, I expect you to put on more clothes to go to sleep. Want me to help you with your ties?"

"You lay one hand on me or my undergarments and I'll give you a wound that'll make the one on your back look like nothing."

"It might be worth it. I'll have to consider the matter."

"Get out of here and call my maid."

"I'm good with corset ties."

"Go!"

"All right, but when you're ready for bed, I come back in here. Understand?" He didn't give her time to answer before he left the tent.

Maddie sat down on the cot. She didn't understand the man at all. One minute she was practically throwing herself at him and he was ignoring her, then the next he was offering to take her clothes off for her.

It was several moments before she realized that Edith was standing over her and whispering.

"I got it."

"Got what?" Maddie asked.

"The fruit you asked for. I had to pay a lot for it though."

Maddie still wasn't thinking clearly and just looked at Edith.

"He make you forget your little sister again? If a man could make a woman forget, he could, but I can't tell that he's interested in women."

"Because he's not interested in you?"

"Jealous, are you? I haven't seen *you* wakin' up happy after a night with him. Or is tonight the first? You sure put on a show for him this time."

"Help me undress, and I did not put on a show for him. I merely sang and played a role as it was meant to be played. It was about—"

"You don't have to explain any of it to me or to anybody else. A blind man could have seen what you was singin' about. The way you was rubbin' on that post and lookin' at Captain Montgomery. Mmmm-hmmm! I'll have to try that sometime."

Maddie could feel her face turning red and was glad for the nightgown going on over her head.

"You want the fruit or not?"

It took Maddie a moment to remember what Edith was talking about. Early the next morning she was to leave the camp, alone, and make the long climb up the mountain to meet the man and exchange letters. And if she did everything he said and did it well, she would see Laurel.

"You still want the fruit, or you gonna just ask him to let you go?"

Yesterday Maddie had decided that the only way to get away from Captain Montgomery was to do something that would force him to let her go alone to meet the man who had Laurel. She knew there was no use trying to talk to him. He'd set himself up as her caretaker, and he wasn't going to relinquish the job.

Sitting in that coach for hours yesterday, she'd come up with nothing more creative than to once again use opium. It would get him out of the way for a good long while, giving Maddie the time she needed to get ahead of him, and Edith seemed to have an unlimited supply of the stuff. Maddie had been able to form a plan that would probably trick him enough to get him to take the opium in some dried fruit.

"Yes," she said softly. "I still need the fruit." As she said it, she felt quite bad. It hadn't bothered her before when she'd seen him drink the whiskey with the opium and now, if anything, he was more of a nuisance and a hindrance than he was before. But since then he'd rescued her from the men who'd taken her and wanted to hear her voice. He had dressed himself like an arsenal tonight, ready to use fists or guns or whatever was needed to ensure her safety. And he'd come to get her when the men had carried her off on their shoulders. And if she were honest with herself, she knew that the truth was that she'd been able to perform *Carmen* only because she knew that he was there watching over her. Had she been alone, with just Sam and Frank to take care of her, she

193

would never have dared to act in such an audacious way. Of course, while she was being honest with herself, she had to admit that she might not have wanted to be Carmen and rub up against a post if Captain Montgomery hadn't been there watching her.

"Bring the fruit in the morning. At about five. That should make him sleep most of the day. Did you get a horse?"

"Just like you said. It'll be waitin' for you." Edith looked at Maddie awhile. "You really gonna go out there in them woods all alone?"

"The woods are safer than a town like this. The woods don't frighten me a bit, but when Captain Montgomery wakes up, he's going to be in a foul mood."

"Is he! I think I might find I have to do somethin' on the other side of town all day tomorrow. I don't want him to find out I had anything to do with this."

"Wise decision."

When 'Ring returned, Maddie was hidden under the covers of her hard little cot, but she listened to him as he undressed and spread his blankets on the canvas-covered floor. She wondered what he was wearing, or, more precisely, what he wasn't wearing.

He turned out the lantern and moved between his rough army wool blankets. "Good night," he said softly.

Maddie didn't answer, but waited, wondering

if there was more to come. She remembered how Toby had said that Captain Montgomery wasn't interested in women. All women, or just her?

"Was I actually good tonight or were you just being kind?"

"You were more than good."

She paused a moment. "I've never done anything like that before. I mean, I've never acted like that before. My life has been rather sedate when it comes to men. I haven't really . . ." She couldn't finish the sentence.

"I know."

His bland assurance that he knew everything there was to know about her made her angry. "Why do you assume you know so much about me when I know so little about you?"

"We learn where our interest lies."

"What does that mean?"

He didn't say a word, and she knew that he wasn't going to answer her. She remembered the way he'd come for her tonight, and she thought of what she was going to have to do to him tomorrow. "'Ring," she whispered.

He didn't speak, but she knew he was listening. "Sometimes a person has to do things that aren't right, or they may not seem right at the time, but in the long run they have to be done whether one wants to do them or not. Do you understand?"

"Not a word."

She sighed. Maybe it was better that he didn't understand. "Good night," she said, and turned onto her side and tried to go to sleep.

In the morning, at five, a sleepy-looking Edith came into the tent, carrying a little wooden box. "Mornin', Captain," she said.

Maddie rolled over and looked to see Captain Montgomery, fully dressed in his dirty, bloody shirt and army trousers, sitting on the stool drinking a cup of coffee. "How long have you been awake?" Maddie asked.

"Awhile. What do you have there, Miss Honey?"

"Dried fruit. One of the men sent it to her," Edith said, pointing at Maddie, "for the singin' last night. I think they're called figs. Ain't never had none myself, and they don't look too good to me, but one of the girls said that they cost a lot."

'Ring took the box from her and looked inside. "They are indeed figs." He held out the box to Maddie. "Have one?"

She sat up in the bed and made a great show of rubbing her eyes. "No, thank you, but you have some."

She tried not to watch as he put his hand over the box, then hesitated. "No, I think I'll wait."

He got off the stool. "I'll wait outside while you get dressed and then I'll escort you to the necessary. Today you're not getting out of my sight."

"Now what you gonna do?" Edith asked as soon as he was out of the tent.

"I have no idea, just help me get dressed and then I'll think of something."

True to his word, Captain Montgomery was waiting for her outside when she was dressed. He offered his arm to her, but she refused to take it. "I can walk on my own."

"Whatever."

She didn't want to talk to him, because she had to think. If he wasn't going to eat the figs, what was she going to do to get rid of him?

She assured him that she could make her way to the necessary all by herself and so walked ahead of him. But she was just inside the place when she heard hissing outside.

"Ma'am, it's us. 'Member us?"

Quickly, Maddie looked around for knotholes in the outhouse and saw about fifty of them. She sighed in resignation. "What do you want?" They were the four men who had kidnapped her and taken her to sing for them. What they had done was wrong, of course, but she couldn't hate any men who wanted to hear her sing as much as these men had. They had kidnapped her so that their friends could also hear her sing.

She listened as the men asked her to grubstake them. In return, they'd give her a deed to half of their three claims. Why not, she thought, and at the same time knew that Captain Montgomery would hate the idea. But then, the fact that she even considered such a proposal was his fault. All his talk of old age and what was she going to do when she could no longer sing had made her think about needing money. What *had* John done with all the money she'd earned over the years? He'd always paid any bills she'd run up, and it had never occurred to her to ask him what had happened to the rest of the money.

"All right," she said. "Go tell Frank I said to give you a hundred dollars each."

"Thank you, ma'am," they chorused. "Thank you. We'll make you a rich woman."

She was relieved when they left and she at last had some privacy. Captain Montgomery was waiting for her outside the little shack. I am little more than a prisoner, she thought. For some reason, all my freedom has been taken away from me.

In the tent, Captain Montgomery held up the box of figs. "Want some?"

"No, thank you. I really don't like them. But you have as many as you want."

"Don't mind if I do." She watched as he picked up two of them and ate them quickly. "They're really good. You should have a few."

"No, I'd rather not." She smiled as he ate another fig, but then frowned as he ate a fourth one. She didn't have any idea how much opium Edith had put in each fig, and she didn't know how much a person could take without sleeping forever.

When he put the fifth fig to his lips, she leaped at him. "No!" She knocked the box to the floor and grabbed the fig from his hand.

He looked at her in surprise, then understanding. "What have you done, Maddie?"

"Nothing I didn't have to do. Please try to understand."

"Understand that you don't trust me? That you

think that I'm so incompetent that I can't help you in whatever it is that you have to do?"

"Yes. I would ask for your help if I could, but I can't. You must understand."

"I don't understand at all." He put his hand to his forehead and swayed on his feet.

Maddie went to the side of him, put his arm around her shoulders, and led him to the cot, where he half fell onto it, pulling Maddie halfway down with him. She pushed at him, trying to get away, but he held her. She relaxed after a moment, knowing that soon he wouldn't have the strength to hold her.

"Where are you going? Who are you meeting? What's so important that you have to risk your life for it?" He had a hold on her neck, not allowing her to move from her position of half on, half off his body.

"I can't tell you. Believe me, I would if I could. I would like to have someone's help."

He closed his eyes for a moment, then forced them open again. "Is it the same man as before?"

"What? Oh," she said, remembering the first time he'd followed her. "I can't say. I have to go. I have a long way to go before tonight."

She tried to move away from him, but he was still awake enough to keep a firm hold on her shoulders. "Where?"

"I'm not going to tell you because as soon as you can you'll follow me. Damn you!" she said. "Why did you have to come into my life and confuse me? I was fine before I met you. I was free.

I had no one who thought he was my keeper, and now . . ."

She gave a violent jerk and pulled away from him. He tried to follow her but sleep was too heavy on him and he fell back against the cot. She went to the trunk and got the map out, then stuck it down the front of her blouse.

She went back to him, bent over him, and touched his hair. With effort he opened his eyes.

"I'm afraid you'll be hurt," he whispered. "You'll get lost."

"No, I won't, and I'll stay on the outskirts of the town. I won't let anyone see me. I'll be back before tomorrow night. Wait for me. And . . ." She smiled at him. "Don't be too angry with me."

"I'll come after you."

She could barely hear him now as sleep was overtaking him. She leaned closer to his lips. "Wait for me," she repeated. "I'll take care."

He didn't answer her as he lay there, and she thought he was probably fully asleep now. As she looked at him she felt a great deal of regret. She was frightened of these men who held Laurel and she was frightened of some of these men who lived in the mountains, these miners who were far from home and the rules of civilization. She smoothed his thick, dark hair back from his forehead. She would feel a great deal safer with him along. And if he'd started in with all his talk and teasing, she'd probably have been able to forget her fears for Laurel for a little while.

"I'm sorry, 'Ring," she whispered to the sleeping man. "I wouldn't do this if I didn't have to."

She started to pull away from him, but then, on impulse, she touched her lips to his. She had thought he was in a deep sleep, but instantly his strength returned to him. His right arm came up around her back, burying itself in her hair, and his left arm tightened about her waist. He slanted her head so that her mouth was firmly against his and then he kissed her.

Maddie had kissed a few men before, but kisses had never much interested her. This one did. She felt as though she were drowning, that his lips against hers were taking her soul from out of her body. She put her arms around his neck and pulled him closer to her, as though that were possible, and then, of their own accord, her feet came off the floor and she stretched out on the cot beside him. But there wasn't room for both of them, so she moved to extend her body fully on top of his.

Abruptly, unexpectedly, his arms released her and fell to his side. Maddie nearly fell to the floor. She had to clutch his shoulders to keep from falling. She lifted her head to look at him and saw that he was at last asleep.

Slowly, she got off him, but when she tried to stand, her knees gave way under her and she sat down on the floor. Her heart was pounding in her ears and her entire body felt weak and shaky.

She sat there for a few moments, breathing rapidly, her eyes wide as she looked at the sleeping form of Captain Montgomery. She brushed the back of her hand against her forehead and felt the sweat that had broken out there.

"*Mon Dieu*," she whispered, and it was a few moments before she could remember who she was or where she was. Then, using her hands, she pushed herself up to a standing position. "I'll be back," she said to his sleeping body as she looked from one end of him to the other. "You can be sure of that. I'll be back."

She went to the tent flap, gave him one last look over her shoulder, then went outside to where a saddled horse awaited her.

CHAPTER 10

Maddie skirted the settlement rather easily. After her performance, she felt sure that any man she met would know who she was and would have an opinion of her that wasn't a true one. What would Madame Branchini have thought of her rendition of *Carmen?*

As Maddie made her way up the mountain, her fears for Laurel increased. What if the man didn't show up? What if this awful man who seemed to be the messenger for the kidnappers attacked her again? She had done what he asked the last time and this time brought him "something shiny," but what if it wasn't enough? She couldn't very well tell him to wait just a minute while she made her way back down the mountain and got the last of the jewelry she had with her. She didn't think

Captain Montgomery would allow her to go alone for the third time.

Maddie tried to think of anything in the world except 'Ring. Even though she had not wanted him to accompany her on this trip, he had made himself useful. General Yovington had hired the three people who were supposed to protect her, but they had never been there when she needed them. But 'Ring had always been there. He'd asked her where her manager had been when the Russian students had kidnapped her, and she'd had to tell him that John had left her to her own devices. But Maddie knew that 'Ring would never leave her alone. He would protect her with his life, just as Toby said he would.

She rode up and up for hours, never seeming to reach the top of the mountain. She ate beef rolled in stale bread as she rode. She drank from her canteen without dismounting. The horse panted and Maddie slowed, but she didn't allow the poor animal to rest. She had to get to the man before sundown. He'd told her that Laurel would be there if she got to him before sundown.

It was late when she started to look at the sky with nervousness. The sun seemed to be dropping at an accelerated rate.

"I wish my father were here," she said aloud to the horse. "I wish Hears Good was here. And Bailey and Linq and Thomas." She sighed. "I wish 'Ring were with me."

She stroked the horse between the ears. "Maybe he could have come with me. Maybe I could have shown him the route and he could have found some other way to get to Laurel. Maybe we could have made a plan to take Laurel and this whole horrible episode would be over. Then I could take Laurel home, go back east and sing for people who appreciate me. Appreciate me even when I have all my buttons fastened."

Even as she said the words, she knew how wrong they were. What if in the fracas that would no doubt ensue there were shots fired and Laurel was hit? She envisioned Laurel. She hadn't seen her young sister in years but, along with a few photographs, her mother had sent sketches, watercolors, and pen and ink drawings of Laurel, so Maddie knew that she'd recognize her sister anywhere.

No, she couldn't risk it. She urged the horses forward. It was better this way, to go alone and give the man—or men—what they wanted. She would exchange letters with him and give him all the jewelry she had and whatever else he wanted. And if the man kissed her again, she'd smile at him. Somehow, that was the most difficult part for her to anticipate. She'd rather part with all her jewelry than give one kiss to a man she despised.

She was so deep in thought that she wasn't prepared when the man jumped out of the trees at her. She worked to calm her frightened horse, then thought that her father would be very disappointed in her if he'd seen her so easily surprised in the woods.

"You're late," the man said, grabbing the bridle

of her horse. He grinned at her, then ran his hand up her leg.

Surreptitiously, she dug her heel into the far side of the horse and made it jump away from him. "Where is she?"

"Who?"

Maddie tried to keep from glaring at him. "You said that after my third performance I'd see my sister. I sang for the third time last night, so where is she?"

"Around. You bring me anything?"

Bullets. Poison. Whips. A firing squad. "I brought a pearl necklace. It's quite valuable. It was given to me by the king of Sweden." She pulled the necklace from her saddlebag and looked at it once before handing it to the man. She'd told 'Ring that money meant nothing to her and, in truth, it didn't. Not money itself, but she loved beautiful things, and the pearl necklace, all the pearls perfectly matched in size and color, was an extraordinarily beautiful thing. He took it into his dirty hands.

"Not bad. Anything else?"

"The necklace is worth a great deal, not only for its intrinsic value but for its historical significance."

He gave her a blank look.

"It is important that it once belonged to a king and it was given to me, LaReina. You can show it to your grandchildren."

He gave a noise that was meant to be laughter.

"Yeah, right. My grandchildren. You got the letter?"

"I want to see my sister."

"You'll see her when I get ready, and now, Miss History, get off that horse and come over here to me."

Maddie's heart jumped to her throat and began to pound. Whatever the man did to her, she had to bear. She could not risk Laurel's being hurt.

She realized from the way he looked at her that he knew what she was thinking. And Maddie could tell that her revulsion wasn't displeasing to him. "Come over here and give me a kiss."

It was perhaps the longest walk of her life as she went toward him and tried to prepare herself for touching the man.

It was at that moment that an arrow went flying toward the man. It missed his head by only an inch and stuck into a tree a foot away from him.

The man's reactions were slow, Maddie was glad to see. She had thrown herself to the ground while the man was still standing and staring stupidly at the arrow. Maddie looked up at the arrow and saw that it was Crow, and she felt some tears of joy come to her eyes.

"Get down," she said to the man. "Indians."

She looked at the naked fear on the man's face and knew that he, like most of the men now in the West, was from the East. His knowledge of Indians was what he'd heard around campfires at night—stories that were the equivalent of ghost

206

stories and had about as much to do with the truth as ghost stories.

"What is it?" he whispered, fear in his voice.

"I hope we aren't being attacked. How are you at surviving torture?"

He turned to look at her, his eyes wide. "Torture?"

"I've heard that the Indians around here have vowed to kill all white men they catch out alone. Their hatred of the white man has increased since the white man has been taking the sacred yellow rock from their land." She hoped that Hears Good was close enough to hear, because if he was, he was having a good laugh over this. Any Indian who had an ounce of brains knew that a good horse and rifle were worth all the yellow dust in the world.

"I'm getting out of here," the man said, and started to get up.

She caught his pant leg. "Wait! I want to see my sister."

"You're more fool than I thought you were if you think I'd bring a kid like her out here."

Maddie felt panic rising in her. It didn't matter that her father's friend, Hears Good, was near her, not if the man didn't have Laurel. She grabbed him by the shirtfront. "Where's my sister?"

"How the hell do I know? I'm just a messenger." He jerked away from her, but she caught him again.

"Where is she? Who does know about her? Who has her?"

"I don't know and I don't care." He gave her a shove that sent her sprawling, then started running up the hill.

Maddie was right behind him. "You said that you'd have my sister here."

As he mounted his horse, he looked down at her. "You oughta be glad I didn't bring her, what with Indians all around."

She grabbed his bridle. "You don't have her, do you? This is all a joke. Laurel is safe somewhere and I haven't been told."

The man reached into his canvas pants. "Here," he said, and flung something to the ground, then jerked the bridle out of her grasp. "I'll see you in the next place. Bring something else. Bring gold." He started to rein his horse away, but then, with a nervous look around, he glared down at her. "None of this ain't any of my business, and I don't care nothin' about any of you, but, lady, I'll give you some advice: They don't like that army man of yours snoopin' around. They don't like it at all, and if he sticks his nose where it don't belong, that little girl is gonna be killed. They're a mean bunch."

Maddie grabbed the bridle again. "Have they hurt her?"

"Not yet they ain't, but then, you been obeyin' them so far, ain't you?" With that, he reined his horse away and started traveling west as fast as the terrain would allow him to move.

Maddie stood there, stunned for a moment, and then she began to frantically search the ground for what the man had thrown down. It wasn't difficult to find. It was a dirty linen handkerchief tied into a knot. She sat down and, with shaking hands, carefully untied the knot.

When she had it unwrapped, she drew in her breath. There, lying on the linen, was the gold and sapphire ring that Maddie had sent Laurel from Italy just last year. Their mother had written that Laurel was so proud of the ring that she never took it off.

Carefully, Maddie rolled the linen back around the ring and held it in her palm. She wasn't going to cry; she wasn't even going to allow herself to feel. They *did* have Laurel.

She looked around her at the trees in the fading light. "Hears Good?" she said softly, but no one answered. Right now what she most wanted was to see and talk to someone familiar. "Hears Good," she said louder, but still no answer.

She puckered her lips and gave a whistle that imitated the call of the mountain lark, but no answering call came to her.

When she tried to stand, she found that her legs were shaking. Unsteadily, she made her way to the tree where the arrow was. She pulled it out and looked at it. It had the two tiny marks on it that were Hears Good's symbol.

"Where are you?" she shouted, but the forest was quiet. Why won't he show himself to me, she thought, and tried to keep her mind on the question. *Anything* to keep her mind off Laurel.

She ran in the direction that the arrow had come

from, but he wasn't to be seen. When she was out of breath, she stopped running. If Hears Good didn't want to be seen, no one on earth, not even her father, would be able to find him.

But why, she wondered. Why would he follow her yet not let her see him?

The answer came to her instantly. Because there was someone else nearby, someone who Hears Good wanted to avoid.

With that thought she began running down the hill, slowing only long enough to catch the bridle of her horse. If Hears Good was nearby, then perhaps her father was also. She tripped over ruts and scrub oak and scraped her hands on rocks as she tore down the mountain.

She was tired and it was full dark when she came to a stream and allowed her horse to drink while she replenished her canteen. She looked all around her but saw no one. It was too dark to see much now, and there was only a quarter moon. Her father had taught her how to travel at night, and she'd heard stories of men who'd traveled for days, moving only at night.

"Come on, boy," she said to the gelding, and picked up the bridle. For what seemed to be the thousandth time, she whistled the call of the mountain lark but received no answer.

Because of the darkness, she had to travel much slower than she'd moved on the trip up the mountain, and with each step she took she felt her mood growing worse. She was tense and angry over Laurel having been taken as well as angry that her friend, Hears Good, a man she'd known all her life, was so near yet wouldn't come to her. How long had he been following her? She remembered Captain Montgomery saying that many people were following her. He must have seen some sign of Hears Good before now.

She stumbled over a rock and fell face forward into thorn bushes. When she came up, she was cursing. At that moment she hated every man on earth. She hated men and their stupid talk of war, these men who had taken a child to use in the war they were trying to start. She hated the miners who liked to look down her dress as much as they liked to hear her sing. And most of all she hated 'Ring Montgomery because . . .

She wasn't sure why she hated him, but she did. Part of her also hated her father because she was so close to him and he wasn't coming to help her. Why didn't Hears Good go and get him and the others? Why—

She was walking along, so involved in her thoughts that it was a complete surprise when a strong arm came out of the dark, encircled her waist, and then a hand slipped over her mouth. The action caused an immediate reaction in her. It was as though she were a keg of gunpowder and someone had lit her fuse. Suddenly, she became a ball of energy and she began kicking and clawing and fighting, and she managed to get her teeth into the palm of the hand that was over her mouth.

"It's me," she heard Captain Montgomery say. "It's just me."

If that was meant to calm her down, it had the opposite effect. When she bit him and he released her mouth, she began screaming at him. "I don't want you. I hate you. Get away from me." She kept fighting him, kicking back with her heels, banging her head against his chest.

He wrapped his arms around her, pinning her arms to her chest. This effectively kept her from biting or clawing him, but her heels were still free to kick, so he lowered her to the ground and threw one of his legs over both of hers.

"Quiet," he said soothingly as he stroked her sweat-drenched face. "It's all right. You're safe now."

"Safe?" she screamed in his ear. "I was more safe with just the mountain lions for company before you came. Why aren't you asleep? I was afraid I'd given you enough opium to kill you."

"It wasn't enough. Here, stop that," he said when she again tried to bite him. He put his whisker-stubbled cheek next to her smooth one. "I'm here with you now and you're safe."

Maddie stopped fighting him because she had to, because he had her pinned so that she couldn't move, but her anger was still raging inside her. "Get off of me! Go away and leave me alone. I don't need you."

He didn't move away even an inch, but still held her securely. "Yes, you do need me. Tell me what's happened. Tell me what you did, where you've been."

She knew she couldn't tell him. She couldn't

tell anyone. Even if Hears Good had appeared, she couldn't have told him either. "I can't tell you," she raged at him, but to her horror there was a catch in her voice. "I can't tell even my father."

He moved his head to look at her. "You can tell me," he whispered.

It was those words that made the tears start. She tried to choke them back, but she couldn't. She tried to find her anger again, but she couldn't renew it. Truthfully, she was glad to see another human being. She was tired of being alone. "I can't tell anyone. Not anyone." The tears won out then, a great steady flood of them.

'Ring moved off her and pulled her into his arms. While holding her, he leaned back against a tree and held her to him, cradling her as one would a child. "Go ahead and cry, sweetheart. You deserve to cry."

Since Laurel had been taken, Maddie had not allowed herself to cry much. She had been very brave and strong as she told herself that she was doing what must be done. But then, perhaps the reason she had been able to be brave was because she had had hope, hope that Laurel was going to be returned to her and that everything would turn out all right. But after tonight her hope was almost gone.

'Ring stroked her hair and held her tightly and securely as she cried. He'd said that she was safe now, and she did indeed feel much safer. And when her head cleared somewhat, she was grateful that he wasn't raging at her for having once again used opium on him. She tried to pull away from him, if for no other reason than that she was very embarrassed. She sat up in his lap. "I am so sorry, Captain. I don't usually do this."

He tucked a strand of hair behind her ear and handed her his clean handkerchief. Maddie was glad for the darkness that hid her red face. The entire front of his shirt and a great deal of his jacket was soaked.

She blew her nose and the unladylike noise further embarrassed her. "I usually have better control of myself than this. I . . ." She trailed off, not knowing what to say. She started to get off his lap, but he pulled her back into his arms and snuggled her head against his chest.

She did try to move away from him, but it wasn't a serious attempt to move and he didn't have to make much effort to hold her to him. His heart against her cheek felt good, and as she lay against him, she prayed that he wouldn't again start asking her to tell him where she had been.

"I don't guess you've had many women cry on you before, have you, Captain? I would imagine most women do their best to present their best side to you. Mustn't let handsome Captain Montgomery see a lady in any way except at her best."

She had meant her comment to be a little snide—anything to save her further embarrassment, but he was silent for so long that she felt guilty about her nastiness. She lay still against him, listening to his heart and trying to think of anything except Laurel.

"Actually," he said slowly. "I held my sister, Ardis, after Davy died. She cried then."

Maddie was quiet, allowing him time to tell her the story if he wished. She didn't want to leave his arms, didn't want to move away from him, and thinking of someone else took her mind off Laurel. "Who was Davy?"

"Davy was the son of a woman who worked for us. Her husband had been killed before Davy was born so we became her family, and with there being so many kids in our family, there was always a lot to do. My sister Ardis was born two days before Davy, and it seemed natural to put the two of them together. They played together, slept together, took their first steps by holding on to each other."

He looked off into the darkness and smiled. "I guess it was a little odd how much they were left on their own, but my mother produced a new child every year for a while, and I guess everyone was grateful that there were at least two kids who didn't need constant attention. As the oldest, with a whole passel of brats following me, I was glad to have one fewer to pester me."

He took a breath and put his hand in Maddie's hair and began stroking it. "Three years ago, when Ardis was seventeen, I received a letter from her asking if I could come home for her wedding to Davy. With those two, a wedding seemed anti-climactic. I'm not sure that I'd ever even seen one

215

without the other." He smiled again. "You should have seen them! They were like a world unto themselves. They talked together constantly, but when anyone else tried to talk to them, they had nothing to say. I was very pleased when Ardis asked me to her wedding because, to tell you the truth, I wasn't sure she knew anyone except Davy was alive."

"You returned?"

"Yes, of course. I arrived in Warbrooke three days before the wedding. My mother was in a dither because Ardis was the first of her children to get married. Ardis was the calmest of the bunch. The only time she showed any agitation was when my mother told her she couldn't see Davy for twenty-four hours before the wedding. I don't think Ardis had gone so much as an hour of her life without Davy beside her, and she didn't very much like the idea of being without him. I think that if it had been up to her, she would have called off the wedding rather than do without Davy for a whole day."

He paused. "Nor did Davy like the idea of separation. He didn't say much—he never did—but we think that's why he rowed out to Ghost Island by himself."

"Ghost Island?"

"Warbrooke is on the tip of a peninsula and there are islands not far away. Ghost Island is said to be haunted by a couple of men, one of them wearing a black mask. Boys often take girls there to frighten them."

"Did you?"

"No."

He was silent, not saying anything, just holding her and stroking her hair.

"What happened to Davy?"

"We don't know. He never came back. When he didn't show up for the wedding we knew that something was wrong. Davy wasn't going to jilt Ardis. Everyone started searching. My brother Jamie found Davy's little rowboat. It had caught on a snag on the far side of Ghost Island. But there was no sign of Davy."

"How did Ardis take the news?"

"She was very, very calm. Everyone else was tearing around, no sleep, only enough food to keep us alive as we searched for him, but Ardis was still and quiet, not saying anything. On the third day after when the wedding was supposed to have taken place, Davy's body washed up on shore."

"What had happened to him?"

"We never knew. After three days in the water, the body was misshapen and the fishes . . ."

"I understand. What about Ardis? Did she cry then?"

"No, she didn't cry then. My mother went to tell her the news and Ardis took it very well. Everyone was so relieved—that is, until the next day at breakfast, when Ardis kept looking out the window. Someone asked her what she was looking for and she said she couldn't imagine what was keeping Davy."

"How awful."

"Yes, it was. No one knew what to do. For two days we all tiptoed around the house, fearful that Ardis was losing her mind. I know they all meant well when they were so careful of her, but I had spent some time with the army and I had seen some things."

"Such as?"

"Things I don't want to remember, much less talk about. But I had seen women, and men as well, who had seen terrible things done to the people they'd loved. They, too, had done the best they could to pretend nothing had happened."

"What did you do?" she asked, sensing that he had been the one to help Ardis.

"I took her to see Davy's body."

She moved to look at him. "His body that the fishes had . . ."

"Yes. I thought it might shock her into facing reality."

"Did it?"

"No. She looked at the body but she didn't see it. She said that she had to get back to the house to be there when Davy returned from Ghost Island."

He took a breath. "My family was quite angry with me when I returned home. They thought Ardis should be in bed. There was an awful scene and everyone was on her side and against me. You would have thought I was a monster and wanted to hurt my own sister."

She could hear the hurt that was still in his voice.

"In the end it was my mother who asked me what I wanted to do with Ardis, and I said that I wanted to take her with me to Ghost Island, just the two of us. My mother packed food and blankets for us and, while everyone else protested, I rowed Ardis out to the island."

"What did you say to her?"

"I didn't know what to say at first, but every time she mentioned Davy I told her he was dead. She ignored me. She acted just as she always did, but there was a certain wildness in her eyes that I hadn't seen before. By the third day I couldn't stand it anymore. She mentioned Davy and I grabbed her and shook her and screamed at her that Davy was dead and that he was never coming back again."

He clutched Maddie closer to him. "Ardis began to fight me, fight me as hard as anyone's ever fought before. She wanted to get away from me. I didn't know what she wanted to do if she did get away, but I wasn't releasing her to find out. I tried to keep her nails away from my face, and when she kept kicking me, I sat on her legs and removed her shoes."

Maddie looked up at him, but he put her head back down.

"I don't know how long she fought, but it was a while. An hour or more probably. I thought she was getting tired, so I relaxed my hold of her and she slipped away from me as quick as an eel. I ran after her but couldn't find her. I guess my senses were dulled or something, because she sneaked up behind me and hit me with something. It dazed me, knocked me out for a few minutes."

"What did she do?" Maddie felt her heart pounding in sympathy for the girl.

"I think she meant to drown herself, for she was swimming toward the mainland. It took me a while to find her, and by then she was so far out that I wasn't sure if that was her head I saw or a lobster trap. I went after her. She's a strong, fast swimmer and I thought I wasn't going to be able to catch her."

"But you did."

"I did. And when she began to fight me in the water, I hauled her up and clipped her one on the jaw, knocked her cold, then swam back to the island with her. We were both freezing, and I knew there was no time to build a fire, so I stripped off her clothes and mine, down to our skin, pulled her onto my lap, wrapped four blankets around us and tried to get us warm."

"And that's when she cried," Maddie said softly.

He didn't say a word for a moment. "When she woke she spoke so softly I could hardly hear her. She said that she and Davy had decided to wait until they were married before making love to each other. They had decided that they knew so much about each other that they would save this one thing for later. She said that she had always known that when she sat, nude, in a naked man's arms, they would be in Davy's, not in her brother's arms and certainly not in the arms of her ugliest brother."

Maddie didn't look at him, for she knew that there were tears in his eyes as well as in his voice.

"Ardis cried then. She cried the rest of the day and most of the night. I built a fire and got our clothes dry and we dressed and still she cried. I got her to eat a little lobster but nothing else. She—"

He broke off, and Maddie knew that he couldn't speak of it anymore. She lifted her arm to put it around his neck and pulled his face down so that it was buried in her neck. "I'm so sorry, so very sorry."

CHAPTER 11

She held his face against her neck for some time. So, this was the cool, perfect Captain Montgomery. This was the man who seemed to know how to do everything. This was the man who told people what to do and how to do it.

She stroked his hair and held him, and it occurred to her that she'd never been as close to a man as she'd become to him. In all the years she'd been traveling around the world with John's help, she'd been able to keep her distance from other people. It had been easy to keep up the façade of being a duchess, but with this man she wasn't able to keep up any façade.

"What's this?" he asked, moving his head and taking her hand in his.

It was Laurel's ring that she'd slipped on her little finger. "Nothing," she said, and snatched her hand away.

"I can tell you anything about myself, but you can tell me nothing about you, is that it?"

She wanted to protest that what he was saying was unfair, that there were reasons that she couldn't tell him about herself, but she didn't. Maddie remembered the man saying that those who held Laurel were angry that an army man was following her.

She moved off his lap. "I have told you at least a thousand times, Captain, I neither want you nor need you. Now, if you'll excuse me, I'm going down to the camp."

He stood and caught her arm. "In case you haven't noticed, it's night and you're tired and you need rest. We'll spend the night here."

Spend the night with him? It was one thing to sleep in the tent with him nearby but quite another to sleep in the open with nothing between them but a little mountain air. "I'm going down the mountain."

He caught her arm again. "No, you're not."

She jerked away from him. "I most certainly am going back to the camp. If you're tired, you may remain here, that is your choice. *I* do not try to impose my will on other people. Now, would you please get out of my way?"

He didn't move. "You're still not going to tell me anything, are you?" he said softly.

"There is nothing to tell." She glared up at him, barely able to see him in the darkness.

"When do you meet him again?"

"Three days," she said before she thought.

He seemed to be thinking about something else. "I don't want you to go back to the camp tonight. There's something wrong in that camp. Something wrong with one of your people, and I don't know which one it is."

"Edith," Maddie said quickly. "I mean, if there is something wrong, I have no doubt that Edith is the cause."

"Toby is trying to find out what he can, but in the meantime I don't want you near the place for a while."

"So, you want me to spend the night here in the woods with you. Alone. Just the two of us. Tell me, Captain, do you plan for us to share blankets?"

"Why, Miss Worth, that thought hadn't crossed my mind. Tell me, do you always have such carnal thoughts, or is it me alone who incites them?"

"Drop dead," she said, and started down the mountain. She heard 'Ring move toward his horse, and he didn't try to detain her again, so she was able to make some progress before he stopped her. Damnation, but he could move silently! She wondered where Hears Good was and if he was impressed with this young man's abilities. Probably not, she thought. Hears Good

223

wasn't impressed with much of anything a white man could do.

"Ah, Captain Montgomery, what a surprise to see you here. Although I should have guessed that you'd reappear. It's not as though I've been allowed any privacy since you came into my life."

"I want to show you something." He picked up her right arm and she felt something heavy being slipped around her wrist. A bracelet? He was giving her a bracelet now, in the middle of the night?

When he dropped her arm, she found it was heavier than she'd at first thought—and it rattled. "What in the world—" she muttered, then she knew what he'd done.

Handcuffs! He had handcuffed her to him. She jerked her arm and saw that there was about two and a half feet of chain linking the two of them together. "Release me," she said through her teeth.

"I will in the morning, but for now I need some sleep, and with the way you have of sneaking around, I just might sleep through your leaving."

She was so angry that she couldn't speak.

"Come on," he said as though nothing were wrong, and when he moved, her arm rose.

She stood where she was.

"Ah, now, come on. You aren't going to be sulky, are you? You must be able to see that this is the only way. I can't protect you if I'm asleep, and I can't let you go down the mountain by yourself. Surely even you can see that."

She swallowed against the lump in her throat. "Release me," was all that she could say.

"Oh, hell," he said in the voice of a man pushed to his limits, then he lifted her into his arms and carried her back up the mountain to where his horse was.

She didn't fight him. She knew from experience that fighting did no good, but she lay rigid, rather like a board stretched across his arms.

When he was at his horse, he set her down and began unsaddling the animal. Every time he moved, the chain rattled and her arm came up.

"I find this situation intolerable," she said in the calmest voice she could manage. "I cannot accept this."

He removed the saddle and went to set it on a stump, and as he walked, he pulled Maddie with him. "You'll get used to it." He turned back to her. "Look, I don't want to have to do this. I thought long and hard before I did it. If you were a woman of reason, maybe I could talk to you, but talking to you is like talking to my horse. You smile and lie and sing so very beautifully and, just as I let Butter get away with things I should discipline him for, I let you get away with things I shouldn't allow either."

Reason? This man spoke of reason? This man, who thought that a horse he owned and a woman who he definitely did not own were one and the same, talked to her about *reason?*

"I am not your horse," she said quietly. "You cannot tie me up as you do your horse."

He ran a handful of grass over Buttercup's sweaty back. "Believe me, I don't want to, but I see no alternative. Are you ready to get some sleep? I'm bushed. I don't know how you keep such hours. Maybe it's all the years you spent in Europe. You want to sleep on the right or the left?"

"I sleep alone," she said pointedly.

"I'll do the best I can to allow you to do that. There's some slack between us with this chain." He pulled her to her horse and began unsaddling it.

"I . . . I have to have some privacy. You'll have to release me to allow me a few moments alone." She made her voice sound as sincere as possible.

"And then you'll come right back here and let me put the cuffs back on?"

"Certainly."

Even in the dark she could see the brilliance of his white teeth as he smiled at her. "Sometimes I may seem like I was born yesterday, but if I have learned nothing else, it's that you, my dear little songbird, are not to be trusted. You can go behind those bushes over there. I promise I won't look."

Maddie's lips tightened. "I've changed my mind."

"Suit yourself, but it'll be a long night. Now, which blanket do you want?"

She snatched the nearest blanket from him. To think that just a while ago she had been feeling sympathy for him. She started to stomp away, but she took only a few steps before she came up short.

Being chained to him was rather like being chained to a tree. If he didn't move, then she couldn't.

"Oh, pardon me," she said, her voice dripping with sarcasm. "I forgot for a moment that I now have even less freedom than I've had since I met you. Now I can't walk where I want or sleep where I want."

"You may not need any privacy, but I do."

"I'll wait for you by the horse," she said a bit too eagerly.

He chuckled. "I don't think so. I think that your delicate sensibilities will have to bear up under the shock."

She turned her back to him. She would have crossed her hands over her chest, but he had to use both his hands, and when he did he pulled hers forward. She noticed that he had pinned her right hand and his left, leaving his more skilled hand free.

"That's better," he said.

"I don't want to hear about it."

"You planning to be angry at me all night?"

"All night? Captain Montgomery, for your information, I plan to be angry with you for the rest of my *life*. Don't you have any concept of the fact that I am a free human being and that I have rights and wishes of my own? That I have as much right to freedom as you do?"

"You don't have the right to get yourself killed and, as far as I can tell, that's just where you're heading."

"*I* am in no danger."

"I see. Then who is in danger?"

"You!" She clamped her free hand over her mouth.

"That is interesting. Very interesting. So, I guess all this sneaking about of yours has been to protect me. You're so fond of me that you're risking your life to protect me."

"No, I didn't say that. I just meant that . . ." She had no explanation for him.

"Come on, let's get some sleep. You're so tired that you're getting your lies mixed up."

She stood to one side, trying to not allow him to jerk her forward every time he moved, but not succeeding, while he spread two blankets on the ground.

"Sorry, but that's about as far as I can get them apart. We'll have to sleep with our arms outstretched as it is."

"This is really ridiculous. Will you release me if I swear to not run away? I will sleep very near you, so near that you'll hear me if I so much as turn over, but please take this off my wrist. It's heavy and it hurts."

He turned toward her, and for a moment she thought he might give in, but then he sighed. "I'd like to, but I can't. Which side do you want?"

She jerked the chain, raising his arm in the process, and went to the blanket on the left, then lay down, her arm straight up, pointing toward him.

"I think . . ." he began. "I mean . . ."

She didn't look at him but stared up at the stars.

He lay down on the blanket that was three feet from hers, and she saw the problem at once. When he was on his back, as she was, his arm was drawn across his chest, as was hers, and since their blankets were so far apart, they had to stretch. All in all, the position was rather painful. But she vowed that she'd endure any pain before she said another word to him.

"You don't think that we could, ah . . . change places, do you? If you were over here and I was over there, this might work out better."

"I am as comfortable as any prisoner can be, Captain."

"I see. Not going to move even if you're in pain all night, is that it?"

She didn't answer him, but stared up at the stars, her whole body rigid with anger. The next thing she knew, he was on top of her, his big body fully covering hers. Out of instinct she began to kick and thrash about.

"Could you be still a moment?" he said in exasperation. "I'm merely trying to get on the other side of you. Since you refuse to move and since you constantly complain that I manhandle you, this is the only way."

He rolled off her and lay on the other side for a moment. "Oh, sorry," he said as he reached across her to get his blanket. As he did so his arm rested on her breast, and for a moment he looked down at her. Maddie held her breath, thinking that he was going to kiss her. But he just whispered, "Sorry again," and moved so that he was no longer touching her.

She cursed herself in a couple of languages and tried to fold her arms over her chest, but that brought Captain Montgomery's hand over so that it lay on her breast. She flung his arm off her as though it were something vile.

"I wish you'd make up your mind whether I'm a rapist or whether I'm not interested in women. Good night, ma'am."

His words made Maddie open her mouth to ask him what he meant by that, but she closed it. She wasn't going to ask him anything. She drew the too-thin blanket over her and closed her eyes. Did she think she could sleep? She was worried about Laurel, she was chained to an idiot of a man, she was cold, hungry, her corset was cutting her in half, and her bladder was full.

When she heard the deep-sleep breathing of Captain Montgomery, she turned and hissed at him. How could he sleep? The most awful things could happen and men never lost their appetites or their ability to sleep. Put food in front of a man and he ate it. Lay a man horizontal and he went to sleep—or he began fumbling with the buttons on a woman's dress.

She turned and looked at him, flat on his back, sound asleep. Around him was a regular arsenal of weapons, all at the ready. She wondered if she could possibly sneak his pistol away from him. Maybe she could threaten him with it, make him release her. She inched her hand forward.

"Why don't you relax and go to sleep and stop playing Indian?"

His voice so startled her that she jumped. "I thought you were asleep."

"Obviously. What's wrong?" He spoke again before she could list her anger. "Besides not liking being here with me."

"I don't like being chained, that's what."

"All right, you've said that. Just go to sleep and it will be morning soon and I'll unlock the thing. This isn't exactly comfortable to me either. You may not have noticed, but there are only three blankets. I think I'm on some cactus."

"Good. It serves you right. I hope you don't expect me to pick out the thorns."

"You want me to tell you a story so you can sleep? Or sing you a song?"

"With your voice? I'd rather hear a chorus of frogs."

"You could sing to me," he said softly. "I'd like that."

"A song for the key," she said quickly.

He was quiet for so long that she turned to look at him. "That's a hard one. To give myself immense pleasure, I might be risking your life. You might be like the sirens and sing me to my death. Or your death if you left without me. Oh, Maddie, this is a dilemma."

A great deal of her anger melted and her muscles began to be a little less tight. "Do you really like my singing? You no longer think I'm just a 'traveling singer'?"

"I'm worried I'm going to hell for that remark and even more worried that I may deserve the punishment. Maddie, you could bring dead men back to life with that voice of yours."

She turned over on her side toward him. "Really? You don't hate opera anymore?"

"Well, maybe I do." He turned a bit toward her. "Opera in general, I mean. But then, it's your voice that I've come to love. I don't care what you sing. You could sing the Lancaster Treaty papers for all I care and I'd love to hear it."

"I have sung some popular songs and I've been told that I'm rather good."

"Good!" He gave a derisive snort. "You're so good I worry that God may soon take you off this earth because He wants you to lead His heavenly choir."

"Really? I mean, Captain, how could you say such things? There are other singers alive today. There's Adelina Patti singing"—her voice dropped an octave—"this week in New York."

"I told you, didn't I, that I'd heard her sing."

"I vaguely remember something of the sort being mentioned."

"I can tell you that the sound of her voice certainly never made my very bones ache with wanting her."

Maddie smiled in the darkness at him, then she lost her smile. "Wanting her? What does that mean? That my voice makes you . . . want me?"

"Well, sure, you know that I like to be around

you. I keep hoping I'll slay that dragon for you and you'll sing just for me."

"Oh."

"You sound disappointed. Did you think I meant something else?"

"No . . . no, of course not. There wasn't anything else that you could have meant, was there? So I couldn't possibly think that you meant anything else, could I have? There just wasn't anything else to think, so of course I understood what you meant." She shut up.

"Good, I'm glad for once that you understand me. As much as I'd like to trade you the key for a song, I can't. All the pleasure on earth isn't worth risking your safety." He yawned. "As much as I'd like to continue talking to you, I think we'd better sleep. Good night, my angel."

Maddie started to protest his calling her that, but she didn't. She was still angry at him, but his words about her singing had gone a long way toward relaxing her. She closed her eyes and in minutes she was asleep.

'Ring turned on his side without moving the chain that lay on the ground between them and looked at her. He couldn't help smiling. She really was impossible. Impossible, yes, but the most magnificent woman he'd ever encountered. Wanted her, he thought. No human in history had ever wanted a person as much as he wanted her. But she wasn't ready yet. As yet she was only beginning to see him as a person. Him, not just any man, but him. And that's what he wanted more than anything else on earth, more than he'd ever wanted anything: he wanted her to want him as much as he wanted her. He wanted her in every possible way that a man could want a woman— but he wanted her to want him in the same way.

He smiled at her in the darkness. I just have to make you more aware of me, that's all, he thought. I have to make you see me as a man. I want some of that passion that you give to your music. He stretched his free hand across the space between them and touched her fingertips. She curled her fingers around his like a baby would. Smiling, he went to sleep.

"Maddie," 'Ring said softly, "wake up."

Slowly, she came awake and she smiled to see him so near her. "Good morn—" she said, but he broke off her words by putting his lips on hers. She experienced a moment's astonishment before closing her eyes. Then his lips began to move against hers, but he wasn't kissing her, he was talking to her.

"Someone's coming. Please obey me. Please don't do anything foolish. Follow my lead."

She nodded against his lips. She wanted to continue kissing him, but she could see that his attention was now on the sounds coming from the woods around them. It was very early morning, the light gray and cold.

Quickly, in one motion, he pulled her into his arms and tucked her underneath him. She knew that he was doing this mostly for protection, for

234

at the same time that he'd pulled her to him he had also moved his pistol under her. He had the other hand on his knife, but she didn't mind. She slipped her free arm around his neck and opened her mouth under his as he kissed her again.

"I can't concentrate when you do that," he said, and she could feel his heart beating against hers. "I'm going to try to unlock these. Maddie, swear that if I tell you to run that you will."

She began to think about what he was saying then. The person he heard (her heart was beating much too loudly for her to hear anything) couldn't be Hears Good because if he wanted to sneak up on someone, he'd do it, he wouldn't make enough noise that he'd be heard.

Before 'Ring could get the handcuffs unlocked, she felt his big body go rigid with tension and his hand clamp down on the gun under her back. He rolled away from her as far as the chain would allow and sat up, but he wasn't fast enough. Standing over them was a man lounging against a tree, holding a pistol aimed vaguely at 'Ring's head.

"What do we have here?" the man asked. "A couple of lovebirds, all chained together. What's the matter, mister, can't keep your girl so you have to chain her to you?" He motioned to 'Ring to toss his gun aside, and 'Ring did so.

Maddie looked at 'Ring, saw the way he glared at the man, but he said nothing.

"What do you want?" Maddie asked. The man didn't look like a robber or any kind of villain she'd ever met. He looked like a gambler or card-

235

sharp. Maybe he'd come to the Jefferson Territory to cheat the miners out of their gold.

"Ah, so the lady can talk but the man can't." He looked back at 'Ring. "You got anything to say, mister?"

"What are you doing here?"

"Seeing what I can find out. You have any money on you?"

When 'Ring didn't answer, Maddie drew in her breath. She hoped he wasn't going to try to play the hero with this man pointing a gun at them. "Yes, in my saddlebag, I have a bag of gold dust," she said quickly.

"Don't give it to him," 'Ring said.

Maddie began to be afraid. Sometimes a simple robbery could turn into murder if the victims refused to be victims. "You can have everything," she said. "Take it all."

"Now, there's a sensible lady." The man took a step toward her. "Do you come with that package? Can I have you too?"

Instinctively, Maddie moved closer to 'Ring, but 'Ring kept his eyes on the man and paid no attention to her.

"The lady seems to like you." The man grinned and Maddie almost smiled back at him. He was certainly a handsome man, and when he smiled like that, something happened to the hairs on the back of her neck. 'Ring noticed her reaction to the man and, out of the corner of her eye, he gave her a quelling look.

The man gave a bit of a laugh. "Jealous, mister?

I would be, too, if I were you. That there is one fine figure of a lady. One real fine figure." He tipped his black hat back with the barrel of his pistol, showing black curls on his forehead. "Now, what am I going to do with the two of you?"

"We'll give you the gold and you can go away," Maddie suggested. She couldn't figure out what was wrong with 'Ring. Usually he had a great deal to say about everything, but now he just sat there saying nothing. A quick glance to his back and she saw that he was trying to unfasten the handcuffs. Oh, no, she thought, he's going to free himself and jump on the man. She wasn't sure what to do, but risking his life for a bit of gold wasn't worth the risk.

The man saved her from doing anything. "You'd better give me the key," the man said softly, smiling at 'Ring. "I think I'd rather have a guy your size chained than unchained."

Maddie let out her breath as 'Ring handed the man the key to the handcuffs, and when 'Ring looked as though he was about to spring and attack the armed man, Maddie rolled against him.

The man jumped away from the two of them. "It looks like the little lady don't want you to try anything funny. That suits me." The man straightened to his full height. He wasn't as tall as 'Ring, Maddie noted, but he was quite tall just the same.

"Now, let's get down to business. I'm going to take everything you two have."

"Like hell you are," 'Ring said.

"Please don't fight," Maddie said.

"Hear that? The little lady don't want us to fight. That's fine with me. I'd hate to have to whip your ass, mister."

Maddie knew that she was going to have to do something to keep the men from fighting. "Take everything," she said. "We don't need anything. Take it all."

"Includin' the big black?"

"Satan?" Maddie said. "Of course. Take him, but, I warn you that he is the devil's own to try to ride. He'll not let many people ride him."

"Satan? Good name for such a fine animal."

The man walked toward the horse, and as he presented his side to them, Maddie sensed 'Ring's muscles coil for the spring. She leaped on his back. "Please don't. He has a gun. You could be hurt."

"I could take him," 'Ring whispered.

"Not with me chained to you. 'Ring, please don't try. They're only possessions. They mean nothing. We'll walk down the mountain and buy more horses. I'll give you the money if you don't have any."

He turned his head to look at her. "You're afraid I'll get hurt? It would get me out of your hair."

She put her head on his shoulder. "Please don't play the hero."

He kissed her forehead. "All right."

The man turned back to them. "You two finish your little confab?"

"Take whatever you want," Maddie said. "Just give us back the keys to the cuffs and leave us alone."

The man smiled at her, and again she was charmed by his smile. She could feel 'Ring turning to glare at her, but she didn't mind. The man smiled again and began putting the saddles on the horses. She held tightly on to 'Ring while the man took the weapons that were around them.

"I'll have those blankets too," the man said.

Again Maddie had to hold on to 'Ring when he started after the man. She handed the blankets to him.

She didn't say anything as the man mounted 'Ring's horse. "The key," she said.

He reached into his pocket, pulled out the key, and looked down at it a moment. "I'd sure like to know why you two are chained together. Seems that one of you don't want the other to get away." He fixed 'Ring with an insolent look. "I sure don't have to chain my women to me." He looked at the key, then grinned at it and put it back into his pocket. "Think I'll let you two stay together."

With that he rode away, leading Maddie's horse behind him.

The man wasn't out of sight before 'Ring was on his feet and starting down the hill after him. Maddie, of course, was fastened to 'Ring, and she went tripping after him.

"Will you stop!" she said as she fell over a tree stump. "He's already gone and you can't catch

239

him, not on foot and not with me chained to you. I wish he had given us the key."

He turned on her. "You seemed to want to go with him. Maybe you wanted to unlock these things so you could go with him."

"I what? I wanted to go with him? Are you out of your mind?"

"I saw the way you were smiling at him."

She glared at him. "I can't believe this! I may have just saved your life by keeping you from jumping on a man who held a gun on you, but now you stand there having a fit of jealousy."

"Jealousy? I am merely stating what I saw. You nearly threw yourself at him. It's a wonder that you didn't ask him to take you with him along with the horses."

Maddie started to yell back at him, but then she relaxed and smiled. His jealousy was rather nice. "He was the best-looking robber I've ever seen. I don't imagine he has to use a gun on the women he robs. All he'd have to do is smile at them and I bet they'd give him anything he wanted."

'Ring stood there and glared at her for a few moments, then she saw him relax. He smiled at her, and Maddie thought that the robber wasn't the only one who could make a woman do whatever he wanted. "Well, here we are, just the two of us, chained together, no horses, no blankets, no anything at all, but three whole days before you have to be somewhere else. Why don't we stay here and have a little vacation?"

Maddie was standing as far away from him as the chain would allow. "Stay here? We can't stay here."

"Why not? You need a break, and you said that it was three days before you had to meet anyone again, so I guess that means it's three days before you have to sing again, so why not stay here? Aren't you sick of that camp and living in a tent?"

"Actually I am, but I can't stay here with you."

"Why not?"

She closed her eyes for a moment. How could he be so dumb? "Because, Captain, you are a man and I am a woman. And on top of that we are chained together. Does that answer your question?"

He stood there, looking at her for a moment, as though he were trying to understand her meaning. At last he said, "Oh, I see. You're concerned that I'll . . . You know. I guess I'm being branded a rapist again. What if I promise that I won't make any improper advances toward you? What if I swear not to touch you? Will that help?"

Maddie looked at him. Three days alone in the woods with a man, and a man such as Captain Montgomery. She shouldn't do it. Absolutely not. Of course she shouldn't. She *should* go back down the mountain, get Sam to cut the handcuffs off, then spend the days peacefully in her tent, alone. Reading. Worrying about Laurel. Alone.

"You'd have to swear on your word of honor," she heard herself saying. "I mean, Captain, I wouldn't want to be fighting you off every minute." Even the thought of fighting him off made chill bumps on her arms. What if she lost?

He looked at her very solemnly. "I swear that I won't touch you. I would swear on my mother's grave, but she is still very much alive, so I guess you'll just have to take my word for my intentions. I swear to not touch you no matter what."

"No matter what?"

He stepped closer to her, and when he spoke, his voice was very low. "I won't touch you no matter how much I may want to. No matter how your hair smells when it's been warmed by the sun. No matter that I would give ten years of my life just to hold your bare body against mine. No matter how the memory of you riding in front of me, your thighs against mine, haunts me. No matter that the nights in the mountains are cold and, because we are handcuffed together, we will have to sleep together, wrapped around each other, our bodies perfectly fitting together. No matter what, I will not touch you."

Maddie closed her eyes. His voice was so soft that even though he was so close to her she could feel his breath on her face, she could barely hear him. He put his hand to the side of her face, his fingertips in her hair, his thumb against the corner of her mouth.

"I swear that I will not kiss your neck or your eyes or the little vein in your temple. Nor will I kiss your round white shoulders, or your waist, or your thighs, or the arch of your left foot. I will not lick the soft skin where your arm bends, or put your fingertips one by one in my mouth and suck on them. Are you hungry?"

Maddie was lounging in a standing position, her knees weak, her whole body turned soft and pliant. "What?" she managed to whisper. She opened her eyes slowly. She could see his full lower lip and she had what was nearly a craving to run the tip of her finger under his mustache and feel the curve of his upper lip. His shirt was open halfway down his chest, and she wanted to bite the hair-covered skin she saw.

"I asked if you're hungry. Are you all right? You look a little pale."

Maddie opened her eyes a little wider and stared at him. Had he said all that she'd heard? "What did you say to me?"

He put his hands under her armpits and jerked her upright to a full standing position. "Maybe we should go down the mountain after all, although I do think you need rest. The last few days are beginning to tell on you."

Maddie shook her head as though to clear it. "I demand that you repeat what you said about . . . about not touching me."

"I swore that I'd not touch you under any circumstances. Isn't that what you were worried about? You did say that you were concerned about what I might do to you, considering that I'm a male and you're a female. I was merely trying to reassure you." He looked up at the sky. "You know, I think we might get some rain. If we're going to stay here, we'd better find shelter and some firewood."

Maddie was wondering if she was perhaps going a little mad. Had she imagined what he'd said? He started walking and, being chained to him, she had no choice but to follow. "What did you say about . . . about sleeping together?"

"I said that it's cold in these mountains and, for warmth, we'd have to sleep together. Look over there, it's an outcropping of rock. We can make camp there. I think there's enough room for us and a fire. Now, how do we start a fire? You don't have matches, do you?"

"No," she said softly, looking at his back as she followed him, then, abruptly, she stopped. "Stop right there! I demand that you repeat what you said to me, the part about my hair and . . . and my foot."

He turned slowly and smiled in a fatherly way. "You have two feet, a left one and a right one, and you have rather nice hair. Anything else?"

Maddie started to say more, but she caught herself. Two could play at this game. Well, maybe she could play. She couldn't imagine telling him that she wanted to see how his upper lip curved. She walked past him, trying her best to act haughty. "I don't need matches to start a fire. My father—" She stopped when he didn't move, the immobility of him jerking her backward.

"Your father," he said under his breath.

She smiled sweetly. "Yes, my father. My father taught me some survival tricks."

"Such as starting a fire without matches? Rubbing two sticks together? Do you have any idea how long that takes and how difficult it is to do?"

"I know exactly how long it takes, and if you'd done it as often as I have, you'd find it wasn't too difficult. I may not carry matches with me, they get wet, but I always carry a fire steel and flint with me. My father said that a man—or woman for that matter—could survive if he had the makings for a fire, a snare, a few fishing hooks, and a knife."

"And I guess you have all these things with you."

"Of course," she said smugly. "Don't you carry them with you whenever you leave camp? One never knows when one may be separated from one's horse. Don't tell me, Captain Montgomery, that you left everything on your horse." She wasn't sure, since he looked away quickly, but she thought he turned a bit red in embarrassment. Now who was feeling uncomfortable?

Her father had taught her what to carry and how to carry it. During the long journey in the rocking stagecoach after she'd left the East, she'd whiled away a few hours by sewing a few pockets on the inside of her voluminous riding skirt. The pockets were as small as she could make them and about halfway down the skirt, so they would not show near the waist.

Now, looking at 'Ring's back, she knew that she was going to have to lift her skirt to get to the pocket, and she suddenly remembered being in

245

the bedroom of a French soprano. Maddie couldn't remember the woman's name, only that her G's were awful, but that day Maddie had seen the singer's—if one could call her that—pantaloons draped across a chair. They were made of fine, exquisitely soft Swiss lawn. The fabric was so fine as to be almost transparent, and it was a lovely shade of pink, the color of a girl's blush. Maddie had laughed at them and said to the singer that they were really quite worthless, that they wouldn't stand any wear. The singer had looked at Maddie in the mirror and said, "They also tear quite easily." At the time, Maddie had had no idea what the woman meant.

Now, knowing that she was wearing pantaloons of heavy, serviceable, long-wearing cotton, she wished she were wearing underwear of pink Swiss lawn. 'Ring had said that he'd give ten years of his life to hold her naked body next to his. She might give five years of her life—not the singing years, of course, but the years afterward—to allow him to hold her.

She lifted her skirt and pulled the fire steel and flint from the hidden pocket on the underside of her skirt, but he didn't look at her.

Then, with 'Ring attached to her, she gathered the dried inner bark of a cedar tree and a bit of cotton fluff from a cottonwood tree near the river. Her father had shown her how to hold the fire steel in one hand and strike it against the flint, and she'd done it very often, but now, with 'Ring so near her, watching her, she couldn't seem to concentrate.

"Here, gently," he said, then took the steel and flint from her. "You don't blow on it like a hurricane at sea, you kiss it. Like this."

They were so close together that their heads were almost touching and he looked up at her with his lips pursed, as though he meant to kiss her. Softly, with sweet breath, he blew against her lips.

"A gentle kiss," he said, looking down at the small pile of tinder. "As though you were kissing a virgin." He looked at her, and the intensity in his eyes made her throat go dry. "Or a kiss to a woman who is very near to being a virgin."

"How?" she said, and to her horror her voice squeaked.

He looked down at the fluff and shredded wood. "A man, at least a man who is concerned about the outcome, that is, can't expect a virgin to be like other women. He can't just one day take her and expect her to want him in return. No, he must first make her aware of what there is to want."

"Oh?" Maddie said. Her voice didn't squeak but it was higher than necessary. "What is there to want?"

"Love. Passion. Touching. Feeling. Sometimes virgins are hard to . . . awaken, so to speak. Sometimes women who have been virgins for a long time have buried their feelings, or have forgotten them and replaced them with other things, and then special things have to be done with those women."

"Special?" A tiny trickle of perspiration ran down the back of Maddie's neck.

"They have to be made aware that there is something in . . . shall we call it life, for them. They have to learn to look at men—or I guess we could be talking about male virgins as well, couldn't we?"

"Certainly. Of course. What should a woman see in a man?"

"How he makes her feel when he kisses her, touches her, holds her." His voice lowered and she had to lean forward to hear him. "How she feels when he makes love to her and caresses her. He has to first make her want those things so that she will come to enjoy them. Sometimes virgins don't even know that love, that kind of love that's between mature, healthy adults, exists. You know, that sweaty, lusty, hard, pounding kind of love, the kind where, at the end, you think you're going to die from the release, a release that leaves you limp and fulfilled as nothing else in the world can."

Maddie's upper lip began to sweat. "Certainly," she said, her voice cracking just a bit. "That kind of love."

"With virgins you need to lead up to that."

"H-how?"

"Talk to her, for one thing. Virgins love words. Tell her that you'd like to kiss her ears and her hair. Touch her breast. Not hard, mind you, that comes later, but just lightly at first. Kiss her closed eyelids. Virgins love that. Make love to her

248

hands." He lifted Maddie's hand and entwined her fingers with his, his thumb rubbing the center of her palm. "Some people don't realize how sensitive hands can be, how very much fingertips can feel, or all the body parts that fingertips can touch and stroke and caress. But you know, don't you?"

She didn't even try to speak but looked at his big hand holding her small one and nodded.

"Yes, virgins need to be wooed and courted. They need to have attention paid to them. A virgin needs to care for a man before she can relax and love him back."

Abruptly, he dropped her hand and pulled back from her. "Look at that. I was so busy talking philosophy that I forgot about the fire."

Maddie looked over the little blaze at him. Her throat was dry and her body tingled from her toes to her hair line. She was afraid to try to stand because she didn't think her legs would hold her.

He sat back and grinned at her. "What an odd subject of conversation."

"Yes," she managed to say.

"What do I know about women, anyway? You've heard why my father hired Toby and you've heard Toby say that I'm not interested in women, so how could I know anything about virgins, or any other type of women, for that matter? Whatever made us talk about this anyway? Oh, yes, I remember, the fire. You know, we really should have used that snare that you say you have *before* we made the fire." He grinned at her. "But then, maybe fires are like virgins and they can be rekindled if you know the right kisses."

He stood up, and as he did so, he pulled Maddie up with him. Her legs buckled under her and he caught her under the arms. "Are you all right? You don't look all right. You're pale as a ghost and you're sweaty. You aren't getting sick, are you?"

"Keep your hands off of me," she whispered. Before I make a fool of myself and throw myself at you, she thought.

"Oh, sorry," he said, releasing her so abruptly that she almost fell. She grabbed his belt as she started down. He, the unaffected so-and-so, just stood there and watched her, his hands held out at his sides to show that he wasn't touching her.

She was able to recover herself before she hit the ground. She stood in front of him, as far from him as the chain would allow. "Let's g-go—" Her voice, that usually perfect machine of hers, betrayed her again.

"Maybe we shouldn't go anywhere," he said with concern. "I'm not sure you're well."

"Rabbit," she managed to say at last. "Catch rabbit." Maddie started walking, pulling 'Ring behind her, so that she didn't see him pull out his handkerchief and wipe at his face then scrub at his sweaty palms, then wipe his face again, then reach inside his trousers and adjust himself, then wipe his face again, then, after watching her walk, close his eyes so hard that he shed a few tears. When she looked back at him, he was smiling at her as though he didn't have a concern in the world.

CHAPTER 12

Maddie had never been so confused. She had always known what she wanted to do with her life and she'd planned it accordingly, but now, with this man, she never knew what was going to happen. She not only didn't know what was going to happen, she couldn't explain what was happening.

She kept asking Captain Montgomery what was going on, but he just smiled at her. One minute he seemed to desire her, then the next he didn't seem to know that she was alive—or that she was alive and female.

He helped her with the buttons on her riding dress (even though they were down the front) and he helped her with the ties of her corset, which they used to make a snare for the rabbits. He laughed at her when finally she could stand it no longer and went behind a bush to relieve herself. After that, whenever she had to go, she made him sing even though the sound was grating to her ears.

She couldn't seem to figure him out. One minute she thought she had him pegged as a pompous know-it-all who wasn't worth her time, then the next minute he was telling her about his sister Ardis. One minute he seemed cold and uncaring and the next he seemed full of pent-up emotions.

251

One second he seemed to desire her and the next he didn't look at her.

What a day it was, Maddie thought as the sun began to set. They had used the fish hooks she'd had inside her skirt to catch a few big mountain trout, they'd lain side by side for over an hour waiting for a turkey that they'd heard to come near them, then 'Ring had pulled the snare made out of her corset ties and caught the big bird. Maddie had plucked it and he'd laughed because he didn't believe she knew how.

In the late afternoon 'Ring had followed a swarm of bees to their hive and Maddie had begged him not to try to get the bees, but nothing would make him stop. He'd lit a torch of dried cedar and used the smoke to dull the bees, but as soon as his hand was in the nest, the bees had come awake and taken after him.

He came down the tree and started running, dragging Maddie behind him, and when she couldn't follow fast enough, he tucked her under his arm and kept running to the stream.

They evaded the bees, but they were soaking wet with icy water. When Maddie started to scold him, he grinned and held up a fistful of honeycomb. Unfortunately, it was honeycomb that was covered with angry bees.

In seconds they were swatting at bees, Maddie trying to keep her balance as she danced at the end of the chain linking her to 'Ring. But, no matter how many bees attacked them, 'Ring still hung on to that comb.

Now they sat together by the big fire that 'Ring had built, huddled in their wet clothes. There was nothing else to wear, nothing to cover themselves with if they should remove their clothes. And there were no hot drinks to warm their insides.

"I'm sorry that I got you into this," 'Ring said. "If I'd been more alert last night, that man wouldn't have been able to—"

"It's all right. Even my—" She had been going to say that even her father had been ambushed a few times, but she refrained herself. "It's not so bad. I've had a good time today. It's taken my mind off my problems."

"Laurel," he said softly.

Maddie drew in her breath sharply. She wasn't going to ask him how much he knew, because he obviously knew more than he should. "I'm tired and I'm cold. I think I'll go to bed." She started to stand up but then the chain rattled. She'd almost forgotten it.

He stood with her. "You'd be safe in your tent now under half a dozen blankets if it weren't for me." He looked down at her. "You want to go back in the morning? We can be there by this time tomorrow and we can get these cuffs off."

"I . . . I don't know," she said, and she really didn't know what she wanted to do. He was the most confusing man. "Why couldn't you have stayed that man I first met? I really hated that man. The way you put your foot on the stool! And that horse of yours trying to eat my coach! Oh, damn you, why did you have to change?"

He smiled at her. "I didn't change. You thought you knew me and you didn't, that's all."

She moved as far away from him as she could get. "I can't figure out who you are. Are you the man Toby talks about or are you that dreadful man I first met?"

"A little of both, I guess, and maybe a few more besides that." His voice lowered. "What does it matter what kind of man I am? In a few more days you'll go back east and you'll probably never see me again."

She looked away from him. "Yes, that's true." She imagined going to John and telling him the truth as to why she'd had to go west and sing and hoping that John would forgive her and be her manager again. She looked back up at 'Ring and thought of pearls in soup bowls and silk dresses created by that new man, Worth, and somehow it didn't seem like a very fulfilling life.

Suddenly, Madame Branchini's words echoed in her head: "You can have your music or you can have a man. One or the other, not both." So far it had been easy to choose.

She shivered at the first drops of rain and clasped her arms about her chest, dragging 'Ring's arm with her.

"Come on," he said, and swept her into his arms and carried her to the overhanging rock ledge. She sat to one side while he used the steel and flint to start a fire on the dried grasses that he'd earlier brought to the ledge, and within minutes he had a fire going. She sat and watched him as he fed deadfall to the fire and soon had a blaze.

At last he sat back, then opened his arms to her. I shouldn't, she thought, I really shouldn't, but she went to him just the same and he held her tightly. "We *do* fit together," she murmured.

"What were you thinking about just now?" he asked, snuggling his chin onto the top of her head.

"You," she said sincerely.

"I'm glad. I'm glad that you're at least able to see me."

"How ridiculous. I've always seen you. From the first moment that I saw—"

"No, you haven't. You decided what I was that first moment, and you haven't changed your mind yet. You thought I was, let's see if I get this right, a pompous, overbearing know-it-all."

"You are, you know."

"No more so than you are."

"Ha!"

On the far side of the ledge the rain came down in cold, heavy sheets, but inside there was a fire and her clothes were beginning to dry, and even the wet parts that were next to him were beginning to feel much warmer.

"It's odd to think that I've known you only a short time," she said. "Sometimes I think I've known you forever. I remember the first time I sang at La Scala. It seems to me you were there, telling me that I'd do a good job, and then you kissed me on the forehead before I went onstage."

She snuggled against him. "Why do you think

I feel this way? No one else has ever made me feel this way. Even as long as I spent with John, as much time as I spent with him, I always distinctly remembered a time when I didn't know him."

"Do you really not know how much alike we are?"

"I can't see that we're alike at all. You can't sing, we've proven that, and there doesn't seem to be much else to my life except singing."

"That's exactly what makes us alike. You said that my childhood must have been spent outside in the sunshine, and in a way it was, but not in the way you mean. I started working in my family's business when I was twelve. I was making major decisions by the time I was fourteen."

"Oh," she said sadly. "Were you very poor? Did you have to quit school?"

He smiled. "Just the opposite. Have you ever heard of Warbrooke Shipping?"

"I think so. I think I may have traveled on some of their ships." She turned to look at him. "Warbrooke? Isn't that the name of the town where you grew up? Do you work for them?"

"My family owns Warbrooke Shipping."

She turned back around. "Oh, then I guess that makes you wealthy."

"Very. Does it make any difference to you?"

"It explains your horse and your perfectly cut uniform and your education and having a servant like Toby."

He didn't tell her how pleased he was that his wealth didn't matter to her. Sometimes, where

256

women were concerned, having money was a hindrance. Sometimes they saw the money and not the man. "Some servant he is."

"Tell me about Toby and why you think we're alike."

'Ring took a deep breath before he spoke. "You and I have been alone. I sensed it a few days after we met, but after you told me about your childhood, I knew you were as alone as I have been."

"But I have never been alone. I have always been surrounded by my family, and later I had John and a hundred social engagements. I have had far too little time alone."

"No, that's not what I mean. Perhaps alone isn't the right word. Different. You and I have always been different."

"*I* have been different, but I can't see that you are."

"My father is a good man, a very good man. He has a heart of gold. He would give the shirt off his back to any man who needed it. He would give up his own life before he'd see one of his children harmed. But—"

"But what?"

"To be honest, the man has no head for business. He can't sit still long enough to do the paperwork required to run a company the size of Warbrooke Shipping, and a sunny day is to him an opportunity to go fishing or go on a picnic with my mother."

"That doesn't sound too bad. Sometimes I wish I had more time to devote to pleasure."

"You can't devote all your life to pleasure when there is a company like ours to manage. There are thousands of employees depending on us. What we pay them feeds their families."

"And your father forgot that?"

"I guess so. Forgot or never realized."

"So that's why you were involved in the company since you were a child?"

"Yes, I don't know how it happened. I was curious, and my father praised me whenever I did anything that helped him. It all seemed to have evolved rather gradually."

He smiled. "And then, too, like your gift for singing, I seem to have a gift for running a business. It was no problem for me to keep all the things in my mind that I needed to keep there. My father said I was like his father, that I was a true Montgomery."

"So you gave up your childhood to do a man's job."

"Did you feel you were giving up anything when you were inside singing and the rest of the world was outside in the sunshine?"

"No, I felt lucky and sad for them that God hadn't given them the talent He had given me."

"I felt about the same. My mother hired a tutor for me and in the evenings I read with him and—"

"Learned languages."

"Yes, I learned a few languages. I think I thought I'd use them when I visited all the exotic

258

places I'd heard the men who sailed on our ships talk about."

"Your mother hired you a tutor and your father hired Toby as a different sort of tutor, didn't he?"

"Exactly."

She was thoughtful for a moment. "But Toby doesn't take care of you, does he? You take care of him."

"More or less."

He didn't seem to want to say more about Toby. "What made you give it all up and join the army?" she asked.

"Two things: something I overheard and a woman."

She didn't say anything for a while because she wasn't sure she wanted to hear this story. "Tell me," she whispered at last.

"One day when I was seventeen I was on board one of our ships. I had been inspecting cargo and talking to the men about the trip when I overheard one of the officers talking to the captain. The officer wanted to know how I could have such a responsible job. He said I was just a kid, what could I know. The captain made me feel good because he said that even though I was still a kid, I knew a great deal about the sea. 'Haven't you heard what they say about the Montgomery children?' the captain said. 'They aren't born. When their father wants another one, he goes to the nearest pier, throws down a net, pulls it in, and takes out another brat. It's a wonder those kids can walk. It's a wonder they don't have fins for feet.'"

"That doesn't seem a bad thing to say. In a way it's a compliment."

"True, but as I listened to the two of them chuckling, I had a vision of my life. I knew that I'd run Warbrooke Shipping forever and that when I was twenty-two or three I'd marry a local girl—if I could find one who wasn't already related to me—and then have some of my own children."

"Taking them from the sea?"

"Wherever children can be had. I could see myself at fifty, having trained my children and now training my grandchildren to run Warbrooke Shipping. I could see myself at eighty, still planning how I was going to get away from Warbrooke."

"I see. And what did the woman have to do with making you join the army?"

"About the time I heard the men talking about me, a friend of my mother's came to visit her. The woman was in her midthirties, I guess, and at my young age of seventeen I thought she was an old woman. She was to spend a month with us, and for the first few days of her visit I don't guess I even looked at her."

"What with lessons at night and working during the day, I don't think you had time to look at girls. Did I tell you that I took my lessons in the evening also?"

"Whoever taught you forgot your arithmetic," he said.

"My father was my teacher."

"That explains everything."

"Stop complaining about my father and tell me about your lady."

He smiled. "She *was* a lady. Anyway, a few days after she arrived, my brothers started coming down with the chicken pox."

"What about your sisters?"

"Carrie wasn't born yet and Ardis went to Davy's house to stay. My mother wanted me out of the house, too, so I wouldn't catch it, and she told her friend that she'd better return to her home. But there was some reason that she couldn't return, I don't remember what, her house was being remodeled, something. Anyway, she asked my father if she could see the way Warbrooke Shipping was run."

"And your father turned her over to you."

"Yes, he did. I was really angry about it. I'm afraid I shouted at my father that I had work to do, *hard* work, and that I didn't have time to nursemaid some old woman. And, besides that, she was a woman, what could she possibly understand about business?"

'Ring closed his eyes for a moment. "She heard me and she came marching into my father's study and told me that she could keep up with me anywhere I went, and she challenged me to find one aspect of business that she, with her mere woman's mind, couldn't understand."

"And did she? Did she keep up with you and understand you?"

"Oh, yes. She did in spite of the fact that I gave her such a hard time. When you're seventeen and run a business as big as ours, it makes one—"

"Vain? Self-centered? Full of oneself?"

"More or less. It was a full week before I gave up and stopped trying to make her clean the Augean stables."

"What?"

"Your father forgot Greek fables too, didn't he? I finally stopped making her prove herself to me, and we gradually became friends. I had no idea women like her existed. In my great wisdom I thought that all women were like my mother. My mother cares only for her family and nothing else."

"But this woman? Your friend?"

"Her father had died when she was twenty-two. Up until that time, she said, she'd never had a thought about anything except the latest dress style or the latest present her most recent beau had given her. When her father died she found that he'd left her a ladies' dress shop that wasn't doing very well and a great many debts."

"What did she do?"

"She said she had three choices. One was poverty, the second was to marry a man and let him take care of her and run what was left of her father's business. But she said that none of the men she might have wanted to marry could run a business and she couldn't bear the idea of living with any of the businessmen."

"And the third choice?"

"To run the business herself. She said she figured that she was quite good at buying dresses, and all she'd have to do was buy a few more and sell them."

"And she did just that?"

"Exactly. She said it was difficult at first but she managed, and by the time I met her she owned six shops and was doing very well."

"How did she influence you to join the army?"

"I fell in love with her. Not real love. I know that now. But I found her fascinating. I had never before realized that I didn't have anyone to talk to. My father was bored by business and he was pleased to leave everything up to me. My mother wasn't interested, and my brother Jamie, who is two years younger than me, was always off sailing. My other brothers were too young to understand."

"And Ardis was with Davy."

"Yes, so my mother's friend was the first person I had to share what I did with. And she was insatiably curious. She wanted to know everything there was to know, wanted me to show her everything."

"And did you? Did you show her everything?" Maddie whispered.

"Yes," he said after a moment. "On the day before she was to leave, we sailed out to one of the islands. We hadn't gone far when a sudden squall came up and we were caught in it. For a while I was afraid we weren't going to make it."

"But for someone born in the sea, it couldn't have been too difficult."

"I guess not. We got to the island and we were drenched. There was an old shack on the place that an old hermit had once lived in, but he'd died a few years back so it was empty." He paused. "We spent the night there."

"And did you make love to her?"

He didn't answer for a while. "Yes. Actually, she made love to me. At seventeen, and with a life like I'd led, I hadn't had much to do with girls, and nothing to do with women."

"Even with Toby's help?"

"*Especially* with Toby's help."

"So, you spent the night with her. What happened then?"

"In the morning we sailed back to the mainland and all the way back I planned our married life together."

"Marriage? But she was so much older than you."

"I didn't care. I imagined a life with the two of us, both of us running Warbrooke Shipping and talking and . . . spending time together."

"But you didn't marry her."

"No. When we got home, I fell asleep and when I woke up that evening, she was gone. I can't tell you how betrayed I felt. She left me no note, nothing. I took it all pretty hard. I sulked and moped and snapped at everyone.

"It was my mother who suspected what was wrong with me. I broke down and told her all my heartache and how I hated the woman for leaving me. My mother said that her friend had given me a gift and I was to take it as that. It took me a while, but I began to realize that she was right. My time with my mother's friend had been something wonderful, and I was to take it as such."

"Did you ever see her again?"

"Once, years later, in New York."

"Did you make love to her again?"

"Actually, I spent three days going over her accounts while she went out with a man twice my age. Nothing can kill romance quite as successfully as thirty-five dirty ledgers full of incorrectly added numbers."

Maddie smiled broadly at that. "So you didn't love her anymore?"

"Not much."

"But you haven't told me how she caused you to join the army."

"After she left Warbrooke I heard the men talking about how my father fished his Montgomery brats out of the sea. I bet my mother wished that were true. She had a difficult time delivering the last child. Anyway, when I saw my life all laid out for me, I realized I didn't want that life. I didn't want to be eighty and still planning how I was going to get away from the responsibilities of the business. I could have climbed aboard any of our ships and gone around the world, but I decided I wanted to see the desert, and also I was sick of responsibility. I wanted to be one of the crew, not one of the bosses. I wanted to know what it felt like, that if things went wrong, it wasn't my fault. So I joined the army as a private and applied for the western campaign."

"And they sent you where you wanted to go?"

"It wasn't so difficult. All I had to do was demonstrate that I could ride a horse."

"And to think: Toby said that he had been hired by your father because you weren't interested in women."

"Toby doesn't know all there is to know about me. He complained that I wasn't interested in the women available to soldiers. The forts are surrounded by places called 'hog ranches.' They're named for the women who inhabit them and the women in them are as clean as their name implies. Everywhere in the army the men are dying of the pox. The only other white women a man sees are those brought in from the East, and they're either the wives or daughters of the officers. You get into trouble with one of them and all kinds of awful things can happen."

"But Toby said you weren't interested in the women he introduced you to."

"The first woman he 'introduced' me to in a little town outside Warbrooke was named Bathless McDonald."

"Bathless? What an odd name. It sounds as though she's never had . . ."

"She hadn't. She bragged about never having had a bath in her life. She was quite pretty, but when she started sticking parts of her body in my mouth, I . . . ah, well, anyway, I found the experience less than enjoyable. I tried to explain to both my father and Toby, but both of them thought I was too finicky."

"Are you? Finicky, I mean?"

"Very. I want only the best. The very, very best." He tightened his arms around her and put his face in her neck.

"Are you ready to go to sleep?" he asked after a while.

She didn't nod or give him any signal that she wanted to sleep, but her body was pliant as he lowered her to the cold, hard ground and wrapped her snugly in his arms. Maddie was far from asleep. She was thinking about the time she'd known him. Only a short time, but it seemed like a lifetime.

She turned a bit in his arms so that she could look at him, look at the way the firelight played on his cheekbones. She thought he was asleep, so she brought her free hand up to touch his lower lip. He didn't open his eyes.

"I am beginning to love you, you know that, don't you?" she whispered.

"Yes."

"You are beginning to take up as much of my thoughts as my music does."

He didn't say a word, but she thought he smiled a bit. "Not many men love their rivals."

She wanted to ask him what he felt about her, but she was afraid of the answer. *How* could she love someone, especially someone like him? He was a man who needed freedom, a man who had no connections with the music world.

"When do you get out of the army?"

"Next year."

"And what will you do?"

"Go home to Warbrooke. My father needs me."

She sighed. And I shall go to Paris or Vienna or Florence, wherever people want to hear me sing. "Good night, my captain," she said, and closed her eyes.

'Ring opened his eyes and looked at her for a long while before falling asleep. It seemed the most natural thing in the world to be holding her. He'd wanted to since he'd first seen her. Making love to her could wait until she was sure about him, as sure about him as he was about her.

By the end of the second day it seemed almost natural to Maddie that she should be chained to this man. They learned how to move together, how to give each other privacy when needed, how to talk and how to be silent.

'Ring's stories of his family had awakened Maddie's curiosity, and she began to ask him all about himself, about Warbrooke and the inhabitants. He told outrageous stories about his cousins the Taggerts, who, along with the Montgomerys, seemed to make up most of the town.

He told her stories of the sea, stories of his

ancestors that were handed down in his family like fairy tales. He showed her how to make knots with her corset strings, and when her hands got tangled up, he laughed at her and showed her again.

Maddie kept thinking about what he'd said about her life having been lonely, and now she could see that it had been. As a child she'd never had time for a friend; her sister had been too busy with her paintings and she and her family had been isolated from other families. There had been Hears Good's sons, but they came to stay only in the summer and then went to their own people in the winter. Her father and his friends had spent a great deal of time with her—all that Maddie could spare, but it wasn't the same as having a friend her own age.

They were lying on the soft, damp grass by the edge of the stream, their chained arms out-stretched. "I never had a friend when I was a child," she said.

"Me neither. Just brothers."

She laughed, but he turned a serious face toward her. "But you still aren't going to tell me about yourself, are you? Even about this father of yours, who is such a paragon of virtue?"

She wanted to, wanted to very much, but she was afraid that if she told him one thing, she'd never be able to stop, and the next thing she knew, she'd be telling him all about Laurel, and there was no predicting what he'd do then. Would he be so protective of her that he'd forbid her to sing? Forbid her to continue on her tour? Tell her that he'd take care of everything from now on, including her little sister that might be killed in the fracas?

When she said nothing, he turned away from her, his jaw set in a hard line. "I'm sorry," she whispered. "I'd tell you if I could."

"If you could trust me, you mean," he said.

"Would you trust me if the life of someone you loved depended on that trust?"

He turned and looked at her. "Yes," he said simply.

She looked away from him, knowing that he was telling the truth. She sensed that he'd tell her anything she wanted to know about him or his family. "But then, you're big enough and strong enough to keep me from doing whatever you don't want me to do, aren't you?"

"I am smart enough to think that the woman I love has sense enough to do what's right," he snapped.

Maddie didn't have time to take in what he'd said before he rolled to his feet and pulled her up.

"Get up," he said angrily. "We need to gather firewood."

"What . . . what did you mean by 'woman you love'?"

"You heard me," he growled, picking up some damp deadfall and shoving it into her arms.

"I don't think I did. Maybe you should repeat it. In fact, I'd like a lot of things repeated, like all that about virgins and my left foot." She was smiling at him, and inside she felt light and joyous.

"You can't hear when it suits you and yet you remember everything your father has ever told you. I hope I get to meet this man someday. I'll look down at him and say, 'Mr. Worth, I—'" He broke off and looked at Maddie, his eyes wide.

"Worth?" 'Ring's eyes widened more, the piece of wood suspended in midair.

"My name?"

When he spoke, there was wonder in his voice. "You said that your mother said, 'Jeffrey, I want you to go east and get a teacher.'"

"Yes. So?" She was acting innocent, but she knew where he was going and it felt good to have her father vindicated.

He looked at her in awe and there was reverence in his voice. "Your father couldn't be Jefferson Worth, could he? *The* Jefferson Worth? The man who wrote the journals?"

She smiled at him so sweetly. "Yes, he is."

'Ring could only look at her. Jefferson Worth was a name of legend, a name like George Washington and Daniel Boone. Traveling with but a few other men, he had explored most of America before it was America. He'd kept journals, made maps. His observations were all that was known about some of the Indian tribes that the white man's greed and diseases had destroyed. He wrote about the animals and their habits, made sketches of the strange plants that he saw on his journeys, wrote about rock formations and hot springs.

"I read his journals when I was a kid and my

little brothers still want to *be* Jefferson Worth. Is he still alive? He must be an old man now."

"Not too old and very much alive. His journals were published when he was just thirty years old, the year after I was born. My mother was the one who saw that they were published. Had it been up to my father, he would have thrown them in a box somewhere and left them."

"Imagine that. Jefferson Worth."

She couldn't resist getting him back for all the things he'd said about her father. "Broad shoulders. Carries pianos around on his back."

"I imagine he could do so." 'Ring's eyes had a distant look in them. "You once asked me where I learned to sneak about so quietly. It was from Jefferson Worth's journals. My brothers and I used to pretend to be him and his men. I was always Jeff, my brother Jamie was Thomas Armour, and—"

"Thomas would like that."

'Ring shook his head. "I can't believe that these men are still alive and that I'm here with Jefferson Worth's daughter. What was the Indian boy's name? It was something odd. We used to fight over who got to play him."

"Hears Good."

"Right. He named himself that after your father took him east and he had an operation on his ears."

Maddie smiled. The story was as familiar to her as though she'd been there with them. "He was deaf and my father took him east. After the operation he said in sign that he was now to be called

272

Hears Good. Up until then he'd been called No Hears."

'Ring was smiling, remembering. "And there was a woman, too, wasn't there? Your father took the first white woman into the territory. She was to paint pictures of the Indians."

"Yes."

"My father bought one of her watercolors. It's of a tribe I'd never heard of, but he and his men spent the winter with them."

"Probably the Mandans. Smallpox nearly wiped them out two years after she painted them."

He paused, thinking. "One of my Taggert cousins always played the woman, but there was something that we used to do to her that used to make her furious. What was it? It was something from the journals."

"I would imagine one of you played Hears Good and stole from her."

"That's right. How could I have forgotten? Hears Good, because he was deaf, had never been able to steal because he couldn't be quiet enough. But when he could hear he practiced his stealing on the woman painter. If I remember correctly, she got awfully angry."

"But she got him back, remember?"

"No. I can't think what she did."

"One night after a strenuous day of traveling when Hears Good was hard asleep—he was only about twelve, you know—she sneaked up to him and stole everything he had, including his loin-

273

cloth. When he woke up in the morning he was stark naked and everything was gone."

'Ring smiled. "That's right. I bet my cousin would have loved to pull that off, but she never did. But my brothers and I constantly sneaked around and stole what we could from each other. Wasn't there something that happened in the end that made the woman forgive Hears Good?"

"Yes. My father and . . . the woman and Hears Good were separated from the others and a band of renegade Apaches up from the south came to spend the night with them. My father didn't trust them, and it was a scary night. The three of them rode out early the next morning and the Apaches chased them and shot at them."

'Ring's face lit up as he remembered. "But Hears Good . . ."

Maddie smiled back at him. "Hears Good had practiced his stealing during the night and had stolen all their bullet molds. They had powder and lead but no way to make bullets. The three of them were able to get away because Hears Good had become such a good thief."

'Ring laughed. "I guess over the years those journals have become like a myth to me. It's difficult to believe that those things actually happened. Where are they all now? All the men who traveled with your father?"

"Actually, my father was one of the men who traveled with Thomas. Thomas was the leader and older and more experienced than my father. But they all live with my father now, and I grew up around them."

"What were their names? Linquist the Swede who snowshoed in the winter and—"

"Skied. Linq skis."

"Whatever. And the old man?"

"Bailey."

"He couldn't still be alive. He must be a hundred now."

"Probably. He looks old enough to be Toby's grandfather, but then, he always has. My father said he wouldn't be surprised to find out that Bailey is only about twenty years old, but Bailey says that he's been in the Rockies so long that the mountains were just hills when he arrived."

"And Hears Good? How old is he now?"

"Hears Good is about forty. But, I don't suppose he knows precisely, or cares."

"Does he live with your family too?"

"Sometimes. He's a blanket Indian." At 'Ring's puzzled look, she explained. "He's what whites sometimes call a wild Indian. He doesn't depend on the whites."

'Ring nodded. That this boy who was his childhood hero should be called a "wild Indian" fit his image of what he hoped the man would become. "What tribe was he?"

"Crow."

It took 'Ring a few seconds to react. "Crow?"

"Is something wrong?"

"No, some pieces of a puzzle have fallen into place, that's all." He looked around at the trees and knew without a doubt that the Crow who'd helped him find Maddie was Hears Good. "He's following us, you know that?"

"Yes," she said softly. "I know."

"This explains a great deal, such as why you know so much about Indians and why you aren't afraid of them."

"I'm afraid when I need to be. I just don't hold the belief that an Indian man is overwhelmed by lust whenever he sees a white woman."

"And how did you come to that conclusion?"

"From Hears Good. You see, there is no finer-looking human on earth than a Crow brave in his prime. Tall, strong, handsome, thick, heavy black hair, skin the color of—"

"I get the picture." It was exactly the picture he'd imagined of this man when he was wrestling his brothers to see who got to be the Crow brave, but he didn't like to hear Maddie describing him. "What did Hears Good do?"

"My father and the others felt sorry for Hears Good because, to the white man's eyes, there is no uglier creature than a Crow squaw. They hated to see a beautiful, magnificent man like Hears Good with Crow women, so, my father thought he'd give Hears Good a treat and take him to St. Louis."

She paused. "My father had a brother who ran a trading post in St. Louis. It was through him that my parents met, but, anyway, Dad and Hears Good traveled to St. Louis. Hears Good was very impressed with the wonders of the city, but, as far as my father could tell, Hears Good never once looked at the white women in all their beautiful clothes. Although the women did look at him. Of course a woman can't help but look at a Crow warrior when he's in full regalia, and Hears Good is one of the finest specimens—"

"I understand."

She smiled at him. "After they left St. Louis, my father asked Hears Good what he thought of the women, and Hears Good said they were a sad-looking group. He thought their tiny waists were awful, said they looked like ants, not women, and that a woman with a waist that small couldn't work or bear children. He also thought their white skin and their sour-looking faces were ugly."

She laughed. "Hears Good also told Dad what he thought of the way white men treated their women, what with taking them off into the plains with no other family members nearby for the women to have for company. He thought the men treated their women like children, dressing them in tight-laced garments and making them work so hard and—"

"I've seen the way the Indians make their women work. They use them as beasts of burden."

"That's because it's accepted that Indian men are worthless."

"Explain that one to me."

"The man has to keep his hands free in order to fight, and to die if necessary while protecting the valuable one, the woman. The woman carries everything but she also owns everything. Trust me, no one works as hard as the white people. The Indians think we're fools."

"Sometimes I agree with them. So, your Hears Good went back to his own people and his own women? I take it he didn't think his own women were ugly."

She smiled. "My father asked his friend to describe a truly beautiful woman, and he did. She should be short and stout, thick-middled, have a wide, flat face with a wide, flat nose, and she should have long, thin breasts that reach her waist."

'Ring took a long moment to look Maddie up and down, his eyes lingering on her bosom that even without the corset was full and upright. "I can't say that I agree with him on that point."

Maddie turned away, blushing but pleased.

As they started back toward the rock ledge, he said, "What happened to the woman? The painter?"

"My father married her."

They turned and looked at each other and smiled. It seemed natural that they should have their lives so entwined, that as a child 'Ring should have played at being her father and that her father's friends should have been his heroes.

For the rest of the afternoon they sat by the fire and talked—or actually, 'Ring asked questions and Maddie answered them. It felt so very, very good not to have to pretend to be a duchess. Years ago John Fairlie, being the English snob that he was, had said that no one in Europe was going to want to hear an opera singer who was the daughter of a man who skinned animals for a living, so he'd come up with the idea that she should be a duchess from the tiny country of Lanconia. It had seemed sensible at the time, a time when she was so full of ambition and wanting more than anything in life to sing for people. It wasn't until years later that she regretted her decision, for it seemed that she was denying her father and his friends.

About five years ago her parents, along with Thomas and Bailey and Linq, had visited her in Paris, and she'd been embarrassed that she wasn't using the name her father had given her. It was as though she were ashamed of it. Her father had laughed at her and said that a name was just a word, that she was his daughter no matter what she called herself.

She told 'Ring about that visit to Paris, how Thomas and Linq as well as her father had been restless and wanted to get back home. "But my father did look handsome in evening clothes." Bailey, however, had loved Paris, and two times her father and Thomas had had to bail him out of jail, where he'd been put for lewd conduct. Her father refused to tell her exactly what Bailey had done.

It began to rain again, and it was cold, so they snuggled together by the fire and ate turkey and rabbit (which they were getting sick of) and Maddie talked more and more about her parents, telling 'Ring about her mother's paintings that were already being acclaimed as having documented a time that never would be again.

279

It was at night when it was so cold that to keep warm they had to lay together, wrapped in each other's arms, that she began to feel her confusion. Never before had she been so aware of the fact that she was such a misfit. She belonged to the silken world of opera, but she also belonged to the wild world of Jefferson Worth. And where did this man fit into her life?

She put her face up to his to be kissed, but he lifted his chin away from her.

"Why?" she whispered. "Why do you say you love me then turn away from me? Why do you look at me so . . . so lustily yet touch me as little as you can? *Really* touch me, I mean."

"Ah, sweetheart, don't you know how many people are watching us?"

"Watching us?"

"There's three of them out there. They've been near you from the first. They follow you, only now I think one of them is following me rather than you. Pardon my fastidiousness, but I don't care for performing for an audience."

"Who are the other two?" She knew about Hears Good, and now she knew why he hadn't come to her the night she'd whistled to him. He'd known that 'Ring was near. She couldn't help smiling. If Hears Good had left her in the care of 'Ring, it meant that the Indian approved of him. That was high praise indeed.

"One is the man who took my horse."

"You mean the gambler?"

"Gambler?" He pulled away a bit to look at her.

"That's what he looks like: a slick riverboat gambler. He should wear a gold brocade vest and a white panama hat. I wonder if he can sing."

"He can't," 'Ring said quickly.

"Mmmm, I wonder. Who else is following us?"

"One of the men you meet," he said, and there was derision in his voice. He picked up the hand that was wearing Laurel's ring. "The man who gave you the ring."

She snatched her hand away from him and hid it between them. "Is that why you don't touch me?" she whispered.

"Other than the fact that I promised, you mean?"

She laughed. "Some promise. You said that our bodies fit together perfectly and that you'd like to put my fingers in your mouth one by one and suck on them and that you'd like to—"

"Shut up," he snapped.

Maddie looked at him and saw that he was under a great strain. "Wasn't there some mention of my shoulders and the inside of my elbow?"

"Maddie, stop talking." There was sweat breaking out on his forehead.

"What else?" She squirmed against him just a bit, as though she were looking for a comfortable place. "Something about my feet, wasn't there? You'd like to kiss my feet. Was that something you've learned? No man has ever kissed my feet before."

"No man has kissed any of you before," he said

in a gruff voice that sounded as though he were in pain.

"Ha! That's what you think. I've had men drink champagne from my slippers. A man once offered me a ruby necklace to go to bed with him. Men have offered me everything to be their mistress. But it is true that no man has ever said that he wanted to make love to my foot before. Shoulders, yes, but feet, no."

At that 'Ring put his hand on her jaw and turned her head so that he could kiss her. And Maddie lost herself in that kiss. She didn't care who was watching them, all that mattered was this man and this moment.

" 'Ring," she whispered, and her free arm went around him. "My 'Ring."

He was the one who pulled away from her. "We can't, Maddie. No, I won't. I'll not perform for an audience. There are too many people watching us."

She turned away and snuggled her back against his front, and between them was such a tension that Maddie knew her body was vibrating with her desire. Her hands were trembling and images kept forming in her mind: When she'd pulled the thorns from him and had run her hands over his legs; the day he'd helped push the coach from the water and he'd removed his shirt; the night he'd come to her wearing nothing but a loincloth.

"Maddie . . ." he said, and there was warning in his voice. "Think of something else."

"How do you know what I'm thinking?"

He held out his hand toward the fire, and when he did so she could see that it was shaking, just as hers was.

"Why did you tell me no the day I took the thorns from you?"

"Because then I was Captain Montgomery to you. I was a good-looking, well-built man and we were alone and you are one passionate woman."

She snorted at that. "Even your sister says you're ugly."

"Ugly in my family is relative."

She groaned. "Spare me. I knew from the moment I met you that you were vain, but I had no idea of the depth of your vanity."

"Who has the best voice in the world?"

She smiled in the darkness. "I get your point. So, now you think it's different? Now you think I see you as anything besides a good-looking man?"

"What do you think?"

She held his hand in hers and looked at it. He had long, thin fingers and beautifully shaped nails. What did she think of him? At this moment she couldn't imagine being without him. From the first he seemed to know her better than anyone had ever known her. He was right that at first she hadn't paid much attention to him except as a beautiful man, but now . . . Now she remembered the times he'd risked his life to protect her, how he'd climbed up a cliff to be with her, how he'd come for her after she'd sung *Carmen*. She thought of all the wounds on his body that he'd suffered because of her. She thought of the times she'd drugged him and tricked him, yet he was still here with her, still trying to help her.

"General Yovington has been helping me," she said softly. "Some men took my little sister Laurel, and if I'm to get her back, I have to sing in six camps, and at each place I am to meet a man and exchange letters with him. They promised I would see Laurel this time, but they lied to me." She held up her hand. "The man gave me the ring I sent Laurel as proof that they have her. He said . . . he said that they would kill you if you didn't stop interfering in this."

She choked back tears. "They say that they'll give me back Laurel at the last town, but I'm afraid. I'm beginning to think they won't do it. I'm afraid they'll kill her because of the stupid war they want to start." She couldn't stop the tears. "And now I'm afraid they're going to hurt you too."

He turned her toward him and held her tightly. He even put his leg over hers as though to protect her completely. "I know, sweetheart. I know."

She cried for some time. "How can you know? You don't know how dangerous these men are. He said—"

"You don't have to tell me, I heard it all."

"Heard it all?" She sniffed and he offered her a wet, soiled handkerchief. "What did you hear?"

"Everything the man said to you. You're safe now, so why don't you go to sleep? We'll talk about this in the morning."

She pulled away from him. "I want to know what you know. What you heard." There was some anger in her voice.

"All right, I'll tell you. You didn't think that I'd let you drug me a second time, did you? You and Edith were so obvious that a blind man could have seen what you were doing. While you were taking so long in the outhouse, I had Toby replace some of your drugged figs with something else. From the taste of them, I think he used horse manure, but at least I wasn't put to sleep that time. I also found out that you cared enough about me to keep me from eating a lethal dose. You and Edith should stop playing around with that stuff until you learn how to use it."

"You tricked me. You pretended to fall asleep. You flailed about that tent as though you were a dying clown. When I think of how . . . You make me furious!"

"*I* make *you* furious? What was I supposed to do? Tell you that I hadn't eaten poisoned figs? You were so eager to get out of there that I was afraid you'd shoot me if I didn't let you go."

She started struggling to get away from him. "So you followed me, didn't you? You knew I wanted to go by myself and yet you followed me."

He gave her a look of astonishment. "Your fine Crow warrior friend is following you and you're grateful to him, but I follow you and you're angry with me. That doesn't make sense."

"Hears Good is protecting me."

"And what do you think I'm doing? You think

I *want* to sneak around among cactus and scrub oak and scratch myself, not to mention my horse? Is that what you think I *want* to do?"

She started to move away from him, but the chain was holding them together, and since he wasn't moving, she couldn't go very far. "I don't like being spied on."

"I don't like having the woman I love doing things that need spying on, so we're even." He softened his voice. "Maddie, I was just trying to protect you. Is that so bad?"

"It is if I don't want you to protect me. I can take care of myself."

"Ha! If Hears Good hadn't sent that arrow flying, that man would have—" He broke off, remembering that man starting to touch her, then he pulled her back into his arms, holding her full length against his body.

"Maddie, let's not fight. I've done what I felt I had to in order to protect you and to find out what was going on in your life. I've never meant to offend you in any way."

Maddie put her hands over her face and started crying again. He held her close as he stroked her back. "Don't cry, baby, there's nothing to cry about. All lovers have quarrels."

With her arms pinned between them, she couldn't hit him, so she settled for kicking him in the shins.

He gave a grunt of pain. "What was that for?"

"I have more important things to cry about than

quarrels with you. And besides that, we're not lovers. We're—"

"Yes," he said softly, "what are we?"

"I don't know. I don't know anything anymore. Six months ago I knew exactly who I was and what I wanted in life, but now everything seems different. I can't seem to figure out anything."

"That's the best news I've heard. Maybe the best news I've ever heard in my life."

Maybe how she felt was good news to him, but it wasn't to her. She put her face in the hollow of his shoulder and inhaled of him.

"Does it bother you that we aren't lovers?" he asked.

"No, of course not. A lady should wait until she's married. A lady—" She stopped because 'Ring kissed her, and as he did so, he slipped his hand up inside her loose blouse and touched the bare skin of her stomach.

"'Ring, I don't think . . ."

"Shhh, sweetheart, be still."

She was quiet as his hand moved up to her breast, cupping it, holding her flesh in his big, warm palm. His thumb touched the peak of her breast. Her breath stopped in her throat. Her eyes closed and she leaned her head back as his lips touched her neck.

"Don't you have any idea what I'd like to do to you?" There was pain in his voice. "Are you so innocent that you don't know how much I want you, how long I've wanted you?"

"No, I . . ."

"I didn't think so. I want you so much that Toby laughs at me. I want to touch you, your skin, your hair. I want to feel the inside of your body. I want to know you, Maddie, know you as well and as completely as any man can know a woman."

He moved his head so that he could touch her ear with his tongue. His teeth made little nibbling bites and the hairs on Maddie's body began to stand up straight.

"'Ring," she whispered.

"Yes, baby, I'm here. I'm always here, always near you, always wanting you."

He was kissing her neck now, but not just kissing it, touching her skin with his tongue. She began to tremble, and when she did, he stopped.

For a moment she lay still in the circle of his arms. She didn't care if the whole US Army was watching them; she didn't want him to stop. She put her hand up to his face and tried to pull him down to her.

"No," he said. "I can't. I mean, baby, that I'm not made of steel. Although for the last few days parts of me have felt as though they are. I can't go on. You just be still and go to sleep. Tomorrow we'll go down the mountain and we'll have time for privacy."

Maddie lay still in his arms, and after a moment her trembling stopped and her mind began to function again. She remembered his saying that for a very long time he'd wanted her. If he wanted her so much, how could he stop? Why wasn't he trembling too?

She lifted her free hand and slowly unbuttoned the top button of his shirt.

"Maddie, what are you doing? You can't—"

She put her lips on the warm brown skin of his chest, rubbed her face in the hair on his chest, and as she was doing so, she unfastened another button.

"Maddie, please don't. We can't . . ."

She moved her lips lower. He was warmer than she was and his body was very hard, with no fat on it, just warm, hard skin over muscle. Her hand slid inside his shirt to touch his ribs, her fingers moving over them to feel the strength of him. He wasn't talking now as her mouth moved lower to his belly as she kissed and then very gently bit his skin.

When she reached the top of his belt buckle she stopped, and for a moment she rested her face against his hard stomach. There was sweat breaking out on her body and her breath seemed to come from deep, deep inside her. " 'Ring," she whispered, but he said nothing.

She pulled away from him enough so that she could see his face. She'd never seen such a look on a human before, except maybe on some of the Renaissance statues in Florence. It was a look of pain and longing and suffering and ecstasy. Everything combined in one look that, for a moment, as seen on this beautiful man, made her heart stop. The look on his face was as beautiful as the best aria ever written. The look on his face was as beautiful as the voice God had given her.

"'Ring," she whispered, and moved back up into his arms.

"I love you, Maddie," he said at last. "I have been looking for you. I left my home and the family that I love, the family that needs me, to find you. You are part of me."

"Yes," she answered. "I think perhaps that I am."

She settled into his arms and let him hold her, not saying anything, just lying there together, her body trembling and alive, but she was content to just be near him now.

CHAPTER 13

In the morning they started down the mountain, breakfasting on another rabbit, and Maddie laughed at 'Ring when he complained about more rabbit.

"This is the man who ate hardtack rather than my vegetables and fresh bread?" she teased. "My father could live on nothing but rabbit and I doubt that he'd complain."

"Your father," he said under his breath. "That old man?"

"Old? How can you say that? Why, you . . . ." She began to chase him, and he ran in front of her, staying very close to her but as far away as the chain would allow, and when she came close

to stumbling, he was there to keep her from falling.

Maddie didn't think that she'd ever had such a
carefree day in her life. For this one day she
wouldn't allow any problems to cloud her mind.

They laughed and teased each other all the way
down the mountain. Maddie soon realized that she
had as much power over him as he had over her.
When she started to fall and he came close to catch
her, she touched him in the most unusual places,
sometimes at the inside of his thigh, sometimes
her breasts hit his body.

He laughed and caught her in his arms and
twirled her around in a circle and then they went
rolling down the mountain, his big body protecting her from the thorns and sharp rocks.

"My pompous captain," she said, laughing with
him, rolling with him.

Maddie heard the horse, but since 'Ring was
kissing her neck, she didn't pay any attention to
it.

"Shhh," he said, lifting his head to listen.

"What is it?"

"My horse."

"Mmmm," Maddie said without much interest.
"You know, it's rather private here." It took her
a moment to regain her senses, but she pushed
away to look at him. "What do you mean, *your*
horse?"

He had his hand inside her blouse. "Buttercup."

It took a moment longer to clear her mind.

Between his hands and his mouth, she couldn't think very clearly. "'Ring, listen to me. If that's your horse, then that means that robber is near us. Are you sure you can recognize the sound of your horse?"

"Perfect pitch, remember," he said, and put his mouth to her neck again.

She had to push at him three times before she could move him, and then she had to use her knees to make any impression on him. "'Ring, listen to me. We have to do something."

"I plan to do something. I'm going to go get my horse. I have a score to settle with that man who robbed us."

Maddie's eyes widened. "I meant that we have to get out of here. The horse isn't that important. Let's go down the mountain. I'll buy you another horse, or—you're rich, you can buy your own horse."

He seemed to be thinking about something very seriously. "No, this is something I have to do."

"'Ring, wait a minute. I know that you take your honor very seriously, but this isn't the time to think of honor. You have no weapons and we're chained together. You can't take on an armed man alone. Let's go down the mountain, then you can get Frank and Sam to help you."

"I don't trust those two. No, I think that now is the time. I think he may be expecting me, that's why he's here."

'Ring stood up, and when he did, he brought Maddie up with him.

She put her hands on his chest. "Don't do this, 'Ring," she said. "Please don't do this. I won't let you do this." She sat down on a fallen tree and folded her arms over her breast.

He looked down at her as though he were amused by her.

"Don't you dare look at me like that," she hissed at him. "I am not being a silly female, and I resent your insinuation that I am."

"I didn't say a word." His mouth was twitching in amusement.

There is nothing in the world more infuriating than a smirking man. She refused to say another word to him but instead stared straight ahead at an aspen tree.

"Not going to let me move, are you?"

She still didn't talk to him, but looked at that tree.

With a chuckle that only a man who is laughing at a woman can make, he bent over and picked her up, his arm about her waist, her backside pointing toward the front of him. "What an interesting position. We could go together after the man."

She pounded the back of his leg with her free hand. "You can't go after him. You can't risk your life for a horse."

At that he turned her around and stood her in front of him. "You're worried about me?"

She gave him a look of disgust. "I don't know why I am. I guess it's just that I'm worried about my own skin. If we're attached and you go where there's . . . there's bullets flying, I might get hurt."

He smiled down at her and smoothed her hair out of her eyes. "I'm glad that you're worried only about yourself."

"Please don't risk yourself—or me."

He continued smiling. "Then I guess I better not risk you. The world would lose a lot if it lost you and that God-given voice of yours."

She let out her breath, glad that he could see reason and wasn't going to try to be a hero and go after the man. She was still smiling at him when he reached into his pocket and withdrew a key. She was smiling when he lifted her bound right hand and kissed her palm. She even smiled when he inserted the key in the lock.

"Thank you," she said sweetly after he released her. It wasn't until he used the key on the band about his own wrist that she realized what was happening. She rubbed her sore wrist, her eyes wide, her voice low. "You had a key all along."

"Of course. Now, baby, I want you to stay here and wait for me. I'll get Buttercup and come back for you. Try to be quiet."

"You had the key."

"Sure. You did hear me, didn't you? I think that Indian friend of yours will look out for you, but I can't be sure, so I want you to be still."

"You had the key."

'Ring looked at her and he saw a woman who was on the verge of getting very, very angry. "You don't think I'd have let that man take the only key, do you? Do you realize what could have happened if there had been any real trouble and the two of us were chained together like a couple of sausages? Surely you thought of that, didn't you?"

"You had the key all the time. You lied to me."

"You, my lovely, are the king and the queen of all liars. Come on, sweetheart, don't you have a sense of humor?"

She was sputtering as a few hundred words tumbled over themselves to get out.

He kissed her. "As much as I'd like to stay here and argue with you, I have some business to attend to. I'll come back for you as soon as I can."

Maddie didn't have time enough to recover herself before he slipped through the trees and was gone. She sat down on a fallen log and put her head in her hands. She thought of the lack of privacy of the last three days, the way they'd had to walk together, sleep together, the way they had not been able to get more than three feet from each other.

At some point her anger dissolved and began to be replaced with laughter. He had certainly repaid her for all the times she'd tricked him.

She was sitting on the ground, her arms tucked about her knees and musing on what he'd done, when she remembered where he was going. He was just fool enough to go up to that robber and demand the return of his horse—and the robber would repay 'Ring with a bullet through his heart.

Maddie could do some of her own silent traveling when necessary, and now she began to move through the shrubs and low bushes with all the sound of a snake. When she was close enough to the robber's camp to hear voices, she stopped. 'Ring seemed to have extraordinarily good ears, and she didn't want him to hear her.

But he must have heard her, for the voices stopped as soon as she could see the men—and the voices were replaced with sounds of flesh hitting flesh. Before she thought about what she was doing, she started moving toward the two men. Maybe she could get the robber's gun and—

She didn't think anymore because Hears Good sent an arrow flying into her path. She put her hand on the arrow and her mouth turned into a grim line. He wouldn't come to her when she called to him, but he stayed around and spied on her when she was with the man she loved.

"Show yourself," she hissed at him, but only the wind in the trees answered her. She was tempted to defy him and go to 'Ring in spite of what Hears Good wanted her to do, but she wasn't a fool. Even if she didn't like his methods, she knew that Hears Good's advice was right.

So Maddie sat down and waited, waited for what seemed to be an eternity. The sun reached its zenith and it became afternoon while she waited for 'Ring to return. Every muscle in her body was tense as she expected at any moment to hear a shot.

When a twig snapped behind her, she turned and saw 'Ring moving through the trees. She ran to him, put his arm around her shoulders. "Are you badly hurt?"

He leaned heavily on her. "I told you to stay away."

"I thought maybe I could help you."

"And I told you I didn't want any help. I told you— What are you doing?"

She'd begun to run her hands over him, to check him for injuries. "I want to know if you're hurt."

He smiled down at her as she knelt and ran her hands over his calves and thighs, then up to his waist, and around his ribs. "Maddie, let's stay here tonight."

"No." She ran her hands over his shoulders and down his arms. "You don't seem to be bleeding anywhere. In fact, you don't even have bruises on your face, yet I heard the two of you fighting. What happened?"

"Not much. I made him listen to reason, that's all."

"Got the drop on him, did you?"

"More or less. Now, about that staying here tonight . . ."

"No, it's too dangerous. I don't trust that robber. Let's get down to the camp. I have to sing tomorrow night and then I have to meet the man and exchange letters."

"About that—"

She put her hand to his lips and wouldn't let him speak. "We'll talk about that tomorrow. Is that your horse making all that noise? What do you think he's eating?"

"Cactus probably. Loves the stuff. I have to pull the thorns out of his nose."

"Just like his master."

He smiled at her, took her hand, and led her to the horse and then mounted behind her. All the rest of the way down the mountain, he rubbed various parts of Maddie's body and told her how much he was looking forward to a little privacy tonight. He hinted at things he was going to do to her.

"In the army, what with a lack of, shall we say, suitable females, I've had some time to use my imagination. I have a few things I'd like to try."

"Oh?" Maddie asked, and her voice broke. She cleared her throat. "What sort of things?"

He put his lips to her ear and began to whisper things to her that made her so limp that, when they reached the camp, she couldn't stand up. 'Ring helped her.

Toby came running to them. "Where you two been?" He was trying to sound harsh, and worry had made his old face look at least twenty years older.

'Ring had one arm around Maddie, and he put the other around Toby. "Talking mostly."

Toby gave a grunt. "With you that's probably true. Now, if *I* had been alone with this little lady . . ."

Maddie didn't listen to any more of their banter. She eased away from 'Ring's side and went to Edith and demanded that water be heated and a bath prepared for her. Edith complained about the late hour, saying that it was almost nighttime and time to go to bed.

"That's just the point," Maddie said so that Edith at last understood.

Edith went off mumbling about it being Judgment Day if her royal highness were going to spend the night with a man, but she put the water on to boil. Maddie had her bath in an enclosure of blankets, and when she was at last clean she went back to the tent.

It was dark inside, and she had to light a lantern to be able to see. 'Ring was sprawled on her narrow cot. His shoulders were wider than it was, and he was longer than the cot, so his feet hung off. He had started to unbutton his dirty, torn shirt, but he hadn't made it before he fell asleep, so his hand was still on the third button. It had been almost four days since he'd shaved now, so his face had a heavy growth of black whiskers on it.

She went to him and kissed his sleeping lips. He gave a little smile, but he didn't waken. "'Ring," she whispered, but he didn't so much as move.

So much for his imagination, she thought. It didn't look as though it were something that kept him awake at night. She gave a sigh and looked with displeasure at the folded blankets in the corner. Once again she'd have to sleep on the floor, but this time she'd not have 'Ring's strong arms around her. She was sure that she wouldn't be able to sleep, but she lay down on the blanket and was asleep instantly.

When Maddie awoke, it was late morning, and right away she knew that something was wrong. Her head was fuzzy from sleep but her senses knew that something was very wrong.

When her mind cleared, she saw that she was on the cot and not on the floor. Sometime during the night 'Ring had picked her up and moved her, but he wasn't asleep on the floor. He wasn't in the tent at all.

She pulled a blanket over her nightgown and went outside. Edith was bending over the campfire, stirring something in a pot, and Toby was sitting on the ground, drinking a mug of coffee. "Where is he?" Maddie asked in a voice that let them know that she wanted no lies.

"He left you a letter," Toby said, and pulled it out of one of the many pockets on his army blouse.

Maddie didn't want to look at the letter, but she knew she had to. With trembling hands, she opened it.

Do not sing tonight. Wait for me.

CHM

She looked up at Toby. Since the letter had been merely a folded sheet of paper, she had no doubt that both Toby and Edith had read it. "That's all? That's all he left for me? How long am I to wait for him? A day? A week? A year? Did he bother to tell any of you where he's gone? Or when he plans to return?"

300

"No, ma'am," Toby said, looking down at the ground. "But then, the boy don't usually tell nobody nothin'. He keeps to himself, he does."

"He just gives orders, you mean," Maddie said, and turned and went back into the tent.

Once inside, she sat down on the cot and looked at the letter. CHM, she thought. His initials, as though she were a stranger to him, as though she were an army person. As though—

She couldn't sustain her anger. She knew exactly where he'd gone: he'd gone after the men who had taken Laurel. It was what she knew was going to happen if she told him why she was singing in the West. She'd known from the first moment she met him that he was the type of man who would take on responsibility. He thought everything was his business and was something that he had to deal with.

She began to dress but her fingers were shaking too much to fasten the buttons, so she called Edith.

"What're you gonna do?" Edith asked.

Maddie knew what she meant. "I'm going to sing, of course. I'm not going to allow Captain Montgomery to rule my life. I'm going to—" She stopped and took a breath. "I'm not going to sing tonight. I'm going to wait for him. I'm going to do just what he wants."

"The miners are gonna be real mad. They brought that piano up here for you, and they been filin' in from all over to hear you sing."

"Well, I'm not going to sing!" Maddie half

301

shouted. "If he can risk his life, I can—" She broke off. She was damned if she was going to break into tears in front of Edith. "Leave me alone. Tell the miners that I'm sick."

Edith grunted her disapproval and left the tent.

For a long while Maddie sat on the cot, her head in her hands, not crying, for she was too afraid to cry. Why did he have to do this? Wasn't it bad enough that she had to worry about Laurel? Why did he have to put *his* life in jeopardy as well?

When she heard someone in the tent, she thought it was Edith. She didn't look up. "Go away."

It was Toby. "I brung you somethin' to eat," he said softly.

"I don't want anything to eat."

"I sure do know that feelin'. He makes a body so mad that you don't wanta eat or nothin'."

Maddie covered her face with her hands. "He's gone after my sister. He's gone alone against I don't know how many men. They'll kill him *and* my sister."

"Maybe, maybe not. You know, it's almost funny you turnin' out to like him so much. I ain't never seen him so mad as when the colonel made him escort an opery singer. The boy said he was gonna scare you and make you turn back. He didn't scare you none, did he?"

"He scares me now."

"Yeah, but you didn't think he was gonna hurt you, did you? You mind holdin' this coffee cup? It's burnin' my hand."

Maddie took the coffee and absently sipped it. "Why should anyone be afraid of him?"

"Beats me, but the colonel back at Fort Breck hates him."

"Hates 'Ring? How could anyone hate 'Ring?"

Toby grinned at her. "You mind takin' this sandwich for a minute? My hand's beginnin' to sweat. You see . . . Mind if I sit down?" Toby took the single folding chair and leaned forward. "You see, Colonel Harrison don't like havin' a full-fledged hero under him, makes him feel—"

"Inadequate?"

"That's the very word the boy uses—that and a lot of other words. The colonel don't know nothin' about nothin', and he's afraid that the boy will get promoted and pretty soon the colonel will be callin' the boy sir."

"But doesn't it take a long time to work your way up through the ranks? Surely the colonel will be retired by the time 'Ring makes a higher rank."

"Not the way the boy is goin' at it. He was a private just a few years ago."

Maddie took a big bite of the bacon sandwich. "He did mention that, and, you know, at the time I didn't even wonder how he was made an officer."

Toby started to get up. "I guess I can tell you the story someday, but you got things to do. You know, with the worryin' and all. I better leave you to it."

"No, please stay. A story might help take my mind off 'Ring . . . and Laurel."

"Well, all right," Toby said, and sat back down.

"It was about four years ago and we was at Fort Breck. Sometimes it seems like we always been at that place. Anyway, we was goin' out on what they call a detail, but it was just to see if we could come up with some firewood. We do a lot of that sort of thing in the army. It's a real borin' job, and that's why so many men, ah . . . leave it, if you know what I mean."

Maddie nodded. Deserters.

"So, we was ridin' out and Captain Jackson was with us. There was about fifteen of us, a lot 'cause the Cheyennes was real mad. It seems the Cheyennes was gettin' sick of the settlers puttin' up houses on the Cheyenne land and killin' off all the game. And the settlers—Lord! but I ain't met a meaner bunch of people—they had the idea the only good Injun was a dead one, so they shot them for target practice. The Cheyennes didn't take too well to that."

Maddie knew all too well what the whites had done to the Indians.

"Since the army was there to protect the settlers—"

"Who had the guns."

"Right you are. Well, anyway, the army was the Cheyennes' enemy, so to speak, so on that day they decided to kill a few white soldiers."

Toby was quiet for a moment. "They come out of nowhere. I think we was singin' one of them talkin' army songs and—"

"Cadences."

"Yeah, them, and we didn't hear nothin'. Them

Cheyennes just run up on us and started shootin'. Captain Jackson was the first to go down—the Injuns probably wanted his pretty coat."

Maddie thought there might be some truth in that.

Toby's voice lowered. "I was one of the first to be shot. Got one in the shoulder and another in the leg."

He took a breath. "All those men just plain panicked. Hell, they ain't no more soldiers than I am. They was just farmers and men runnin' from the law, whatever, and they joined the army to fill their bellies. Hardly any of 'em could ride a horse, much less shoot. When the Injuns started their attack, half of 'em fell off their horses."

"'Ring took command," Maddie said.

"That he did." Toby grinned. "You ain't never seen nothin' until you've seen that boy in battle. I swear, he seems to get bigger. He started shoutin' and orderin' ever'body about and they didn't know what to do, so they did what he said."

"And what about you?"

Maddie wasn't sure, but she thought she saw tears in Toby's old eyes. "He slung me over his shoulder and carried me. I told him it weren't no use, that I was already dead, but he didn't listen to me. No, he carried me and did his yellin' just the same."

Toby gave a noisy sniff. "Anyway, he got all the men in a circle in the ground. There weren't no cover, but there was this hole, like."

"A depression?"

"Yeah, that's what it was. He made ever'body keep down and he wouldn't let nobody panic. He said that help was on its way and that they'd be out of it soon."

"Was help on its way?"

"Hell no! Oh, pardon, ma'am. The soldiers at the fort thought we was out gettin' wood, wasn't nobody gonna help us do that."

"And you knew this at the time?"

"I did, and the boy did, but them farmers didn't. They wanted to believe the boy, I guess, so they did. The boy wouldn't let 'em shoot unless they thought they could kill somebody."

Toby grinned. "You shoulda seen him. He was cool as you please, givin' shootin' lessons to the men. You woulda thought we was target practicin' instead of bein' attacked by a couple hundred Cheyenne. And them Cheyenne, they took their time. I think they was enjoyin' the sport."

"As much as the settlers enjoyed killing the Cheyenne?" Maddie asked.

"Just about the same, I'd imagine. We stayed there all day and all night. We was about to run out of water, and the men started quarrelin' over the water."

"What did 'Ring do?"

"Kept it all himself and doled it out a swallow at a time. We didn't know if we was gonna die from thirst or the Cheyennes was gonna get us."

"Why didn't he send for help?"

"Who was he gonna send? I was shot too bad, and if the boy left them men, they'd go crazy and they was all too scared and too dumb to know how to get past the Injuns. There wasn't nothin' we could do but wait and pray."

"So how did you get out?"

Toby laughed. "If there's one thing you can count on in the army, it's confusion. Back at Fort Breck, the CO, that's army talk for commandin' officer, was a drunken old sod and the men got sick of him—they always did about ever' six weeks—and they decided to desert, that is, after they'd taken a couple barrels of his whiskey."

Toby closed his eyes in memory. "Here we was, layin' in this hole, dyin' of thirst, fightin' for our lives, and along comes a whole passel of drunken soldiers desertin' from the army. I don't think the Injuns knew quite what was goin' on, so they stopped shootin' at us for about ten seconds and the boy made his move."

"What did 'Ring do?"

"I was kinda in a daze then, so I don't really know for sure, but the boy got the men in the hole up and runnin' and they jumped up on the horses with the drunks and ever'body started yellin' and kickin' them poor horses and got the hell out of there."

"And you?"

Toby looked away for a moment. "He carried me all the way. I told him not to, but he's one hardheaded so-and-so."

"That he is. Won't listen to reason."

"No, he don't."

"So, you all got back to the fort safely."

"There was a few men that didn't make it, but not many." Toby chuckled. "The boy told the army people that the deserters were concerned when we didn't come back from the woodchoppin' foray and that they was out lookin' for us. The CO had been too drunk to notice that we hadn't come back so he wasn't gonna call the boy a liar. The CO was smart enough to see the advantages of the whole thing. He made the boy an officer—although he said he didn't wanta be—and gave him a medal and he got pieces of paper for the rest of the men."

"Commendations?"

"Right, that's it. We all got us a piece of paper sayin' we was minor heroes instead of just a bunch of wood-choppin' drunks."

Maddie smiled at him. The whole story sounded like the 'Ring she'd come to know.

Toby stood up. "I reckon I better leave you now, ma'am," he said as he walked to the tent entrance, and Maddie nodded.

CHAPTER 14

What followed for Maddie were three days of hell. She wasn't very good at waiting. She was used to controlling her own life and now, between Laurel's kidnapping and 'Ring's disappearance, she'd never felt so out of control.

If it hadn't been for the miners, she thought she might have lost her mind. The miners gave her someone to vent her anger on. They were lonely men and they had heard of her singing and they wanted her to entertain them. At first she'd merely told them no, mumbling that she had a sore throat or some such nonsense, but then their pleadings began to annoy her.

She turned on one group of miners and let them have it. She yelled at them with the full force of all her lung power. She told them that she did not want to sing for them, that she *would not* sing for them.

The men stood there and stared at her in awe. She could be very loud when she chose to be. One man, still blinking from the force of Maddie's voice, said softly, "I guess you got over your sore throat."

Maddie turned away from them, but that didn't stop them from pestering her to sing for them. She couldn't walk anywhere without a miner following her and asking her to please sing. They gave all kinds of reasons, one man saying that his family would be thrilled to hear that he'd heard LaReina sing. Another said that he'd consider his life having been worth living if he could just hear her sing. Their flattery became outrageous, but it didn't move Maddie. She spent most of the day in a woody copse near the edge of the camp and watched the road.

Edith sometimes brought her food, but it was just as likely to be Toby who brought the food to her.

"No sign of him?" he asked.

"None. Why couldn't he have told us where he was going? At least the direction he was taking. How could he have known where to go?"

"Maybe he went after that man you were meetin'."

Maddie took a deep breath. "That's what I'm afraid of." She looked around at the trees. "I think he may have had someone with him, though."

"That Injun friend of yours?"

She looked at Toby sharply.

"The boy didn't tell me much, didn't have time 'fore he left, but he said somethin' about some journals and some Injun that can hear things."

"I think Hears Good went with 'Ring. Hears Good will take care of him." I hope, she added to herself.

Toby didn't ask any more questions, but turned to leave, then looked back. "Oh, yeah, them miners that you grubstaked come back. They found these rocks." He held out his hand and in it were four black rocks.

"What are they?"

"Lead mostly."

"Worth anything?"

"Not much."

Maddie gave her attention back to the road. It didn't matter much to her one way or the other whether the men had discovered gold or not. All she wanted was her sister and 'Ring to return.

By the third day the miners gave up on her and stopped trying to persuade her to sing for them. They no longer tried to entice her with promises of a piano and even a roofed building housing the piano. They walked past her on the road and tipped their hats to her but they said little.

Maddie didn't know or much care why the men were at last leaving her alone, but she was glad. She wasn't aware that both Sam and Toby had placed themselves on the hill above her and looked down on her like a couple of guardian angels—or vultures as the miners saw them. Toby was outfitted with enough weapons to make him look like a pirate, and Sam had his size to intimidate anyone who bothered Maddie.

By the evening of the third day she was beginning to give up hope. She knew that this time 'Ring's luck had run out. This time he hadn't been able to save himself, much less a company of soldiers, from the dangers that he faced. Maddie tried to get angry at him. She'd tried to tell him that the men who had taken Laurel were dangerous, but he wouldn't listen to her. No, he thought he knew everything. He thought he could do anything, that he was all-powerful. He thought that he didn't need anyone, that he could do everything by himself.

She was trying to whip herself into a really good rage, but it didn't work. She told herself that she'd lived all her life without him and she could be quite happy again without him, but she couldn't make herself believe that. She'd never before thought of herself as lonely, but now her whole life seemed lonely. She remembered being alone as a child, being alone as an adult. When those Russian

311

students had kidnapped her and John had left her on her own, at the time it had seemed perfectly natural, but now it made her feel lonely that no one had come after her.

She sniffed and wiped away a tear at the corner of her eye. She was *not* going to cry over him. He had chosen to do this and it's what he wanted to do.

She tried to think rationally about what she was going to do. If he hadn't returned by the following day, she would start the journey to her father and get him and his men to help her find Laurel . . . and 'Ring. What was left of 'Ring, she amended. If he hadn't returned by the next day, she would know that he was dead.

Perhaps her father could track him, find him. Maybe 'Ring would only be held prisoner somewhere and the men wouldn't have killed him as they said they were going to do. Maybe—

She couldn't think anymore because it seemed that a tight band was about her chest. "Oh 'Ring," she whispered.

She leaned against a tree and closed her eyes. No matter how she looked at it, his death was going to shatter her.

She wasn't aware of Toby on the hill, the way he squinted his old eyes and looked down the long, rutted road. She wasn't aware of Sam, following Toby's look, and also standing. Maddie was too immersed in her own grief to be aware of much of anything.

She felt his presence before she saw him.

Slowly, she turned and there he was. 'Ring was dirty and his clothes were ragged and he was carrying something wrapped in a blanket in his arms, but all she saw was him. She walked to him and put her hand up to his cheek. It was scratched, with long furrows running down the side, and some of the scratches were still bloody.

She stood there, touching him, not saying anything, just looking at him until tears began to form in her eyes.

He grinned at her. "I've been out fighting dragons for you."

She didn't hear him at first. She was too glad to see that he was alive to be able to hear.

"Here," he said, and then he dropped a heavy bundle into her arms.

She staggered under the weight, but 'Ring caught her before she fell. It took Maddie several moments to realize what the bundle was.

'Ring pulled the blanket back and Maddie saw the sleeping face of her pretty twelve-year-old sister. Maddie hadn't seen her for years, but she'd recognize her anywhere, and she was wearing the diamond and pearl brooch that had been given to Maddie by her grandmother.

Maddie looked up at 'Ring in wonder.

"She's a terror," he said, rubbing his cheek. "I don't know why anyone in his right mind would kidnap her. Personally, I'd rather take on a couple of grizzly cubs than that one."

Maddie just looked down at her sister, then up

at 'Ring. She couldn't yet believe that either of them was safe. "She . . . she scratched you?"

"Nearly tore my eyes out. I kept telling her that I was sent by you, but it seems that her kidnappers had also told her that. She bit Jamie."

"Help me with her," Maddie said. "Is she well? Has she been hurt? Has anyone harmed her? How did you find her? Oh 'Ring, I—" She couldn't say any more, for the tears were too strong.

'Ring caught both Maddie and Laurel, then helped lower them to sit on the ground, Maddie in 'Ring's lap and the sleeping Laurel on the top. Maddie leaned back against him and held Laurel tightly to her.

"She must be awfully tired."

"It's hard work terrorizing two grown men."

She leaned her head back against his shoulder. "Did she really put up a fight?"

"I'm bleeding from a dozen places."

"Tell me what happened."

"No, not now. Now I want food and sleep and you'll want to talk to your hellion of a little sister. Have you got enough room and food for two men?"

"If I have to shoot a buffalo myself, I will."

"I'd laugh if I didn't know you were telling the truth."

"Who helped you?"

'Ring nodded toward the road, and she looked up to see a man coming toward them, limping slightly as he walked. She recognized him immediately. He was the man who had robbed them and left them in the mountains with nothing. As he approached, he drew his gun and pointed it at them. Maddie stiffened.

"Put that gun down," 'Ring snapped, and the man, with a grin, put the gun back in his holster.

"You asked a robber to help you?" Maddie asked.

The young man grinned at her. "I prefer highwayman."

"Ha!" 'Ring snapped. "This is my infant brother Jamie. He enjoys playing dress-up and trying to frighten women."

"It seems to run in the family."

A few hundred thoughts went through Maddie's mind as she looked at him. Her first thought was anger at 'Ring and his brother for playing such a trick on her on the mountain. The two of them pretending to be robber and victim, with her the innocent bystander. Later there had been that little play they'd put on, pretending to fight. No doubt that was when they'd planned their rescue of Laurel.

Aside from her anger, she was looking at this man and remembering that Toby had said that 'Ring was the ugly one.

Jamie had curling black hair; thick, black spiky lashes over brilliant blue eyes; a chiseled nose; a full, sensuous mouth over a square jaw; and a cleft chin. Not as tall as 'Ring, "only" about six foot, but as broad and as strongly built.

Maddie turned to look at 'Ring. "You *are* the ugly one."

Jamie laughed at that, a rich, deep laugh. "Brains as well as beauty. You've done well, brother."

'Ring didn't seem in the least bothered by her pronouncement that his brother was better-looking than he was. In fact, he kissed her neck. "She does have brains, at that," he said, and there was pride in his voice as well as a bit of astonishment.

Jamie gave a jaw-splitting yawn. "You, brother, may need love more than you need sleep, but not me. If no one minds, I think I'll take advantage of that tent. Is there a bed in there?" He addressed this last question to Toby, who was coming down the hill.

"Might of known one of you youngsters would turn up," he grumbled. "Come on, I'll get you some grub and see you get a bed."

As Jamie walked past them he winked at Maddie.

Maddie sat still, holding Laurel, her head back against 'Ring.

"No lecture? No anger at me for leaving you?"

"None," she said. "I'm just glad that you're safe, that's all."

"No questions about how my brother came to be here? Nothing?"

She adjusted Laurel in her arms. "Tomorrow I shall sing for you. Just you."

He tightened his arms around her, and for a moment they sat in the growing darkness without saying a word.

"Did you wait here by these trees for me while I was gone?" he whispered.

"I was scared the whole time you were away."

He kissed her neck. "Your hellion of a little sister was perfectly safe. The men had left her in the care of an old woman in a falling-down cabin in the mountains. They thought she was a city-bred child and that she'd be terrified by the woods."

Maddie gave a snort. "Not Jefferson Worth's daughter."

"True. When Jamie and I got there, she'd escaped the old woman and two men were tracking her. She was difficult to find."

"She would be," Maddie said with pride. "Did Hears Good follow you?"

"I think so. We never saw any sign of him, but a couple of times I thought I heard him."

"Then he meant for you to hear him."

"Maybe so. Anyway, Jamie and I found her."

"And she didn't want to go with you?" Maddie was beginning to smile, now that she knew that both of them were safe.

"A dragon," 'Ring said with some awe in his voice. "I don't think I've ever seen anyone fight so hard. I was truly tempted to wring her little neck."

"I'm glad you didn't. Now, I think we should get her to bed. I think both of you are exhausted."

'Ring started to say that he wasn't, but he was nodding off asleep as he rested against her. Neither he nor Jamie had had much sleep in the past few days. "Maybe you're right."

It was a bit of a struggle getting all of them up and walking toward the tent. 'Ring started to take Laurel, but Maddie insisted on carrying her, so 'Ring put his arm around Maddie's shoulders and they walked back to the tent together.

Toby had already made Edith spread blankets on the floor of the tent for 'Ring and Laurel to sleep on. Jamie lay on the cot, sprawled just as 'Ring had done a few days before.

"I'll get him out of here," 'Ring said.

"No, let him sleep. He can have the cot. I just wish that I had a couple more for you and Laurel."

'Ring was too tired to argue with her. He looked at the blankets spread on the floor and the next minute he was lying down and asleep. Maddie lowered Laurel onto another blanket, and for a long moment looked down at her sleeping face. Only a child could sleep through all she'd been through in the last few hours. She kissed her sister's forehead, saw that she was covered, then blew out the lantern and left the tent.

Toby was waiting outside for her. "They all right?"

She smiled at him. "Fine. Just tired. Any coffee left?"

Toby poured her a cup and handed it to her. "You find out what happened?"

She sat down on the ground by the fire and told him what she knew.

Toby looked at the fire and nodded. "I didn't get much out of that young scamp either," he said.

Maddie smiled at his tone. It was obvious that 'Ring was by far Toby's favorite. "Why was Jamie here?"

Toby shook his head. "I tell you, that family of theirs is strange. Their daddy told me once that sometimes in their family a girl's born that can see things that are gonna happen. Not things that have happened, but things that haven't happened yet."

Maddie held the warm cup in her hand and nodded. "I've heard of it. Sometimes it's called second sight. I can't imagine a fortune-teller in 'Ring's family."

"Oh, they mostly keep it quiet. But whenever there's one of them girls born, they name her Christiana. There's one of them now, lives on the coast, not the Maine coast, but way out west. This one's only a girl, younger than your little sister in there, but she once saved a church full of people from burnin' or somethin', so they know she's got this 'sight.'"

"She knew that something was wrong?"

"It seems that months ago she was playin' with her dolls and she told her mother that her Uncle 'Ring was gonna be in trouble." Toby smiled. "Her mother sent a man all the way across the country to tell the boy's father, and the old man sent the youngster out here to help the boy."

Maddie drank her coffee. "So Jamie found his brother and followed him."

"When we was watchin' you, 'Ring saw the kidnappers followin' you, and he saw the Injun, and then he saw somebody else, couldn't figure out how he fit into it all."

"And that was Jamie."

"Yeah."

She shook her head. "So Jamie saw the two of us handcuffed together and decided to play robber, no, highwayman, and take 'Ring's horse and other goods." She was silent for a moment, thinking of all that 'Ring had known and she hadn't. No wonder he had been so calm when the man took his horse; no wonder he hadn't wanted to go after that precious horse of his. He knew it was safe with his brother. 'Ring had also known that they were safe as they camped for three days, since his brother was keeping watch over them. And also, 'Ring had had a key to the handcuffs all the while.

She thought of the way he smirked at her when she'd been so afraid for him when he wanted to go after the robber. She thought of the fistfight they had pretended to have. 'Ring had known that she was not far from the camp and had been listening. She remembered being puzzled by the fact that she could not find any marks on him after his fight.

She stood and looked down at Toby. Maybe she should be angry, but she wasn't. Whatever he'd done, he had returned Laurel to her. "I'm going to bed," she said, then turned and went inside the tent. She slipped into 'Ring's arms and, in his sleep, he drew her to him. Maddie pulled Laurel to her and went to sleep.

"Are you all right?" Maddie asked Laurel the next morning. They were alone in the tent, both of them sitting on the cot. "And don't lie to me. I want the truth."

Laurel told of her experiences in a string of curse words and exclamations that, had Maddie been another woman, might have horrified her. But Maddie knew how Laurel had grown up. It wasn't until Maddie had been away from her father and his friends, not until she'd been in the opera world for some time, that she realized what an unconventional childhood she had had. Her family had been isolated from other people, and her friends had been old mountain men. Instead of learning sewing and how to pour tea, like most young ladies, she'd learned to dress out a buffalo, to trap beaver, and how to bead buckskin. When she started to sing professionally, she realized that the only songs she knew were opera arias and a few filthy little ditties that Bailey had taught her. She could survive in the wilderness on her own but, before she met John, she couldn't tell silk from canvas.

Maddie smiled at her little sister and brushed her hair out of her eyes. "I was worried about you."

Laurel looked at her sister with some awe. She didn't remember her older, famous sister very well from the few short years that they had spent together before Maddie left, but Laurel had kept scrapbooks of everything that she could get about Maddie. There were posters and clippings and pressed flowers and every letter that Maddie had sent her.

"They said that you needed me," Laurel said. "I went to the men because they said that you'd had bad medicine."

Maddie smiled, for Laurel's words took her aback.

"I was froze fer you and that's why I went with them," Laurel said softly, her heart in her eyes.

Maddie smiled and took her little sister's hands in hers. "I was froze fer you too, but I couldn't get there." She touched her sister's cheek again and realized how much "civilization" had changed her. In the civilized world, people didn't admit that they were longing for someone else, or "froze fer," as Laurel called it. No, in the civilized world people hid their feelings or lied about them. And when they were told that someone needed them, or, as Laurel said, had bad medicine, bad luck, they didn't just drop everything to go help them.

"I went with them," Laurel said, her mouth in a tight line. "The man was a damned sky pilot, but he gave me some high wine and I went to sleep." She looked at Maddie. "But he got his. He took a pill and dropped his robe."

Maddie's eyes widened. A man pretending to be a preacher had taken Laurel and drugged her, but it seemed that he had been shot and had died. "Did you kill him?"

"Naw, some vide-poche did it."

Maddie was glad to hear that one of the other bad men and not Laurel had killed the kidnapper. She hugged her little sister. "I'm just glad that you're safe. You seemed to have given 'Ring a hard time."

Laurel pulled away to look at her sister. "He thought I'd believe him when he showed up at that house. Just expected me to go with him, like he was God Almighty Hisself."

Maddie had to pull Laurel to her to keep her sister from seeing her smile. She could imagine 'Ring telling Laurel what to do and how to do it, just as he'd first told Maddie what she was to do. "He tends to be like that," Maddie said, "but I have hopes that he will learn. Were the kidnappers bad to you? Did they harm you?"

"They tried to scare me, but I put a little buffalo tea in their food and that kept them away from me."

Maddie frowned. It was one thing to be brave, but another to be dumb, and putting urine in the food of kidnappers was definitely dumb. "Laurel, I think—"

Laurel recognized the tone of an impending lecture when she heard it. "Speakin' of buffalo tea, you got any food? I'm so wolfish I could eat whangs," she said, speaking of the fringe on a mountain man's garment.

Maddie laughed. Her sister was fine, and even from the little of what she'd heard, she was beginning to pity the poor kidnappers. They were no doubt merely hired men, just as the man she'd often met in the woods said that he was, and they'd had no idea how to deal with a twelve-year-old hellion who put urine in their food.

"Go on, go eat," Maddie said, then, as Laurel started to leave, she caught her hand. "When you're talking to the others, try to keep it clean. Otherwise they won't understand you and you'll shock them."

Laurel's mouth turned into a grim line. "That . . . that man of yours, he . . ."

"What did 'Ring do?"

"He turned me over his knee, that's what."

Maddie had to bite the inside of her mouth to keep from laughing. Her father had threatened to do just that whenever his daughters cursed, but he was much too soft-hearted and had never once been able to strike them. Their mother had not been so inclined though. "Just pretend you're talking to Mother."

Laurel nodded. "I figured that out. What kind of men are these easterners? Are they *men?*"

"Yes," Maddie answered. "They're men. Go on, get something to eat." As Maddie watched her little sister leave the tent, it occurred to her that perhaps the reason she'd never been interested in the men in Europe was because they didn't seem like men to her.

She stood and brushed off her skirt. Yes, the eastern men were men, different from the men she'd known as a child, but definitely men.

Later in the morning Laurel told Maddie that she did not want to return to the East, that she wanted to go home to her parents.

'Ring looked at the child and said, "It will be a while before I can escort you. But I'll take you as soon as I can."

Before Maddie could open her mouth, Laurel spat at 'Ring. "You! Who needs you to take me anywhere? I can go on my own."

Maddie started to interfere in this argument until she realized that her inclination was to protect 'Ring.

'Ring looked a bit bewildered by Laurel's attack. "I only meant—"

"You meant just what you said. Why, you—" Laurel broke off at a look of warning from Maddie. "We don't need you, do we, Maddie? We can go on our own." Laurel's chin came up. "Besides, we have Hears Good."

'Ring snorted. "He just watches. He never helps directly. Besides, I'm beginning to believe that he doesn't exist. I think he's a figment of your and your sister's imaginations."

Laurel looked as though she were ready to chew nails, and Maddie had to cover her mouth to keep from laughing. Her little sister had no idea that 'Ring was teasing her and enjoying her sputtering.

Laurel looked at the trees and said loudly, "I need you."

Maddie was curious whether Hears Good would show himself when given such a direct request. She had no doubt that he was near enough to hear them, for Hears Good had always been very curious and had always found the arguments between white people to be endlessly fascinating.

Laurel stood there with her arms folded across her chest and her foot tapping, while 'Ring made exaggerated motions of scanning the trees.

"I don't see your phantom Indian," he said.

Maddie could see Laurel beginning to lose her confidence in the appearance of her friend, and Maddie wished that Hears Good would show himself. She gave a whistle and waited.

Just as she'd begun to think that Hears Good was not going to show himself, he stepped from the trees—and all eyes were on him.

There is nothing, absolutely *nothing* on the earth more magnificent than a Crow warrior in his prime—and Hears Good was that: handsome, tall, proportioned as man was meant to be proportioned, skin the color of the earth, and he carried himself with the knowledge of what he was.

Maddie did not go to him, did not speak or touch him, not when he was being a warrior. As a child she and her sister and Hears Good's children had crawled all over him, had teased him and played tricks on him, but not when he was being a warrior; then they stood back and looked at him in awe—as 'Ring, Jamie, and Toby behind him were doing now.

As quickly as he appeared, Hears Good slipped back into the forest.

It was a moment before Laurel spoke. "There.

Does that suit you? Do you think *he* can take us back to my home?"

'Ring wasn't listening to her. He turned to his brother and they smiled at each other. It was as though they had seen a childhood legend come alive and they weren't sure that they yet believed it.

Jamie went to his brother and put his arm around 'Ring's shoulders. "I get to be Hears Good next time," he said, using a phrase that was obviously one he'd used often as a boy.

"Only if I get to be Jefferson Worth," 'Ring replied.

Laurel looked at Maddie. "What are they talking about?"

Maddie laughed. "Boys," she said. "They are being boys."

"They still askin' her questions?" Toby asked as he squatted by the fire and ate another helping of bacon.

Maddie yawned and nodded. Right after Hears Good's appearance, 'Ring and his brother had called Laurel into the tent and, since then, they had been in there asking her questions about where she had been held and why. At first Maddie had been protective of her little sister, but then she'd realized that Laurel was enjoying having the full attention of the two handsome men—even if she was more than a little cool to 'Ring. Maddie could see that her sister especially liked the blue-eyed Jamie, and Jamie gave the child very grown-up looks.

As Maddie was leaving the tent, she passed Jamie, bent over, and whispered, "You hurt my little sister and I'll break more than your heart."

Jamie laughed as Maddie left the tent.

Now Maddie felt like singing, and she realized that in the past few days she had not wanted to sing. It was the first time she could remember in her life that she hadn't wanted to sing. But now she wanted to sing and she wanted to sing for 'Ring.

"Didn't the miners say that they'd brought the piano up here and put it in a building?" she asked Toby.

"It's up there on the hill. It was just a lean-to, but they put a roof of sorts on it and a front wall."

"Good," she answered, and started up the hill. It was just a small place, hardly big enough for the piano and a chair, but it would do. She smiled as she thought of 'Ring's coming reaction to her singing. It was one thing to hear an opera singer on a stage and quite a different thing to hear her in a small room.

It didn't take her long to arrange with Frank to play for her in the afternoon. Edith made them lunch of fried ham and biscuits. Maddie wanted to talk to Laurel, but she seemed interested only in Jamie and kept watching him. Maddie narrowed her eyes in warning at Jamie, and he lifted his hands in a gesture of innocence.

At last Maddie stood. "I'm going to have a lesson now," she said as though it meant nothing. "Perhaps, 'Ring, you'd like to join me."

He smiled. "I might like to do that," he said, and followed her up the hill to the little cabin.

Inside the cabin he closed the door behind them, she walked to the piano, then turned to Frank, who was already seated at the keyboard. "'Ah, fors' è lui,' please," she said softly.

'Ring sat down in the chair she had placed opposite the piano and smiled at her. The lovely aria from *La Traviata* was already one of his favorites, and he'd heard her sing it twice before. Yet, for all the times he'd heard Maddie sing, he'd never been alone in a small room with a voice such as hers. When heard on a stage one realizes that it takes a powerful voice to be heard to the last seat, but it is difficult to understand the full depth, the full power of an opera singer's voice when sitting in an audience of a hundred or so people.

At first 'Ring merely enjoyed the music as Maddie sang about whether or not she should love Alfredo. But when she got to the part where she was singing of how perhaps their souls were meant for each other, he opened his eyes a little wider. Her voice, partly from talent, partly from training, came from inside her chest, deep, deep down within her. When she sang *follia,* Italian for "it's madness," the sheer volume of her voice made his chair begin to vibrate and with it, his body.

She sang of the burning flame of love, of a love that was mysterious and unattainable, the torment and delight of her heart.

It was on the exquisite trill of *gioir*, "Enjoy myself," that he sat up in his chair and looked at her. He'd never seen anything as beautiful in his life as this woman. He knew that he loved her, had loved her for some time now, but now he was looking at her differently, not as a person, but as an incredibly desirable female.

Frank surprised 'Ring as he made an attempt to sing Alfredo's part as he stood outside Violetta's window and sang that love is the pulse of the whole world.

It was Maddie's trills on her first reply to Alfredo that made 'Ring begin to shake. It was a slow inner tremor that spread from the core of his body until it reached his limbs. He held on to the chair as though he might come apart if he didn't.

Maddie saw the blood drain from 'Ring's face and knew she had a very special audience. Crystal-clear she sang the notes, and her A flats were perfection.

At the second set of trills, 'Ring began to sweat. Her voice surrounded him, went through him, and when she sang of fluttering from pleasure to pleasure, he felt the words as well as her voice.

It was at the end, at those final magnificent high C's that he looked at her. He started at her feet and moved up.

When Maddie saw his eyes on her body, she, too, began to tremble, for it didn't take much knowledge to see that what she saw in 'Ring's eyes was lust. At the moment it didn't matter that she didn't know whether the lust was for her or for her voice. It mattered only that it existed.

Before the last note died, somehow 'Ring managed to make his way out of the cabin. He shut the door behind him and leaned against the wall and tried to get a cigar from inside his shirt pocket.

"There you are," Toby said. "I was lookin' for you and then I heard the caterwaulin' and I knew where you'd be. You all right?"

"I . . ." 'Ring whispered.

Toby immediately went into action. He put his hands on 'Ring's chest and guided him to a tree stump to sit down. When 'Ring kept fumbling at his shirt, Toby removed a cigar, lit it, then handed it to 'Ring, but 'Ring was shaking so much he could hardly hold it.

"What's wrong with you?" Toby demanded.

"I think I've just visited the Garden of Eden," 'Ring said.

"Huh?"

"Eaten of the Tree of Knowledge."

Toby still didn't understand, so when Jamie walked up he grabbed him. "Can you make any sense of him?"

They stood there looking at 'Ring, sitting on the stump, still shaking, doing his best to smoke the cigar to calm himself.

"Says he's been to the Garden of Eden, eaten some fruit."

At that moment Maddie opened the door. She took one look at 'Ring and sneered at him. "How dare you leave the room while I'm singing," she said, and slammed the door, then angrily started walking down the hill toward the tent.

'Ring looked around Toby and watched her walk: full hips, a tiny, corseted waist. She turned and he saw her profile of breasts in front, a curvy backside.

Toby looked from 'Ring to Maddie then back at Jamie. "I'll be damned," Toby whispered. "He's been struck at last." Grinning, he pulled 'Ring off the stump and pushed him toward Maddie. "Go talk to her," he said, laughing. "Bring her back up here. I'll see that ever'body's out a your way."

'Ring managed to make his legs work long enough to get down the hill to her tent, but his hand was shaking so badly that he could hardly pull the flap to her tent back. He was only halfway inside when what looked to be a picture frame came sailing past his head. He slipped inside the tent and the flap closed behind him.

"How dare you?" Maddie screamed. "How dare you leave before I finish singing?" She grabbed a small jar of face cream and threw it at him.

'Ring caught it and started walking toward her.

"I am waiting for your explanation." When he didn't say a word but just kept slowly moving toward her, she grabbed a perfume bottle from the top of the trunk and tossed it. He caught it in his right hand.

When he reached her, he stretched both his arms around her, set the objects on the trunk

332

behind her, then stood for a moment, looking at her.

It was when she looked into his eyes that she saw what he was feeling, and her heart leaped to her throat. She'd seen something of this look in men's eyes before, but nothing anywhere near the intensity of this. He had never frightened her before, but this wild-eyed man did frighten her somewhat.

"'Ring, I—" she began, but he didn't answer her. Where was the civilized, controlled man she'd spent three days with on the mountain? This man was neither civilized nor controlled.

Before she could think, he tossed her over his shoulder and carried her out of the tent. Jamie, Toby, Edith, Frank and Sam, and Laurel were all outside, not to mention about twenty miners. She closed her eyes against seeing them, for she sensed that it was no use trying to talk to this man who carried her. This man was not the man she knew.

He carried her up the hill to the cabin, shut the door behind them, set her on her feet, and looked at her with eyes that were burning with intensity.

"'Ring, you know, I think I forgot to do something. Maybe I should—"

He caught her in his arms as she started toward the door. As he held her, his hands moved down the back of her until he encountered the curve of her fanny, and he clasped the roundness.

Maddie held still a moment, her eyes wide, then

she looked up at him. His eyes were not only darker, his breathing different.

Slowly, he lowered his mouth to hers and lightly kissed her.

He had kissed her before, but this was different. Now there was an intensity there that she'd not felt before. She blinked at him, then swallowed and backed out of his arms. "I think I, ah, I need to talk to Laurel."

He took a step toward her.

She put her hand on the door. "I think I heard someone calling me."

'Ring reached over her head and dropped the latch on the door so that no one could get in.

Maddie backed toward the piano and he followed her. "Did you see that your horse is being taken care of? You know how the animal eats everything. I would hate for him—"

He backed her into a corner, put his hands on either side of the wall by her head, leaned forward and kissed her, long and softly. When Maddie started to melt toward the floor, 'Ring caught her by the waist and pulled her close to his body. When he released her mouth, she looked away from him, her breath coming in short gasps. Nothing ever had made her feel quite like this. She looked up at him, her body growing hot just at the sight of the intensity on his face. "I . . . I don't know what to do," she whispered.

"I don't know all that much either," he whispered. "But I'd sure like to learn."

She gave him a weak smile. "Maybe we should hire teachers."

His hands started working with the many tiny buttons at the back of her dress, and he gently kissed her neck, her cheek, her eyes. "I'll teach you if you'll teach me."

"Yes," she whispered, her fear beginning to disappear. "Oh, yes."

"Maddie, I . . ." he said, and she could feel his fingers trembling on her dress.

She wasn't sure what happened next. The buttons wouldn't easily come unfastened, so he gave a pull and the fabric tore away, the dress landing in a puddle about her feet.

He kissed her again, this time not so gently. He spared one hand to turn her head sideways and she opened her mouth under his. She didn't know which of them groaned, but it was a B flat.

She didn't even feel her other clothes fall away, but within minutes everything lay at her feet and she stood in the circle of his arms, wearing only her stockings, caught with lacy garters at her knees, and her heeled shoes.

He held her hands, stepped away, and looked at her. The little cabin was dimly lit from a single window, making the light in the room golden.

Maddie felt her body blushing under his look, but he put his fingers under her chin and lifted her face. "You're as beautiful as your voice," he said.

High praise, she thought, the very highest praise. "I want to see you," she whispered.

'Ring ran a trembling hand down her shoulder to the curve of her breast, then downward to her waist, moving his fingers over the flat softness of her belly. Finally, he looked back at her eyes and gave her a crooked smile. "Men aren't half as interesting-looking as women."

She put her hand to his chest, eased one button loose and slipped her hand inside, feeling the hair on his chest, the warm skin, the shape of his hard muscles. Slowly, she unfastened one button after another, put both her hands inside his shirt, and eased it off his shoulders. As she did so she looked up at him and saw that there was passion on his face, but there was something else too. Something akin to wonder. From what she knew of him, she knew that there hadn't been a lot of women in his life and she knew that all this was almost as new to him as it was to her. This thought sent a new thrill through her. She had always imagined that she'd someday love a man who knew all the arts of lovemaking, a man who'd take her to bed and teach her everything—she'd certainly had enough men offer to do just that for her. But she sensed that 'Ring was a student as much as she was, and somehow this pleased her very much. Perhaps it was the difference between being given a gift of a new pair of shoes or a pair that had been worn by many other people.

She put her arms around his chest, felt her breasts against his skin.

He held her tightly to him. "I never imagined," he said softly against her hair. "I never had any idea what they were talking about. Toby said that this was something that a man *had* to have."

He began to tremble again, then he held her away from him and looked down at her, his eyes dark. "I don't want to hurt you, but I do feel a, well, a sense of urgency."

She laughed. "Hurt me?" she said, laughing, then bit his chest. "Hurt me? I'd like to see you try." She bit him a couple of more times before he allowed his lust to overtake him.

Years of suppressed passion exploded within him. Years of looking but not seeing; years of wanting but denying; years of loneliness came to the surface.

At first Maddie smiled as he eagerly began to kiss her body, bending down to her, his hands at the small of her back, pressing her bare legs against the rough wool of his trousers, his belt buckle gouging into her soft belly, but when his mouth fastened onto her breast, she stopped smiling. Her eyes opened wide, then she gave a little moan and leaned back against his arms, allowing him to support her full weight.

He pushed her against the wall, holding her in place with one hand against her shoulder while he used his mouth and free hand to explore her body.

"How beautiful you are," he murmured, his mouth on her hip. "How very interesting."

"So glad I please you," she managed to whisper.

He held her upright with his hand on her stomach while he ran his mouth down her legs, rolling down each garter as he went, then tossing her shoes aside. He finally came back up to her mouth. "You have fine soft hair on your legs," he said, sounding like a scientist observing a different form of wildlife.

She could just blink at him as she put her arms about his neck.

"Oh, 'Ring, make love to me," she whispered.

"As soon as I finish playing the overture," he said against her lips, making her smile, then he turned her around. "Let's see the back of you."

He held her against the wall as he ran his hands over the back of her, kissing her down her spine, around her buttocks, then down the backs of her legs. When he reached her heels he nipped at them, making her squeal with pleasure and lift first one foot and then the other.

She turned to face him. Her body was hot with wanting him, and she'd had enough of his power over her. She wanted a little power of her own. She slipped away from his grasp when he reached for her.

"Maddie," he said, his voice full of yearning, his hands out.

When he looked at her like that she knew she would be able to deny him nothing. "Off," she said, pointing to his trousers.

He grinned. "Mustn't disappoint a lady."

She watched as he sat on the floor and pulled his calf-high boots off, then stood again and slipped his trousers and knit underwear down to his ankles and easily stepped out of them.

Maddie stood back against the wall and took

her time looking at him. Having grown up around mountain men and Indians, she'd often seen men wearing nothing but breech cloths, but somehow 'Ring was more magnificent than they were. And in the middle of his body was rampant evidence of his desire for her.

She looked back at his face. "Is all that for little ol' me?" she asked, and was very pleased to see him blush all the way to his shoulders.

"Come here," he growled, reaching for her, but Maddie ran a few steps to escape him.

'Ring stood where he was, his mouth agape as he saw parts of her jiggle.

Maddie suddenly felt very powerful, for it was she who had absolute control of this magnificent man. She opened her mouth and sang the second set of trills from *"Ah, fors' è lui."*

'Ring was on top of her in a second. All two hundred pounds of him hit her and knocked her to the floor—and his aim was perfect. His mouth hit hers precisely, and all his maleness entered her femaleness in one smooth move. Out of instinct her legs went around his waist as he began to move within her. At first he was slow, slow and deep, but within seconds, as she lifted her hips to him, he began to move deeply and quickly—and Maddie met his every move.

She wasn't aware they were scooting along the floor until her head hit the wall. Her neck bent and her shoulders began to slide upward, and 'Ring's mouth made contact with her breast. In his urgency he sucked a little too hard, a little too painfully, and Maddie cried out. Her legs locked even tighter about his waist.

When she was bent nearly double by the wall, 'Ring tightened his arms around her waist and lifted her, never losing their connection, then stood up with her clasped about him. He took a step toward the piano, but then he paused. She opened her eyes to look at him, saw he seemed to be considering something.

She wiggled against him, and he closed his eyes, and the next moment she found her back against the wall. She held on for dear life as he began to move again. Excitement began to build and build in her as her nails dug into his back and her ankles locked, holding him close.

"Yes," she said, and took his earlobe in her teeth. "Yes." She stuck her tongue in his ear and he slammed into her with such blinding force, that for a second she couldn't see as she saw bright white light and her body rocked in tremors.

It was minutes later that she was able to breathe again, and she could feel 'Ring's heart thudding against her breast.

He took a few steps backward with Maddie locked around him, then he knelt with her, pried her legs from his waist, smiled at Maddie's groan when their connection was broken, then lay down on the floor, Maddie held securely to him.

"I didn't know," she whispered as she lay with her head on his shoulder, her fingers twining in the hair on his chest. He didn't say anything, so she rose on one elbow and looked at him. She ran her fingertip over the frown lines in his forehead. "What is making you frown?"

He kissed her fingertip and held her hand against his chest, then looked at her. "I understand now what drives men. I understand what my father was talking about."

"Your father talked to you about women?" She snuggled her head back against his shoulder, thinking how well they fit together.

"Tried to." Suddenly he hugged her so tightly she almost cried out. "Maddie, my beautiful LaReina, I would like to give you as much as you've given me. First your voice and now this." He ran his hand down her arm.

She stretched luxuriously, moving her legs by his. "You've given me Laurel."

"That wasn't enough to repay you for this."

She laughed. "What if I told you I wanted the moon?"

"I'd give it to you."

She rose up on her elbow to look at him. "And what do you want in return?"

"All of you. Every bit of you," he said as he kissed her.

"There's a lot of me."

He looked down at her breast. "I think I can handle all you have."

"With what?" she said, looking down at his legs.

"I'll teach you . . ." he said, and grabbed for her as Maddie squealed and tried to get away from him.

She didn't succeed.

Laurel sat by the campfire near Toby. The sun was going down and it was growing cool. She looked over her shoulder, up the hill at the old shack where her sister and . . . and that man had been for three days now. Her eyes widened. "Toby, I think that place is shaking."

Toby looked behind him and stared at the shack with interest, then, wisely, he nodded. "Who's got shakin' shack," he said to the miners who were around them.

For several days the miners had gradually been leaving their claims, until now not one man had done any work at the streams for three whole days. Instead, their interest had been given over to the opera singer and what was going on in her life. They had first become interested when Maddie refused to sing and had instead spent her days standing under a tree and looking down the road, rather like a sea captain's widow watching for a man who wasn't going to return.

They had become even more interested when 'Ring and his brother had returned with a sleeping child. They'd gathered around Toby and asked lots of questions. If the woman wasn't going to sing for them, the least she could do was provide them with stories.

Toby had been regaling the men with incredible stories of 'Ring's exploits (and about the minor help he'd received from his "little" brother) when they heard Maddie's singing coming from the cabin. They were very quiet as they listened, then they were astonished to see Captain Montgomery leave the shack, the opera lady leave behind him, and then there was some shouting (*What* a voice the woman had! You could probably hear her ten miles away) then the captain threw the woman over his shoulder and took her back to the shack. Not any of the miners had said a word, just stood there watching that shack.

It was when they heard a female squeal followed by a crash that one of the miners said, "I got twenty bucks that says they don't come out 'fore mornin'."

"You're on," said another man.

It had started out as a simple diversion, but when Edith took breakfast to the opera singer and her man the next morning, and the couple asked her to bring them the jar of rose-scented oil from Maddie's trunk, that's when the betting began in earnest.

They bet on the amount of time that Maddie and 'Ring would stay in the cabin. Since there were so many miners, they had to take bets on the hour that they would emerge. Toby found that young Laurel had had proper training from a man named Bailey and she knew all about odds on betting. Jamie had protested against someone of Laurel's youth and innocence being involved in such a thing as betting on the sexual habits of her sister. He said this even as he put ten dollars down that said his brother couldn't last more than forty-eight hours.

Laurel, for all her youth, knew something about men. She knew that Jamie wanted to get her away from the others so he could drill her with thousands of questions about the kidnappers. She told Jamie that unless he let her handle the bets, she wouldn't answer one question for him. When Toby laughed and said that Laurel had beaten a Montgomery, Laurel began negotiations for how much of the betting proceeds she was to receive from Toby for handling the transactions. Toby said that he'd give her a nickel for each bet that she recorded. Laurel had laughed in his face and started the negotiations at fifty percent. After much haggling, they settled that Laurel was to get thirty percent of whatever Toby made. She answered Jamie's questions while she took bets.

"Shaking cabin," Laurel said, looking at her notebook. "Tim Sullivan." She opened the box (she also took care of the bags of gold dust) and paid the man. "I told you not to take that bet," Laurel whispered to Toby. "You were bound to lose."

"What do you know?" he growled. "You were the one that wanted that five hundred candle bet. And the honey bet. And the bathtub bet."

"Ah, but we made it back when they asked for the milk to put in the tub. Nobody had milk bath."

Jamie lounged against his saddle, his long legs sprawled out in front of him, looked at old Toby and the pretty little Laurel, and shook his head. Two days earlier he'd stopped saying that it wasn't seemly for Laurel to participate in this kind of betting, that she was just a child. He was beginning to think that this "child" was older than he was.

"No more bets, Jamie?" Laurel asked him as she counted the bags of gold dust in her box. She had somewhere obtained a weighing scale to accurately measure the gold that she and Toby took in.

He pushed his hat down over his eyes. "The pride I have in my brother is more than enough reward for me."

"Shhh," Laurel said, and all the men around her became very still, their eyes on the cabin on the hill.

"What is it?" Toby whispered.

Laurel smiled. "That's *Carmen*."

There was immediate confusion as the men began scrambling to reclaim and pay off their bets. They didn't know one opera from another, but Laurel did, and she'd made a list of what Maddie sang. The men had drawn the songs from a hat, then wagered on the corresponding times when they believed she would sing from the opera they had drawn.

There was a loud crash from the cabin and a corresponding shout of triumph from the miners.

Laurel looked at her book. "Fell off the piano for the sixth time," she read. "Caleb Rice."

Caleb grinned as Laurel weighed the gold dust, poured it into a bag, and gave it to him.

"That was your bet," Laurel said to Toby. "I told you not to take it."

"Who woulda thought they was dumb enough to fall off the piana *six* times," he snapped at her.

"Caleb Rice did," Laurel answered calmly.

Jamie got up and left after that, and he vowed that should he ever do what his brother was doing, he would do it in the utmost privacy. He walked to one of the many tents that served the miners as a saloon. Of course, for the last three days the tents had been empty. The men hadn't stopped drinking, but now they bought their bottles of watered-down whiskey and took them back to the campfire where Laurel and Toby sat taking bets.

The man Jamie wanted to see was in the saloon tent. After all, Jamie had given orders that the man was to be given as much whiskey as he could drink. With years and years of experience behind him, Sleb could drink a great deal. He was starting on his third bottle.

"How're they doing?" Sleb asked as he looked up at Jamie. His words weren't slurred, but his eyelids were nearly closed.

"All right," Jamie answered, taking a seat. "They just fell off the piano for the sixth time."

Sleb nodded gravely. "I remember one time backstage in Philadelphia with a pretty little mezzo . . ." His voice trailed off and he shut his eyes in memory.

For a moment Jamie thought that perhaps he'd gone to sleep. "Anything more you have to tell me?" he asked softly.

346

Sleb opened his bloodshot eyes. "Not a thing. I've told you everything I know." He picked up the whiskey bottle and looked at it. "In fact, I don't guess my life is going to be worth much after what I've told you." He gave a derisive snort. "But then, I don't guess it was worth much before I ever met you." He held up the bottle. "Drink?"

"No, thank you." Jamie stood. "I guess I better get back. They might decide to come out of that shack, and I want to be there to talk to my brother when he does. Of course, they're going to need sleep sometime or other."

Sleb gave a dreamy sort of smile. "That time in Philadelphia I went four days without sleep. I was younger then and I thought I was going to be the greatest singer who ever lived." He reached for the bottle again.

Jamie bit his tongue to keep from speaking. He'd never yet met a drunk who didn't think that he was the only one to ever have suffered in his life. Deliver me from the self-pity of drunks, he thought, and left the tent.

'Ring idly ran his hand over Maddie's bare stomach. For three and a half days now his body and its needs had been his only concern. It was as though he'd had no mind at all, like he was an animal and was driven only by lust and longing.

He grinned.

"Share that with me?" Maddie asked, trying to ease her back. They had hit the floor rather hard a few times.

"I was thinking of my father. He'd be proud of me."

"You? Ha! What have you done? *I* am the one who has had to work. *I* am the one who has had to . . ." She trailed off. She was too tired to even argue. "Yeah, I guess he would be proud of you. I'm not sure my father would be proud of me, though." She yawned, then put her hand on his chest. "This has been wonderful but . . ."

"But what? You're not giving up, are you? Why, we've just started. There are several more things I'd like to try." He said this, but he didn't make a move to pounce on her as he would have a day ago.

"I wonder if Jamie has found out anything from your little sister," 'Ring said, looking at the ceiling.

She smiled. "If you're thinking of your brother, then I guess the honeymoon is over. And too bad, because I was thinking of a few more tries at that piano." Even as she said the words, her back began to ache.

Neither of them commented on the other's bragging. They just lay there in each other's arms, now comfortable and familiar with each other's bare skin, and knowing intimately every inch of the other's body.

"You think we should get dressed?" Maddie asked after a while. "Maybe I should see about Laurel. Maybe you should talk to Jamie. Maybe—"

He rolled over so he could look down at her.

"Yes, I think it's time we left. Are you all right? Not too bruised and battered? Too sore?"

"There isn't any part of me that isn't sore," she said, looking up at him. "There isn't any part of me that isn't bruised, but it's been a wonderful few days." Her eyes sparkled. "I think I learned as much in these three days as I did in the first three years with Madame Branchini." She ran her fingertips down his unshaven cheek. "I got to see your upper lip too."

He kissed her softly. "Maddie, I—"

She didn't allow him to finish. She didn't feel there was a need for words. They were two people who had needed each other, needed each other physically and emotionally, and they'd found each other. "I know the way you feel, for I feel the same way. You were right when you said that we had been looking for each other."

He looked down at her bare breasts. "I had certainly been looking for you," he said with a leer.

She laughed and pushed at him. "Help me dress—if there's anything left to my poor dress —and let's go see what's happened to the others."

She was shaky when she stood up, and 'Ring had to steady her. Now that she could think again, she was a little embarrassed as she looked at him, and remembered all the things they had done in the last few days. But they had each felt possessed, and nothing on earth could have stopped them.

He kissed the tip of her nose. "Don't look at me like that. This is just the first of many times together. Turn around and let me tie this contraption of yours."

Smiling, she faced the wall while he pulled her corset strings tight.

It was an hour later that Maddie and 'Ring sat with Toby, Laurel, and Jamie around the campfire. When they had left the shack, Maddie had been embarrassed, knowing that all the people in her camp were going to know what she and 'Ring had been doing for the past few days. But when she opened the door, she saw a perfectly normal camp, with Edith bent over the fire, stirring a pot, Toby and Jamie lounging by the fire, and Laurel writing something in a little notebook. Maddie smiled. If Maddie was a singer and her sister Gemma was a painter, maybe Laurel was going to be a writer.

"Good evening," Maddie said softly, and they all looked up at her.

"Oh, hello," Laurel said, beaming up at her older sister. "Have you two had a nice vacation?"

Maddie was glad for the growing darkness that hid her red face. "Yes, thank you, and have you been well cared for?"

"Oh, yes," Laurel said, eyes wide. "Toby helped me pick wild flowers. I'm pressing them into a book."

"And selling them for a thousand dollars each," Jamie muttered.

"What's that?" 'Ring asked.

Laurel glared at Jamie. "He thinks I should sell my pictures."

"Or take over the management of Warbrooke Shipping," Jamie said under his breath, then, "Ow!" as Laurel leaned over and pinched him.

Laurel smiled at her sister. "You want some coffee?"

Maddie took the cup that Toby handed her, then handed a cup to 'Ring, but 'Ring's attention was fully on his brother.

"Out with it," 'Ring said, taking a seat on a log that had been pulled up near the fire. He didn't notice that the bark was already getting shiny from the many behinds that had used it in the last few days. Maddie took a seat next to him, trying not to grimace with the pain she felt. There were unmentionable parts of her body that were very, very sore. 'Ring felt her stiffen and turned to give her a knowing little smile. She ignored him and looked at Jamie.

"What makes you think your brother has anything to say?" she asked 'Ring, but not looking at him.

"I know him and he's bursting with it. Can't you tell?" 'Ring answered. "Well?"

Jamie couldn't contain his smile any longer. He wanted—and planned—to tell his brother about the wagering that had been going on the past few days, but now he had something much more important to tell him.

"I found out everything."

Maddie drew in her breath. *What* did he know?

Jamie looked at her and seemed to enjoy her embarrassment. "I found out about the letters and your General Yovington."

Maddie's cup stopped on the way to her lips. Laurel was safe and, what with her preoccupation of the last few days, she hadn't thought of the kidnapping. Now all she wanted to do was get out of this country and go back east, where she could sing. After she visited her family and returned Laurel to them, she planned to do just that.

"What about him?" 'Ring asked. "How did you find out? *What* did you find out?"

"While you were, ah . . . otherwise occupied, I had a chance to talk to the brat here." He gave Laurel a look that 'Ring couldn't interrupt. "Her answers to my questions led me to a man called Sleb."

"The man who sang with you," 'Ring said, looking at Maddie.

"Right," Jamie said. "He used to be a pretty good tenor, at least to hear him tell it. But in the last few years he's fallen on hard times."

"A bottle."

"Right."

"So what does this old drunk have to do with Maddie and Laurel?" 'Ring smiled at Laurel. She was such a sweet-looking child. She could be an illustration for an angel, but he knew all too well what a mouth she had on her. He just hoped that Maddie didn't hear her.

"Sleb worked for General Yovington's brother in a town named Desperate."

352

"Heard of that place," Toby said, and the way he said it made 'Ring look at him.

"So's half the baser element of society," Jamie said. "The two Yovington brothers own most of the town and the big gold mine at one end of it."

Maddie hadn't said anything up to this point, but now she spoke. "General Yovington helped me find Laurel."

"The reason he could help you was he was the one who arranged her kidnapping."

Maddie put down her coffee cup and stared at Jamie.

"It seems that the two brothers had invested their life savings in that gold mine, but it yielded nothing."

"Maybe that's why they called the place Desperate," Laurel said, and Toby nodded at her.

"Maybe. I guess their lives did look desperate. They're both in their fifties, with nothing waiting for them to comfort them in their old age. So, a few months ago the brothers got together . . ." He looked at Maddie. "Your general was out here to look over some forts and he got with his brother and heard the news that their gold mine was empty. They decided that if they couldn't get the money legally, they'd get it illegally. For the last couple of years there's been a lot of gold mined out of these mountains and they decided to take that."

"Stealing!" Maddie said. "They meant to take the gold these poor men have worked so hard to get?"

"That they did. The only problem was getting it out of the mountains without arousing suspicion. Gold is heavy, and the miners might, well, notice somebody riding around with hundred-pound saddlebags."

"So they used me to go from town to town."

"Exactly. That big ol' Concord of yours can hold a lot, especially if it's been fitted out with a false bottom as yours has." Jamie paused while the others absorbed this information. He was rather proud of himself for having found out what he had.

"And the letters?" 'Ring asked.

"Blank. The objective was to get Maddie away from the wagon, that's all. The letters were a ruse."

"Money," Maddie said with feeling. "All of this had to do with money. I thought I was doing something, I don't know, political. I thought I was at least being used to help a cause that someone *believed* in. But all I was was a common, everyday thief."

'Ring looked at his brother. "Which one of Maddie's people was in on it? They had to have someone inside."

"Frank," Jamie said softly, "but he won't bother us again."

'Ring nodded, but he didn't ask what had been done to Frank. "Why did they choose Maddie?" he asked. "Any singer, or magician, for that matter would have done just as well. They just needed someone who could travel freely from camp to camp without arousing suspicion."

Jamie grinned. "It seems that the general's brother loves opera. Apparently, opera is his major interest in life." He looked at Maddie in wonder.

She nodded at him. She had often met people like the general's brother. Men with stars in their eyes when they looked at her.

Jamie shook his head in disbelief. "You should hear about this town Desperate. It's full of criminals. It's backed up against a mountain and there's only one way in and one way out, across a narrow land bridge. And Yovington's brother runs the place like his own little fiefdom, hangs any man who crosses him. Men say they'd rather be hung than—"

"Hanged," Maddie and 'Ring said in unison.

Jamie rolled his eyes as though to say Spare me from lovers. "Whatever. Nobody in his right mind wants to go there."

Jamie smiled. "But the oddest thing in the town is this man Yovington's love of opera. He heard that Sleb was once a singer onstage and that he'd been an opera teacher before the drink got him, so Yovington shanghaied Sleb to train singers for him. Pays ol' Sleb in whiskey."

"I've never heard of another singer in this part of the country."

"None whose name you remember anyway," 'Ring said just so she could hear.

Jamie laughed. "There are none, but Yovington

gets ol' Sleb to train . . ." He glanced at Laurel. "Sleb trains ladies of the evening."

"Oh, whores," Laurel said, nodding.

All three men looked at Maddie as though in condemnation. Maddie shrugged. "Bailey." She looked back at Jamie. "These women couldn't have been very good."

"Horrible. Dreadful. Sleb says that cats have better voices than these women."

Maddie ignored 'Ring's knowing smile.

Jamie continued. "But Yovington said he had a real good imagination, so he had these women following him around wherever he went. Sleb said the men could stand Yovington's hangings and they could stand the cold and the loneliness, but they could *not* stand the singing of those women. Every three months or so the men would run the woman off and that would give them some peace before Sleb could train another one."

"And that's why he kidnapped Laurel?"

"I guess he thought he could kill two birds with one stone, one golden stone, that is. Sleb thinks that when you got to the end and had sung in all six towns and the kidnappers hadn't returned your sister, Yovington was going to send you a message saying that he'd found your little sister and would you please come to Desperate and get her." Jamie looked at Maddie. "I'm not sure he meant to release you after he had you. Sleb thinks he meant to return Laurel to you only if you married him."

"Marriage?" Maddie said, horror in her voice.

356

'Ring smiled at her. "I've heard of worse ideas."

Maddie looked away, hiding her red face.

"We'll leave in the morning," 'Ring said to his brother, and Jamie nodded.

"Leave for where?" Laurel asked.

"It's my guess they mean to make heroes of themselves," Toby said, and his tone told what he thought of the idea.

Neither Jamie nor 'Ring said a word.

"'Ring," Maddie said softly. "Where are you going?"

"To Desperate, of course."

Immediately, her heart began to pound, but then she tried to calm herself. Her mother had always said that there was nothing so unreasonable as a man who had his mind made up. "*Why* are you going to Desperate?"

"Unfinished business."

She started to raise her cup to her lips, but her hands were shaking too badly. "Guns," she whispered. "You mean to go in there with guns. You mean to do some killing. You mean to get yourself killed."

"I have no such intention," he said indignantly. "I mean to take Yovington off his mountain and see that he's brought to trial for what he's done."

"It isn't any of your business. You should leave this to . . . to people in authority."

"And who would that be?"

"I don't know. The army. Yes, that's it, take your army up there."

He gave her one of those indulgent smiles that

men seem born knowing how to do. "This has nothing to do with the army, and, besides, the army assigned me the job of taking care of you and it's you who Yovington has hurt the most."

She stood up and looked down at him. "Yes, it's me who the man has hurt the most, and it seems that it's my right to say what I want. I have Laurel back now, and that's all I want. Tomorrow you can take me back to my father's house, and we'll leave Laurel there."

He looked up at her. "I have to go after Yovington."

"You have to have revenge, that's what. That's all this is, revenge, nothing else."

He caught her hand in his. "No, it's not revenge, it's something that I have to do."

She looked down at him and knew that there was nothing that she could say that was going to change his mind, and she suddenly saw what love really was, that it was accepting a person as he *was*. Not trying to change him into what you wanted him to be, but accepting him just as he was. He was a man who took his responsibilities seriously, a man of honor who would do whatever he thought needed to be done, regardless of any danger to himself.

She blinked back tears of fear as she looked down at him and squeezed his hand in hers.

He smiled at her, then pulled her to sit on the log beside her.

"What happens now with you two?" Jamie asked, trying to lighten the mood. He asked as though the answer were a foregone conclusion. Women may hate to talk about justice, but it was his experience that they loved to talk of marriage.

'Ring smiled. "Oh, the usual thing with lovers, I guess. You and I are going to see what we can do with the kidnappers, and when I return Maddie and I will be married at the fort." He looked at her. "I guess you'll make an honest man out of me, won't you? You weren't taking advantage of me in the last few days, were you?"

Maddie was too upset by his pronouncement that he was going off to wage a minor war to give him her full attention. She looked at her coffee cup and nodded. It wasn't the marriage proposal she'd hoped for, but after what they'd done the past few days, she had expected him to marry her. If nothing else, he was an honorable man, she thought with some anger, and blinked away more tears.

Toby looked from one Montgomery to the other, then at Maddie. "Where you two gonna live?" he asked softly.

"In Paris," Laurel said with wonder in her voice. "Bailey has told me all about Paris."

Maddie opened her mouth to speak. An opera singer lived all over the world. But before she could say a word, 'Ring answered for her.

"We'll live in Warbrooke, of course." He winked at Laurel. "We'll visit Paris and maybe you can go with us, but I have a business to run, so we'll have to live in Warbrooke." He turned to Maddie. "You'll love it there. It's on the sea and it's beautiful."

Maddie was quiet for a moment. "Where do I sing?"

He reached for her hand, squeezed it, then released it. "I'll build you the most magnificent theater you've ever seen."

Her voice was very soft. "With plush seats?"

"Whatever you want. If you want silk brocade, I'll buy it for you."

"And a gilt ceiling?"

"Of course. I'll hire some craftsmen from Italy to carve cherubs on the ceiling. Sweetheart, it'll be the most beautiful theater in America." He looked at Jamie. "Hell, we'll make it the most beautiful theater in the world."

"And who will hear me?" Maddie asked.

He smiled at her. "Anybody you want. I don't think you have yet to realize what kind of family you're marrying into. You want the President there? We'll have him come up." He smiled broader. "We could have your cousin, the king of Lanconia, visit."

Maddie didn't smile. Her eyes were very serious. "Will you pay them to applaud me? Will you buy flowers for them to toss at my feet? Will you buy me diamonds after each of my performances? Or will you just toss me a tidbit as you would a trained dog?"

'Ring's face lost its laughter. "Wait just a minute. You're taking this the wrong way. I don't think of you as a trained dog. You're the woman I love and I want to make you happy."

"By buying me?"

'Ring looked at Toby and Jamie, and a wide-eyed Laurel who was watching them. "Maybe we ought to talk about this in private."

"Why? So you can touch me and make me forget the good sense that I was born with? No, I think we should talk about this here and now and in front of witnesses. I am *not* going to spend the rest of my life in some isolated community where I sing only for you and your relatives. Oh, yes, and for whoever you pay to hear me sing."

"That is not what I meant at all. You weren't listening to me."

She set her coffee cup down and stood. "No, you are the one who wasn't listening to me. Either you weren't listening or you don't actually understand about my voice. I am one of the best singers in the world. I am one of the best singers who has ever lived."

'Ring forgot about the people around them. "Sometimes your vanity surpasses itself."

She turned to him, her face intense. "No, you don't understand. Not *really* understand. I don't think that I'm the most beautiful woman who ever lived. I'm really only average-looking. I'm not the most intelligent, and, as you point out rather frequently, I'm not the most well educated. I'm not one of those women who inspires love from all she meets. True, men have wanted me, usually for my voice, but I have never—at least not until I met you—had anyone love me who wasn't related to me or wasn't a friend of my father's, not really

361

love me. And I have never had a woman friend in my life."

"What does this have to do with us . . . and where you sing?"

"This has everything to do with my voice. My voice is what I do have. I don't have brains or beauty or a particularly good character, but I do have the best voice of anyone alive today, one of the best voices that has ever been given to a human being. Don't you see? I have to *use* what I have. You have an obligation to go back to Maine and help your father run that company of yours because you're good at business. I have an obligation to share my voice."

He gave her a patronizing smile. "There's a great deal of difference between a 'company' the size of Warbrooke Shipping and performing in operas. I don't think you realize how big Warbrooke Shipping is. We are the transporters of the world."

She nearly sneered at him. "Do you print that on your stationery?"

He looked away. The motto wasn't on stationery, but it was on several plaques about the office.

She took a deep breath, trying to calm herself. He *must* understand. "I'm sure that you help a lot of people. But, truthfully, if your family didn't own the ships that people sail in, then someone else would. I, on the other hand, with my voice, am irreplaceable. No one can take my place. No one on earth can do what I do as well as I do it."

"You're wrong if you think just anyone could

run a business the size of Warbrooke Shipping. My family has owned the business for over a hundred years. We're trained to run it from the time we're children. Each son— Where are you going?"

"You're not making any attempt to listen to me. You have your mind made up that what you do is important and what I do isn't important, and you're not going to listen to what I have to say. I see no reason to discuss this further."

He was on his feet instantly and caught her arm. "You can't just walk away. Don't you realize that this is our life you're talking about? If you don't live with me in Warbrooke, what's going to happen to us?"

Her voice and face were very calm when she spoke. "What are *we* going to do if *I* don't do what *you* want?" She jerked her arm out of his grasp.

"Look at you," she said. "I sensed that you had money the moment I first met you. You walk with that air about you, of someone who has always been able to buy whatever he wants. This time you decided you wanted to buy an opera singer. You wanted to buy her a pretty cage in the form of a theater full of plush and gilt and famous people. You wanted to buy her diamonds and silk gowns. And in return, whenever you wanted to hear your little opera singer, all you had to do was look at her and say, 'Sing, little bird,' and she would do so. After all, you had bought and paid for her, hadn't you? She was yours to command as you wanted, just as all those many men who work for you are yours to command."

"You don't understand."

"It's you who doesn't understand."

"What am *I* supposed to do if you want to keep on performing in public?" He made it sound as though she were a strip dancer. "Am I to follow you around from city to city? Hold your cloak? Maybe you'll let me see to the stage sets. Maybe I should have cards printed that give my name as Mr. LaReina. Do I get to be a duke?"

She looked at him and there was sadness in her eyes. "I have never lied to you about what was important to me. I have always told you that my voice is the most important thing in my life."

"I'm not asking you to stop singing," he yelled at her. "You can sing from morning to night for all I care. I *want* you to sing." He stopped shouting. "Maddie, I can't do what you want. I know you think Warbrooke Shipping is just a business, but it's more than that. It's . . . it's tradition. I don't know how to explain it. Tradition is an important part of my family and my family is important to me. The Montgomerys are as important to me as your singing is to you."

She understood very well what he was saying. It was the end. Even though she knew that, she knew that she could not give up what meant life to her to become his pet performer. "I can't do it," she whispered. "I would die. I would shrivel into nothing and die if I had to give up my life in order to receive your love."

"I'm not asking— Oh, hell! Jamie, you talk to her. See if you can make her see reason."

Jamie didn't say a word and 'Ring turned to look at his brother. There was disapproval in Jamie's eyes.

"Don't tell me you *agree* with her?" 'Ring half yelled at his brother.

Jamie's mouth tightened. "It's not as though you were an only child. You have six brothers and, granted, none of us is quite as good as you are at running Warbrooke Shipping, but we manage. In fact, we manage quite well without you."

"I saw the last quarterly reports. I saw how well all six of you have managed without me."

At that Jamie stood, his handsome face distorted with rage, and for a moment it looked as though the two men would come to blows, but Jamie was the first to turn away. He looked at Maddie. "You're better off without him. He's not worthy of you." At that Jamie turned and walked away.

Maddie started to follow him, but 'Ring caught her arm.

"You can't leave now. We have to settle this."

She was trying to hold back tears. "It is settled." She looked up at him and the tears spilled over and ran down her cheeks. "Madame Branchini was right. She said I could be a singer or I could be like other women."

"You are like other women," he said softly. "You need and want love just like every other woman, and, Maddie, I'm offering you love.

Please don't turn me down. Please don't think that I'm making you give up your singing."

"But you are, and you don't even see that you are." She jerked her arm from his grasp. "Don't you realize that I never asked to be given this gift? No one came to me sitting on a pink cloud with a little book in hand and said, 'Maddie, we're planning your life. Do you want to be a singer or do you want to have a normal life with a husband and children and friends?' No one asked me what I wanted."

"What would you have chosen?" he asked softly.

The tears began then. "I don't know. I don't know. What is is. I can't change what I am."

"Neither can I."

She couldn't speak anymore, for her throat had closed up with tears. She put her hand to her mouth and ran from him.

'Ring stood staring after her. There had to be some way to make her see reason, he thought. There had to be some way to explain to her—

"Ow!" he said, and grabbed his shin, then looked at Laurel in astonishment. She had just kicked him. "What was that for?"

"You made my sister cry and you made Jamie mad. I hate you." With that she turned and ran after her sister.

'Ring turned back to the fire and Toby, who was still sitting there. With a hand that shook, 'Ring poured himself a cup of coffee and sat down.

"Don't look like you're none too popular," Toby said.

"She'll get over it," 'Ring answered. "By morning she'll see the light and—"

"And what?" Toby asked.

'Ring didn't say a word but looked into his coffee cup.

"It don't matter none," Toby said. "Women are a dime a dozen. They're always around. Always underfoot. Why, I bet that within a week you can get yourself another woman. Colonel Harrison's daughter likes you a lot. I bet she'd be glad to go back to Warbrooke with you. She'd like to have you buy her diamonds and silk dresses. In fact, sometimes I think that one of the things she likes best about you is Warbrooke Shipping. In fact, I sometimes think that's what most women like about you boys. It would bother me some if I was contemplatin' marriage. You know, if I was as rich as you tradition-lovin' Montgomerys and a woman wanted to marry me 'cause I was so rich. Don't seem to bother you, though. In fact, with you, if a woman don't want your money, you try to give it to her anyways. That's good, lets you know where you stand with her."

'Ring threw the coffee on the ground and stood up. "Toby, you talk too much and you don't understand anything." He walked away from the campfire.

"True," Toby called after him. "I ain't as smart as you." He looked back at the fire and snorted. "There's rocks smarter 'n that boy."

367

CHAPTER 15

Maddie pushed Edith away and saddled her own horse. When the animal blew out its belly, Maddie punched it in the stomach and pulled the cinch tight. It was cold in the early morning light, but she didn't feel the cold. She hadn't slept any during the night, but lay awake and looked at the ceiling of the tent and listened to Laurel sleeping and the sounds of the night.

'Ring hadn't come to her and she hadn't expected him to. All during the night she had cursed herself, asking herself why she'd ever thought that she could have a life like other people's.

She leaned her head against the horse for a moment and thought of her mother. Her father had received all the credit for his travels and his journals, but those in the family knew how much he owed to her mother. If it hadn't been for the quiet calm of Amy Littleton, Jefferson Worth would have died anonymous, just as hundreds of mountain men before him had.

Maddie had a great need to see her mother, to talk to her, to ask her advice, just to be held in her strong arms. She closed her eyes and remembered what her mother had told her on the night she'd first sung for her father, the night that her mother had said that her father was to go east and get Maddie a teacher.

Afterward Amy Worth had tucked her daughter

into bed. "What is going to happen to me?" Maddie had whispered to her mother.

Amy took a deep breath. "For some reason God has blessed you—or cursed you, depending on how you look at it—with a talent. He has singled you out from other people. He's made you different. And from now on nothing in your life is ever going to be the same. I know you're young, but right now you have to decide whether you want to honor this gift or hide it."

"Oh, honor it," Maddie had said easily.

Amy did not return the smile. Instead, she grabbed her daughter's shoulders and pulled her up so they were face-to-face. "Listen to me, Maddie, and listen hard. If you decide to honor this gift, you will never, never have a life like other people. There will be wonderful highs, but there will be agony such as other people never know. You have to take *all* of it, you understand me?"

Maddie had no idea what her mother was talking about. To her, singing was only pleasure and nothing else. It was adulation and attention from adults. It was hugs and kisses and praise.

Her mother was searching her daughter's face. "I'll allow your father to get a proper teacher for you only if you want it."

"I do. I like to sing."

Amy gave her daughter a little shake. "No, not *like* it. You have to love it. Maddie, a talent like yours is an all-or-nothing thing, and you have to want to sing more than anything else on earth."

Maddie understood a bit then. Already singing

was everything to her. It replaced schoolwork and games, pretty clothes and playmates, and everything else that others considered good in life. She'd rather sing than do anything else. "I want to sing," she said softly.

Amy had seen the fire in her daughter's young eyes, and she'd let out her breath, then clasped Maddie to her. "May God protect you," she whispered.

Now Maddie at last knew what her mother had meant. Until now she'd found no conflict with what she wanted and what she had. Oh, there were times when she was tired and she wanted to be alone yet there was a group of people clamoring for her to sing. Sometimes she yearned after the solitude of her father's mountains, and sometimes she was sick of being wanted, not for who she was but for what she could give people, but all that was more an annoyance than anything else. And she'd always known that if she wanted badly enough to leave Paris or Venice or wherever, she could. But now she seemed to have no more choices left in her life.

"Maddie."

She lifted her head but she didn't turn to look at 'Ring.

"Please don't leave like this," he said. "Let's spend the day here and talk."

She turned to look at him. "Will you travel with me as I sing?"

"I have to run the family business. I've stayed

away long enough, and as soon as my tour in the army is finished, I have to return."

"Then we can be married and live apart. I will do my best to get to America to see you at least every other year."

His expression answered her.

She looked back at her horse. "Why did you do this to me?" she asked softly. "Why did you make me fall in love with you?"

He reached out for her, but she moved away. "Maddie, these things happen. I never meant—"

She turned to look at him. "Yes, you did. You wanted me and you did everything in your power to get me. You were like someone who saw something lovely in a shop window and you saved for it, planned how to purchase it."

"That's absurd. I fell in love with you. It happens every day. If you'd just—"

"*When* did you fall in love with me? Tell me the exact moment."

He didn't know what she was talking about with this purchasing talk, but he couldn't help but smile when he remembered the moment he realized that he loved her. "It was after the miners kidnapped you, on the day that I was bringing you back from where they'd taken you. We had been talking and it was so easy between us. I thought you were so different from other women, and then you looked up at me and I knew that I loved you."

She looked back at the horse. "That was some time ago. After that what did you do?"

"Maddie, these questions are ridiculous. We love each other. We can work this out."

"We can work it out by my singing in the theater you build for me?"

"I can't see that that's so bad. We'll make Warbrooke into a haven for opera lovers. People from all over the world will come there to hear you. I'll build a hotel just to accommodate them, and, of course, we can transport them on Warbrooke ships."

"Buy me. Buy me. That's all you can think of. If you have your way, I'll die never having achieved anything on my own. On my tombstone will not be written that I was a great singer, but that my husband bought everything for me."

"Maddie, you're not being reasonable."

She turned on him, tears in her eyes. "Reasonable? You don't know what reasonable is. All you know is what you want. You've been so spoiled in your life that you have always had whatever you wanted. If you wanted to run the family business when you were just a child, then you were allowed to do so. If you wanted to join the army, then you were allowed to do that too. And now you've decided that you want a little songbird for a wife, so you expect to be allowed to do that as well."

"Maddie, you're becoming hysterical. And you don't know what you're talking about. I've always had to work for what I have."

"Like you worked to get me?" Her voice was rising in anger. "You planned your attack on me like you'd plan a battle campaign. You decided that you wanted me, you figured out how to get me, and then you put your plan into motion."

"You make me sound cold-blooded. I admit that I did do a bit of planning, but I can't see that it was so wrong. I love you and I want you."

"Do you? Do you know me from . . . from Edith? Or did it just fit into the plan of your life to marry an opera star? Wouldn't it look nice with the illustrious Montgomery name to tie it to the great LaReina?"

"You're going too far now," he said softly.

"Oh, I'm not to step on the toes of the magnificent Montgomery name, is that it? Oh, God, 'Ring, why did you do it? Why did you work so hard to make me fall in love with you?"

"Because I loved you and I wanted you to love me in return."

"Me!" She almost shouted at him. "Me? You don't know anything about me. I told you long ago that unless you know about my singing then you know nothing about me. You seem to think that knowing what kind of food I like or my favorite color is knowing *me*. Those things have nothing to do with me."

She could see by his face that he didn't understand a word she was saying. Her anger left her, and she turned back to her horse. "I wish you hadn't done it. If you'd wanted a housewife, someone to wear the pretty dresses you buy her, someone to be at home waiting for you when you returned, then you should have found her and married her. You should have chosen to love a woman who was what you wanted in a wife and left me alone." She leaned her head against the horse and fought back tears. "Why couldn't you have been content to just take me to bed? That seems to be what most men want from a woman, but not you. You wouldn't even make love to me until I loved you. And now you make me choose between you and my music."

"I'm not asking you to give up your music."

She began to tighten straps that were already tight. "No, you're just asking me sing for you while I'm in a cage." She turned on him. "Damn you! Damn you to hell, Christopher Hring Montgomery! Do you even know enough about me to realize that I am not a frivolous woman and that when I love I love forever? I have seen so many singers, singers with great voices, who gave up singing after only a few years simply because they fell out of love with singing. But me, once I love someone or something, I love them forever. I don't change affections for people or animals or for what I do."

He put his hand on her arm. "I don't know why you think that I love someone I don't know, but it's you I love. I saw a long time ago that you love with all your heart. When I found out that you were here singing for these men who don't appreciate your voice, and all because you wanted to save a sister you hadn't seen in years, I was sure that I loved you. Maddie, don't you yet see how much alike we are? I could never love someone who didn't have the intensity that I have. Were I to marry one of those little women who is content to live her husband's life, I would terrify her." His hand tightened on her arm. "You can't leave me. After I deal with Yovington I have to go back to the fort. Wait for me there. We can work things out. Maybe after we're married we can go to Paris or London every summer and you can sing there."

"How can *we* ever work anything out? You don't know the meaning of compromise. *I* am the only one to compromise. Just me. Never you. You don't compromise at all. If you decide we're to spend three days chained together, then it's your decision and yours alone. You never even ask my opinion. If you decide you're going to go after my sister, you go, never saying a word to me, just sneaking off and leaving me a note signed with your initials. Now you're telling me I'm to marry you and do whatever you want for the rest of my life."

She glared at him, then shook her head. "You really don't understand, do you?" She sniffed back her tears and put her chin up. "Let me explain it to you as clearly as I can. You are not the only person in this world who has to do what he must. Just as you feel that you have to go after the kidnappers all alone and anyone else's opinions be damned, I have to sing. I have to sing for other people, not people who are purchased by you, but people who *choose* to hear me sing. I am not going to live *your* life, I am going to live *my* life." She jerked out of his grasp.

"You mean that you're going to walk away from me, don't you? You're going to give up what we have without even trying to work out our problems?"

She swung into the saddle and looked down at him. "You are the one who doesn't seem capable of seeing anything but your own point of view." She picked up the reins to the horse. "I hope your high principles keep you warm at night." She started to move away from him, then stopped. "Like hell I do! I hope you're miserable for the rest of your life. I hope that every time you read that I'm singing somewhere in the world, it makes you cry." At that, she kicked her horse forward.

CHAPTER 16

Maddie stood by her horse and looked out over the beautiful landscape that was near her father's house and felt like crying. But she couldn't cry— or at least she was not going to cry. She'd done enough of that already.

It had been three weeks since she'd left 'Ring, three miserable, long weeks. When she'd arrived at her father's house, she'd been glad to see her parents and the old mountain men, but being near them hadn't made her feel a whole lot better. Hears Good had ridden into the front yard ten minutes after Maddie and Laurel had arrived, and he'd regaled his friends with stories of Maddie's escapades with the army officer. There had been a time when Maddie would have found the stories hilarious, but not now. She had done little more than greet her family, then she went outside and left them to their telling of stories.

It was her mother who had come after her, and it was in her mother's arms that Maddie had lain while she choked out the truth of what had happened. Maddie told of her fear for Laurel, of her fear while singing, and, most of all, she told of her love for 'Ring.

"But he wants to put me in a cage," she said.

Her mother had said very little, had just listened, making no comment.

For the first two weeks of Maddie's stay her father's friends had tried everything to make her stop moping. Bailey sang three new songs for her, terribly vulgar things, and asked her help with the tunes, but Maddie just said that he was doing fine on his own. Her father asked her to go hunting with him, but Maddie didn't want to go. Linq asked her to help him find young trees to make new skis for the coming winter, but Maddie said that she'd rather stay at home. Thomas said he was writing about his adventures as a young man and needed Maddie's help, but she couldn't keep her mind on the subject. Hears Good tried teasing her, but she just looked at him with blank eyes.

Laurel lost patience with her sister. "You're better off without him!" she yelled. "I didn't like him at all. He thought he knew everything. He thinks he's the only one who can run that company of Jamie's, and I bet that Jamie could run it all by himself. He—"

"Jamie couldn't stop flirting long enough to do anything," Maddie said tiredly. "You know nothing about 'Ring. He takes care of people. He takes on the responsibility of the world. And now he's going to be all alone."

"He won't be alone. He'll find someone else. And you'll find another man and he—"

"It took us all our lives to find each other, and we won't find anyone else. I will continue singing and . . ." She trailed off. Until she'd met 'Ring she'd thought she'd had everything there was to have in life, but now nothing seemed to mean anything without him.

"Why don't you sing?" Laurel asked softly. "Everybody wants to hear you sing. Bailey says that you don't remember how. He says that that man made you forget how to sing."

Maddie blinked back tears. The last time she'd sung had been for 'Ring, when they had made love for days on end.

Now, standing on the hill, looking out at the countryside, she didn't know what she was going to do with her life.

"Still haven't made up your mind?"

Maddie turned to see her mother standing behind her, and she smiled. The rest of the world thought that Jefferson Worth had single-handedly explored the West, but Maddie knew how much her father's life had been involved with his wife's, and how much Amy Littleton had influenced him.

"Made up my mind about what?" Maddie asked.

"About how much love means to you." Maddie didn't answer, so her mother kept talking. "When your father asked me to marry him, I was so very happy. I immediately started talking about our life together, how we'd go back to Boston and live in my father's house. I said that Jeff could run my father's freighting business. I even talked of the beautiful clothes that I would buy for Jeffrey."

Maddie looked in puzzlement at her mother. She knew that her mother's father had been quite wealthy and that one of Jeff's objections to taking a young woman up the Missouri River to paint had been her life of ease and luxury. But Maddie couldn't imagine her father living anywhere but in the West, couldn't imagine his wearing anything but buckskins.

Amy continued. "For a while I thought I was going to have to give him up. I was sick unto death of the dirt and the sickness of the West. I was tired of the same food day in and day out. I was tired of men and their filthy habits. I wanted to go back east and live with people who could say a whole sentence without using a vulgar word. I wanted books and music and porcelain dishes. I wanted pretty clothes."

A few years ago Maddie wouldn't have wanted to hear this about her parents. Always before she wanted to think they'd been in love forever, that they'd never had any problems. "What did you do?"

"I left him. I knew what I wanted, and he couldn't give it to me. I went back east and lived for a whole year without him." Amy smiled in memory. "But I hadn't bargained for how much I had changed in that year. I wasn't the same young lady who had left. I was annoyed with my women friends when they were so easily frightened by things like a skittish horse. When you've been trapped without water for three days while Apaches are shooting at you, a nervous horse doesn't mean much. And I was always shocking people with my observations. I could not bear the pretense of 'society' any longer."

"So you went back to Dad?" Maddie said.

"By then they had a steamboat going up the river, and I got on it and went to him."

"And begged him to take you back."

Amy laughed. "Not quite. In fact, a long way from begging. I told him what he'd have to do to keep me." She smiled. "It didn't take much to see that he was as miserable without me as I was without him. I told him I wanted a proper house and that I was not drifting about the West as he tended to do. I said that he was free to travel whenever he wanted, but I was staying in one place."

Maddie looked back toward the mountains and smiled. It had worked for her parents because every summer her father had gone exploring, visiting his friends in different tribes, and some of the old mountain men still living in the hills. For five of those summers Maddie had gone with him, and Gemma had nearly always gone with their father.

"Am I to go to 'Ring and tell him that I must sing and he must go with me?" Maddie asked.

"I don't know. I just know that I loved your father and I went with him and I have never regretted it."

"In that case it was you who had to give in, but now 'Ring is the one who has to give in to me." Maddie put her hands over her face. "I don't even know if he's alive. He went to that awful town after that man who took Laurel. If 'Ring is killed, it will be my fault. Laurel was taken because the man wanted to hear me sing, and if 'Ring—"

Amy put her arms around her daughter. "You can't blame yourself. It was his decision."

"All decisions are his," Maddie said bitterly.

That night she didn't sleep much but lay awake, staring at the ceiling. She came up with no answers, but long before the sun rose, she got out of bed and dressed.

Outside the long adobe house it was still dark, but her father was waiting for her.

"I'm going after him," Maddie said, her mouth set in a firm line. "I shouldn't and I may regret doing it, but I'm going after him."

Her father gave her a little smile. "I thought you would. We Worths usually go after what we want. You wanted to sing and you did it."

"And now I want this man."

Jeff grinned at his daughter. "You get that from your mother."

Maddie looked up at him. 'Ring had said that Jefferson Worth must be old by now, but he was still quite handsome and Maddie couldn't imagine being alive when he wasn't. On impulse, she threw her arms around his waist and hugged him.

Jeff stroked his daughter's hair. "We're wastin' time. Let's go get him."

By the time they were ready to go, their horses saddled, and their packs filled, Thomas, Bailey, and Linq were ready to ride with them. And when they were mounted, Amy, Laurel, and Hears Good joined them.

Maddie couldn't bear to look at them. Always, her family had been there for her.

"Let's go save this boy of yours," Bailey said impatiently. "I been wantin' some excitement. Too quiet around here. Though what we're gonna be able to do with a bunch of women and children along beats the hell outa me."

"I can outshoot you," Laurel said. "You're too blind to see past the end of your nose."

"Jeff, that girl of yourn ain't respectful," Bailey grumbled.

Maddie smiled at her father, and they started down the mountain.

It was on the second day of travel that quite suddenly Thomas and Jeff halted, Hears Good dismounted and slipped into the trees, while Linq and Bailey moved the three women into a circle of protection.

Maddie held her breath. It had been years since she had lived like this, where every movement might mean danger. All of them were as quiet as they could be while they listened. At first Maddie could hear nothing, and she wondered at her father and the other men for being able to hear so well.

When she did hear something she wasn't sure what it was, but then her eyes widened and she sat up straight. "It's him," she whispered.

Her father turned and scowled at her. He had taught her not to speak when they might be in danger.

But Maddie ignored him as she kicked her horse forward and started down the mountain, the others close behind her.

She hadn't sung a note for over three weeks, but now, atop the galloping, slipping horse, she began to sing. She wasn't sure what she was singing, but she thought it was from *Carmen,* when Carmen sang about her soldier.

'Ring came tearing up the side of the mountain toward her, and when he reached her, he pulled her onto his horse and began kissing her eagerly.

"I couldn't do it," he said. "I couldn't lose you."

Maddie didn't care about any words, she just wanted to hold him and feel him and touch him. They sat on top of the horse kissing, their bodies entwining, while around them people began to gather, Maddie's family on one side, 'Ring's on the other.

After a while the two families began to grow restless, and Jamie nudged his horse forward. "I'm James Montgomery and that's my brother 'Ring," he said to Thomas and Jeff. There was a bit of awe in his voice at meeting these men who were legends to him.

It was 'Ring who became aware that he and Maddie had an audience, and he kneed Buttercup forward so that they were hidden from view in the trees.

'Ring pulled Maddie away from him. "We have to talk," he said.

Maddie was afraid of talk. When they kissed or made love, everything between them was fine. It was only when they talked that they got into trouble.

"Later," she whispered, kissing him again.

"No," he said firmly, then he dismounted and lifted his arms for her. When she was on the ground, he held her at arm's length. "I want to say this now, while I still can, because I'm not sure that I'll have enough courage to say it again."

"Courage?" Maddie's heart began to pound. "Courage to tell me what?"

He moved away from her, his back to her. "Courage to say that you were right," he said softly.

Maddie blinked at the back of him, then walked to stand before him. "Right about what?"

"Well . . . maybe you were right about several

384

things." He looked at her and she saw that there were dark circles under his eyes. He hadn't been doing any more sleeping than she had. "I started to Desperate. I had every intention of taking Yovington back to stand trial, but I kept hearing you say that I was after revenge."

He looked away. "I guess I've lived too much of my life alone." He smiled at that. "Alone in a family of nine kids. I don't know how I managed it, but I did."

He looked back at her. "You were right when you said that I've always done what I wanted. My family never tried to stop me from doing anything I wanted. I don't guess I did learn the meaning of compromise."

She went to him and put her hand on his chest. "What happened on the way to Desperate?"

"I realized that for once in my life I might not get what I wanted. Toby says that I've been spoiled, that Montgomery money has always been able to buy anything and I wouldn't know how to cope without that money. I thought he had no idea what he was talking about. Money doesn't help you when you're being shot at by a bunch of Indians."

He looked down at her and caressed her cheek. "When I left you, I thought you were just having a tantrum. That seemed reasonable to think, considering that you're a woman and an opera singer. I thought I'd go get Yovington and then take you back to Warbrooke and everything would be just as I planned it to be."

He paused and took a breath. "It was Jamie who made me realize that what I wanted might not be."

"What did he do?"

"He said that he was going to miss your singing. Then Toby said that he was going to miss the caterwaulin' too. I laughed at them, said that they'd be able to hear you all they wanted when we got home." 'Ring paused. "Jamie said, 'Not this time, brother. This time you lost.' Until that moment I don't guess I'd thought that anything you'd said to me was anything more than a little-girl fit."

He took her hands in his and he held them so tightly that he hurt, but she didn't protest. "I didn't sleep that night. I just lay awake, thinking about life without you. I couldn't imagine it. I tried to tell myself that if you wouldn't come to live with me that that was your loss and that I'd find another woman, but it wasn't any use. It took me years to find you, and I'm not going to let you go."

He started to draw her into his arms, but she stepped out of his reach. "Tell me everything. What did you do about Yovington?"

He smiled at her and ran his hand through his hair. "I don't think my family will ever let me hear the last of this, but I did what you said."

"What *I* said?"

"I turned Yovington over to the army. Jamie and Toby and I lit out for Fort Breck, told Colonel Harrison everything, and he took soldiers after

Yovington. I insisted that my name be kept out of it and that the colonel take all the credit, so maybe ol' Harrison will get a medal or something."

"And forgive you for making his life miserable?"

"I hope so. I have another year to go before I get out of the army."

"And then what?" she asked.

He took his time before answering, and Maddie sensed that what he was about to say was difficult for him. "I thought about what you said about being in a cage, and I tried to understand what you were saying. My talent seems to be in running a business the size of Warbrooke Shipping, but what if my father were some rich man who had to do nothing for his money and, to indulge me, he bought a business for me to run? I'd never know if I was any good or not." He smiled. "It's a great feeling to successfully negotiate a deal, to know that because of your brains and planning that you've won. I guess it must be like that when you sing for people who have come of their own free will to hear you, not because they owe your husband's company a favor."

He took a deep breath, and when he spoke, she knew that he meant what he said. "I cannot ask you to give that up. I will go wherever you go. I will follow you around the world as long as you can sing," he said softly.

She looked at him for a while before she spoke.

"And what will you do while I'm singing? Manage the props?"

"Maybe I can look into Warbrooke Shipping interests in other parts of the world. You ever sing in Hong Kong?"

Maddie was afraid to move. This was what she had wanted. He *did* love her. Her. Not a woman he'd created in his mind, but her, Maddie. And he also loved LaReina, a woman who had something to do in her life besides be there for her husband whenever he needed her. He loved what she was and who she was and he was willing to give as well as take.

She gave him a smile, trying to hold back her tears of happiness. "You know, I was thinking. Maybe I could sing around the world in the winter and I could spend the summers in Maine with you, and sing in that theater you plan to build for me."

He stood there with his arms at his sides, not touching her.

"That is, if you think that could work. Could you leave your business for half the year?"

'Ring put his hand to his jaw and flexed it. "I can still feel where Jamie told me that my brothers were quite capable of running Warbrooke Shipping without me."

"I'm willing to try it if you are," she said.

It was a full minute before 'Ring spoke, then he grabbed her and whirled her around and around. "It'll work. I'll *make* it work." He kissed her then, long and lingeringly.

" 'Ring, let's stay here and—"

"No," he said firmly. "I want to meet your father and the others and I want us to get married right away and I want to start handling your finances."

"My finances? What makes you think you can handle *my* money? You don't have enough of your own to manage?"

"No wife of mine is going to be cheated, and I plan to see that—"

"For your information, I asked my mother about the money, and she's had John Fairlie send her four accounts a year about how much I earn and she's invested it in things."

"Invested it in 'things,' huh? I'm glad to hear that someone in your family has some sense when it comes to money. I'd hate our children to grow up unable to run Warbrooke Shipping."

"Our children are going to be singers, or maybe artists, and you are not going to run their lives like you try to run mine. And furthermore—"

She stopped because he was kissing her, and she forgot whatever else she was going to say.